These Granite Islands

~ ~ ~

These Granite Islands

a novel

SARAH STONICH

LITTLE, BROWN AND COMPANY
Boston New York London

FIRST EDITION

The characters and events in this book are
fictitious. Any similarity to real persons, living or dead,
is coincidental and not intended by the author.

Excerpt from "Marina" in *Collected Poems 1909–1962* by T. S. Eliot.
Copyright 1936 by Harcourt, Inc., copyright © 1964, 1963 by
T. S. Eliot, reprinted by permission of the publisher.

Library of Congress Cataloging-in-Publication Data

Stonich, Sarah
These granite islands : a novel / Sarah Stonich.
p. cm.
ISBN 0-316-81583-7
1. Married women — Fiction. 2. Female friendship — Fiction.
I. Title.
PS3569.T6455 T47 2000
813'.54 — dc21   00-020358

10 9 8 7 6 5 4 3 2 1

Q-FF

Book design by Fearn Cutler de Vicq

Printed in the United States of America

For Sam and his
great-grandparents
Julia and Joseph

I made this, I have forgotten
And remember.
The rigging weak and the canvas rotten
Between one June and another September.

— T. S. ELIOT

Acknowledgments

The writing of this book was supported in many ways. Money and time came from the McKnight Foundation, the Oberholtzer Foundation, the Ucross Foundation, and the Ragdale Foundation. Ragdale's Sylvia Brown was particularly helpful with many kindnesses and commiserations.

Patient readers include: Susan Bonne, Catherine McKee, Valerie Stonich Schooley, Danielle Sosin, and Pat Weaver Francisco. Thanks to Wendy Sherman for her faith and audacity, to Judy Clain at Little, Brown and Company, and to Linda Biagi for bringing this book to overseas readers.

My gratitude for a remarkable friendship (and space to work) to Terry Anderson. Appreciation to the staff at Electronic Media, the Sisters of the Villa Maria at Old Frontenac, and the Rap-in-Wax Lodge. Thanks to Georgina for reminding me that books and life are magic, and to William for laughing along with all of us.

Thank you, Woody. Your patience and kind support made this book possible.

These Granite Islands

~ ~ ~

They worked side by side through the warm days, and in the evenings they traveled the fringes of town to the reedy shore, walking arm in arm the way women no longer walk. There they would sit, Cathryn doing most of the talking, her words bridging the whispers of waves.

Words. Histories, stories, the funny, tragic things women say only to each other.

"It's a woman's duty to astound a man, at least in the beginning."

"What do I want in life? That's easy. Tulips, *white* tulips. White lilies, even."

Other words, more serious, that made Isobel shield her eyes against the low sun as she listened. But she did not try turning those lines inside out to examine their meaning until much later, long after Cathryn was gone and that summer was memory.

When she asked Cathryn how she could be unfaithful, the reply was this: "When I'm with Jack Reese I feel as if I've been skinned, that's how well he knows me, sees me. And there I am, all gore and pit like a burst plum, and still he finds me beautiful, still he loves me."

A tear fell then to the pebbly sand, where it was taken by the lazy tongue of surf. One drop of a woman's sorrow or happiness pulled away, absorbed into the grey song of a glacial lake.

Looking away from where the tear had fallen, they glanced in the same direction but saw different things. One noticed the long shadows cast over the water, the other saw distant islands strewn like musical notes.

~ 1936 ~

The summer began with the island, and the island began with Christmas of the winter before. Church bells heralded Christmas, and so in a way rang in the existence of the island. Isobel remembered easily now, clear as the carillon resounding from the bell tower at Our Lady of the Lake on a snowy afternoon.

On Christmas Eve Victor came home, not with gifts for their children, but with three peppermint candy canes.

In the back porch he shed snow, his stomping punctuating Isobel's questions. "Presents?" He grinned, his tone was derisive, sly. "Bah, Isobel, any child can have presents on Christmas." He shrugged in through the kitchen door.

Isobel, baffled, sat back down. "Aren't our children any children?"

What could possibly make any child different from another on Christmas? If there was one universal emotion among an age, she thought, it would be the thrill of children everywhere upon waking Christmas morning. Christian children, anyway. What was he up to?

"Don't tease, Victor. What can you mean, you've bought no presents?"

He leaned to her hair and said in a conspiratorial tone, "Oh, Izzy, I've bought better than presents."

Isobel could smell the alcohol on him. She shot out of her chair. "What can you be thinking, coming home drunk on Christmas Eve!"

Victor patted her into a sitting position and splayed himself into a chair. "Good God, Isobel, can't a man have one drink on a holiday? It's Christmas, for Christ's sake!" He chuckled at his phrase and repeated it, tapping a knuckle on the table. "Christmas, for *Christ's* sake."

"Oh, I see. Drunk and blasphemous. Victor! What about —"

"The presents?" He pulled a tight roll of documents from the inner pocket of his coat and laid them on the table before her. "Right here." He spread out a deed and a legal description. He took a small photograph from his breast pocket and slapped it down.

From what Isobel could tell with a cursory glance at the papers, he had bought land.

"Land? Victor, I don't understand."

"It's an island, Izzy, a gorgeous place."

Isobel squinted at a purchase agreement and gasped. *Fifteen hundred dollars!* As much as she'd made in the last year doing seamstress work. Victor's signature sprawled next to the date, spelled out formally, *December twenty-fourth, nineteen hundred and thirty-five.* Ink from the official seal of the county land office bled into the description. *Five and one half acres, island parcel, tract 78, Lake Cy-*

press. Isobel picked up the photo. Five and a half acres. It looked like nothing. It looked like exactly what it was, a mound of pine-studded granite jutting from a plane of black water. As she looked at the picture, the question burned her throat.

"You didn't ask me?"

Victor offered empty palms in response.

In sixteen years of marriage they had always been together in every decision, no matter how trivial. Just that morning they had lightheartedly debated whether to have creamed potatoes or roasted for Christmas Eve dinner. Victor wouldn't so much as place an advertisement for the tailor shop without Isobel's approval. If new machinery was purchased, it was only after the two had put their heads together and both had concluded that model X was better. Whether the living room walls would be papered in pine green or olive was worth days of discussion; deciding on a name for a baby could and sometimes did take weeks. But in the end they agreed. Always. Together. Isobel glared at the snapshot. The kitchen was quiet save for the distant bells from Our Lady of the Lake, ringing in Christmas Eve.

As the last chime faded, Isobel rose from her chair and slapped her husband's face in one clean motion. His head jerked neatly sideways and stopped abruptly, as if he meant suddenly to examine the wall.

In the echoing silence she looked at her palm as if it were a stranger's. Shaking, she hung her apron on a hook. Calling upstairs for Louisa to come down, she turned to the sink and waited, counting the footfalls, the seconds it took for her daughter to bounce down the back steps. The door squealed open.

"Yes, Momma?"

In a barely controlled voice, she instructed Louisa to baste the turkey at intervals, check the yams, and set the dining room table. The girl nodded curiously at her mother, sneaking a sidelong glance at her father, still facing away in his strange posture.

Isobel turned on her heel and pushed out of the room, away from Victor. She imagined him rubbing his cheek and staring at the swinging kitchen door until it bumped to stillness behind her.

She climbed the stairs, rasping knuckles along the dark beadboard, veering into the room she shared with Victor. Snapping on the light, she pawed through her underwear drawer until she found the envelope of money she'd saved from her dressmaking. She carefully pulled bills from the thin packet. Victor's smug face loomed before her and she stuffed three of the dollars back into the envelope.

She was grateful Thomas and Henry were out of range. Earlier she'd seen their snow-blurred movements from the kitchen window. All afternoon they'd struggled over an igloo at the edge of the creek, their caps cardinal bright against bare trees and colorless blocks of icy snow.

Downstairs, she pushed her felt cloche over her eyes, shouldered the porch door open against a low drift, and aimed herself downtown to stretch her bit of savings into a decent Christmas for her family.

Main Street was nearly deserted, most shops already closed for the holiday. Isobel blinked through fine lashings of snow and plucked her way through ankle-deep drifts. Each time her foot came down, slush shot up to spatter her stockings and hem.

She saw a figure move toward her and she pulled her scarf up high, but not fast enough to avoid Mrs. Sima's eye. Sima's butcher shop was next to Victor's tailor shop. Mrs. Sima trotted closer, trailing a wake of snow, her voice ripping through the curtain of white.

"Isobel Howard!"

She took refuge in her hat, pretending she hadn't heard.

"Mrs. Howard!"

As Isobel turned she managed a surprised look, suddenly glad for pelting snow that explained away the red sting in her eyes.

"If you're looking for Victor, dear, he's left the shop . . . oh, hours ago now." Mrs. Sima rubbed her arms like a channel swimmer. "About noon, I'd say." Powdery snow rose from her fur coat. When Isobel only smiled, Mrs. Sima cocked her head sideways. "You haven't lost him, have you?"

Isobel blinked, her smile cast in place. "I don't think so, Mavis. Why do you ask? Had you thought I would?"

After a beat, the woman chortled. "Ha! Ha, well . . ."

"Well?"

"Well, isn't this a perfect Christmas Eve? Made to order!"

"Yes." Isobel nodded at the doorway of the mercantile. Large, garish boxes were gift-wrapped and propped in a tower against a display window coated from the inside with false snow.

"Here's my stop, Mavis."

"Last-minute shopping? Goodness, I had everything bought and wrapped by Thanksgiving."

Isobel put her hand on the door. "Always prepared, Mrs. Sima, just like a Boy Scout."

"Ha. You tell your family for me to have a very merry —"

"Yes, merry. Same to yours." Isobel slipped into the door, but not before hearing Mavis muttering into her fur, *"Butter wouldn't melt . . ."*

If the children were disappointed the next morning at the tin banks, adventure books, and sketch pads she had found on picked-over shelves at the mercantile and the dime store, they didn't show it. Nor did they display any false enthusiasm. Receiving their perfunctory kisses and lukewarm thanks, Isobel fought tears. She was tired, had been up late cleaning the kitchen and wrapping gifts. She had restlessly tossed all night next to Victor's snoring bulk. Still wearing her bathrobe and slippers, she sank into an armchair. Victor took down the roll of documents tied to the tree with a silver ribbon.

The deed to the island thrilled the boys to awe as Victor described the island's rocky ledges, the copses of aspen, the mysterious peat bog that could suck your foot under if you were careless, the precipices of granite, a small beach where every stone was the perfect skipping stone broken from the slope of shale that stood like a giant's foot in the shallows of the north end. The palisade log cottage needed just a bit of fixing. He explained how they would have their own permanent camp, accessible only by boat and complete with tents and bonfires. A paradise. They would be like the Rough Riders out on expedition.

Louisa remained curled around a cushion near Isobel's feet while the boys fought for space on their father's knee, grabbing at the photograph of the island until it was bent and smudged.

"Are there owls?"

"Are there badgers?"

"Daddy, are there bats?"

And in unison. "Are there bears?"

Victor shook his head. "No badgers. No bears, but we'll have teddy bear picnics, just like Roosevelt's children."

Isobel looked up, puzzled. "Teddy's or FDR's?"

Victor ignored her. "We will be Lewis and Clark" — he winked — "paddling the wild, charting our own wilderness." The boys threw their arms around their father's neck and shoulders. Through a tangle of limbs Victor gave Isobel a sidelong look of triumph. Payback for the slap. Isobel slumped, glaring at the tree.

She managed to put the island out of her mind until after the ice melted from the big bay in spring. Victor packed her into the car one April evening and drove her to the boat landing at Chalmer's Point.

"I just know you'll feel differently after you've seen it, Izzy. It's a marvelous place."

While Victor fiddled with an anchor and readied the boat for launch, Isobel kicked off her shoes, pulled a pair of borrowed opera glasses from her handbag, and climbed carefully onto the hood of the Ford. Satisfied her weight wouldn't dent the metal, she clambered higher to stand on the slope of the black roof.

When Victor looked up from his task, he was astonished to see his wife balanced like a bowsprit atop the car, searching the horizon. Loose tendrils of blond hair skipped across her cheekbone, and her skirt billowed around her calves. Oblivious in her perch, Isobel held the glasses to her eyes, scanning the lake and focusing the tiny binoculars. She slowly swept her gaze level with the far shore, her motions concentrated and minute. Suddenly she went very still.

Isobel stood, a slender woman with clear skin and the sculpted features of her European ancestors. Her light hair was cast gold with the same bright evening light that made her squint and washed her skin the colour of a tea rose. Breeze moving off the lake carried ribbons of chill that pressed her blouse to outline her small breasts and angular shoulders. Victor walked slowly to the car, stepped onto the running board, and reached out to hold one of her ankles.

To steady her?

His hand wrapped easily around. Pressing his thumb lightly into flesh and sinew, he felt a twinge at the fragility of his wife's bones. Clouds reflected in the enamel of the

Ford and shifted with the fast-changing black pool, her skirt casting its movements.

Victor wondered, had he never held her ankle? If he had, he'd not taken any real notice. He had lived with Isobel for sixteen years. Could it be he'd never touched this fine place? Her feet were small and narrow, so highly arched that he could slip a leaf underneath and pull it out the other side without her knowing. The warmth of her under his hand brought a sudden sharp desire to him.

They hadn't made love since before Christmas.

She hadn't openly rebuffed him, but had simply managed to be asleep each time he got into their bed. In the mornings she was up and dressed before he woke.

Perhaps after getting out to the island?

His own hand felt rough as he felt upward along her calf, taking care not to snag her stocking. Tailor's calluses ran in crested ridges across his fingers, and he wondered idly if he could file them down with the stone he used to grind scissors blades.

He laughed that he was even considering such a vain notion.

Isobel lowered the opera glasses to her chest and smiled crookedly at him.

He grinned hopefully. They used to go off, just roam away from the house, even if only for a half hour after the children were asleep. They would talk, and she would laugh and hang from his arm and he would tell her jokes or stories he'd heard, aping the voices of the townspeople, relaying what recent gossip he'd been privy to in the shop. Not very long ago, yet it seemed ages, the last time he'd made her laugh. It couldn't have been as long ago as autumn?

They'd been walking under the turning maples in their neat neighborhood. As he kicked leaves, Victor spied something on the ground. He picked up a scrap of white paper, folded it to a square, and held it to his collar, mimicking Father Thiery's oil-thick Irish brogue. He whispered somberly into her ear.

"Why aye, lad, I'm as fond of curly little darlin's as the next feller, but in yer capacity as a shepherd-in-training, these types of impure thoughts about the lambs might . . . What's that, boy? Well, perhaps it's not so great a sin if ye were thinkin' of good St. Francis whilst . . ." When Victor wriggled his eyebrows in mock consternation, Isobel laughed so she had to lean against the neighbors' fence. "Now, did you say *flock,* son?"

She folded herself into a crouch and wiped her eyes with her knuckles. Victor looked down the street and back, waiting for his wife to stop laughing. He held out his hand.

"Up now, there's a girl."

"I can't!" There was an edge of hysteria in her voice.

He knelt next to her, the cloying accent back. "And why's that, my child?"

"Stop it!" Her tears were mixed now, and her answer was a hiccough. "B-b-because I've wet myself." She slapped his chest. "You've made me . . . I've peed on Mrs. Perlin's sidewalk!"

They both started laughing then, but hers was thin, and as she walked awkwardly away she gave him an accusing look. "Having three babies will do that to you."

"Aye." The accent thickened. "Wonder what four'd do, lassie?"

She looked at him with disbelief before pulling free of his arm. "Victor, not everything is a joke."

Steadying herself against a sudden wind from the lake, Isobel gingerly climbed down from atop the car, taking the hand he offered her. The gravel was a shock after the smooth metal of the hood, and as she limped to her shoes she brushed off her skirt in sudden industry.

He was reminded of her demeanor in the shop, her

movements there swift and economical. She had worked nearly every day since Thomas, their youngest, had started school. She'd bring lunch, and while he ate she'd work on the account books or wait on customers. If she had a dress order or alteration or was sewing something for the children, she bent quietly over her machine through the afternoon, rising promptly at the sound of the school bell so she could rush home to greet the children.

She glanced at the lake, at the far speck of the island, before turning to look into her husband's eyes.

"I've seen it. Now take me home."

CHAPTER TWO

~ *1999* ~

*I*sobel felt herself rising through dark water. It was a
slow ascent from slate depths, light teasing in a far shimmer above. Air bubbles trapped on the underside of the
boat gleamed like wriggling snails. Victor was leaning over
the gunwale, his face wavering just over the surface, beckoning to her, his fingertips dents of mercury in the water.

She kicked with all her strength, and with each kick she
was leaving the dark below. Finally she was freed to the
foaming surface, revealed into the heat of summer. Breathing air blanched with sunlight, she reached out for the boat
and he caught her hands. His flesh was warm, his fingers
twining comfort through hers as her body rose, weightless
and rescued.

I've missed you, Victor. You don't know how.
Finally here.
With you.

But as she mouthed the words, his fingers slipped from hers and she sank back with the weight of years. When she closed her eyes she could hear her name being called as though through a shell. For a long time she rested there, somewhere near the silty bottom. An uneasy sea creature, suspended.

Deep and curled.

And later her name called again. And again.

She opened her eyes to a great dryness, and through the kind haze of her cataract wavered the profile of a man.

Not Victor. But someone.

Someone she knew once.

He had her wrist, was holding it lightly between his fingers. She began to cry, but tears were cinders stopping at the corner of her eye.

She pulled away. Who? She could not name him. His features faded in and out of a bright glare. When she tried raising a hand to shield her eyes from the reflected sunlight, she found her hand fast on the gunwale, frozen there as if to steady herself and the shifting canoe. A different boat altogether.

"You're awake." The timbre of the man's voice matched his face, rugged and broad, matched an echo from bright years past. Who? Silver calipers somehow clasped about his neck. Isobel blinked. Strange thing to wear in a boat.

The man leaned in, his voice washing over her. "Isobel, can you speak? I just have a few questions." She turned and peered at him.

Don't we all?

He spoke a few more words, all running together in a stream save one. *Stroke.*

She tried to hoist herself up. Somehow she was in the canoe, no longer beneath it.

Where's my paddle?

"Isobel, can you tell me when and where you were born?"

Stupid question.

She stared at his neck, at the curious silver hooks pinching his flesh. He had the muscled neck of a man who worked with his body. When he cocked his head, sunlight assaulted her. She squinted, trying to raise her arm, but it wouldn't move. The man turned his back to her and made a sweeping motion with his hand. Light crumbled.

It took a moment for Isobel to adjust to the sudden dimness. The unbroken horizon and the expanse of water were transformed, condensed into stiff lines until they took on the dimensions of an ordinary room. With the pulling of a shade, Isobel's boat squared itself into a narrow bed. Her hand on the gunwale was a mottled talon clutching a metal safety railing. Fluorescent light flickered above her head with a static hum, and the strange ornament worn by the man formed itself into a common stethoscope.

A doctor. Of course. Still, that did not explain the man's familiar shadow. A name nearly came to her and slipped as suddenly from her possession as the boat had. As Victor had.

With the slow revelation of her circumstances, Isobel felt a sting of remorse. She was not dead after all, only groggy. Alive enough to feel aversion at the nasty film coating her lower teeth. Someone — a nurse? — had removed her upper plate so that when she ran her tongue over her gums their nakedness surprised her. Stroke? She wanted to go back to her dream, the cool satin of her floating space.

The man impatiently repeated his question.

"Isobel, do you know your birth date? Your birthplace?"

Birth date, birthplace. What did he really want? She had been in the hospital before. There would be examinations, tests. They seemed to be forever testing her, drawing vials of blood from the parchment crooks of her arms, strapping her body onto metal gurneys to run her through churning and blinking machines, as though she were being processed. During those grim moments Isobel always felt an uncharacteristic paranoia; that the essence of her was being shifted or manipulated somehow. The technicians tended to say her name overoften during the more uncomfortable moments of these procedures, as if hearing her name like a mantra would reassure her. Of what? That she was not breaking down, cell by cell? That her destiny — and theirs, for that matter — was not set, that they would all somehow, through some series of miracles, escape their arid fates of bone and ash.

Reduced by a wind.

Afterward, safe in her bed, Isobel always felt a little foolish for her drama and chastised herself for acting like a child. Or worse, an old woman.

Stroke.

Perhaps if she was polite, obedient, the man might go away. Isobel cleared her throat with a gummy croak and answered, lisping a little without the wall of her upper incisors.

"May seventeenth, 1900, in Cypress."

Nodding, the man bent to make a note on the chart, frowned, and looked back at her. "Cyprus? You mean the island near Turkey?"

Isobel heard his question clearly, but the tug of sleep was stronger than any desire to correct him. She smiled and closed her eyes against the blur of his curious face.

By the third day, Isobel was nearly herself. She'd grown accustomed to being alive; she even felt resolve, a near optimism about continuing on. As she took in the room's false cheer of yellow wallpaper and orange plastic chairs, she remembered the fleeting moments of her stroke.

Seized. Seconds of clarity, a series of impressions etched into crisp scenes she could run through her head like a reel of vignettes. First there was the pain. *Hit!* she had thought. *Hit from behind, right here in my kitchen.* She felt a ping somewhere just up-brain of her ear, and her eyelid shuttered itself fast. Flesh prickled along her cheekbone and down her neck, the invisible force that was peeling her hand from its mooring leapt to her leg and tried to trip her.

No one's hit me.

I'm alone. Dying. It's crawling on me.

Finally. Finally I'm giving way. But why now?

Oh God oh dear God.

But as she clutched the cabinet, starting her slow slide to the floor, she experienced wonder — even awe — the type she hadn't felt since childhood, mostly at the irony that she had questions even as she was slipping down to her death.

Now?

Now. At the drainboard, putting away a coffee mug I've always hated?

The mug had a stylized *M,* as part of the insurance company's logo, and the letter resembled a textbook diagram of fallopian tubes and ovaries.

Why have I never thrown the thing away? Sun glinted on the handle as the mug fell from her open hand.

In daylight? Ridiculous. Nobody should have to die at midday! Like childbirth, wouldn't dying be more appropriate in the solitude and cover of night?

She felt a puzzling satisfaction that questions resolved themselves as quickly as she could form them. They simply didn't matter.

Death? It suddenly seemed more a courteously posed

invitation than a frightening inevitability. Willing resignation came over her, and she suddenly craved the rest her new state would offer. Yes. Death. Willing as a bride. When she let go her grip on the countertop, she had felt — instead of the hard smack of linoleum and ensuing blackness — a spiraling sensation of peace, warm and comforting as any embrace.

Sitting up now and dressed in a wrinkled nightgown and thin hospital robe, Isobel took a spoonful of watery Cream of Wheat and wondered aloud whether her son Thomas had remembered to stop by her apartment and water her orchids.

"Yes, Mother. This morning."

At the voice she smiled. "Oh, you're here. I thought you left ages ago."

"That was yesterday." He lowered his newspaper and tucked a pencil above his ear. As the paper fell to reveal Thomas's face, Isobel realized with a start that she'd almost expected a gap-toothed nine-year-old to emerge from behind the comics to snap his gum. She'd expected the green-eyed boy who'd been able to wring her heart with a wink. He could do that before things shattered for him. For them all.

She blinked and looked again. The overhead light reflected in the sheen of his high forehead. Her son was grey-haired and tired-looking; his tie was pulled loose down his starched shirt. His wife takes such care of him, Isobel mused, can't she keep him from looking so old?

Another male voice came to her from the foot of her bed.

"Good morning, Isobel."

When she glanced up, the spoon fell from her hand with a clatter, lukewarm porridge splashing over her knuckles. Creamy dabs peppered the brown liver spots on the crepe of her skin.

The doctor held a chart, the rubbery loops of his stethoscope dangled from the pocket of his white coat. Underneath he wore a plaid shirt, blue and green hatched with grey.

"My name is Dr. Hertz." His eyes were puffy and his hair had not been combed.

It took her a moment to find her voice. "I believe we've met." She recovered her spoon. "Dr. Hertz, you say?"

"Uh huh."

The old woman peered at him, leaned forward. After the three of them shared an awkward silence, Isobel laid the spoon away and drummed the fingers of her working hand on the plastic tray. "Since you are on a first-name basis with me, perhaps it should be reciprocal?"

"Hmm?" At first the doctor did not catch the bite in her tone. He had been listening for signs of slurring.

"Doctor? Your first name?"

"You are better, aren't you? Joel. My name's Joel."

Isobel looked into the doctor's face and motioned with a hooked finger for him to come closer. "Since I'm old enough to be your grandmother, *great*-grandmother, I'll call you Joel. And if you like, you may call me Mrs. Howard."

Thomas grinned, watching the exchange. She was reeling in another one.

The doctor reddened slightly and ran a hand through his sandy hair. "I didn't mean to be disrespectful." He tried to suppress a smile, dimples appearing at the corners of his mouth.

Isobel's brow arched. "You still remind me of someone."

"Still?" He checked a tube on the IV snaking into her vein-riddled hand. "Anyone special?" When he glanced up she was staring out the window. He waited for her to continue, but she seemed to have lost her train of thought.

His tone was a little weary. "I take it you know where you are now?"

Isobel sighed. "St. Joseph's Hospital in St. Paul. Geriatric wing, I suppose. And I believe today's date is September the second, maybe third?"

"Close enough. So, how are you feeling, Mrs. Howard?"

Isobel looked at him. "Call me Isobel." Her smile was a lopsided display of unnaturally white dentures. Her uppers had been located. "I'm fine. Aside from this arm, I'm feeling fine. And how are you?"

The doctor blinked. "I'm fine too, thank you." With his pen he made a few stabs at the chart, then he hung it at the end of the bed. "I'll be back later to check on you." He shifted away and nodded to Thomas on his way out. "Your mother's doing very well, considering."

Isobel suddenly rolled to her side. "Joel?"

He stopped in midstride and turned. He had rounds to make. "Yes, Mrs. . . . Isobel?"

"I remember now."

"Your stroke?"

She waved the air in dismissal. "Never mind that. I remember who you remind me of. Your hair, your profile, even that shirt you're wearing. You look very much like someone I knew when I was your age." Isobel could tell he was fighting the urge to look at his watch.

"No kidding. Who do I remind you of?"

"Now, why can't I say his name? I know it." She poked her temple. "It's right here . . . the man who disappeared."

Thomas righted himself in his chair and leaned toward her. He opened his mouth to speak but stopped short, biting his mustache.

Dr. Hertz stepped forward. "Disappeared where? In Cyprus?"

"Oh! What was his name?" Isobel raked at the blanket. "No, not *in* Cyprus. It was at the lake, near Cyprus."

"Ah." The doctor nodded knowingly and retreated to the door of the room. "Good-bye, then." As he turned away he shook his head. *Dementia.* From what he remembered from his geography, Cyprus was a bone-dry crust of earth surrounded by ocean. Not likely to have any lakes.

~ ~ ~

Plaid shirt. Plaid shirt. Isobel's eyes would not move above the collar of his shirt. She recognized the fabric as Pendleton. Quality wool. She reached tentatively to shake the hand of the man wearing it. She'd been almost afraid to look at his face, but when Cathryn's arm tightened around her shoulders she looked up.

He had deep-set green eyes under a thatch of wavy blond hair. Certainly good-looking enough, Isobel thought. He did not look nervous or guilty as Isobel expected he might. As he should. She slowly pulled her hand away. When the man spoke it was with a deep and even tenor, the voice of a public speaker, a politician, an unexpected voice for an ordinary man.

"My name is Jack Reese."

Isobel recalled Cathryn's saying he had studied in the seminary. She could imagine him at the pulpit, where his voice and stature would serve him well. Cathryn poured tea and hovered near, uncharacteristically quiet as her lover and her friend became acquainted.

They sat near the back of the tailor shop. Isobel had locked the door and flipped the sign to the *Closed* side. She'd pulled the shades and took the further precaution of placing the trio of chairs well away from the windows. She perched uncomfortably on the edge of hers, warily eyeing Jack, hands knitted to her knee.

Jack cleared his throat and began, immediately deflecting attention from himself by asking Isobel a number of friendly questions. He asked about Victor's tailoring business. He asked after her new millinery work, her children. How did she think her husband and sons were faring out on the island? Isobel glanced icily at Cathryn, then back to Jack.

"It seems as if you already know enough about me."

His manner remained genial as he persisted. At first Isobel's answers were curt and unembellished. He had so many questions, all asked with a genuine sincerity, as if he were truly interested in her life. He pressed her to elaborate on certain points and edged his chair close to hers, leaning forward to lightly touch her arm whenever she faltered or paused. Without realizing it, Isobel began talking more freely. After an hour it dawned on her that while she had been talking, not one of her rehearsed questions had been asked. Suddenly impatient, she interrupted to ask him about his own life.

"You have family?"

"Yes, mostly in Philadelphia. My father was killed in Belgium in '18, but my mother's still alive, and I have a brother in Cleveland. I don't see them often enough."

Isobel couldn't stop herself, the question faltered at her lips and stuttered out. "Have you d-done this before? With a married woman, I mean?"

He shook his head, not breaking her gaze. "I understand your concern." He didn't flinch. "You've a perfect right to ask. Of course not. Never."

After a moment she continued, this time her voice a bit more mellow. She asked about his work with the forest service, about the isolation of the job.

"Not so different from the seminary, really," he said. "Alone in a tower, waiting, or alone in a cell, waiting and praying . . . for what, I'm not sure. Clarity, I suppose." He laughed. "Perhaps my failure in the seminary had something to do with the fact that I had no clear idea what I was looking for."

Isobel surprised herself by placing a hand over his to encourage him. "But there must have been something that drew you to the Church. Something must have made you want to become a priest."

"To be honest, I'm no longer sure. I thought I would be needed." He laughed and shook his head. "I supposed that I would save souls."

"Save souls — from what?"

He leaned in, his face growing serious. "Why, from hopelessness. From loss of faith."

Isobel nodded wryly. "And now you're a ranger. That must've been quite a change for you."

"Not really. I was attracted by the solitude. Both vocations share one luxury. Time."

"Time for . . . ?"

"Oh, for thinking, reading." He paused, looked warmly at Cathryn, then back to Isobel. "Time to take note of small, seemingly inconsequential things." Jack picked up a simple panne velvet cap Isobel had just finished. He lightly touched the bunting feathers at its brim.

"Have you ever, for instance, had an entire afternoon with time enough to sit and watch a bird build its nest?"

Seeing Jack's earnest gestures, listening to him describe his afternoon of observing one bird, she realized he was not what she'd imagined. But then, what traits did define the sort of man who would steal another's wife?

A ruthless plotter? Someone desperate? As his conversation drifted to the landscape, the outdoors, and the botanical studies he'd made of the region, she realized the man before her was neither. His eyes were light with vulnerability, and in his shyness he preferred the company of birds and plants.

"Plants?"

"A passion of mine." He glanced up at Cathryn and smiled. "One of them. This area is a paradise for the amateur botanist."

"And you are . . . ?"

"An amateur? In most things, yes." He spoke of his finds in the field, even pulled out a pencil to sketch a rare species of fern he'd happened upon. In describing the setting, the light on that day as he went along his woodland trek, Jack Reese was somehow able to make the discovery of a flowerless plant sound romantic.

Isobel wondered if he would speak as effusively of Cathryn if she were to ask about their love affair. She would like to have gotten him alone, but just as she was thinking it, Cathryn came up behind his chair and laid her hands lightly on his shoulders, glancing nervously at her watch in the same motion. Jack beamed.

"I'll take you both to see those ferns if you like. They're growing out by the old Finnish farmsteads on the west shore."

Isobel swallowed, looking to the floorboards beneath her feet.

Cathryn coughed softly. "Jack, perhaps an outing isn't a good idea."

Jack turned around and looked squarely at Cathryn. "Of course. I'm sorry, I just . . ."

For a moment all three concentrated on points away from each other. Jack bent to straighten the laces on his high leather boots, while Cathryn examined some line of interest on her palm.

Isobel filled the silence by telling a joke that her daughter, Louisa, had told the night before.

". . . and then the first stitch said to the second stitch, '*Suture* self!'"

When Jack broke into infectious laughter, Cathryn smiled. His smooth face creased, the corners of his mouth punctuated by precise dimples, white teeth shining even and square.

If it were only desire that drove Cathryn toward Jack, Isobel thought, she might better understand. When Jack touched her arm, she had even thought, *No wonder*

Cathryn must have him. But at the moment the two seemed unaware of anything so mundane as the physical. As Cathryn's hand fluttered forward to push back a curl fallen over Jack's brow, Isobel saw the look pass between them. Need? Had Jack found his calling in her? Was Cathryn's troubled soul the one he would save?

She peered at his clear, guileless eyes and wondered, *Will he be able?*

When he moved to go, Jack took Isobel's hand but had difficulty meeting her gaze. "I'm sorry we had to meet in such awkward circumstances."

"I understand," Isobel replied, though more in response to her own thought than his apology. "I understand now." She realized she was still grasping his hand. "I'll do what I can to help."

When Cathryn kissed her cheek in thanks, Isobel turned to her.

"Just don't ask me to lie." But Isobel knew if they asked her, she would.

~   ~   ~

The *Reader's Digest* left on Isobel's bedside table was still unwrapped.

"Aren't you up to reading?" Dr. Hertz nodded to indicate the magazine.

"Oh yes. I think I am. I like to read. I was thinking just this morning I would like to have a novel."

"What kind of novel? A mystery?" He winked. "A romance?"

He was every bit as handsome as Jack, maybe even more so, with his jaw looking as though it were borrowed from some statue. But the doctor's manner was too easy, he seemed glib and world-weary. One of the things that had endeared Jack to her was his almost boyish innocence. His inexperience with disdain. The uncrushable hope.

She sighed. "No, no. A real book, maybe some short

stories. Maybe Joyce." She looked up at him and mused. "I never did finish reading Joyce. I meant to do that, read all of his work. I just don't know where the time went." She poked a sharp finger into the hard flesh of the doctor's forearm. "You think I'll live long enough to finish Joyce?"

He laughed, feigning ignorance, "I'm just your doctor. I don't know any Joyce."

"Right." Isobel looked distant. "Maybe I'll try Proust. He used to read Proust aloud to Cathryn while I sat guard in the boat."

"He?"

"The man you look like." She smiled and tapped her forehead. "I've remembered his name. Jack Reese."

"And he is . . . ?"

"He's the man who disappeared in Cypress."

"Cyprus? So, we're back to that."

"Yes, Cypress, the town I lived in then. That's where the tailor shop was, that was where I made Cathryn's hats."

"Cyprus is a town?'

Isobel was tiring. "Yes, Cypress, Minnesota. It's also a lake. A very large lake. You're not from around here, are you?"

"Nope." Dr. Hertz frowned at the temperature readout on the monitor. "D.C." He had been due at the desk five minutes earlier. "So, a man named Jack who looks like me disappeared in some lake up north?"

"You mean you look like him. Yes . . . well, no. No one ever found them . . ."

"Them?"

"Jack and Cathryn."

"So, *two* people have disappeared now?"

Isobel scowled. "Not now, for heaven's sake. Years and years ago. A lifetime."

The pager at the doctor's belt beeped and he tipped it out to read the neon digits flashing at the tiny window. He absentmindedly patted Isobel's hand. "I want to hear this, but I have to go. Promise me you'll keep that thought."

When Isobel looked up he was gone.

Keep that thought. As if it were one. With her false teeth and her working hand, Isobel managed to tear open the wrapper of the *Reader's Digest*. She squinted at the table of contents. Everyone else had been testing her, perhaps it was time to test herself, see what damage had been done to her mind. She pawed forward to the serial article, "It Pays to Increase Your Word Power," smiling at the title's ironic clumsiness. She felt for her bifocals, aimed their shaking stems at her temples, and managed to settle them. The small print blurred, and she felt a flash of despair.

My eyes. Now my eyes too.

She turned on the bedside light and held the book close, nearly touching the page to her nose. The words she could make out were familiar: *augury, recalcitrant, sonorous, lugubrious.*

She scanned down the page to a word she did not recognize. Isobel rolled the awkward syllables on her tongue and again read its definition. The magazine fluttered slowly to her chest.

Strange how you know of something all your life and find only at the end there has been a better word for it all along. The syllables bumped pleasantly against her dentures as she read aloud, "*Tintinnabulation:* The sound of the pealing of bells."

CHAPTER THREE

~ ~ ~

*I*n May, Isobel Howard turned thirty-six years old. She woke early to find the sun not yet risen and the house perfectly quiet. She lay motionless next to her husband, the deep silence revealing a jewel within her cache of memory. She had only to reach up and wrap her hands around the glad weight of it.

Had it been there all this time?

She'd been very young, only four or five, and had just been bounced from the back of a careening toboggan full of schoolchildren. Lying on her back on a slope of blue snow in bitter twilight, she squinted through her pain at the dry crystals pirouetting in the dissolving glint of day. The toboggan slid out of sight and downward over a horizon that could have been the end of the earth. The air had been knocked from her small chest, and the pain tore as she waited for breath to return.

She knew instinctively not to move, and after a moment found that when she did stay still, the sting lessened.

As the pain slowly ebbed, Isobel marveled at the stunning silence. She was suddenly aware of herself from all angles, feeling every fiber of her body, the smallness of her limbs, the soft shell of her skin, the solidity and blood-pumping wonder of it. The perfection.

If she had been left, forgotten there, surely she would have been content to lie on her snowy bed for the night. Perhaps forever.

Unmoving, with no breath to cloud her view, she took in the entire curve of a sky streaked with lavender and indigo shouldering in from the east. She was buoyed between snow and sky, weightless, held up by an earth that was turning for her and with her. She was a part of all that surrounded her, yet at the same time distinct. Acute.

For an indelible moment she knew a plain serenity.

After what had seemed like an hour — but could only have been a moment or two — the squealing of rubber-soled snow boots approached, and the distant shout, "There she is!" came to her as if through a sheet of ice. The earth throbbed beneath her, and a metal boot buckle jangled near her temple. The shadow of a figure bent low to obscure her vista. Gritty snow kicked up from a boot sprayed her cheek, and she shook her head, blinking her way back to the world.

The sky, the air, the snow, and her breath — back now and pouring freely from her nostrils like dragon's steam — were reduced to molecules along with the brief seconds of the already falling-away moment. Time compressed itself into a crystalline trinket, lodging on the highest shelf of Isobel's memory.

A treasure. Kept there for her.

As she lay next to Victor, her thoughts shifted to her own children, and she wondered if they experienced such instances, if they had stored similar moments of their own. It occurred to her that if they did, they would have no language to tell her, as she had possessed no language at age five to describe her fleeting but unforgettable sensation of awe and belonging. Of her three children, she supposed Thomas would be the one, with his guileless face and his hunger for awe, so like Victor in his belief that all things were for him. Thomas was an open well, his mouth always wide with laughter, pulling in the affections of all, even dogs and strangers.

Yes, certainly Thomas. Louisa tentatively considered everything in her path, even gifts. Henry was somewhere else altogether, his serious mind obscured by some vapor floating just above the rest of the family. Isobel shook her head in wonderment for the hundredth time over the vast differences among her children.

She swung her feet to the floor, padded to the window, and listened, waiting for some noise from outside to drift in and breach this new silence. What would it be this time? A delivery van, the wind, distant trains, first birds of the day? She looked out over the trees of the angled yard. Just beyond the vegetable garden and the narrow creek was a dense barrier of woods. Past the woods, several alleys of cheap houses sat apart, neatly sequestered from the rest of Cypress by the geography of a ridge, a cliff of weedy clay. Built for Finnish families, the shacks listed on the outcropping of terraced soil. This area had been dubbed Finn Row, and children were warned to stay away by parents wary of the Finns' socialist leanings, their strange-smelling food, and communal bathing. Most of their houses were shingled in raw cedar softened by weather to a pale driftwood colour. A few had been painted the childish sharp blue of the Finnish flag, and these structures were strewn chock-ablock like gems over the grey landscape. Darkened by the hour, they were mislaid chunks of lapis lazuli, the name of the stone as difficult on Isobel's tongue as the names on the mailboxes in front of those houses, the vowel-laden surnames of Aukee, Heikkala, Tuumi. Tribes of stony immigrants who made the same thin wage mining alongside the Welsh, spending their days bent together underground among conflicting accents and the shatter of hydraulic hammers. They emerged from the shafts each night to split off into distinct lines, Welsh veering off to their boarding-houses and dinners of pasties and dark beer, and Finns to their tidy shacks and broad-faced wives cooking potatoes and fish. While the Welsh slept, the Finns rallied in furtive meetings to voice distrust for mine management, clergy, or non-Finns, and to read manifestos of questionable doctrines. They sat naked on the wooden benches of their saunas, drinking a liquor distilled from fetid chokecherries, and sometimes deep in the night Isobel could hear them singing, liquid, foreign melodies curling upward on smoke and steam rising from cinder-brick chimneys.

Beyond the cluster of these houses was another buffer of trees, then the steep drop to the grid of town, where buttery light from streetlamps began to flicker away as the sky lightened. The small park and its wind-battered band shell near the public beach defined the edge of town, and spreading from all points beyond was the immense stain of Lake Cypress.

Closing her eyes, Isobel pressed her forehead to the cool windowpane. Her long silence was finally broken by a faint whistle floating over the Mesabi ridge. The iron mine's first shift. Five A.M. Soon the crushers would roar.

Seven days a week, twelve hours a day, the machines pummeled great hunks of ore into rubble small enough to be loaded into railcars headed to the smelters in far towns.

The constant pounding was a pulse reaching all of Cypress. Some days, with the wrong wind, the noise bit into Isobel's ears; on a good day it was a mere pulse, faint and monotonous as repeated whispers.

Victor stirred slightly and pulled the blanket to his ear. He rolled onto his stomach with a sigh. She should dress. There was a basket of hemming she'd brought from the shop; she could finish that and have lunch boxes packed before the children were up, when she would cook breakfast.

Suddenly remembering the date, she sat again on the edge of the bed. May seventeenth, her birthday. The memory of her moment on the snow-covered hill had been a gift.

The crocheted coverlet had slid from the bed to the floor, and as she leaned down to retrieve it her eyes traveled along the darkened objects in the room — the burled maple bureau, the hooked rug, the wooden valet standing in the corner with Victor's coat draped over it to make a third, comical figure in the room. Faint light glinted off the convex glass of two oval portraits, Isobel's parents: her father, handsome in spite of his sternness, and her mother, looming and sunken-eyed, her black dress straining over a dowager's hump so prominent even the photographer's sympathetic angle could not obscure it. She was sixty-five and looked eighty, spent from stillbirths and embraced bitterness. Isobel turned to the dresser and caught her own reflection in the mirror.

For the first time in years, she prayed, not so much asking as insisting, "God, don't let me die without more moments of that calm." She murmured to the walls, "That's all I want."

She laid her hand on Victor's warm back and began to lean into him. She could wake him. They could make love now, and afterward he could say how sorry he was. She'd been waiting. How long now? Months. She had purposely denied him, and he had not sought her out in the way he used to, never tried to impose on her feigned sleep. He didn't seem to want her. She suddenly sat up.

She'd had his babies, seen them through poverty, worked with him in the shop. When she stood next to him now she felt she was an extension, a fixture no longer seen or heard but relied upon just the same. He was conscious of her in the way he was conscious of his own arm. She couldn't remember the last time he'd told her a joke, coaxed her out of the house for a walk, tried to please her in some small way. He could have rolled to his side just this minute, laid his hand on her hip, and whispered something airy.

She wondered, for the first time in years, if he might have someone else, some other ear to whisper to.

She quickly pushed the thought aside before it could settle against her ribs.

Rising heavily, tired now as if she hadn't slept, she padded to the bathroom, past the rooms of her sleeping children. She ticked off a mental list of the chores ahead, quickly forgetting any notion of her birthday.

After dinner, when Louisa was in the kitchen, supposedly scraping dinner plates and putting away uneaten food, Isobel heard a muffled giggling and a sudden, tinny crash from behind the dining room door. She rolled her eyes and began to rise from the table, but Victor motioned her to sit back down. "Drink your coffee, Iz."

Henry shot out of his chair and snapped off the overhead light.

Isobel sighed. "What on earth?"

Louisa backed out of the swinging kitchen door, weighted with the cake. Victor hopped to her side and attempted to relight a candle that had fallen sideways into the icing.

"Ta da!"

The effort was placed in front of Isobel. A sloping, three-layered affair, lemon icing massed on one side of the platter like a sugared glacier.

Isobel put her hands to her cheeks in mock astonishment. "Oh, so that's why all the flour was on the kitchen floor!"

Victor nudged her knee, frowning.

She looked at him. "It was a joke, Victor."

Louisa looked down. "I worked very hard to make that cake."

Isobel was about to say something blunt to Victor, but caught herself as her gaze swept round the table. Her children's faces were halved in shadow and candlelight.

"Well, it's lovely."

Henry would be taller than Victor soon. Isobel noted how much prettier Louisa was when she smiled. Thomas leaned forward on sturdy fists, the luster in his eye aimed at the candles.

"Just lovely."

Louisa was shy as she offered her mother the knife she'd dipped in warm water.

"After you blow out the candles, can I help cut?"

Victor cleared his throat. "Wait a sec. Isn't anybody going to sing?"

When they were in bed Victor pulled the magazine from Isobel's hands. "What is it?"

"*Harper's.*"

"No, I mean, what *is* it?"

"What is what?"

"Izzy. You've been short with the children, you're . . ."

"I'm what?"

"I don't know. You tell me."

"There's nothing to tell, Victor."

Victor stared at her.

"It's my birthday. You know I've never liked my birthday."

"It hasn't been your birthday every day for the last five months."

Isobel sat up and gathered her nightgown around her ankles. "Fine. Do you want to have one of your talks?" She pursed her lips and examined the lace of her sleeves.

He struggled to his elbows. "You've lost your sense of humor."

She laughed.

When he asked her the third time what was bothering her, she shrugged and gave him a pained smile. "Don't worry about me."

"I'm not just worried about you, I'm worried about all of us."

"Oh Lord, Victor. Please."

Victor suddenly heaved himself to the edge of the bed. "I don't know what's going on with you."

Guess, she wanted to say. Guess what's going on with me.

He snapped off his light and snorted into his pillow, "Haphy birfday."

She thought of touching him. He would look at her then and she could ask, what do you know of me?

She stared at his back for a long time before turning off her own light. She sensed the faint movement of his shoulders and the slow rise of his back as he breathed, saw by moonlight the vulnerability of breath that matched her own. Air in and air out. Same air. She would touch him, finally. *She* would apologize, get him to talk. It had gone on long enough. As she reached over, he took in a serrated breath and exhaled with a gentle snore.

She fell back on her pillow. They hadn't spoken of the island since the day he drove her to Chalmer's Point. The island. It topped the list of hazy unrests she did not want to think about. In the darkness her discontent seemed ripe, a thing to be turned away from before it burst and rotted.

Victor began preparations to outfit the island. Isobel watched from the back porch as he and Henry loaded the flatbed trailer. Onto it went precious sacks of flour, salt, rice, cornmeal, dry macaroni, a case of tinned beef. She crossed her arms, silent as half her kitchen went onto the trailer — pots, cutlery, jelly glasses, most of the blue willow dishes. She waited. When Victor went into the cellar, she dashed out to retrieve a painted china teapot, slipping in a chipped brown replacement. She winnowed through the box of bedding, pulled out the better linen sheets that had been wedding gifts, and tossed in cheaper flannel.

The mercantile had delivered a barrel of kerosene, five gallons of lamp oil, coils of hemp rope, canvas sheeting, rough planks, several folding cots, and a two-burner cookstove. All on credit, Isobel thought grimly. Victor and the boys somehow fit all these items onto the trailer with inches to spare. Louisa brought out a few things her father wouldn't have thought of and placed them on top of the neat palisade of boxes — straw hats, a first aid kit, mosquito netting, a wax bag filled with cakes of soap.

Henry declared himself the only one to be trusted with the new camp spade and wrenched the tool from Thomas's hand. Isobel sat down on the wicker porch swing and shook her head. It looked for all appearances as if they were preparing for an expedition to the Klondike, not just a few weeks of camping.

After lunch they pulled the trailer behind the Ford to Chalmer's Point, where its contents were transferred to the boat that carried mail to the lake's island residents and the Ojibwa families living along the remote north shore. As they loaded the bow, Isobel hung back near a piling.

Doug Green, the skipper, leaned against the railing, intently smoking a cigarette down to its end. "Quite a haul you got there, Victor."

He grimaced as the boys and Victor unloaded more from the trailer, as if puzzling how and where on deck he would ever disperse so much weight.

Once everything was in place, Victor paid Doug for the overweight and slipped him a dollar tip.

"Well, you're off to Lucy Island, then."

Doug looked up. "Lucy Island still? So you haven't re-named it? I thought you'd be calling it Howard Island by now, or Isobel Island. Something."

Thomas ducked around the mail boat's steering wheel, touching everything he could reach on the greasy control panel. "Yeah, Papa. Let's name it after Momma!"

Isobel pressed herself into the piling, pretending not to hear. Victor cleared his throat but did not speak. He scooped Thomas up under one arm and lifted him out to deposit him on the dock, climbing out after.

Doug saluted and promised Victor the load would be left on the island's dock to await their arrival the next day.

"How's the forecast, Doug?"

"Dry as a bone, Vic. You won't be needing that tarp."

Sunday they all piled into and onto the old Ford. The boys stood out on the running boards and clung to the car as it bounced along. Isobel embarrassed Thomas by hold-ing tightly to his wrist as he clung to the side mirror. She didn't let go for the entire trip, even though they crept slowly in the loaded car. Items thought of at the last minute sprouted from the open trunk along with bedrolls and car-tons of clothing. Two thin horsehair mattresses were rolled and tied to the roof so that the car appeared weighted by a giant scroll. The children yelled and waved to anyone walking along the road leading down the hill. Victor leaned on the horn at every passing car or truck. As they traveled down Main Street, Henry swayed from the car to slap each lightpost. They rolled past the closed post office, the imposing facades of the bank, the land office, the library. The fry cook at Jem's Diner leaned against the brick wall, one leg up like a stork, oven mitt dangling at his belt and a curl of smoke at his lip. The only other downtown business that was open was the movie theater, and matinee patrons milled on the sidewalk to form a ragged line to the ticket window.

The car slowed as they passed the tailor shop, where Victor punched out a rhythm on the horn and waved furiously at the darkened windows. Another block and the car left the pavement to sway along gravel past the lumberyard. They passed the road to the marina and the steep trail leading up to the mine. Woods enveloped them for a few miles and the children settled, holding their arms straight out to swipe at the tags of birch leaves. Bluebottles and mayflies met quick deaths on the windshield and grill.

At Chalmer's Point, Isobel kissed her sons good-bye. When she rubbed the grime on Thomas's round cheek with her thumb, he squirmed from her reach. She turned to Henry.

"You have the first aid kit? Remember, butter on a sunburn and Vaseline on wood ticks, not the other way around." She handed him a bulging paper sack. "Apples and carrots. Keep them in a cool spot. And try to get Thomas to eat something besides potatoes."

Louisa hung back. Victor loped to the shore, where he swept his daughter up and whispered into her hair. She giggled and kissed him on the ear before she slipped blushing from his embrace.

Every available bit of space in the boat had been loaded with mattresses, boxes, boys. They were ready.

Victor made a great show of throwing his arms about Isobel and dipping her back in a dramatic swoop. Louisa covered her eyes and the boys moaned as their parents kissed. Victor pulled her up, whispering, "That wasn't so bad now, was it?"

A warm wind caught Isobel's hat, and it cartwheeled across the grey boards. Louisa scampered along to retrieve it before it could sail off the end of the dock. Victor's glance caught Isobel squarely, a smile ticking briefly at the corner of his mouth as he turned to jump into the stern.

As the boat coughed away, Victor saluted and called out above the din of the motor, "See you at the end of August!"

Louisa and Isobel stopped and turned. Isobel cupped her hands and yelled, "August?!"

As if he hadn't heard, Victor did not stop waving or smiling. Smoke spewing from the outboard motor rose to veil him in a yellow-green haze the colour of an old bruise.

~   ~   ~

"I've been talking again, haven't I?"

Thomas shifted in the hard plastic chair next to Isobel's bed.

"Only for a while, Mother. Go on if you like. Please."

"You were falling asleep."

"I was not. I was listening."

Isobel looked at her son, the sheen of baldness creeping through his grey hair. "You're a busy man, too busy to listen to an old woman prattle on."

"You weren't prattling."

"I do that now, sometimes. I'll be thinking and suddenly realize I'm prattling aloud like an old crow. Sorry."

"It was interesting. The things you said about us, the island."

"Oh yes, the island."

Thomas waited, but she didn't finish. Often now she seemed to just drift away, lose the thread. Sometimes it seemed deliberate, as if she were using her age as some corner away from the world when she found it tedious. The entitlement of years, the decades piling up. Hell, she was a sliver away from being a century old! When her doctor first spoke with him he had used the term *senility*. Thomas had laughed aloud at that. "My mother? She's anything but." He'd shaken his head. "Don't let the numbers fool you. She's sharp as a razor."

Was she being evasive now? They sat in strained silence until a candy striper came in. She offered his mother a snack, but she waved away the Ritz crackers and apple juice. She knows what she wants and doesn't want. Never a question there. As the girl swung around Thomas with her tray, he playfully snatched up the little paper cup and popped a cracker into his mouth. He winked at the girl. After he'd watched her walk out the door, he turned back, his voice suddenly serious.

"When you were talking earlier, you didn't mention that dead man again."

Isobel sighed. "First we chew and then we talk, Thomas. Dead man? You mean the missing man."

"Yes, the one you said looks like your doctor."

"Oh, Jack. Jack Reese. Hmm, I was thinking of him just yesterday. You must've missed him. Don't worry, he'll be back later in the story."

"So this is a story? I thought it was real history. I even remember something about a search party." There was an edge in his tone that made Isobel look quickly up at him. Suspicion?

"History. Story. It's all the same, isn't it?" Isobel put on her glasses and peered over their rims. "You can't remember that summer, can you?"

"On the island? Sure I do. That first year . . . how ungodly hot it was." Thomas smiled into the paper cup in his hand. "Dad made hammocks out of old blankets so we could sleep outside. He made us strip each night, and we picked the wood ticks off each other by firelight. Dozens.

We'd drop 'em into the coals and listen for them to pop. *Phweet, phweet,* that's exactly how they sounded."

Isobel shuddered. "Nasty."

"We thought it was great." Thomas laughed. "I caught my first fish there, on a leech. Now, that was nasty. Henry tried to make me bait the hook myself, but Dad ended up doing it for me. I caught a little sunfish. Couldn't have been more than this long." Thomas spread his thumb and forefinger. "Henry thought I should fillet the poor thing, but Dad came to its rescue, said throw it back, let it grow up and become a decent meal."

His mother's eyes fluttered as if they might close. Thomas felt a flash of tattered emotion that surprised him. He crushed the paper cup in his hands and closed his own eyes. He could see his father that day in the boat, the hair on his brown forearms gone blond from months on the island, sleeves rolled high to show his wiry biceps. His nose had peeled from sunburn, and his fishing hat was cocked low, the little cigar clenched sideways between his molars as he grimaced over the squirming leech.

Sixty years? Something like that. But it was as if his father were there in the room, slouched between his chair and his mother's bed. Thomas could almost smell the cigar, its smoke cloaking the stink of bait drying between the ribs of a wooden boat. The memory was so precise, so bright-edged, that Thomas opened his eyes quickly, as if ready for the ghost.

But there was only his mother, staring past his shoulder to the window, as if she were alone.

He wondered if she ever thought of him.

Isobel made herself look at her youngest child. Sometimes it was like seeing a ghost. Thomas's shoulders had begun to round, his jowls had thickened, and his eyebrows were wild. Victor, if he'd lived. She felt very tired.

Thomas had been her last baby. After Victor died she'd felt his eyes move away from her in a cool, confused shift, as if — in the mired reasoning of a grieving ten-year-old — he held her somehow accountable for his father's death. When he had most needed her and she him, he had refused her solace and bore his sorrow in more silence than any child should.

He'd come back, of course, but never the entire way, not with her. He was kind and dutiful, loving really. She knew he loved her. He joked with her just like Victor used to, and they occasionally sparred, but he never forgot flowers on Mother's Day and always bought her expensive Christmas gifts. He came for dinner every Thursday and they played Scrabble in companionable silence. They watched the news and sometimes they talked, even about personal things, fears, hopes. But she'd never won back the fierce shimmer that had once passed between them.

"You better get back to your office, Thomas. Go count some beans. They'll be bringing my lunch soon."

Thomas brushed her temple with his mustache. "Yes, ma'am. Still the boss."

~   ~   ~

Driving home from Chalmer's Point with Louisa beside her, Isobel was silent, her mouth a hard line. She realized she and Victor had never actually discussed how long he would be gone with the boys. He had tried to speak with her only that morning, but she had busied herself tending to a cut on Thomas's arm. Just a scratch, but she made a great task of dabbing iodine and searching for gauze and scissors. She had walked away from Victor, ignoring him as she had every time he'd started a conversation regarding the island.

Had he simply forgotten to mention how long they would be gone? Was their absence meant to be retribution for her indifference over the last months? She clutched the steering wheel. She did not know. Could not. In the same way she couldn't know how a man could be married to a woman — live with her, sleep with her, and move through the world at her side for nearly half her life — and not know of her dread of water.

In their first days alone, she and Louisa cleaned, scrubbing the house and tucking away toys and clothes and books, room by room. Their work dredged up forgotten treasures lodged behind radiators and nested in parcels of dust. Long-forgotten items suddenly offered themselves up — a horn jackknife, old coins, a tiny crucifix, crayon stubs, a tarnished silver chain, and, oddly, a chipped glass eye that must have belonged to some previous tenant. With each of these items rubbed clean and laid away, Isobel felt she was preserving some small history.

The house sparkled as if it indeed were a sort of museum, its atmosphere one of anticipation, as if people were on their way but somehow delayed. As she and Louisa worked, the walls absorbed their echoes: the squeal of windows being polished, the snap of linens unfurled over air-freshened mattresses, the slurring and slopping of mops being rinsed, wrung, and rinsed again.

With the boys away, the voices of the house began to make themselves heard. She and Louisa took to pausing when faint whisperings interrupted their tasks. Mice nested fiercely in the attic walls, constant in their chewing of newspaper insulation. Bats seethed, settling in the eaves each morning. A low chorus of water pipes sang odd rhythms in the walls. The structure seemed a nervous giantess, shrugging and shifting her beam-and-rafter bones, as if trying to better fit into her garment of clapboard and cedar shakes.

At night Isobel walked the hallways, placing her hand

on the doors of the boys' bedrooms, picturing them sleeping on the island, limbs tangled among bedding, damp cheeks puffing gently. Victor would be draped awkwardly on his cot, an elbow or knee jutting over the side. He would snore a little, perhaps fluttering a hand out in his sleep to brush a spider or a hair from his face, dreaming.

After a week Isobel realized that the house, with minimal dusting, was going to stay clean, possibly for the summer. The usually daunting task of laundry was reduced to rinsing out a few undergarments, stockings, and the occasional frock that Louisa wore while weeding the garden.

Meals were simple and small, and as the weather grew warmer their appetites withered. They abandoned the formality of the dining room to eat on the porch or at the kitchen table. Louisa harvested the first greens from the garden while Isobel boiled a vegetable or two, cut and buttered bread, and poured lemonade in the quiet kitchen. She took to drinking her coffee over ice. She sent a note to the dairy asking them to deliver a quart of milk Mondays and Thursdays instead of the usual two gallons.

One early evening Isobel sat in the kitchen reading newspaper accounts of the bad weather in Oklahoma and Arkansas. She pitied the mothers in the grainy photographs, dead-eyed migrants bending in blighted fields or leaning hard against unpainted buildings. They peered at the camera so unabashedly Isobel knew there was no vanity left in the gaunt faces. The women were hollowed by merciless winds and nursing babies. Their exhaustion groaned from the pages, and Isobel felt a twinge of guilt for her own full belly, her comfort.

Her own children were safe. Her fears that the boys weren't eating properly or being carefully watched suddenly seemed ridiculous as she examined the faces of migrant children. Of course Victor would take care of them; had she thought otherwise?

He had temporarily relieved her of her motherhood,

but if the act had been malicious she could not imagine it. It occurred to her for the first time that he had taken the boys not so much deliberately away from her, but to gather them to himself. Because he wanted to be with them, show them a time. Be one of them. Because he could.

From the beginning he had been an eager father.

She'd envied that, never felt herself to be a very natural parent. When she told Victor she was pregnant the first time, she'd burst into tears. He took her hand, puzzled, while trying to suppress his own excitement.

"We'll get a good midwife, Iz. Or we could get a doctor. You can even have the baby in the hospital if you like."

"It's not that part I'm frightened of."

"What, then?"

"What if . . . Oh, what if it's born blind, or doesn't like me? What if I can't make it happy?"

He looked at his wife. He'd heard pregnant women were sometimes unpredictable. "Oh, Iz. It's a baby. Our baby. It'll be fine. It'll love you. Look, I love you, and I'm a lot smarter than some baby."

When she stepped on his foot he made kicked-dog yelps and hobbled to the icebox. Hopping back and apologizing there was no ice cream to go with it, he handed her a pickle. As she bit in, pale juice squirted over his collar.

He touched the tiny swell at her belly, wonderment in his voice. "Oh, Mrs. Howard, what have we here?"

When Henry was born Victor rooted himself outside their bedroom door for the duration of her labour, rocking in place with his eyes squeezed shut against his own helplessness. Each time she fell quiet between gritty moans he was sure she had died. And when it started up again he felt rushes of relief and a terrible pity, wishing only that he could absorb his wife's pain. Toward the end her cries were drawn with agony, and when those cries began Victor moaned along with the awful sound and pressed his forehead into the doorframe, so that for weeks afterward he had a strange, ridged bruise running from his temple to his eyebrow.

When she produced a last, garbled scream, he tried to barge in, but the midwife had locked the door against him.

Later, when he was finally let in, he was astonished to see Isobel smiling weakly and trying to button together a clean nightgown. He nearly folded in relief, catching himself with a hand on the bedstead. The midwife quickly covered the basin she was carrying and bustled out the door.

"Don't you touch that baby. I'll be back in a minute with more cloths."

He ignored her and scooped up the naked infant, still streaked with slime, and held it up to the window to examine.

"Well, well, well. Will you look at that, Iz!"

He leaned down to kiss his wife and laughed, nodding to the first-blush light coming in through the panes. "I had it all planned while I was waiting. I was going to call her Dawn, but you see here, she's got all the wrong plumbing."

Isobel's fingers thrummed the table. Yes, Victor had always been very at ease with the children.

At the hour she looked up at the cuckoo forcing his head out of his tiny chalet and marveled, certain she had never had the luxury of sitting and listening to a clock tick. Late sun glinted off the taps over the scrubbed sink. She sat opposite Louisa across the polished table, a bowl of grapes between them, a dome of waxed cheesecloth to keep away flies.

Louisa was a strangely reserved child, making only the softest impression with her presence. Isobel realized that her daughter was not, as she had suspected, overwhelmed by her boisterous brothers, nor was her spirit trodden in the chaos created by them. Alone with only Isobel, the girl seemed to take on a new dimension, quiet but happily, deliberately quiet, an observant child with an expansive inner life.

Like an island, Isobel thought. Most all of her hidden.

After they had settled into the quiet rhythms of just the two of them in the house, Isobel tried to draw the girl out in conversation — doing nearly all of the talking herself while Louisa nodded, polite but stubbornly mute, her fringe of wheat-coloured bangs rising and falling over blue-grey eyes.

She told the girl a bit about her own childhood, about growing up above the bakery, before it was a tailor shop, back when it had been her father's business and her family lived upstairs. She described her room above the ovens, deliciously warm in winter but unbearable in July. How the smell of yeast and rising dough was so pervasive it insinuated itself into her clothing and hair, so that schoolmates would sometimes tease, calling her Isobread.

She said little of her own mother. She found herself hoping that when Louisa was grown, with children of her own, her remembrances of her first family might be fond.

She tried to explain the loneliness of growing up as she did, as an only child. She was glad Louisa had brothers to play with. "You see, that way no one is left alone."

Louisa, pointed chin shelved on a palm, looked at her mother and with her chewed nails tapped a tattoo over the freckles on her cheek.

"But I am alone."

Isobel frowned. "What do you mean?"

"I'm alone. Even when they're here. Isn't that why I'm staying home and they're all out on the island? 'Cuz the boys are just like Papa, and I'm just like you."

She was smiling as she declared it so.

~   ~   ~

CHAPTER FOUR

On Saturday Isobel walked to the tailor shop. Victor's sign on the door, *Sorry, closed till September,* was crooked. She removed it and hung the sign Louisa had fashioned the night before. The girl had worked so hard bent over her pasteboard, the tip of her tongue anchored sideways, that Isobel couldn't bring herself to point out the misspelling. *Open Mournings, Eight Till Noon.* She took another sign from her basket, this one she had made herself with a laundry marker on parchment in a hurried longhand. *Millinery.* She spread the sign across the window under Victor's gold and black letters and taped it into place. If the summer went well, perhaps in the autumn she would hire a sign painter to permanently assign the word in gilded paint.

The tools and most of the materials she needed were here, squirreled away in drawers and cupboards around the shop. She spread boxes on the worktable. One held the feathers, and those she separated by colour and species. Since her sons had been old enough to leave the yard, Isobel had offered a bounty for each perfect feather brought home. Henry and Thomas scoured the woods and searched the riverbanks for abandoned nests, and their prizes emerged from skins of tissue paper in subdued hues — pheasant, grouse, and guinea hen, waxwing and partridge. A more colourful selection lay beneath — carnival splashes of jay, scarlet tanager, blue bunting, yellow finch, and oriole. Exotic feathers and whole, preserved wings ordered from catalogs had arrived in vellum packets tagged with the Latin names — *Ortalis vetula, Anser cygnoides, Paroaria, Estrilda.* One caught Isobel's eye, *Gracula religiosa,* and she smiled at the name, thinking it rather showy for the simple mynah bird.

She picked up an oil-black feather with a brilliant red slash, running the edge of the feather over the back of her hand. More waxed boxes read *Duck: All Kinds.*

After arranging the feathers and relabeling the drawer tabs, Isobel went through a basket of magazines, copies of *Vogue* and *Harper's,* and the fashion pages torn from previous weeks of the *Minneapolis Tribune.*

She'd planned this moment many times in her head, but always with the knowledge it would be a far-off thing, a someday endeavor to be resumed when the children were in school or old enough to help run the house, or when Victor wasn't so busy. Now, surrounded by these things once again, Isobel felt time dissolve, so that she was no less eager than on her first day in the Pasal Millinery, twenty years before.

When was it? Last autumn Victor had made the glib comment about having a fourth child. Thomas had finally started school, and she was only just beginning to see her way clear. There would be no more babies if she could help it. It didn't matter what she had promised so many years ago. She wasn't filling an order. Victor had made promises too. She clearly remembered his pointing to the sunny corner of the shop and saying, "That's where you can do your hat business, Izzy, right there."

She dove into cupboards and found square bread tins containing ribbons and ribbon scraps, brilliant arrays of grosgrain, satin, and plaids, all tightly packed by widths, from a slivered eighth to five inches wide. She arranged the rolls by texture and colour — crimped, knotty, pleated, watery silk and heavy velvet. Tins were crammed with false flowers of velveteen. The last was heaviest, and she hoisted it to the worktable to begin sorting the brooches with broken clasps or missing rhinestones, mateless earrings, and beads of all varieties — glass, porcelain, clay, horn, ivory, and bone. All items were pawed through and tossed into sectioned trays.

In an old flour bin she found lengths of tanned snakeskin and dyed leathers, scraps of alligator and bits of fur, dyed lengths of horsetail, suede and leather lashings, braided hemp. A stack of cigar boxes held pounded silver disks, pieces of antler, and several dozen perfect clusters of tiny pine cones.

As she dragged an old spool case from the back room, Isobel vaguely wondered if Victor might guess what she was doing to fill her time.

The boxes and drawers and trays fanned out on the vast worktable, their contents representing years of hoarding and waiting. She hadn't seen many of the items for years, and she had to fight to keep from falling into a haze of reminiscence as she worked. Picking up a short length of pearl beading left over from the bodice of her wedding gown, she recalled Victor's pledge: that it would be the one and only article of clothing he would ever make for her.

Isobel clearly remembered those weeks of sewing, and Victor's face as he was chided by superstitious friends about the consequences of making her gown. He'd been warned, "Seeing your bride's dress is bad luck enough, but making it? Vic, you're asking for disaster."

Victor hardly looked up from the lengths of tawny voile spilling from his lap, snapping a thread with his grinning teeth.

"Been courting disaster for months. Can't hardly let her down now, can I?"

Even Isobel thought his idea to make her dress was overly romantic, almost silly. But when she entered the church on her father's arm and saw Victor waiting at the altar, the gown shifted minutely on her shoulders, and she suddenly experienced a stark comprehension, not only of his labours, but his intent. His allegiance to her stitched in silk, pronounced in the lace cuffs and repeated in rows of beadwork. Happiness hinted at in the hems teasing her ankles, his desire trailing in the folds and weight of the train.

Monday she was at the shop early. She swept and scrubbed and polished until the odors of steamed wool, mothballs, and sewing machine oil were softened by Castile soap and lemon wax. By ten A.M. the combs had fallen from her hair and the braid coiled atop her head had slipped sideways nearly over an ear. Her face was streaked with sweat, and in her haste she had forgotten to bring an apron, so that her skirt had two filthy smudges where she had repeatedly wiped her hands on her hips. Her stockings were run from kneeling on the rough floor.

She was moving a heavy suit form away from her corner, half lugging, half dancing it to the rear of the shop, when she began to sing a low, off-key song that rose in a crescendo as she wrestled her ungainly partner along the boards.

Her singing voice could move Victor to hysteria. He would slap helplessly at his knees and shake his head, mute laughter hissing from his throat. Wiping his eyes after a round of "Old McDonald," he would turn to the children. "Well, if there's another war, we'll always be safe. Who needs bombs when we have your mother's voice?"

Isobel was singing at the top of her lungs when a strange woman stepped into the shop, her silhouette framed darkly against a backdrop of bright haze and a passing swarm of mayflies. Isobel nearly dropped the suit form to the floor. It righted itself violently on its heavy iron stand, bouncing against Isobel's chest and nearly knocking her down.

Had she seen the woman somewhere before? She couldn't be sure. Someone from the resorts or summer cabins? The stranger was stifling a laugh with the back of her hand. Isobel took the dummy by the shoulders as though to chastise it. It wobbled for a second, teetering on the uneven floorboards as if it might fall.

Isobel attempted to straighten her braid with one hand, while wiping the other on her dirty skirt. She smiled in greeting. "Look at me! You'll think I'm mad. Well, I'm not. Really, ask anyone. I'm Isobel." She reached for the woman's white-gloved hand. "Isobel Howard." But instead of grasping the proffered hand Isobel merely touched the woman's forefinger, pressing it in a tiny shake. "And as you can see, I'm quite filthy."

The woman clasped Isobel's dirty hand and pumped it vigorously. "I'm Mrs. Liam Malley. And I am quite clean."

"Malley? Oh, you must be that Chicago woman!" When the words spilled out, Isobel's hand flew to her mouth.

Mrs. Malley's own mouth twitched and she nodded somberly.

"Yes, that's me." She looked dubiously around the shop. "I saw your sign." The room was empty of hats of any kind. "You're Cypress's milliner?"

Mrs. Malley was tall and wore her thick sable hair

wrapped into a chignon. She was slight-shouldered and small-waisted, a slim pear. Her clothes, Isobel noted, were simple but well tailored from fine grades of fabric. She wore a thin, cap-sleeved blouse and a straight linen skirt nearly to her ankles. Her jewelry was modest, a gold four-leaf clover at her collar, a plain wedding band, freshwater pearls in her ears. Her hat was the only truly distinctive article about her, a demure mustard-coloured wedge with slim pheasant feathers trailing behind. A city hat, thought Isobel. Simple, elegant. The face beneath its brim was attractive — fetching, as Victor would say — with a thin nose, wide mouth, and very pale green eyes. Dark, arched brows made her appear slightly curious. Her regal neck made her seem taller than she actually was. Isobel tried not to stare.

I could make hats for such a head.

She invited the woman to sit down, apologizing for the mess in the shop and again for her own state. As she spoke, she put water to boil on the small gas burner near the irons. She took down two dusty cups and wiped them clean with a piece of muslin.

"Welcome to Cypress, Mrs. Malley. I can offer you some tea, but there's no milk, I'm afraid. And, honestly, I can't really claim to be the milliner. Not yet, anyway. I confess I might have put the cart before the horse by pasting that sign up. Truth is, I haven't worked for years, other than dressmaking. I'm just getting my things together again, but I don't even have any current patterns . . . " She eyed the woman's hat, wondering how she might politely ask to examine its interior for clues to its construction.

She was chattering on nervously but couldn't stop. She realized she hadn't spoken to an adult in over a week.

" . . . so, you see, I'm sorry if you've come to buy a hat. I'm simply not ready. I don't even have all my supplies yet. It will be a week, at least."

Mrs. Malley was still standing, had made no move to sit

on the offered chair. She picked up the string of pearl beads from the worktable to examine them. When finally she looked up at Isobel, she seemed uncertain. "Have we met?"

Isobel blinked. She was sure now they had not; she would not have forgotten those eyes. Mrs. Malley's gaze was startling, the irises extreme in their colour of the silvery side of a leaf. But there was some reflection in her eye aside from the odd lightness which Isobel found unsettling. Distraction? Preoccupation? She had the sudden inexplicable thought that Mrs. Malley was struggling to place herself as she touched surfaces and scanned the room. She seemed to be taking an inventory, as if to fill a hollowed moment with detail, to anchor that moment and gain some foothold in it.

When she spoke, the words seemed perfunctory and vaguely hollow. "Thank you for the offer of tea, Mrs. Howard, but I should really be getting home." She handed Isobel the beads and turned to the door. "I may stop by another time."

Isobel stepped forward. Perhaps they *had* met. "Wait."

The woman glanced back only for an instant. She smiled and said, "Thank you," before slipping away into the glare of the street.

So abrupt was Mrs. Malley's odd visit that as she sat later, sipping tea at Victor's cluttered desk, Isobel wondered if she'd imagined it. She drained her cup and went back to her tasks.

~   ~   ~

Isobel shut her eyes against the glare of all the metal; too much. The rails of her bed, the towel dispenser, the frame of the wheelchair, each offered warped miniatures of the room.

She clawed backward, trying once again to recall that

first meeting, to ferret up some ancient detail, trying to identify anything special, anything that might have portended such a bitter end. How ironic that her first encounter with Cathryn was so mundane she couldn't dredge up anything other than having thought the woman a little distracted and slightly familiar.

Isn't that just how it happens. A person need only walk over your threshold and your life can become forever changed, lived under a different sky.

~   ~   ~

She laid the pearl beads from her wedding dress away. Fate always seemed to come traipsing through one door or another. When she met Victor, she'd just finished her apprenticeship at the millinery in Duluth and was working at her first paid position. He had come in to pick up a bolt of soleil and loitered at the counter for a full hour after the transaction. He had a charming, lopsided grin that veered left. He was lean, gap-toothed, and energetic, his hair already thinning. He joked and smiled at Isobel incessantly, straddling the limits of decency in an attempt to get her to giggle or blush, but she remained stubbornly composed and uncoloured and kept at her task of cutting a stack of felt rounds. She'd had to shoo him out the door at closing time.

When she stepped out after locking up, she scanned the empty street with a disappointment that surprised her. He might have waited to walk her home, or even to tease her more. With her head down she walked toward her tram stop. Turning the corner, she nearly ran into the flower Victor held out, a paper iris fashioned from a scrap of butcher paper with a pipe-cleaner stem, its stamen a twisted Juicy Fruit wrapper. His grin was sheepish, suddenly shy. He nodded toward the darkened window of the flower shop across the street and shrugged.

"Closed."

Isobel took the flower but could not repress a smile as she sniffed at the paper. "Doesn't smell like much, does it?"

Within six months they were married.

During their courtship Victor was uncharacteristically reticent when Isobel asked about his life.

"But I'm going to be your wife, Victor. You have to tell me something."

"Well, it *is* awfully like a Dickens tale." He was smiling as he said it, but his smile stitched sideways and he focused on a point far over her shoulder.

His father, a railway worker, had died in a switching accident when Victor was only eight. His mother, frail to begin with, grew more weak and distracted. She could neither take proper care of Victor nor make ends meet on her small pension. One day she walked Victor to St. Matthew's Boys Home and begged the nuns to look after him until she regained her stamina.

He waited two years for some word. When the priest came to sit on his bed to tell him his mother had died in the TB hospital in Superior, he could not remember her face.

He had twin brothers ten years older. One had gone west. The other, he told Isobel — only after they'd been engaged for a month — had been convicted on counterfeiting and swindling charges, and was serving out a prison sentence in Wisconsin.

The story had made the Duluth papers, and the nuns who taught at the Catholic school annexed to St. Matthew's discouraged Victor from taking vocational classes that might expose him to inks and printing presses, particularly papermaking and engraving.

"They needn't have worried. My real dream was to be a ship's captain."

The window over his bed in the boy's wing had a fine

view of Duluth's harbor, and the activities of the port inspired his imagination. His sleep was light with expanses of seas the colours of all eyes. He dreamed of the racket of foreign harbors and of climates where he imagined things as exotic as olives or bananas grew, places where darkskinned people danced barefoot and spoke in melodies. He set himself on the bows of ships skirting shoals of islands forged of sand and sun and all hues of green.

If his studies were weak, he was given slack for his good nature. He was kind to the younger boys in his ward. The children of St. Matthew's were expected, among other things, to mend their own clothing. Victor took pity on frustrated boys who fumbled with wormlike fingers over their tasks; usually they ended up tearing or otherwise making worse a simple chore. He took the needle and coarse thread from their hands, knowing it would be easier for him to darn the sock or stitch the hem himself than watch them struggle — in the same way he could not watch a boy in a fistfight without knowing it would be easier to take the blows himself.

Victor showed a talent for settling arguments between the boys who were as rough as motherless boys would be. With the older ones, he turned his nimbleness with a needle into a kind of currency, trading the patching of jeans and sewing of buttons against more unsavory chores of spreading manure in the vegetable garden, washing the tile floor of the bathroom, or disinfecting the long bank of stained urinals.

In his elevated social status in the confines of the orphanage, he found he never needed to steal. If he wanted to sneak to the belfry for a smoke, he could always find some boy with a stash of tobacco who either owed him a good turn or simply liked his company. If he needed a nickel, he would offer to run errands for one of the nuns who trusted him to return with the right goods and proper change, if only late. His navigational skills — even in a town with the landmark of a great lake — were poor. He was forever confusing his whereabouts. *Not so much lost as wandering.*

The policemen who brought him back time and time again became more patient with the boy as they grew to know him; a few even began to look forward to the break in their beat when they might come across him turning circles at some intersection, trying to make sense of the numbered street signs. Walking back to St. Matthew's, Victor always had some embellished story to tell the policemen about his journeys, things he had seen or conversations overheard that he twisted into humorous tales. By the time they dropped him at the gate, the policemen would shake the priest's hand and grin as Victor sauntered off toward the dormitory. They would say things like, "Fine boy, Father. Smart, real smart," then shake their heads. "Odd, though. Compass all cattywampus."

He couldn't tell his right hand from his left. His failure in all but simple mathematics was not for lack of effort, and he often sneaked away to the belfry more often to study on the sly than to smoke, embarrassed at his shortcoming and afraid to let the other boys see him laboring over his sums like a girl.

He would never be a ship's captain, not even second officer. Even merchant marines needed enough sense to navigate by the stars. He could become a dockworker, a labourer, a criminal like his brother, or he could find a trade. He buried the dog-eared math books at the bottom of his wooden locker and asked one of the nuns if she'd teach him to run the pedal sewing machine in the laundry.

Victor took a bow. "And that is the fascinating story of how I became a tailor instead of a sailor."

~   ~   ~

Thomas got up to slowly pace the room. "He never said much to us about the orphanage, only a few funny stories about the boys and the nuns. Did he ever find out about his mother? Those two years?"

Isobel rubbed her numb arm. "Not much, only that she worked for a time as a maid, in a hotel, I think."

"But didn't they write to each other?"

"Oh, I'm sure she couldn't read or write. She'd never been to school."

Thomas stopped and turned, his shoes squealing on the linoleum. "So, my grandmother was an illiterate chambermaid." He looked at the floor and exhaled through his nose. "Christ. How did I get to be almost seventy years old and not know that?"

Isobel shrugged. "Swept under the rug. You know, he always wondered if his own shortcomings might have been passed on. He worried you'd all inherit his . . . oh, there's a name for it now, what is it?"

"Dyslexia."

"Yes, that's it. Lord, he struggled. When he was having a hard time with numbers he'd just leave the account books and receipts on my side of the bed."

"And you'd do his work?"

"Of course. I'd do the books at night and leave them under his coat. Later on I'd just do them at the shop."

"Did he ever thank you?"

She looked at Thomas. "Certainly not. He was too ashamed." Her smile was stiff. "You know, he made me promise something. He made me promise — and he didn't mention Henry — that you would go to college. That was only a few weeks before he died. I remember afterward thinking how strange, as if he knew."

Thomas saw his mother's chin waver, and dug in his pocket for a handkerchief. "Did you really think he knew he was going to die?"

"Oh, I don't know anymore."

He was about to speak when a food service worker came in without knocking. A youth with a greasy ponytail set Isobel's dinner tray down with a metal *clank* on the table and turned without a word.

Thomas glared at the youth's back and asked, "What, no candles?"

"Oh, be nice, Thomas. They work hard."

Isobel lifted the aluminum cover to a mound of beige food. She glanced at her menu slip. "Low-sodium chicken stew, and this, I think, is either turnip or potato." She pushed the tray away and fell back into her pillow. "I'm too tired to eat, anyway." The tear that was threatening ran slowly down her temple and into her hair.

"Let me see that."

Isobel grimaced. "Don't, it smells."

Thomas plucked his suit coat from the chair and picked up the tray. "I'll get rid of this. Listen, Hugo's is right around the corner. How about some pasta? Ravioli? What'dya say to a pizza?"

Isobel shifted and swallowed. "Pizza?"

Out in the hall Thomas slid the food tray into the rolling metal rack. He leaned back against the wall and pressed his thumbs into his temples, the throb of hospital sounds beating to his pulse. He shook himself into his suit coat and moved toward the elevator.

~   ~   ~

Not long after they met, Victor took Isobel to a cockfight in Hayward. Before the first round was half over, he turned to the empty space where she'd been. He found her in the parking lot, leaning against the dusty bumper of his car, hand over her mouth as if she might retch.

"Hey, where'd you go? I had two dollars on that fight."

Isobel closed her eyes. "Is this your idea of a date?"

He sidled up to her and stroked her arm, suddenly contrite. "Sorry. Next time I'll take you bowling." He nodded toward the back door of the bar. "It was kind of smelly in there."

"Victor."

"You see." He dropped his cigarette and ground it into the dirt. "I've never done this before."

"Really? You seemed like an old hand in there, cheering on those horrible birds."

"Not the fight. Courting."

She slit an eye on him. "So now you're courting me?"

"Well, yeah. I mean, yes." He laughed. "You think I'd bring just any girl down here?"

When she turned to open the car door he laid his hand over hers.

"So what do you say?"

"To what?"

"What do you say we get married and have a dozen blue-eyed babies?"

Isobel laughed, but when she met his glance she saw he was serious.

"Is that a proposal?"

"No." He dropped to one knee in the gravel and took her hand. "This is. Isobel Marie, will you be my wife and mother our blue-eyed babies?"

She tried to pull him up. "I'll think about it."

In her bed that night she wondered about the strange boy. Man, really. He was nearer to thirty than twenty. He was rough, streetwise, and not at all what she imagined her first suitor would be. When she moved to Duluth she had taken rooms in the east end of town, near the Normal School. She'd thought how lucky she was to be near the campus. She would meet nice college boys, studious young men, serious and sensitive.

As she drifted off to sleep she smiled, thinking of Victor on his knee in the dingy parking lot, his voice raised to be heard over the din of a cockfight.

He did take her bowling, and afterward she pressed him for more details of his life.

"Ah, you don't want to hear more about me."

She folded her arms and leaned back. "I have all night."

"Fine, then. You sure?"

She didn't move.

"When I was seventeen I was apprenticed to a tailor named Joseph Beeks. You'll not have seen the shop, it's down by Docklands."

"What was he like?" Isobel leaned forward.

"Ah, what's the word? I read it once." Victor thumped his temple. "Garrulous. That's it, fits him to a tee."

Beeks, he told Isobel, disliked the monotony of his work but loved a rowdy story. He allowed himself one furtive dram of whiskey for every hour he sewed, and at the hour the old tailor would hold up a hand for silence, then cock his head sideways to determine by sound the location of Mrs. Beeks. If her off-key humming and cooking noises from the kitchen assured she was at a safe distance, the bottle would come out of the bottom drawer and the whiskey was poured. Beeks would gulp, wipe out the glass, and stash the bottle. A ritual.

Once Victor asked, "Why bother with the glass?"

Beeks slapped the table. "Why bother! Only tramps and drunkards drink from the neck, boy. Speaking of necks, I'm reminded of a story 'bout a Hottentot priestess and her pygmy lover . . . "

Mrs. Beeks was a kind, faded woman who appeared to be built of a series of hinged, uncooked bread loaves. Her hair was a powdery white, she smelled of boiled milk, and she had a tendency to hug Victor in a suffocating clench whenever he was near enough to grab. She apologized once a week to Victor over Sunday dinner, loaded with regret that she had not known of his plight years earlier, for surely she and Mr. Beeks would have adopted him away from "that place."

Not wanting to disappoint her, he let Mrs. Beeks choose

to believe whatever grim miseries she imagined he'd endured at St. Matthew's. She was a good cook, and the room she gave him at the back of the shop was clean, his linens were fresh, and the bookshelf was crammed with dozens of adventure books left behind by their grown son.

Evenings Victor walked through the warehouse district, the great landmark of dual lighthouses at the pier leading him to shore. There he would soak his stinging, needle-worn fingers in Lake Superior and read from young Beeks's stories. Trading one water-numbed hand for another to turn pages, he sat at the edge of the lake and read slowly through Africa and India on the backs of water buffalo, camels, and elephants. He dug for diamonds in Peru and climbed Machu Picchu, went to the pole with Admiral Peary.

His fingertips grew rigid with calluses, but after five years he could tell by touch if a quarter-inch stitch was straight and tight without looking. After the apprenticeship was complete, he stayed on as Beeks's assistant. It did not occur to him to go to a bigger city or find a better-paying position. He could not have said whether his inertia stemmed from contentment or laziness. When Mrs. Beeks died, he mourned her as he might have mourned a fondly remembered grandmother. Mr. Beeks mourned more actively, no longer hiding his whiskey or limiting himself to his once-an-hour "medicinal" shots. The bottle was now within easy reach, the old man pouring shot after shot until his dirty stories degenerated to obscene mumblings and he could neither sew nor walk straight. Victor could hardly leave then.

He corrected Beeks's mistakes, appeased disgruntled customers, and cooked large, starchy meals in hopes that potatoes and rice would soak up the effects of the alcohol. He watched as the old man drank himself to liver disease.

Out of spite for his son who never visited, fondness for

Victor, or some addled sense of gratitude, Beeks redrew his will and left the tailor shop and its contents to his young assistant. After the funeral the only change Victor made in the shop was to clear out the spent bottles and shift over to the old man's chair. He did not bother to change the name of the shop, certain he would be gone within the year.

A tailor shop in the heart of the waterfront was no place to meet girls. Victor often went to the cinema, but his favorite films, the westerns and horror flicks, were seldom attended by single females.

He wandered occasionally to dance halls or bars near the wharf, where he would idly flirt with the barmaids and listen to stories of returning sailors. He fell in with a pretty but irritable waitress named Nell. She even moved into the rooms above the shop for a time. But she left him after a year, frustrated at his reluctance to marry, leaving behind an acrid note and the broken shards of his favorite coffee cup.

Isobel felt a flash of unease. "So you didn't marry her, yet you . . . is that honorable?"

"She wasn't the one."

"But I am?"

Victor pinched the tip of Isobel's nose. "You'll do."

The girls from the Pasal Millinery held a bridal shower for her. Isobel's landlady had agreed to let them use the front parlor of the boardinghouse, and there they spent an afternoon giggling and playing shower games, making up wedding-night rhymes pairing her name and Victor's.

"Victor Howard?" Carol frowned. "Nice name, but crummy for rhyming. All I can think of is coward."

Ruth pulled a scrap from her purse and shot up from her chair. "How about this?

Izzy's garden was full of delights,
A flower so sweet and so bright,
Demure, and just ready for plucking.

Victor laid her right down
On that hard stony ground
To give her a jolly old fu . . ."

"Ruthie!"

Carol cackled, spilling her soda, "You cheat! You wrote that before. This is supposed to be spur of the moment!"

Ellen tapped at the stem of her glasses and frowned, repeating several times aloud, *"Mrs. Howard was deflowered?"*

Isobel rolled her eyes.

Kathleen, who had been sitting quietly in her chair, suddenly waved her arms. "Okay, I've got one!" She stood and laid a hand across her bosom, clearing her throat for effect.

"Fair of hair, sweet of heart, Isobel,
Was a maiden, an innocent gal.
When Victor arrived,
She was filled with surprise,
At the length and the breadth of his swell."

Ruth screamed and then shook her finger wildly. "That's a limerick. It's not fair, she's Irish."

Isobel laughed. "Oh, I think that one takes the prize." She reached into the pile of wrapped party favors.

"Wait. You have to make up one too."

"Oh, no. No-no-no."

They made her sit in a corner with a piece of paper until she came up with one.

"Okay, this is what I've got. No apologies.

A tailor who hadn't a care.
Had the lass Isobel in his lair.
Victor had picked her,
Young Howard had wowed her
with a smile and a dimple, so there."

There was a collective moan and a titter. "Izzy, that's the dumbest poem ever."

She shrugged. "It's all I've got."

Isobel opened gifts, mostly linens, all hand-stitched.

"Oh, they're so beautiful." Her exclamations were sincere even after the third set of hemstitched pillowcases and the second batch of identical tea towels. Cream-colored dinner napkins piled up at her side.

Victor had promised to come but was a full hour late. Isobel made light of it. "Oh, probably gone down the wrong street or something."

Carol poked her. "Sure it's not a case of cold feet?"

Isobel laughed. "His feet are boiling. He just has trouble getting one in front of the other."

Carol pulled a box from behind the divan. "Open this one quick. We didn't want to give it to you in front of Victor."

She took the package. "Another present?"

They all perched around her.

"Well, don't just sit there. Open it."

"Thank you."

"You thank us *after* you open it." Kathleen giggled.

The box was light. The wrapping fell away, and she inhaled when she saw the name of an expensive Minneapolis boutique embossed in the top.

"Ruthie picked it up for us last time she went to visit her brother. We all voted on the colours."

She unfolded the layers of tissue to reveal a nightgown and robe set, featherweight grey-blue silk with jade straps and piping. She held it up over her dress.

"Oh. Oh . . . it's just gorgeous."

Ruthie turned to the other girls. "See, it does match her eyes. I was right."

Isobel felt a sudden bond with these girls. Looking into their friendly, carefree faces, she suddenly wanted to go on being one of them.

When Victor finally did jab the doorbell the party was winding down and most of the food was gone. He was flushed and grinning, holding a wrapped bottle of black-market wine aloft in offering.

"Hello, battle-axes."

Ruthie laughed and leaned over to Isobel, whispering, "Heck, he's cute enough to wait for."

Carol stood to offer her hand. "Natty suit."

Kathleen tugged the elbow of Carol's sleeve and said through her teeth, "He's a tailor, goose."

As Victor worked the cork out of the wine bottle, he looked around. "Glasses?"

Ellen whipped the tortoise frames from her nose and handed them blindly to Victor, who roared as he splashed a bit of wine onto the thick lenses.

Someone dashed to the kitchen to rinse tumblers. The girls gathered in a circle, and after Victor poured they all raised a toast to the future. Glasses met, arms forward to form the spokes of a human wheel.

There was a quiet throat-clearing from the far side of the room and the circle broke apart. Isobel was still sitting on the couch, arms crossed, surrounded by torn gift wrap and boxes.

"I suppose there's a glass for me?"

They met the next day at the sandy shore stretching beyond the lighthouse. When Victor walked down the long expanse of beach, she'd had to run to catch up to him. He had rolled up his trousers, and his bare feet were white in the surf. He was looking out over the water. Isobel was breathless as she took his hand.

He turned. "Would you rather be on an ocean, you know, in a boat, or would you rather see it from shore?"

"Shore. No contest."

"Why?"

"Uh, why? . . . Well, *because*. Because boats smell and

they leak, and . . . because it's so much prettier to look out to sea than to look from sea to land. Isn't it?"

Victor shrugged. "Maybe."

The wind had picked up and began pushing thunderheads in from the lake.

"Victor, what do you want?"

"I prefer a boat."

"No, I mean now."

"Now? A cigar would be nice."

She gave him a look. "Vic, I mean with us."

"Oh, you mean what do I *want?*" Without dropping her hand he leaned to pick up a flat stone. "Well, I've had some time to think about that, Isobel."

He skipped the stone out over the surface of the lake and counted its hobbles. "Six! Did you see that?" He faced her. "I think that's my record!"

She folded her arms until he went on.

"Okay, here it is. I want a wife who laughs at my jokes, but only the good ones. I want my children to have lots of brothers and sisters. I want a real house. In a town, not a city. I want someone to talk to about the things I'm interested in."

In the months they'd been together this was his second display of sincerity. It suddenly occurred to Isobel that what she was embarking upon would last the rest of her life. Victor, for all his outward nonchalance, wasn't going into the marriage lightly. He would rely on her, for all the reasons he had said and more.

She looked out over the water. It was unbroken, no far shore. An ocean, really.

Would she be able to give him what he wanted? She thought she was willing to try.

He picked up another stone and handed it to her. "And you?"

"Me? You mean what do I want?"

She fell silent. She honestly hadn't thought about it, not beyond what kind of songs she wanted sung at the wedding, or what kinds of curtains she would hang. She threw her stone and they watched it dance, impossibly, six times. An omen? Victor hooted and scooped her up.

She laced her fingers behind his neck and they grew silent. A deepening settled between them in the time it might have taken for her stone to drift to the bottom of the lake.

He needed her. The tough, silly boy needed her. And he wanted to know what she needed in turn. She swallowed.

"I want us to be together. To make all our decisions together, to talk about everything, like partners. To have children. We want the same things, Victor."

He shook his head. "You saw it, right? It skipped six times."

"I saw."

Victor groaned and fell to his knees. "You're heavier than you look, woman." They rolled to sit on the sand, plowing their fingers and toes through the sugary layers. They watched a freighter move under the bridge. Isobel swatted at sand flies and laughed after squashing one just over Victor's ear. As she flicked it away he suddenly turned and kissed her.

"I love you."

"You do?" She almost turned away.

"Yes, I do." He squinted, as if relieved to have finally said it. "Wanna know why?"

She nodded.

"You're mouthy when you get angry. Lots of women just sulk or holler. You're not too sweet and you're not coy. Let's see, what else? You told me once my bald spot was — what — *adorable,* I think you said. You see things the way they are, not just the way you want them to be. Oh, did I mention that you look real edible in that dress?"

She smacked his arm.

Victor sprayed her leg with a palmful of sand.

"Right. One more thing." He squeezed her hand and steered it toward the surf. "See those colours? There, just before the wave crests, where it's blue and grey and green all in layers? The lake only looks like that before a storm." He touched the tender skin at her brow. "Your eyes are the same. You're like that water. You don't give away much, but it's there all the same, just underneath."

As their eyes locked Isobel felt a sudden falling in her throat. Looking away from him to see smoke from the freighter ribbon to meet low clouds, she smiled.

"I love you too, Victor."

CHAPTER FIVE

~ ~ ~

Victor closed Beeks's tailor shop, put the building up for sale, and crated up the best of the machinery and supplies. When the building sold, the cash would buy them a new start.

After the wedding Victor cheerfully moved Isobel back to Cypress. He had great hopes for the Iron Range. It was a growing region, loaded with potential for an independent merchant.

Following the red moving van full of the Beeks's better furniture, they drove a hundred miles north. Once in town, they stored their belongings in the back of an old stable and took a room at the Welsh boardinghouse until they could find a place to live.

They poked their way through ten houses before Victor

took her up the hill at the edge of town to look at a tall, butter-colored farmhouse with flaring porches and a crumbling limestone chimney. The yard was three overgrown acres. When the owner left them alone in the back garden to talk it over, Victor swept a brittle hydrangea away from a stone bench so Isobel could sit.

He was too fidgety to settle down, but Isobel was very still, looking skeptically at the house. The porch floor off the back sagged under the weight of a discarded cookstove. A shutter on the attic window twisted free like a broken wing.

"Izzy, a little elbow grease . . ."

"A lot, Victor." She turned to him. "A lot of elbow grease."

"Wallpaper is cheap, Izzy. And I can find someone to fix that chimney."

"Let's hope."

The house sat high on a ridge, separated from town by a stand of young red pine and a quarter-mile-wide shelf of weedy clay propped up by low cliffs. It was easy to see how the place had failed as a farm; the slope was too angled, the soil too hard. Most of the acreage had been sold off long before, and what had been orchard was now a growing neighborhood of two-story houses.

"Clapboard's rotten over on that corner, see?"

"That? That's nothing. Look at those windows. It's got a fine view of the lake, doesn't it?"

By his glassy look Isobel knew he was envisioning the house spruced and painted, not the hulk before them.

"Well, it's awfully big, Vic."

"Yeah, plenty of room."

It was the only house they'd seen that they could afford. They signed the contract.

Victor made a three-piece suit for a local brick mason who was getting married. In return the mason tore down and rebuilt the chimney. A plumber came and spent an ominous hour peering at the old boiler before rubbing his whiskers and pronouncing, "She's a leaker."

Isobel winced. "And?"

"S'pose I could patch her up for now, but you're gonna need new."

"New what? New patch?"

"Hah! Boiler."

The money they had saved for their honeymoon was spent on a reconditioned boiler that didn't look much better than the old one. During the weeks they should have been at an island resort in Michigan, Isobel learned how to glaze windows and scrape paint from clapboards without gouging. She didn't mind the missed honeymoon, was even a little relieved. She'd secretly dreaded the ferry ride, imagining Lake Huron as wild as the Atlantic; she hadn't wanted Victor to see her vomiting over the side, weak and afraid.

They spent days peeling stained wallpaper and a filthy week replacing the sash weights in every window of the house. Victor sold the nickel off the old cookstove and had the bones of it hauled away. He spent four miserable days under the porch, shoring up its beams. A constant stream of foul language rang from under the decking to the second story, where Isobel patched plaster, papered walls, and painted what seemed like miles of trim. She regularly crept down to set a glass of lemonade or a cold beer near the hole in the broken porch skirting. Victor's dirt-creased hand would reach out and grope for her leg, his voice rasping like Dracula's, "Tank you, my lovely." He would drain his glass in gulps, laugh maniacally, and then worm back underneath. The pounding and cursing would resume.

Every night they fell wrecked to their mattress on the floor of the living room, and when they woke, squinting against the sun streaming through curtainless windows, the first thing they did was reach for handkerchiefs to clear plaster dust and soot from their noses. Years later Victor would tell the children that those early days of their marriage were "the most fun I've never had."

Isobel attacked the garden, hacking out brush and laying out a tiny vegetable plot, where she grew anemic tomatoes and pale lettuce. She pulled up overgrown roses and peonies and encouraged the lower flowering vegetation to take over the yard.

Victor crouched next to where she knelt at her task. He scratched his scalp and pointed to her latest crop of transplanted prizes. "Creeping Charlie and bunchberry might be considered weeds in some gardening circles, Iz."

Isobel pushed the kerchief back over her forehead and leaned over her trowel. "Well, you know what they say, Victor, 'One man's weed.' Look, it's pretty and it doesn't need to be mowed or tended. I don't give a hoot if it's crabgrass."

Victor pointed out a freshly planted spot near the birdbath. "But this *is* crabgrass, Izzy."

Isobel bit back a smile and made a motion to throw the trowel at Victor. "Oh, just hush. Just shut your —"

He knelt in front of her. "Mouth?" He covered hers.

Her voice was muffled by his kiss. "I was going to say *trap*."

Isobel's father retired just after the wedding, and the closing of the family bakery assured Victor of a spacious storefront for considerably less than market value. Isobel's parents packed and got on the train headed for St. Paul and their new apartment near the state capitol. Victor blew a riot of insincere kisses to the back end of the caboose, until Isobel thumped him hard. When the train was out of sight, he nearly sprinted to the old bakery to begin remodeling.

He rented out the upstairs apartment to a cheerful Welsh widow whose miner husband had died of gangrene after nicking his forehead on an iron cleat in an underground tunnel.

As Victor dismantled the huge gas ovens and prepared to haul them out back, he inclined his head toward the south quadrant of the shop, bright with light from a trio of many-paned windows. He grunted as he lifted an iron stovepipe.

"That's where you can do your little hat business, Izzy, right there."

Before she could even think, the first baby was on its way.

She'd made some progress in the shop, another bank of shelves cleaned, nests of thread bound by dust were pulled from corners. Leaning back, she wound a string of copper and glass disks around her wrist, remembering the blind Indian she'd bought them from during an autumn trip to Fond du Lac.

Victor had stopped the car at a roadside market to buy pumpkins and to let Henry out for a few minutes. While he took Henry to the outhouse behind the gas station across the road, Isobel wandered over to a low table where an ancient brown woman was selling trinkets. When she said hello, the woman's only response was a low grunt and a suspicious sniff. After Isobel picked out some disks and handed over her money, the old woman felt the dollar bill as if to determine its authenticity and tossed a few coins in change on the table, mumbling something indiscernible. Suddenly she reached out and laid a gnarled hand on Isobel's flat abdomen.

"*Abinoojiins.*" Her voice suddenly precise. The woman nodded, her face blank as stone, her eyes milky and unblinking. She repeated, "*Abinoojiins. Bizaan.*"

"Pardon?" Isobel stepped back, recoiling from the trails of warmth where the woman's fingers had touched her. "Pardon me?" she repeated.

The old woman did not respond but stared sightlessly at

Isobel's torso, nodding solemnly. Isobel shuddered and turned away, leaving her change on the table, only to bump into a much younger Ojibwa woman. The woman smiled at her and explained, "She mean the baby. Quiet baby. Still."

"Still baby?" Isobel glared back at the old woman. "She's crazy."

Suddenly feeling ill, she clutched her beads and wobbled to the car. Nauseous and sweating, she watched blackflies drill at the windshield and waited for Victor to return with little Henry.

She did not tell him of the old woman's prophetic warning, but endured the next seven months of her pregnancy in a daze, resigned to the grim knowledge that the baby growing inside her would be born dead.

Isobel kept her eyes closed for the entirety of her brief labour, blindly stroking the arc of her stomach. The midwife wiped tears from Isobel's face, and after the final push, Isobel heard the sharp intake of the midwife's breath. She turned to face the wall. The birth had been quick and surprisingly easy compared to Henry's. She brought fistfuls of sheets to her face, pressed them to her eyes. After a few moments of silence, it occurred to her that the poor midwife did not know what to say. Isobel weakly offered, "It's all right, Ida, I know."

"You know? What do you know?" Ida placed the wrapped infant on the bed next to Isobel. "It's a girl. A very red-faced baby girl. Lovely, born with a caul. That's good luck, no? See how quiet she is, Isobel? Not a peep."

Isobel looked at the bundle, saw the tiny lips move on the creased face. She struggled to sit up and completely unwrapped the baby, recalling the words of the two Ojibwa women. *Bizaan* — quiet baby, still baby. The naked infant slowly waved her curled fists and stared crookedly into her mother's face with fierce concentration. The tears in Isobel's eyes blurred her vision and fell to the tiny shoulder.

Quiet baby.

She pressed the infant to her and laughed. The name came to her in a whisper. *Louisa.*

~   ~   ~

Thomas leaned in as his mother's voice faded. For the last fifteen minutes she'd mumbled in her sleep, something about an Indian. Gibberish mostly, and then suddenly *Louisa,* whispered but clear.

Her name was a jolt. He hadn't heard her mentioned for years. He never brought her up, and certainly his mother didn't. When he thought of his dead sister the odd tightness in his neck came back.

He pulled the shade against the city skyline and poured a glass of fresh water in case his mother woke up thirsty. He checked his watch. Ten. That late?

She'd said *Louisa.*

He supposed every parent had their favorite.

~   ~   ~

Louisa surprised her by coming into the shop at noon, bringing tomato sandwiches, apples, and a bottle of lemonade. She had prepared the lunch herself, packed it, and brought it down from the house. When Isobel was finished eating, the girl quietly cleaned up the mess and put out a hand to take away Isobel's empty paper cup.

Isobel took Louisa's hand, shaking it solemnly. "Thanks, sweetheart. That was a lovely lunch."

Louisa blushed and turned away, but not before Isobel saw her broad smile. "You do your work, Momma, and I'll do mine."

"Yes, ma'am."

While Louisa sat down to cut out doll clothes, Isobel went to the pattern drawers and pulled out templates for standard hat forms — cloche, tam, and basic disk. She studied them and shook her head, tossing most into the trash barrel. They were woefully out-of-date. She would need more current patterns, along with bolts of ourson, flalean, and heavy felts. The money she had saved during the last few years would only go so far. Biting a thumb, she sat down with a pencil and paper.

After an hour the column of numbers was two pages long. She began to cross off items that weren't absolutely essential. She'd have to order small quantities from suppliers she could count on to be fair. She would have to scrimp, be inventive, make do with older equipment.

She found the old steamer, stiff with rust and disuse. Looking for oil and rags, she opened a cupboard door. A mannequin head rolled out at her like a macabre prank. Isobel rocked back on her heels as the wooden head struck her foot. She almost began to cry.

There was no aspirin in the shop. At two she rested for five minutes, gulping tea while standing at the threshold of her quarter of the shop. She had moved most of Victor's things from this corner and had incorporated them as neatly as she could into the rest of his clutter. She sighed. *He'll skin me alive.* She sent Louisa home to find the tin of Bayer.

As she scrubbed down the front window she saw Mrs. Malley cross quickly from the pharmacy into the butcher shop. She'd nearly forgotten the awkward moments of the other day. She'd heard the gossip about Mrs. Malley, of course. Everyone in town had. A month before, while waiting to buy stamps at the post office, Isobel heard two of the mine owners' wives talking.

"Malley, you know him, that big Irishman, he's brought his wife from Chicago — to get her out of the heat, I suppose."

"Seven monogrammed trunks full of clothes. You've seen her, like some duchess."

"How she affords *that* on an engineer's salary."

Their voices rose in excitement.

"And haughty, too. After I followed her into the pharmacy I said, 'Welcome to Cypress,' and if she wasn't stiff as a board to me!"

"Did you say seven trunks?"

"Full of gowns, I s'pose. Furs, who knows what else . . . "

Isobel stepped closer to the women, tempted to chime in with the suggestion they might be full of nonsense. The trunks, of course.

In the wake of the gossiping women, Isobel learned the Malleys had no children, even though Mrs. Malley, as one of them said in disapproving tones, "has the hips for it."

"Maybe she's got bad tubes," offered the other with a shrug.

"Well, there must be something wrong with her . . . *he* certainly looks healthy enough."

The Malleys had rented the big cottage at the end of Granite Point for the season. "Imagine," said one of the women, a sting in her affected clip, "two people bumping about in that big place all by themselves." Isobel, after finishing at the counter, dropped her letter into the slot.

Walking to the shop she recalled what Victor had told her about Liam Malley. He was a structural mining engineer, who had been in Cypress since February. The mine had had trouble over safety issues when a minor cave-in had left miners skittish and restless. He'd stayed on to oversee the construction of an improved shaft in the third level.

Victor had said the first time he'd seen Malley was back in April, after delivering uniforms for the mine's brass band. There had been a walkout after one of the Finns had pilfered a report Malley had written, a report suggesting the mine's west arm was unsafe and recommending it be shut down until stress tests could be completed. Manage- ment had decided to keep the entire mine running until they could get a second sounding from another engineer coming in from Alberta.

After dropping off the uniform order, Victor stayed and watched the walkout and the ensuing confrontation, and later he described for Isobel the line of Finns who had posted themselves in a barrier around the entrance shaft.

"They were rooted like a stand of timber, with the Welsh miners grousing off to the side. Those Welsh were itching to get back to work, you could tell, but they didn't dare cross that line, so they just shuffled around. Three su- pervisors and two managers barred the steps to the office. Ted Barry, the youngest manager, sweated through his un- dershirt so rings looped nearly to his belt. But he wasn't the only fidgety one. Management wanted those Finns back at work, and someone had been sent down to the river to fetch Malley from his fishing.

"When Malley pulled up in his car, he parked midway between the factions. The Welsh were fuming by then. They were being docked pay right along with the Finns.

"He unfolded himself from behind the wheel, a big fel- low, still in his hip boots. He took in the two sides and said to neither, 'Looks like a nasty game of chess here.' He was met by one of the managers and a rep from the line of Finns. He towered over the both of 'em. They spoke up at him for a bit, him nodding all serious. He never looked up, never looked down.

"These fellas talked at him till they were both blue, and just once Malley raised a finger to the brim of his fishing hat and pushed it high to his forehead. That must've meant he was done listening, 'cause both men shut their mouths and stepped back then.

"He just kicked his rubber boot into the dirt and took a breath. He plunked fists on his hips — I remember the back of one hand was glittering, fish scales, I suppose. When he talked his mouth was hard under his mustache. He didn't seem to be talking to anyone straight on, but when that Irish brogue echoed off the tin walls of those buildings, all the men went still.

"'I done my share of mining,' he said. 'Ten years in open pit. And I'll tell you, lads, *that's* filthy work. Makes pulling ore outta this place look like a day at the fekkin' *Taj Mahal*.' He turned toward the Welsh. 'You know what I'm talkin' about here. I been in your country, I seen your nasty coal holes. But you gotta know too, this ain't coal mining, and yer fellows here' — he nodded to the wall of Finns — 'are well right in this walkout. Just as the big boys here running the place are right to get another man in to check my numbers.' He scratched his neck. 'I'll say one thing, though. If my report isn't right, if I'm wrong and that shaft proves herself safe, I'll eat all the bloody iron you can pull from that western arm.'

"There was nervous laughter from the Welsh. The management on the steps shuffled in place as if needing to go to the toilet. The Finns were silent as ever.

"'I'm not union, and I'm not management either. And I'm no miner. No more.'

"He nodded to the men in suits on the stairs. 'I imagine there's plenty of rock to be pulled from the lower rooms in the south arm, lads, and it's safe as a cradle. Why not put 'em working down there till your other hired man checks out the western arm.' It wasn't a question. The suited men looked hesitantly at one another and Liam shook his head. 'It'll cost you no more than five minutes per man per shift to go down that next level. And on what you're paying that doesn't add up to diddly, certainly doesn't add up to anything like the trouble you could have here.'

"That settled, he turned and faced the Finnish men and wagged his finger just once between them and the Welsh.

'And whatever you've got between you, clean it up. Men who don't work together die together. That goes true in any goddamn mine.'

"He was in his car then, fist on the wheel and head turned, backing away from the three groups of men. He hadn't even bothered to turn off the ignition."

Isobel herself had seen Mr. Malley only a few times. He was handsome, at least from afar, and dark. The mine owners' wives had whispered *Irish* as if it were an affliction. But he was just one of the many men who came and went in Cypress. Someone who had a job to do and would leave when that job was done. He didn't frequent the Welsh tavern or eat at Maki's, the Finnish café. Nor did he visit the brick houses of the mining executives or sit in on their card games at the Masonic Temple. He didn't socialize so far as she knew, and if he drank it was in the privacy of his rented cottage. He took his meals between Jem's and the hotel dining room in the company of a newspaper and a pipe. On spring days, before sunset, he could be spotted fly-fishing from the Marko Dam, a lone figure thigh-deep in the river, casting his line to reflect the fading sun like undulating gossamer. He was a formidable but otherwise unremarkable man who only became remarkable after his extraordinary wife arrived.

And now there was Mrs. Malley, her business at the butcher done, walking in front of the tailor shop window. Isobel rapped on her side of the glass and the woman turned, startled. When Isobel waved her in, a softening passed over the woman's features. Relief at seeing a familiar face? Once inside she shut the door with her back as if glad for an escape from the street.

"Hello again, Mrs. Howard." Mrs. Malley looked around the shop. "You're still in a bit of a mess, aren't you?" She seemed changed, her gaze more steady, her smile easier.

Isobel laughed. "Oh, this? Nothing out of the ordinary. Will you stay for tea this time?"

"Oh! That would be lovely, but I wouldn't want to keep you from —"

"My mess? Believe me, there's nothing here that won't keep. I've been waiting sixteen years to get going here. A cup of tea can't slow me up much further."

Mrs. Malley grinned and set her shopping basket down. "In that case, it would be my pleasure." She peered into the rear of the shop and saw the clutter of open boxes and equipment. As she took off her hat and gloves she turned to Isobel.

"Listen, what do you say we have that cup of tea, and afterward I'll help you straighten up?"

Isobel nearly laughed. "Mrs. Malley, that's very kind but —"

"Cathryn. You must call me Cathryn." The woman laid a hand on Isobel's arm. "Please. I have the whole afternoon ahead of me."

Isobel examined the woman for a second time. Mrs. Malley's sophistication and reserve, her clothes, her very carriage, defined her as an outsider in Cypress. She was here for an entire summer. She felt a sudden pity toward the woman. Though Cypress was her home she saw it for what it was, an ofttimes cold place with a tight social layering Victor called the three *M*'s — management, merchants, and miners. Not much in between. Isobel shook her head. The gossips would eat Mrs. Malley alive.

"All right, Cathryn. Lord knows I could use the help."

When Cathryn smiled, Isobel watched her face change from attractive to stunning. Something deep in her irises shone, as if there were a suppressed energy that she was holding in check. Isobel recalled part of a thought she had had a few days earlier about Louisa. *Most all of her hidden.*

~ ~ ~

CHAPTER SIX

*L*ike an island.

"What did you say, Mother?"

"Did I say something? Sorry, I was gathering moss."

"So, this woman, Cathryn, she's a part of that summer?"

Isobel smiled. "You could say that."

Thomas had a paper sack between his feet. He'd settled heavily into the chair next to the bed and pulled out a bagel and a cup of coffee. "Mind if I eat this here?"

Isobel thought he looked tired. "Go ahead, but aren't they going to miss you at the office?"

"I'm the last person they'd miss. No one likes having the boss around all day."

"Hooey. They love you."

Thomas had started the accounting firm after college. He'd inherited Victor's lopsided grin but none of his clumsiness with numbers.

"Oh, maybe they like me. They're planning some retirement bash for me, I'm afraid. When I was coming out of the john the other day I heard someone whisper, 'Karaoke.'"

"Oh, with the microphone? Isn't that . . . ?"

"Humiliating?"

"Will it be a big party? How many people do you have down there now?"

"Thirty-three. Hired two more last week."

"Good Lord." Isobel raised a brow. "Doing well, then?"

"Well enough."

"So that explains this nice private room."

Thomas tucked a flag of loose sheet in under Isobel's foot. It was not only private, but at the end of the hall. It hadn't been easy to swing that. He'd attempted to make it homey, bringing a few of her violets, a framed oil from her bedroom, her favorite afghan. Just today he'd picked wildflowers from the open meadow behind his house. The manager of her apartment building had sent a dozen roses, but he'd discreetly tossed them out before his mother could see them, slipping the sender's card into a bunch of purple asters instead. Her opinions on roses were clear: they were ostentatious and she disliked the cloying smell. She said they were given by people with more money than imagination, and insisted there wasn't an occasion that warranted roses except secret assignations.

He sniffed now at the wildflowers, their odor mixed with the smells of the hospital. The air was rimed with the indistinct medley of sickness, flowers, and medicine. No amount of sweet aster could disguise the fact that they were in an institution.

The bagel tasted strange. He put it down and looked at his mother.

He'd been the one to find her. After letting himself into her apartment, he'd called out, and when there was no answer he'd assumed she was napping. He thought he'd get himself a beer and watch the news before waking her up. He didn't know how long she might have been sleeping, but he figured another half hour wouldn't hurt. She'd seemed tired lately, and he wasn't surprised. She was wearing herself out with those daily marches she insisted on taking. He wiped his feet and glanced in the hall mirror, straightening his tie under the loose drape of flesh at his neck. He mumbled, "I'll look like a turkey soon." Making his way to the kitchen he rambled on. "But I s'pose by the time *I'm* ninety-nine I'll be wishing I looked as good as a turkey. Jesus. Now I'm talking to myself."

He hoped there would be a cold bottle in the fridge.

When he saw her splayed on the linoleum he lost his footing. He laid his palm flat on the kitchen table and leaned hard, as if he might sink into the pattern.

He thought he'd prepared himself.

Christ. Oh, Christ.

She was so old, of course he'd imagined her dead. Many times. He'd even planned the funeral in his head, working out what kinds of music she'd like, what readings. Any day of the last thousand could easily have been her last. But she'd kept going on like some well-oiled engine. As the years went by he'd begun to take for granted her seemingly unyielding clutch on life.

But as he stood in the kitchen a stiffness began to creep over his own limbs. His knees locked.

"Oh, Mother."

An ancient bitterness rushed to him. He had been so young when his father died. No one could explain to him what he was in for, the greyness of it. He'd been a boy lost in the confusion and dark corners of a family grieving and lost themselves.

He saw now that age didn't matter, ten or sixty-nine, he'd be in the abyss again, the grey as impermeable.

He knew that he hadn't asked the questions he should have, wasn't ready to let go of her after all. Not even close.

"Not now. Not *now*, Momma." His words echoed in the room.

He made himself move. He crouched over her and gently pulled the hem of her dress down over her knee.

When she moaned he jerked backward, almost falling. It was then he began to cry, great sobs of relief nearly choking him as he righted himself and crabbed over to the kitchen phone.

The smell of coffee made her wriggle up straighter in bed. "That's not hospital coffee, is it?"

Thomas blew on his steaming cup. "Starbucks next door."

"Do you think I could have a sip?"

Thomas dug into the paper bag. "Almost forgot." He handed her a full take-out cup. "I brought you your own."

The coffee warmed Isobel's hand and she breathed in the smell of it, sighing, "I'm not supposed to have caffeine."

"One cup? Probably won't kill you."

Isobel smiled and pointed to the bag. "Sugar?"

"And rot your teeth?"

"I don't have any teeth."

"Well, you did. Where'd they go? They were right here a minute ago." He took two packets and poured one into the glass her dentures had rested in earlier. "Sweet tooth?"

"Thomas! You've ruined my Efferdent!"

When she stopped laughing he turned. "Mother, I want to ask you something."

"Ask away."

He edged closer. "D-did you love . . ." Thomas faltered, the stammer he'd developed as a boy came tripping back to knot his words. "Dad. I mean did you r-really love him?"

Isobel stared at him. "My God, Thomas, have you ever thought I didn't?" Her exhalation tore the flag of steam rising from her paper cup.

~   ~   ~

Cathryn came to the shop early the next day, bringing pastries from the Swedish bakery. Isobel tentatively took the waxed bag from her outstretched hand.

"Ah, have a seat, Cathryn. I can make us coffee." She looked at the clock, wondering when she would have time to fill out the many order forms on the desk.

Cathryn took off her coat. She was wearing a work apron over her crepe dress. "Rest easy, Isobel. I'm not about to keep you from your work. I've come about a job — volunteer, of course."

Isobel blinked. The day before, when Cathryn had helped her in the shop, they'd both worked so diligently at their tasks there was hardly any conversation. When Cathryn had finally left, with her nails ruined and her hair dusty, Isobel thought she might never see the woman again.

"But isn't this summer your holiday, Cathryn? Why on earth would you want to be stuck inside here all day?"

"When I could be sitting out in that blasted sun, doing nothing?" Cathryn pointed to the jumbled bolts of fabric she'd moved the day before but hadn't had time to put in order. "For instance, those still need some attention, and you'll be too busy with your paperwork." She patted Isobel's arm. "You get busy. I'll do the coffee."

By lunchtime Cathryn had measured, tagged, and neatly arranged all of the bolts in Victor's high wall of shelving. It was a tedious job, but she seemed happy to do any task. Gabardines, tweeds, and woolens neatly lined the shelves like somber lozenges.

Isobel approved, but her apprehension was obvious. "I feel terrible that I can't pay you, Cathryn."

Cathryn stopped, as though considering this. "Liam and I manage all right as it is."

Later Isobel would remember this modesty when Cathryn, somewhat embarrassed, disclosed a memory of her mother letting her play with the contents of the many velvet cases she'd kept in her bedroom safe — pendants and brooches Cathryn was allowed to drape over her forehead and wrap around her wrists, diamonds and sapphires to wear on her toes. "I thought they were toys." One of the necklaces had been worth a city block, Cathryn admitted. "It's in a museum now, thank God."

"And the rest?"

She shrugged. "Oh, around, in among my things."

She argued with Isobel about the job. "Oh, *please?* I'm not skilled, so it would be more like an apprenticeship. Just let me help out until you get established." She crossed her arms in defiance. "I'm here until September." Cathryn smiled. "But of course you can boot me out anytime."

They shook hands in mock solemnity and Cathryn began with the dirtiest tasks. She sneezed at the filth rising from her rag, but it only seemed to make her more determined to get the place into shape. Isobel watched from the corner of her eye, sure that Cathryn — most likely unaccustomed to such work — would tire of the novelty and be gone by the end of the week.

Cathryn tackled Victor's mess. She backed out of the cubby under his desk with ringlets of dust dangling from her chignon. "When your husband comes back, he'll be so surprised he won't begrudge your claiming your wee corner for the millinery."

Isobel shrugged. "It's hard to say what he would be-grudge."

Cathryn opened her mouth just as the door chime sounded.

Louisa slipped into the shop.

Isobel smiled. "You're early."

That morning they'd left the house together, in their new routine, each carrying a bag lunch. They'd held hands until splitting off in different directions halfway down the hill, Isobel heading downtown and Louisa veering off to the Finnish neighborhood, where she'd taken her first summer job, helping Mrs. Hokkanen with her new twins.

Louisa had her notebook clutched under her arm, and Isobel smiled at the sight of it, knowing its margins were dotted with figures in the girl's laboured writing; the running tally of her wages — five cents an hour — in one column, and in two other columns, the total of diapers she'd changed each day, how many had been "number one," and how many had been "messes."

Louisa said, "Whew!" but then stepped back when she saw the strange woman just behind her mother, a tall woman who looked like a model in a magazine, rag in hand and pearls at her ears.

Cathryn turned. The girl was nearly a miniature of Isobel, leaning in the vestibule, her hands clasped behind her back.

"Oh, my goodness. This must be Louisa." The girl nodded once but did not move. Cathryn walked slowly over and dropped to one knee.

"Hello. My name is Cathryn. What's yours?"

The girl's voice was low. "But you know my name. You just said it."

Isobel frowned. "Louisa. That's hardly polite."

"No, no, she's right." Cathryn offered her hand. "Let's try again. Hello, Louisa. It's a pleasure to meet you."

The girl meekly took her hand. "Hello too."

"You have a lovely name."

Louisa nodded in agreement.

"When I was your age, one of my favorite authors was named Louisa. Have you ever heard of Louisa May Alcott?"

"No."

"Oh, you haven't? Well, is there a library here in town?"

"Yes, ma'am."

"Perhaps we could go together sometime. I could read you some of Miss Alcott's stories."

"I can read." The girl was hesitant, hung back.

"Of course you can." Cathryn did not break from the girl's steady gaze. "Louisa?"

"Yes, ma'am?"

"I was just thinking of doing a little project, but I can't manage it alone, and your mother is very busy right now. I wonder if you might have some free time?"

Louisa nodded, and Cathryn pointed to the cutting table. The girl followed her and settled onto a stool. There was a mound of discards from her earlier chore of trimming bolts; scraps too short for a vest or a sleeve were heaped and ready to be thrown out. Cathryn reached into this mass and fished out a fistful of fabric. She found a small scissors, fetched a piece of paper, and did a few sketches, handing the girl the pencil every so often so she could add her own lines. Referring to this paper they quietly spent the rest of the afternoon cutting and sewing by hand.

Isobel occasionally looked up from her desk to see Cathryn gesturing or indicating with her scissors, or directing a line with a finger, mute as Louisa. If Isobel walked by on her way to the bathroom or to the storage hall, they shielded their project as though it were a great secret.

At dusk they finally let her look.

As far as Isobel could tell, they had accomplished their collaboration with less than ten words between them. It was a waggish collage of twill and herringbone horses appliquéd against a background of pinstripe hills, a lake of satin in the distance. There was a checkered sky with plaid clouds, and their two sets of initials knotted together at the low corner in brown and green floss. *L.H. & C.L.M.*

It was late when the three of them walked to the drop box at the post office.

Isobel let Louisa drop the stamped orders for supplies into the slot.

"Not much to do now but wait."

"And plan." Cathryn smiled.

Isobel looked up to the rising moon. It was nearly ten. "Oh dear, how will you get home?"

Cathryn pointed back to the shop, where a bicycle rested against the lamppost. "My crimson steed, how else?"

"But it's dark!"

"So it is." She pulled a flashlight from her purse, flicked it on, and held it aloft, posing. "Who am I, Louisa?"

The girl reached out to position Cathryn's purse so that it rested in the crook of her arm like a volume.

"There. You're Lady Liberty!"

"Right!"

The next morning Cathryn was waiting at the stoop when Isobel turned the corner onto Main Street. Along the entire length of the block, heads were cocked in the direction of the tailor shop, and several people were staring at the well-dressed woman loitering at the door. Most of the shopkeepers greeted Isobel as usual when she passed, but they blinked excessively or let their greetings trail off, as if to give her an opening to explain why the mining engineer's wife was so often in the shop. She smiled, remarked on the rising temperatures, but offered nothing else. Her annoyance soon tempered to amusement at their blatant curiosity.

Mrs. Harding, the druggist's wife, was at least bold enough to ask. Sweeping her section of sidewalk to where it met the curb, she leaned over the end of her broom. "Goodness, Miz Howard, what *are* you ladies doing in that shop all day?" She stared at Cathryn until Isobel felt obliged to introduce the women. Mrs. Harding dropped her broom to cross the street. As she held out her hand, she strained to see the things in Cathryn's basket, and frowned to discover only a loaf of nut bread and a tin of China tea. She jumped back when Cathryn held the basket out so she could get a better look.

Mrs. Harding nodded to the window. "I, ah, I see the new sign you put up there. Millinery? Is that like haber-dashery? Is it something to do with Victor's tailor busi-ness?"

"Sort of. It's —"

Cathryn cut in. "It's boat-building, Mrs. Harding." Her face was a mask of sweetness. "We're constructing an ark."

The woman frowned, as if she were about to consider it. Isobel slapped Cathryn's hand and chuckled an apology as she turned the key in the lock. "Hatmaking, Mrs. Hard-ing. Just hats."

She turned to Cathryn once they were inside. "I'll get you your own key."

"Thanks. I'm glad you came by when you did. I was beginning to feel like some zoo animal out there."

Isobel sighed. "I know. Wait until you meet Mrs. Sima."

"Oh, I have. She's invited me to tea." Her hand flut-tered. "Unfortunately, my social calendar is just jammed."

They went about fine-tuning the details — pressing patterns, sharpening cutters and scissors, oiling machinery, cleaning surfaces that were already sparkling, and lining up spools and hand tools that had already been lined up.

They pored through catalogs and magazines, looking for styles that pleased them, patterns that Isobel would modify or copy. In her eagerness to be working, she found some old scrap felt and began to cut out a simple cap. She let Cathryn cut the band and lining. A passerby might have peeked in and surmised they were partners, scheming as if they'd hatched the idea of the business together.

Cathryn was spending more time in the shop than she did in her rented house at the lake. When Isobel said she was afraid Cathryn would become bored, she balked.

"But I love this place!" She looked down. "Please, if I'm in the way just let me know, and I'll go."

"You're not in anyone's way. Good Lord, Cathryn, look at how much you've done here. I was just wondering if I'm keeping you from something."

Cathryn stuttered. "F-from what? I'd rather be here than alone."

The strain on Cathryn's face showed in the fine lines at her brow. Isobel touched her shoulder.

Of course. How stupid. Mr. Malley worked such long days and was away overnight to neighboring mines so often. She had to be lonely.

As if reading her mind, Cathryn asked, "Aren't you lonely with your husband away?"

Isobel's hand fell as she thought about it. "I suppose I haven't had time to be very lonely. Actually, I . . ."

Cathryn sat down next to her. "What?"

Isobel reached up to wipe away a surprise tear. She couldn't believe she'd begun to cry in front of someone she barely knew. She tried to make light of it. "Well, before

Victor left we'd been going through a little rough spot. You know how it is when you've been married a long time."

"Yes, I do know. Listen, I don't mean to pry but . . ."

She found herself accepting a tissue, and for the next hour gave Cathryn the barest details of how she and Victor had grown apart.

"And then he took them to the island. Not to spite me, I'm sure, but still . . ."

When Isobel looked up to see Cathryn staring into the distance, she immediately regretted her confession.

"Oh, you see? Now I've said too much, I've upset you too."

Cathryn took her hand. "No, you haven't. I was just thinking it's good to be able to listen to someone else, help ease another's troubles for a change."

"Of course, exactly. You have your own troubles."

Cathryn's look was wry. "I have a husband, don't I?"

There was only the briefest pause before they started laughing.

When Cathryn wasn't busy at some task, she would drag a chair to sit near the windows to read or embroider. She explored and reexplored the dim recesses of the L-shaped storage hall off the back entry. The hall ran the entire length of the building, separating the tailor shop from the butcher shop next door, and as far as Isobel was concerned, its only saving grace was that it acted as a buffer from the disquieting whine of meat saws and the *thunk* of cleavers.

The hall was lined floor to ceiling with dozens of oak cupboards fronted with milky glass, the wood nearly black with seasoned shellac. One high window that had been painted shut since Isobel was a child allowed only a dusty square of light. She associated the hall with the crisp husks of dead flies and the close smells of brass and dust.

But the darkness and claustrophobic dimensions of the hall did not seem to bother Cathryn, who would disappear into the space for hours, clutching a rag and a can of Brasso to attack the half-moon drawer pulls and latches tarnished to molasses. Once Isobel went back to find that Cathryn had climbed the rolling ladder with her sleeves pushed high and was scouring furiously at a particularly stubborn handle.

"Good heavens, Cathryn, come down. It must be a hundred degrees up there!"

"Almost finished, Isobel. Just give me another hour."

"An hour?"

She reluctantly left Cathryn to her polishing. Finding herself near the rear door of the shop, she turned to survey the main room. With hands on her hips, she rolled a critical eye around its perimeters, trying to imagine how it might look to a newcomer, someone like Cathryn.

She didn't see the room so much as sense it. The planes and quirks of the space were held within her. Without looking at the windows, she knew the locations and sizes of the air bubbles trapped in the many panes. She had acquired the habit of noting the time of day by glancing up to see which panel of beadboard was hit by the trajectory of prism light from the beveled glass of the door.

The room was the same light olive colour her mother had chosen thirty years before. The walls stretched up to meet a pressed tin ceiling that had been varnished countless times, giving it the odd appearance of having been coated in honey. Sometimes when a heavy truck rolled by outside, the odd shard might shake itself loose, a bit of false amber to be plucked from Isobel's hair or from a crack in the floor.

She had been two years old when her parents had bought the building. Her childhood was distinctly mapped on the floor in front of her in pattern and shadow. A long path worn by bakery customers led to a dark spot where the old pastry cases had been. Black dimples recorded the weight of marble pastry slabs. Mismatched patches of maple defined the curve where crescent-shaped brick ovens once squatted.

Isobel had only to scan this floor to recall lying on her belly on warm wood, or the freedom of skipping out the back door, the limb-flailing skid of slipping on flour. The taut breathlessness of crouching undetected under a table. How many times had she hidden like that?

Those childish escapes of daydreaming were often perforated by sounds and voices from above: oiled baking sheets gliding together, the sandy spray of cornmeal, the *ppppring* of timers, her mother's tired rail, her father's defensive retorts echoing against the hard surfaces.

The harsh tones of her parents' voices changed only when customers came in, smoothing to a fleeting civility that quickly curdled after the customers left and the jangle of the bell-rope over the door had stilled. Isobel had vowed that when she grew up and had her own family, she would always speak in reasonable tones, even when furious.

Long ago she stopped wondering why her parents had been so unhappy, though early on she suspected herself, naturally, being born a girl after a string of stillborn baby boys.

Her father had ordered flour in fifty- and hundred-pound sacks. Each morning a sack larger than herself was emptied into the great steel bowls and bins. She spent hours underneath the marble pastry slab, where she would reach up to run her fingers along the fissures of its unpolished side, flour whispering down the edges in diminishing curtains. Daydreaming and drifting along with the rays of sunlight thick with it, she often imagined the journey the flour would have taken in its many forms, from seed to wheat, then milled to powder. Using her fingertip, Isobel would draw these scenes into the thin film covering the worktables — the hopeful farmer planting furrowed rows, storm clouds hinting at travails, the triumph as the horse-pulled combines cut quilt patterns through tresses of wheat. She romanticized the end of the harvest by drawing a check-aproned wife and fat-cheeked children by the farmer's side, plump as the stalks being heaped onto wagons. The farmer's family was always smiling. A kindly mother and father, two or maybe three boys, and a girl, always a girl her own age.

The flour had been stored in wooden cupboards that tipped out from the walls, metal-lined bins that now held Victor's better woolens, protecting them from moths. Sometimes, laying out a length of Poirot or Shetland twill, Isobel would notice a crease coated with decades-old flour and brush it away, her past and present merging under her fingers for a brief moment.

Isobel's parents had done well in Cypress. The town was prosperous, with two new mines opening to bring more customers to the bakery. Isobel had always felt a little guilty to be better off than the immigrant children who lived in the crowded shanty neighborhood or along the reedy south shore of the lake. In school she often felt awkward and overclean, the skirts under her stiff pinafore crinkling too precisely as she sat next to girls wearing faded cotton jumpers. Year after year, her deskmates tended to be plagued with sagging stockings, grimy necks, and pidgin English. When none showed interest in becoming friends, Isobel had an idea to win their favor. She took to stuffing sweet rolls or cookies into her pail and offering them to the girls at lunchtime. The foreign girls ate in close knots, heads bent protectively over their battered opened pails, their indecipherable patter defining her exclusion. Her treats were accepted and quickly eaten, but the knot would tighten against her again as they washed down the sweets with gulps of thick milk.

On her way home Isobel would feed the leftovers to the grackles, dropping crumbs along the alleys. By the time she gave up trying to make friends and stopped bringing treats, the grackles were trained to follow her home, clustering at her feet in waves of oiled satin the minute she left the schoolhouse.

For weeks the birds persevered, until one hopped onto the toe of her boot and nipped her ankle. She kicked it away and ran, a carnation blooming through her stocking. Once home she'd lied to her mother about the blood, saying she'd cut herself on a fence post. It was her first lie, and the ease of it surprised her.

There were only two other girls in her school who had been born in Cypress. She asked her parents to transfer her to the town's other school. Most of the merchants sent their children to the Catholic school, but Isobel's parents saw no advantage in wasting good money on educating a girl, and they made no bones of saying so.

In fourth grade she tearfully asked her teacher if she might be moved to another desk. "Can I please sit with an American girl?"

The teacher sat her down. "They are all American girls, Isobel. You should be ashamed of yourself." She was given a lecture on equality, all the while fighting the blush that raced up her cheeks. Her punishment had been to sweep the school sidewalks clear of snow for the entire month.

When she turned twelve, Isobel worked alongside her parents after school. She knew they expected her to stay on with them in the bakery, but after four years of rolling out yards of dough for strudel and peeling apples from the seemingly bottomless crate, she knew she couldn't do it. The texture of raw flour between her fingers made her jaw ache and cinnamon made her sneeze. She did not mind the work particularly, but when she saw her mother, flushed and muttering into the ovens, she envisioned her future self.

She told Cathryn of the day, while cutting squares of petits fours, she had informed her parents she'd apprenticed herself to a milliner in Duluth. She'd seen the ad, had written the letter, and had received a favorable recommendation from her teacher. She'd passed the interview and would be leaving at the end of the school term. Her mother froze over her rolling pin and glared.

"Vot are you saying?"

"I'm going to make hats."

"You vill do no such ting."

Isobel had expected this. "I'm sixteen, I'll do what I want."

With icy silence, her father took his apron off and walked out the back door. Isobel knew her father admired her determination; she knew too he hated himself for not having more.

As the door slammed, her mother slouched over the marble slab, the rolling pin trembling slightly in her hands.

Isobel cried, "Can't you be a little happy for me?"

Cathryn sighed. "Ah, well, there's probably not a sixteen-year-old girl alive who hasn't disappointed her parents one way or another."

"You too?"

"I was a grand champion, did it up real fine. I got it all over in just one night, the night of the Lake Forest cotillion. My coming out."

"Coming out? Like a debu —"

"Debutante, right. Cultured-young-lady-of-society. You are looking at a former, fantastically failed debutante. I was never very good at society. Mother always said my behavior was 'uneven at best' during social functions." Cathryn clapped her hands and rocked. "Ever notice how the word *function* is also used for going to the toilet? Anyway, between Miss Charlemaigne's School and endless private tutoring, I knew everything there is to know about etiquette." Cathryn dipped in a broad curtsey. "Manners! And I can use them too, when I feel like it. Inciting me to use them always was my mother's purpose on earth. Poor dear, she so wanted me to be a socialite like her, but I wasn't built for it. Too moody, she said, too *unpredictable*.

"The cotillion, of course, was a big deal — champagne fountain, orchestra, the cream of the boys from the academy, only the best boys from the best families. Did you know, Izzy, the social magnitude of a function can be gauged by how uncomfortable one's gown is? And mine was killing me — it had enough stays in it to build a boat." She leaned forward to whisper. "So I went back behind the cloakroom, where there was this little restroom, to try to shift things around. Well, didn't I get the surprise of my life in there. My ticket out of that ballroom was kneeling right there on the floor."

Cathryn's accent was suddenly British. "The re*cep*tion line is *veddy* important at these things. Utterly important, really, how one comports oneself. Can make or break a future, you see?" Her smile grew vaguely wicked. "So when Mr. and Mrs. Jarvis, of Jarvis Trust and Indemnity — very hoity-up banking family — came through the line, I was ready. In my best voice — I had three years of elocution at Miss Charlemaigne's, and believe me I could *carry* — I said my how-do's to Mrs. Jarvis and then I turned. 'And here's *Mr.* Jarvis! Sir, I'd be delighted to shake your hand, but didn't you just have it down Bobby Addison's trousers a few minutes ago?'"

Isobel hissed out the sip of tea she'd just taken. "You didn't!"

Cathryn was doubled over. "I did! I was sorry to ruin things for that poor boy, but Mr. Jarvis was a horrid man. It was the least I could do."

"And your mother?"

"Nearly died of mortification. She practically disowned me."

"What happened?"

"I was freed. I applied to art school, and they didn't lift a finger to stop me. I took life drawing classes with naked models and cut my hair and dated racy men. I went abroad, alone. That did it. By the time Liam came along, with no pedigree in sight, they let me marry him anyway. Gladly. They were relieved, I think, to be rid of me."

"And now?"

"My parents?" Cathryn sighed. "Asleep with the angels, poor dears."

~ ~ ~

CHAPTER SEVEN

*I*sobel stayed away from home two years. When she did come back it was only reluctantly, bringing Victor to meet her parents. He endured endless cups of watery coffee and the stream of her mother's chatter. When Victor finally asked what he'd come to ask, for Isobel's hand in marriage, her father nodded solemnly, rose, shook Victor's hand listlessly, and ambled away to the kitchen. Isobel followed him and reached out. He would not look at her.

"Your mother and I were hoping for better."

Isobel's hand fell away. "I wasn't."

She walked Victor downstairs to the street. At the door he whispered, "Those people aren't your parents. Your true mother and father were stolen by gypsics" — he nodded up the narrow staircase — "and were replaced by that pair of wayward pallbearers."

After they married and moved back to Cypress and Isobel's parents moved to St. Paul, the grim bakery changed as if a page had been turned. The gentle hum of well-oiled sewing machines and the hiss of steam redefined the space, and cheerful industry lifted the gloom. Sixteen years of Victor's pack rat habits were represented in the clutter of his worktables; racks bulged with garments tagged with cryptic handwriting. In spite of the chaos, he was economical and swift in filling orders, and though his demeanor might have seemed casual to an outsider, Isobel knew that as he whistled or tapped his foot or idly talked, his real attention was on the cloth in his hands. His standards were as rigid as his manner was leisurely. He insisted on hand cutting his canvas linings, and he sewed every shoulder seam by hand, whether the suit was for a potato farmer or a partner in the Vermilion Mine.

His customers found Victor affable, with a sympathetic ear, an anecdote for every occasion, and an informed opinion on political and economic developments, whether in Cypress or Washington, D.C. He kept up by reading every paper available, and three were delivered to the shop daily, the *Minneapolis Star,* the *Duluth Herald,* and the *Cypress Tribune.* Customers traveling to Chicago or cities east would always remember Victor by bringing him newspapers from those places. Men popped in with little repairs their wives could easily handle at home, and while the client sat in one of the three plush theater seats salvaged from the Lyric, Victor would reattach a loose button or turn under a frayed trouser hem and hash over recent news. More than once it had been suggested to him that he might run a successful campaign for mayor.

"Bah, I'm just a working stiff. My backside isn't wide enough to fill that particular seat. Besides, fellas, who the hell'd make your suits?"

As the Depression took hold, business thinned customer by customer, until the money was barely enough to keep Victor's growing family fed. The mines were still in operation, so Cypress was better off than many places, but people had grown wary, saving what they could in case the worst hit. Tailored clothes were a luxury seldom indulged in. After the first panic, Victor found himself with dozens of abandoned orders worth hundreds of dollars in labor and materials. With scant new business in sight, he resorted to delivering the finished garments to customers' doors. Like a reluctant bill collector, he took the first suit on his rack out to the farmstead of a crusty old Finn.

"Listen, Arno, I reckon you don't have the money for this, and if you do, you'd be a fool to part with it. But I'm willing to barter." Victor took in the shabby farmhouse, the field of overturned stones, the herd of thin goats grazing. "So, what is it you might have extra of around here?"

The Howards were delivered a crock of goat cheese and five hundred pounds of red potatoes, half of which were traded to a neighbor for venison sausage and butter. When the Swedish pastor needed new vestments, two parishioners came to the house and built a small sauna off the back cellar. In this manner Victor was able to provide for his family in the lean years, trading and retrading stores and services — a dozen jars of sauerkraut, one Sacher torte every Saturday for six months, fifty Mason jars of pickled beets, a barrel of cornmeal, a Malamute puppy, ten gallons of pine-green paint, a crate of salt cod, a thirty-dollar credit at the hardware store, train tickets to Duluth, piano lessons for Louisa, and so on. Some things had no takers, and Isobel found herself at the height of the Depression saddled with strange excesses and luxuries — a mound of raw angora from the widow who raised long-haired loppits, twenty-five boxes of French-milled lavender soap too fancy to use, reams of Italian stationery yellowing in gold gift boxes, and ten sour-faced carved wooden dolls the children refused to play with. The dolls were eventually put to use propping open windows around the house and the shop. One of the wretched things still glowered naked on Victor's desk, a nail driven through its neck, a paper cravat of bills jammed onto the point.

Isobel picked up the ugly doll and tossed it into Victor's desk drawer. The shop had always had an overwhelmingly masculine air, like a barbershop. Now, as she looked around, she could see the atmosphere had begun to lighten; it was clean, the windows opened to fresh air, vases of daisies Louisa had picked brightened the rear counter, and the revolting spittoon had been shoved out of sight under one of the theater seats. She'd hung lace curtains behind the display window and placed potted violets on the sill. Now Cathryn's presence added the element that made her recall her days in the Pasal Millinery: the light sounds of women at work.

She was glad for Cathryn's company. After the first weeks of nearly frantic chatter, they had settled into a more relaxed routine, one that included silences, companionable for the most part. But sometimes Cathryn's silence seemed less easy, as if accompanied by some heaviness descending, as if she'd stepped away to some low inner plateau. Barely aware she was doing it, Isobel tried to intercept these moments with quick volleys of gossip, or jokes or some interesting item. She came to realize that what she did to cheer Cathryn was exactly what Victor did when *she* was moody.

After closing up shop, strolling down the sidewalk to Jem's Diner, her arm linked through Cathryn's, Isobel realized she hadn't had a real friend in years. After leaving the millinery, she'd kept in touch with Kathleen by mail, but that correspondence had dwindled to only a Christmas card each year and an occasional letter.

———

Cathryn brought a flat wooden paint box and a roll of heavy paper. She set up her easel by the large windows and began to paint simple watercolor sketches of hats. She warned the sketches weren't perfect; most were vaguely remembered hats she'd seen on women in Chicago or in her travels abroad. Several paintings were thrown out before Isobel could even see them, Cathryn apologizing that her hand was rusty.

"I haven't kept up. I'm afraid I'm out of practice."

Isobel peered over her shoulder. "But you're so talented. Why did you ever give up painting?"

"Oh, I don't know why. I should really give it another go. I suppose I've no time anymore."

"But Liam is away so often, what do you do with your time?" Isobel tactfully did not bring up Cathryn's childlessness, but she couldn't help wondering what a woman alone might do all day.

Cathryn looked startled. "I . . . I do various things." She thought for a moment and then ticked off her daily activities on paint-tinted fingers. "I listen to music, I do my needlework. When Liam's home, I cook. Back home in Chicago there are always exhibits to see, concerts to hear. I shop. I have a few friends, of course, but they all have families now." Her eyes brightened. "I do read an awful lot. There's a beautiful Carnegie library not far from our house in Oak Park, and I volunteer there twice a week. You know, stamping and reshelving books. Very glamorous. Oh, and there's a second-hand bookseller just a few blocks away. I go there and spend hours. I even thought about clerking there, but Liam, well, he thinks it best I stay home. Just as well, I suppose. I'd probably spend all my earnings on books I have no room for. Say, I should bring you some I've brought with me. I've far too many to ever read in one summer."

"Oh, I wish I had more time for reading."

Cathryn waved her hand in dismissal. "Pish. Time comes to you for the right books."

In the idle time between rearranging the shop and the day the supplies arrived, Isobel sewed three plain summer dresses for Louisa, and Cathryn began embroidering their yokes with designs outlined in fine tailor's lead: two kissing thrushes perched on a pine bough with distant clouds shaped like hearts, half a dozen squirrels scampering over oak leaves — one tripping over the acorn in its mouth. The stitches of these works were so tiny, the floss and needles so fine, Isobel worried the task would take up Cathryn's summer. The last dress Cathryn worked on was Louisa's favorite, and the girl checked its progress regularly, creeping to peer over Cathryn's shoulder. Sensing the girl's shyness, Cathryn never turned around to look straight at Louisa. Feigning surprise, she would exclaim, "Oh! There's my shadow! Goodness, I'd thought I'd lost you." And then she would hold up the blue linen yoke for Louisa to examine. There, in Cathryn's exquisite stitching, three cartoon-like fish wearing bowler hats rode their bicycles, racing toward a full moon.

Over twenty years later, on a summer afternoon, Isobel would walk into grown Louisa's house to see one of her granddaughters wearing the very dress. Isobel knelt to kiss the child and as she did, she noticed that the last bicycle-riding fish had never been completed. After staring a moment at Cathryn's unfinished embroidery, Isobel burst into rare tears. Louisa put an arm around her mother, whispering into her grey curls, "Momma, I haven't forgotten her either."

It was Louisa who first noticed the birds had gone silent. "Auntie Cathryn, what do you hear?" They were at the edge of town, Cathryn walking her bicycle, her sandals swinging from the handlebars. Isobel trailed behind, watching as their footfalls roiled up soft dust to coat their bare ankles. They stopped and Cathryn stretched her neck in listening.

"Why, nothing. What do you hear, Louisa?"

"Nothing. They're gone. The birds are gone."

Isobel began to listen for them over the next days. She watched the woods and gardens during her travels from her house to downtown and back and was surprised to find Louisa was right. The chimney swifts had disappeared, the robins were gone. Even the crows had left. It must be this heat, she thought, so little water. They've gone looking for water.

In bed she strained to hear night birds. The owls and maniacal-sounding loons that usually announced the nights ceased announcing them.

What few birds she did sight, starlings, flew close and silent to the ground, as if not trusting their wings at any altitude.

Cathryn brought a portable gramophone and recordings by composers with names Isobel could hardly pronounce: Scriabin, Dvořák, Puccini. She laid a thick seventy-eight on the machine and a pure voice filled the shop.

"Opera?" Isobel looked unsure. Three practice hats were spread before her on the worktable — a russet-brown disk with auburn mink trim and metallic netting, a low teal-coloured cloche trimmed with pounded copper and a band made from a peacock plume, and a tiny black Robin Hood affair with a cluster of tarnished silver acorns and burgundy silk oak leaves. She rested her elbows on the worktable, comparing the hats with those in a Parisian fashion magazine that Cathryn had found. Cathryn leaned over her shoulder. "Izzy, you've got it! Those are almost identical copies!"

Isobel chewed the inside of her cheek. "Yes, perhaps

that's what's wrong." She wrinkled her nose. "Honestly, I think this one" — she picked up the teal — "might be prettier with pheasant. The peacock is completely lost on this colour." She carefully detached the feather and started digging around in her trim boxes.

Cathryn paced the shop, pausing now and then to straighten the items on a shelf or sweep an already clean corner. Isobel, oblivious, sewed and tacked to the music of Puccini, her needle flowing along with the melody.

The days grew longer and Isobel was in the shop by seven. Louisa's mornings with the twins wore her out, but afternoons she trudged to the shop, where she settled down to observe and then proceed to emulate nearly everything Cathryn did. If Cathryn was working on a watercolour, the girl would stand patiently until Cathryn would give her a piece of paper and a brush of her own. If Cathryn arrived with a flower tucked over her ear, Louisa would dash out and return wearing a roadside bluebell or even a dandelion. Most of the time the girl sat blended into the bolts of fabric, sewing on a sampler or drawing pictures, but always watching Cathryn from the corner of her eye.

Isobel watched all this while pretending not to. She noted her own gladness at seeing her daughter and new friend form a charming if odd bond and left it at that. She knew speaking of it might make Louisa draw back in shyness, or become more self-conscious than she already was.

Louisa's presence was so unobtrusive that one Saturday Isobel closed up the shop, locking the girl in for an hour before realizing what she had done. Racing back, she stopped short at the door. Louisa — wearing a hat recently finished for Cathryn — was pinching the handle of a teacup, pinkie extended, murmuring and nodding to her invisible companion while the gramophone scratched out the strains of a distant aria.

———

It occurred to Isobel that she did not miss the rest of her family as much as she should. She admitted this to Father Thiery during confession. His deep laugh drifted through the confessional screen.

"But you're working so hard, child, your mind is taken up. They'll be back soon enough."

Her penance had been one Hail Mary.

Isobel tried to picture the island she had only glimpsed in a blurred photograph and once at a great distance through opera glasses. What could they be doing out there all this time? She imagined the boys swimming for hours, blue with cold, no one sensible enough to pull them from the frigid lake. She did not fear they might drown — unlike herself and Louisa, they all swam like otters. But one of them was bound to catch a chill, get sick.

Then they'll be home. The minute one of them gets ill, they'll be back. Isobel's chest tightened at the thought.

No, no. Victor was very competent. Isobel told herself that he would most certainly take charge were anything to happen.

As if to allay her fears, a packet of letters arrived from the mail boat. Henry wrote in terse fashion, recounting the daily routine of island life.

I've learned to cook in a Dutch oven buried in coals. I've made camp bread, but could use a better recipe. Thomas is being a pain, eats half the berries I send him out to pick. The mail boat brings drinking water out twice a week, we boil the rest out of the lake. We miss the icebox. My kingdom for a Choco-Bar!

I'm fine how are you? Must be very bored without us, huh?

Victor's letter was brief.

Fishing is good, we've had Walleye or Perch for dinner nearly every night. They complain a little and ask for chicken and cheese and cold milk, but mostly they are good sports. We're reading Twain aloud each night.

I carved a cribbage board from a piece of maple I found, but it was too green and it warped before I even finished sanding it. The thing rocks on the camp table every time someone pegs a point. They think it's hilarious, that's the thing about kids, Izzy, they'll laugh at the same joke a thousand times. Miss you, V. —

Isobel noticed how he had signed off, not *Love,* but *Miss you.*

She saved Thomas's letter for last. As she looked at the wide crayon scrawl, the paper was overlaid with an image of his chubby hand.

Dear Momma,

Sometimes we sleep out side. There are Lightening Bugs and the dragonflies are like fairies. Henry says No Such Animal. Daddy says yes there is, and that If I'm lonely for you not to be too sad, maybe you fly over the water and visit us while we sleep. So now you are a Fairy over my bed!

Love and a lot of Kisses,
Thomas Arthur Howard

She could almost see Victor leaning over the boy, their two faces shadowed in concentration beneath the dim light of a lantern, Thomas curled around his crayon as Victor coached him on and helped with the spelling.

She folded the letter into a tight square and tied a ribbon around it. She would put it in her bottom drawer along with the pouch of milk teeth, locks of baby hair, and the handmade Mother's Day cards. She laid out clean stationery and dipped her pen in fresh ink. She wrote a brief note to Henry and a somewhat longer letter to Thomas, decorating the margin of his with a sketch of a dragonfly with the profile of a woman's face in its wings. She wrote that she had made a new friend, and that Louisa was fine but missed them all very much (even though Louisa showed no such sign, except for the night she'd had a bad dream and had climbed into Thomas's empty bed).

As she sat down to write to Victor, she despaired at the blankness of the page before her. She could have described Cathryn and her new friendship, she was eager to, but she couldn't think how without disclosing what she'd done in the shop. It occurred to her that she wanted the millinery to be her secret, a surprise. She realized what a long time it had been since she'd had anything interesting to offer Victor. He always had a story to tell over the dinner table, while she usually had only reportage and dry facts: what needed to be done around the house, how much a pound of beef cost at Sima's, concerns over the children's grades or health, or what mischief they'd gotten into, what they needed in the way of clothes or school supplies.

The letter she finally began seemed just as dry.

Dear Victor,

Things are going well. Louisa's watching the Hokkanens' twins in the mornings and helping me in the afternoons. The garden is a lost cause even though we water every day. This weather!

With so little to do at home I've reopened the shop. A few customers have asked after you. I measured Mr. Vincent for a coat — he said he'd wait for the trousers until you got back (I believe he'd rather you took his inseam measurement!).

It sounds as if you're having a time out there. I'm sending a package back with Doug Green — lemons and apples and a few vegetables, some chicken on dry ice I hope will keep. With luck the chocolate won't melt all over everything. The yeast packets are for Henry.

It's been an interesting summer so far. I hope you are all right.

Love, Isobel

As usual her writing did not express her emotions, as if there were a stutter somewhere between her thoughts and the hand moving her pen, a missed connection. She wanted to say something more, wanted something of herself to emerge. She laid her hands flat on either side of the page. A piece of petrified varnish that had dislodged itself from the ceiling earlier sat glittering near the edge of the table. She had meant to throw it away, but now she picked it up and held it to the light, smiling. She tucked it into the envelope along with her letter. An old private joke. Better than words.

Isobel and Cathryn speculated on what styles and colours might be in fashion the following spring. Cathryn brought recent magazines sent from Chicago and they pored over the pages, their heads bent in happy collusion. Isobel made a few more sample pieces with what scraps she could scrounge — a waxed linen boater, a felt cloche. Easy pieces. Good millinery was more intricate than dressmaking, and not something blithely resumed. It took weeks for her fingers to limber to their former dexterity, to recall the cadences and intricacies of the work, to develop the proper calluses and strengths.

When the long-awaited crates of supplies arrived she and Cathryn tore open the wrappings and ran their hands over the hard bolts of felts and silk linings. Cathryn plucked up the inventory list, and in a dramatic posture, one hand sweeping toward the precious pile, she trilled, "Dusty-Olive, Vivid-Midnight, Forest Fawn, Berry-Brown, Brandy-Wine, Pomegranate, Violet Sky, Pearl, Ecru, Et Ceterahhhh!"

The new tools fascinated Louisa, who endlessly worked the shiny crimpers and punches on her own collection of paper cutout hats.

In the mornings, while Isobel formed and steamed and tacked, Cathryn read aloud the daily excerpts from a serialized novel in the newspaper, that summer it was *So Big,* by Edna Ferber. Louisa and Isobel became caught up in the daily travails of the protagonist, hapless, sophisticated Selena, who stubbornly insisted her life would be beautiful even though she'd wound up on a Dutchman's fallow vegetable farm south of Chicago.

Bits of the novel took place in the city, and Louisa was continually interrupting Cathryn's reading.

"Have you seen that hotel, Auntie Cathryn? Have you been to that street?"

"Yes."

"Is it grand?"

"Grand enough."

"And the shops, are they grand too?"

"Not so grand as this one. Louisa, I've never heard you ask so many questions. I guess I'll just have to bring you to Chicago myself. Show you the sights."

She began to read again, but was soon interrupted by Isobel.

"This Selena character, she has so much promise. How could she let herself give in like that?"

"Give in?"

"You know, to her fate."

Cathryn put the newspaper down. "Is it a matter of giving in? Don't we choose our fates, after a fashion?"

———

Cathryn brought books for Isobel to read, volumes of Tennyson, Teasdale, and e. e. cummings, translations of Rainer Rilke.

At night Isobel lay in bed, holding the slender bindings tentatively, afraid she might not understand or even like what she read, afraid she would be expected to talk about the poems with Cathryn in a vernacular she did not possess and could not grasp. She'd left school at sixteen for the trades, and while she could lay linoleum so it wouldn't bubble, care for a colicky baby, or alter a wedding dress to make a bride five months gone appear virginal, she sometimes felt a delicate chasm between herself and Cathryn which exhibited itself not in the disparity of their social standings, but in language. In the same way she felt set apart from the immigrants of Cypress, with their accents and odd phrasing, she felt duly separated from Cathryn's world. In conversation Cathryn seemed to float just out of Isobel's reach on a cloud of sophisticated adjectives, words she herself understood only after hearing them repeatedly in context. Like a dinner guest waiting to see which fork the hostess will pick up next, Isobel tested new vocabulary aloud only after sure of putting it to proper use.

Cathryn read voraciously. Isobel concluded literature might be the doorway into the world Cathryn inhabited. She reasoned that if she read what Cathryn did, she might gain some insight into her friend's character, the ecstatic moods, the often pained silences.

She read. She didn't understand all of the poetry, but she found herself drawn to the economy of words. She was equally intrigued by the silences between these words and what they summoned or did not summon. A few poems she found beautiful for what they managed to evoke without being overt, and these she liked best, could even recognize bits of herself in them. Others made her uneasy, and she felt the poets had been indiscreet when they laid their pained, raw hearts open for all to examine.

In the late nights, after Louisa was asleep, Isobel would straighten her pillows and tip the lamp to send light pooling into her lap. She let herself fall into the volumes, her lips sometimes moving along, whispering those lovely lines that reached her.

One Saturday Isobel left Cathryn to watch the shop and boarded a train for Duluth with Louisa. She needed a few things and was too anxious to wait the time the post would take. After finishing up at the fabric supply house, they walked down the hill to the Pasal Millinery. Her old friends Kathleen and Ruth still worked there, and when they heard who was in to buy supplies they rushed to the front.

Kathleen had grown fat, her Irish rosiness aged to ruggedness, as if she'd spent the last sixteen years working fields of rye.

"Isobel Marie, look at you!" She opened her massive arms. "You're little as a bird. I'll crush the breath from you. And this can't be your daughter!"

Ruth was more formal, shaking hands so that Isobel had to abandon her intended embrace. She looked so worn and haggard Isobel barely recognized her.

"Oh, Ruthie!"

Her reply was a rebuke.

"Izzy, *you've* not changed one bit."

They made a fuss over Louisa, showing her the workrooms while Isobel picked out canvas linings and floss. She found it difficult to concentrate, and as she plucked up random colours of thread, she realized she'd half expected that Ruth and Kathleen would have remained girls, that living unmarried and childless would have somehow preserved them.

Later Kathleen served tea and admired Isobel's appearance, pinching at her waistline in disbelief. "You've had *three,* did you say? Tell us their names again!"

They leaned in, hungry for news. Isobel felt slightly guilty, suspecting suddenly that her life might, as they had insisted, agree with her. She said little of the new millinery and nothing about being free for the summer. She grew anxious to leave suddenly and said something vague about the time of the train. As she said good-bye to Ruth she pulled her into the hug she'd intended earlier. Ruth felt dry and stiff, and her return embrace was feeble.

When Kathleen wrapped her arms around Isobel she whispered, "Now, don't be a stranger." She suddenly lifted Isobel off her feet, and even Ruth laughed.

Isobel gathered her parcels and stepped away. When Ruth and Kathleen stood side by side she remembered them as they had been, two girls with nothing ahead of them but possibilities. Ruth wanted to be a buyer for a big department store; she would travel and see the country. Kathleen was determined to marry and have babies, perhaps move back to Donegal one day.

Once outside she did not look back through the window. Instead she bent as though to speak to Louisa, averting her gaze, knowing they were still standing there, knowing they had hardly moved.

Was a person really able to choose their own fate? It seemed there were two paths to a fate — the one you chose, or the one you allowed to choose you.

She wondered if Cathryn had decided her own fate. As she walked east along Superior Street, Isobel thought about the path she herself was on. Had she chosen it, or had it chosen her?

The return train wasn't until early evening. They had a late lunch at the Hotel Duluth. It was Louisa's first fancy restaurant, and she surprised Isobel by being prim but friendly with the waiter, ordering with a sophistication that belied her age.

"And tea, please. A cup for my mother too."

"With lemon or milk, miss?"

Louisa blinked. "Both, if you don't mind."

Isobel caught a familiar mannerism and smiled into her napkin. Louisa was playing the role of Cathryn.

After lunch they roamed Canal Park and the lakeside garden, but they still had over two hours until the train. A man hawking tickets offered to let them ride up the aerial lift bridge for half price.

Louisa pointed. "You mean that bridge, the one that goes up like an elevator over the water?"

"The very one, miss."

"But why would anyone want to do that?"

The man was taken aback. "Well, I . . . "

"Thank you, sir, but I don't think so. My mother would regurgitate."

"Re-what?"

"And I would too, probably. Have a nice afternoon."

As the man walked away he stuffed the tickets into his pockets and grumbled.

"Why are you laughing, Momma? Wasn't that more polite than saying *vomit?*"

Heading for the depot they found a tiny bookshop on a side street. As Isobel stood among the shelves she was attracted to an olive-coloured binding. When she picked up the book it fell open to a poem, complete on its two pages.

She gave Louisa a coin and sent her next door to the soda fountain. After finding a chair near the back of the shop she read the poem twice. Glancing around to make sure she was alone, she read its lines again in a low whisper.

As she dug into her handbag, she realized it was the first book she'd ever bought herself. She blushed when asking the clerk, "Do you think I could have it gift wrapped?"

CHAPTER EIGHT

~ ~ ~

Monday morning Isobel walked into the shop to find Cathryn standing over the shards of a broken vase, palms pressed to her eyes as if to hold them in place. Purple columbine and white iris lay amid a pool of water slowly soaking into the floorboards.

Isobel knelt. The vase was shattered as if it had been hurled to the floor, not merely dropped. The stems of the flowers were broken and the irises looked as if they'd been crushed.

"They were so beautiful, and the vase . . . and now it's broken. I've broken it." Cathryn's shoulders convulsed. "I've ruined it!"

Isobel stood and looked curiously into her friend's

swollen face, but Cathryn turned away. "I'm sorry, I'm sorry."

When Cathryn began to rock, shifting from one foot to another, Isobel saw white petals sticking to the heels of her shoes.

She steered Cathryn to a chair near the window. "Cathryn, it's all right."

She covered her eyes again.

"Do you hear me?"

"I'm sorry."

"It's all right. It's just a vase. See? Look." She pried Cathryn's hands downward. "It's just a broken vase and some silly flowers. It'll only take a minute to clean it up."

By the time she'd swept and mopped up the mess and made a pot of tea, Cathryn had washed her face, reapplied her lipstick, and was doing the crossword puzzle in the *Cypress Tribune* as if nothing had happened, her voice steady and bright when she asked, "Izzy, what's a five-letter word for 'fanciful journey'?"

Isobel, balancing a teacup and a plate of shortbread, stared at Cathryn. "I don't know . . . dream?"

"Ha! Wrong, but that's good. I like that, Izzy, a dream really *is* a journey after all, isn't it? A somnambulant journey."

"A *som* — ?"

Cathryn ignored her. "Ah. *Jaunt,* I think. Yes, that fits." She read clues and checked off words as she filled in the squares of her puzzle, drinking her tea and rapping her pencil in a beat whenever she became stuck.

After a half-hour she abandoned the unfinished puzzle and began pacing the length of the shop.

Isobel kept watch from the corner. "Cathryn, you'll wear these floorboards to slivers."

She dutifully sat down and worked on her embroidery, but popped up out of her chair after only a few minutes to stand next to Isobel and watch her fit a muslin lining into a beret.

"Izzy?"

"Hmm?"

"Would you teach me how to drive?"

"Drive! A car? What on earth for?"

Cathryn grasped Isobel's hand and cried, pleading and girlish. "For fun! Oh please, Izzy!"

Isobel was not an accomplished driver herself, but she could hardly disappoint Cathryn. Her friend's blind faith gave her confidence enough, so that Saturday noon she cranked the old Ford to life and drove the bumpy logging road to the end of Granite Point. She thought she was getting close to Cathryn's house when the road dipped to a low spot curving near the lake. Across the bay she could make out the end of the point and the cottage tucked in under the cliff. The ruts of the road were muddy here, even in the dry weather. At this low spot there was a wooden dock with a long cedar-strip canoe resting upon it. The cottage was only a few hundred feet away by water, but the road inclined sharply to swerve off into the woods, growing more rugged and narrowing until the pines towered in an arch, obliterating all sunlight but dusty shafts. Isobel knew she was getting close only when she recognized Cathryn's red bicycle leaning against a tree.

She pulled up to the parking slope. If there hadn't been another vehicle parked there to define the edge, Isobel might well have landed the Ford directly on Cathryn's roof. The wide timber structure was barely visible below, flanked by white pines and camouflaged by moss padding the cedar shakes. The roof was gently speckled, and only the broad chimneys at either end discriminated the structure from the terrain. Isobel descended a narrow set of steps carved into the stone and at the bottom found herself on a path of flagstone leading alongside the cottage. All hues of lichen had attached themselves to the log exterior, and orange mushrooms sprouted next to the foundation.

The steep gables and oddly placed windows reminded her of a fairy-tale book she'd had as a child, *Gnome's, wizard's, witch's lair, all who enter here beware . . .*

Isobel's foot caught as if grabbed and she shrieked. When she looked down to see her ankle snagged by Virginia creeper, she laughed and untangled the vine.

Once someone had attempted a garden along the front of the cottage, but wild cinnamon ferns and sumac had taken over. A bright wave of sweet woodruff thrived in the sour earth of pine needles, and a raft of bergamot drifted toward the door. The slender clematis on the stone pillars of an arbor was shouldered to the side by a rigorous curtain of climbing wood rose.

She knocked timidly at the thick door, fully expecting it to be opened by some crone, but a delighted Cathryn wearing a bright blouse and carmine lipstick popped out to greet her in a tight hug. She looped her arm through Isobel's and swept her inside.

"There you are!"

The entry was weighted on one side by a heavy winding staircase with banisters and rungs of twisted willow; the floor was cold slate. Three tiny coloured windows above the door let in shafts of bottle-green light.

"What an odd house, Cathryn."

Cathryn laughed. "Just wait, I'll take you on a tour." She led Isobel through the low kitchen, its ceiling branded with blackened rings above each gaslight, the wooden walls painted a shiny vanilla that reflected the aqua linoleum. A corner of screened windows framed a table laden with stacks of books and a vase of marsh cinquefoil.

The dining room paralleled a long porch with wicker chairs all painted a dull brown. An adjoining living room was nearly consumed by a stone fireplace the length of one wall. Two horsehair sofas and several rocking chairs were placed around the hearth.

Isobel felt something tickle through her sandal and jumped back. The bearskin rug at the edge of the hearthstone was massive. Glass eyes peered into the firebox, and its yawn was crowded with yellowed teeth as long as Isobel's fingers.

"It's all right, Izzy. You can step on him if you like. Can't *bear* to myself. Ha."

All the windows in the house opened upward to attach to the ceilings with hooks, so that reflections of the outdoors and interiors met in wavering grids overhead. The logs of the interior walls had gone dark and were dotted with beads of clear pine sap, hardened orbs that held reflections of reflections.

There were two empty first-floor bedrooms connected by a small parlor with twisted twig armchairs. Off the parlor was another set of stairs within a shaft of cabbage-rose wallpaper, a tight bower leading up.

The first upstairs room was large, its windows facing the lake. An immense carved bed was softened by a damask coverlet and a half-dozen finely embroidered pillows. Cathryn's scarves and necklaces hung from the empty canopy frame, and a trunk at the foot of the bed opened to a mound of books.

Isobel picked up a framed wedding picture from the bureau. Cathryn and Liam were linked on the steps of a cathedral, a dozen attendants flowing behind. Two priests and a bishop stood well off to the side, as if fearing to tread on the endless gown coming like a flood from the recess of the vestibule.

"Good Lord, Cathryn, that dress!"

"Yes. It was something." She laughed. "You can believe my shoulders ached pulling the thing. That aisle seemed endless! After the wedding Liam nearly had to ride one of the horses, there was barely enough room in the carriage for me and the train."

Isobel touched the frame. "And your groom, how handsome, he looks so . . . "

"Happy? Yes, Liam was happy. In love then." She flashed a grim smile of her own, shrugged, and slipped out the door. Isobel followed her down the corridor of doors opening to four smaller, slope-ceilinged bedrooms, all furnished with willow headboards and bare, grey-ticked mattresses. Clear glass oil lamps near each bed emitted a smell of clean kerosene, and the pale yellow floors were evenly dusted with a powdery chaff sifted in through window screens.

Cathryn had been breathily singing out the rooms as they went through the house. *"Parlor, big porch, stairs, this room, that room, bedroom, bedroom . . ."* When they reached the tiny hall off the upstairs corridor she sang, *"Other porch, husband!"* At the sound, Liam Malley turned from his fly-tying table in the far corner of the screened porch.

Cathryn's husband rose, ducking to avoid a rafter, as Isobel came forward to shake his hand. She had never seen him close-up and was immediately struck by his unusual colouring, eyes of startling blue fringed by thick lashes the same shade as his blue-black hair. His skin was white save the steely sheen where his whiskers had been closely shaved. His features were young, as if he were a great overgrown boy, but his mouth was old, the lips withheld. When he smiled it seemed a weighed decision.

Isobel spoke first. "Hello."

He remained silent, his wariness was palpable. His hand dwarfed Isobel's, but his touch was tentative, as if her hand were an egg.

He sat back down to his task.

Isobel cocked her head, unable to tell whether he was gruff or simply shy.

She mentioned the warm weather they had been having, and Mr. Malley nodded solemnly without looking up. "No good for trout." After a long pause he added, "All right for a picnic, though."

Isobel smiled at him, puzzled. He seemed misplaced in the cottage, his bulk too awkward for the space. A bear in a rabbit warren. He turned in his chair and reached for his pipe. As he tamped in the tobacco he seemed to relax.

"I've seen your husband around, Mrs. Howard. We've never met, though. He's the tailor, isn't he? Makes the uniforms for the mine's brass band?"

"Yes, he does."

"And you, you make hats?"

Isobel shrugged. "Just starting again. Your wife's been a great help to me."

He raised his brow at Cathryn through a plume of smoke. "She spends a lot of time in the shop. That's good, that's fine. Keeps her occupied then, doesn't it? Idle hands and all that." He peered in Cathryn's direction, but she folded her arms suddenly and turned to the window. Liam inclined his head, and when he spoke it was as if he only had half his attention to spare. The rest was trained on Cathryn, even though he no longer looked directly at her.

"Yes. Can't have too many hats, can you?" He suddenly looked down as though searching the surface of his table.

"I hope not." Isobel turned to Cathryn, but she was still focused out the window. She pointed beyond Liam's shoulder. "What a lovely setting you have here. Just look at that stone." Great outcroppings sloped gradually from the house to scallop into the water.

Liam looked up, a mild shift. "You know that stone?"

"No, I don't."

"That's Ely Greenstone." He rolled his *r* on the word *green*. "We're very close to the Laurentian divide. Have you been to see it?"

Isobel shook her head.

Liam pulled out a chair and nodded for Isobel to sit. She settled onto its edge. Cathryn leaned on the sill, rapt on some point outside.

"You should, y'know. It's a sight. The divide is really a fold, a great folding of the crust of the earth. Exposed all the root rocks of former mountains round here."

"Former mountains?"

"Sure, all the Saganaga granite, the quartz shelves."

Cathryn laughed nervously. "Oh, not a geology lecture! Really, Liam, you'll bore our poor guest to tears."

He ignored her, becoming more animated as his sentences were peppered with words that sounded very much like desserts to Isobel, *peneplain, strata, cherty*. He talked about the Knife Lake sediments, slates, impure quartzites, volcanic tuffs. "Agglomerate ten thousand feet thick, this very house is sitting on it."

Cathryn was suddenly behind Liam, hands on his shoulders, patting him to silence. "Next thing you know he'll be dragging us over to Giant's Ridge for a field trip."

"Oh, I don't mind, it's rather interesting . . ."

Cathryn swept around Liam, and as she passed him he reached out to touch the small of her back. She did not stop but motioned Isobel up from her chair. "Up, up! Enough for today, class." She took a curt bow toward her husband. "Professor."

She led Isobel to the door. "Let's get going on that picnic, Izzy. We don't want to miss a minute of this glorious sun!" At the second mention of a picnic, Isobel glanced curiously at Cathryn, who warned a silence by pressing her lips. She made a tight face toward the chair where Liam sat and backed stealthily down the hall.

Isobel turned at the doorway. "Ah, it was a pleasure to meet you, Mr. Malley."

"Same here." He picked up a tiny hook between tobacco-stained fingertips. "Mrs. Howard?"

She turned back.

He nodded to the hallway. "You'll take care with her."

"Pardon?" Isobel waited.

Cathryn's voice came from far down the hall. "Ta, Liam!"

Isobel stood, thinking he might explain, but he didn't, only looked her in the eye once before turning away, suddenly intent on the window Cathryn had glued herself to earlier, searching the landscape as if to find what had held her attention so long.

Downstairs, Cathryn took a wicker hamper from the counter and pushed Isobel neatly out the door.

Jostling along in the car, Isobel asked, "A picnic, Cathryn? You didn't tell him where we're really going? That I'm teaching you to drive?"

"Goodness, no. He'd only fret. Besides, what's wrong with having a little secret?"

"Secret?"

Cathryn took a silver case from her bag, opening it toward Isobel. "Cigarette?"

Isobel tightened her grasp on the wheel as the car bumped into the ruts. "Perhaps later, after our *picnic*."

All her life she had embraced an abiding distrust of horses, water, and any mechanical device larger than a sewing machine. Why Cathryn, or anyone else for that matter, would want to drive a car for pleasure was a full mystery. Isobel had learned how to drive only out of necessity and after twenty years still shuddered at the sound of ignition.

She had decided the safest place for Cathryn to learn would be somewhere well out of the way where they could cause no one harm, just in case.

"Perfect!" Cathryn clapped her hands together and hooted as they drove through the gates of the Cypress cemetery.

After they parked Cathryn insisted on peeling back the vented hood to examine the valves and pistons. She even reached in to feel the warm cables and pipes, tracing them to see how and to what they connected. Unlike Isobel, she didn't seem at all frightened of the smelly engine and its black rumblings.

"Oh look, Izzy, this must be the carburetor!" Isobel backed away and sat down to watch from a distance, jumping up after realizing she'd settled on a tombstone. Cathryn leaned into the car's open hood.

Isobel pulled at quack-grass engulfing the limestone angel on a child's grave. The hood of the Ford crashed back into place and Cathryn calmly wiped her fingers, stuffing her blackened handkerchief nonchalantly into the pocket of her immaculate skirt. She called out to Isobel, who had moved down the long row of headstones to tidy another neglected grave. Cathryn cranked the starter herself and when the engine rattled to life she threw her hands up in triumph. Jumping in behind the wheel, she motioned wildly and yelled, "C'mon, Izzy, or I'll go without you!"

Cathryn tested the brakes, pressed the clutch, and put her foot to the accelerator. The car lurched a few times and veered from the road into the grass. Isobel covered her eyes, regretting their location. "Please, please, please don't hit anything."

"Any*one,* you mean."

They bumped back onto the lane and then they were moving, Cathryn steering through the narrow road between grassy plots and mausoleums. Shifting was difficult, but by midafternoon Cathryn was slipping fluidly from first gear to second with hardly a jerk. "Why, it's just a rhythm! That's all there is to it, Izzy. It's as easy as swimming or making . . . dancing."

After the lesson they laid out a blanket and ate their lunch under a canopy of aspen. Cathryn was flushed with her triumph and ate quickly, crumbs from the Cornish meat pasties dusting her blouse. "After lunch we'll try the open road, Izzy. I can't wait to use fourth gear!"

Isobel dropped her head, moaning.

"Now. Don't be such a ninny." Cathryn pulled a bottle of wine from the hamper. "Here, this might buy you some courage."

"Where did you ever find that? Not here in town?"

"Oh, no, madame." She turned the dusty bottle so Isobel could see the label. *Chateau Alsace, 1922.* Working the corkscrew into the bottle, Cathryn frowned into the hamper. "It's from our cellar back home."

"Is this another secret?"

"Do you mean did I tell Liam I was taking a teeny bottle of wine?" The back of her hand flew to her mouth in a theatrical swoon. "Oh my, I do believe I forgot!"

Isobel looked into the basket. "And you've forgotten wineglasses too? No matter." She tipped the bottle toward her lips. "We'll make do."

Cathryn scanned the graves. "You see that headstone, Izzy, the one with all the swirly lines in it? Do you know what kind of flower is growing there?"

"No."

"Saponaria. Isn't it pretty?"

Isobel peered at the grave, but Cathryn nudged her shoulder and pointed in another direction. "And see over by the pond, that white cluster of blossoms? That's called grass-of-Parnassus. Isn't that a name?"

"Sounds like a line from a dirty limerick. You can see that from here?" Isobel squinted.

"Oh look, Izzy, blue gentian!"

"Since when are you the botanist?"

Cathryn shrugged. "Since . . . since I've started to take notice."

At the far end of the cemetery, a stooped figure parked his wheelbarrow and began chipping lichen from the base of the stone pillars supporting the iron gates. The sound reached the women's ears only after his hammer and chisel were lifted, a delay between the retreating glint of metal and the grating sound on stone. Cathryn watched the man at his task for a moment before musing, "What happens in the gap, I wonder?"

"The gap? You mean the silence?"

"Yes, the silence, the gap in between. If noise can delay itself, what else might be floating around out there that doesn't reach us right away?"

"Such as?" Isobel kicked off her shoes and began stripping a dandelion.

Cathryn lit two cigarettes and handed one to Isobel. "Oh, emotion, for instance. Something that is felt for you by another person, say anger, or even love. What happens in the time it takes for you to realize it's there?"

Isobel thought about this for a moment and was about to speak when Cathryn pulled her skirt up over her knees. "What wonderful sun!" She began to unbutton her blouse with one hand. "I'm going to get some colour."

Isobel took in Cathryn's peach silk chemise and noticed the fine embroidery at its V. She felt a sliver of envy. It had been years since she wore anything like it, anything daring. She picked a bit of tobacco from her tongue.

"Dangerous daywear, Cathryn." Isobel glanced over toward the maintenance man.

"It's a dangerous day, Izzy. I've learned to drive and now I'm going to sunburn my back." As Cathryn rolled over, Isobel noticed a pearlish cord running through her flesh, a wide scar just over her collarbone, silvered with light.

"What's that on your neck?"

She reached quickly to touch it. "Oh, my surgery?" As her fingers drummed over the mark, alarm fluttered across Cathryn's face, and Isobel had an image of a dark curtain falling.

"My, I'd almost forgotten it. I had a little cyst there. Maybe the sun will fade it." She reached for the wine, and when she turned back she was smiling again. "More anesthetic, nurse?"

Across the cemetery, the maintenance man lifted his head, as if hearing distant birds. He put down his tool and shaded his eyes to peer toward the noise. Loons? One of the marble angels at the base of the far knoll sported a broad-brimmed straw hat, its long ribbons ticking in the breeze. Beyond the statues, two women reclined under the trees, half-sitting, propped on their elbows. Thin strips of smoke rose from the cigarettes in their hands. The man was upwind, couldn't make out what they said, heard only a singular cough and the audible wails of laughter as the women fell out of sight behind the tall grass.

On the way to Isobel's house they stopped to pick wildflowers. They gathered crowded bouquets, their arms spilling with the flowers Cathryn had spoken of. In the kitchen Cathryn and Louisa arranged them in a large spongewear crock, the girl rapt as Cathryn recited the proper names, teaching as she poked each stem into the mass of colour. Louisa's eyebrows snailed in effort as she paired the names with the flowers, pursing her mouth and watching Cathryn's lips, holding back until she was sure she could pronounce the Latin words properly, speaking only when she could do so precisely.

Isobel sat on the counter and watched this exchange. She saw herself in the girl's efforts, realizing how often she herself held back when it came to new things, taking on new situations. Victor accused her of being cautious to a fault, but she'd never really understood what he meant. It touched her how Louisa wanted so badly to pronounce the words right the first time. She saw they had this in common; both would choose not having a thing if it involved risk.

"I went and picked up your mail while you were having your CAT scan. Just a few bills and this package from Cypress."

Isobel squinted at the return address. "From Louisa?"

"Louisa?" Thomas peered over his glasses. "Mother?"

Isobel looked out the window. "Robert, of course, I meant Robert."

"Yes, it's from Robert." His brother-in-law still lived in the house he'd shared with Louisa during their marriage, the same house Thomas and she had grown up in. "Look here, it says 'book rate.' Seems he's sent you some book." Thomas opened the package and handed her a thin volume, its green binding furry with mildew.

"Oh, wonderful. He found the one I wanted."

"And here's a note."

"Will you read it, please?"

Thomas cleared his throat. "*Dear Isobel, Glad to hear you're doing so well. I'll send along some pictures of the grandkids before they head back to school (I barely see them myself, between their dates and weekend trips). Both my girls say 'hello and kisses to Gran.' Stay well, Robert.*"

Isobel took the note. "Did he send something else? I'd asked for a magnifying glass."

"You need a magnifying glass? Has your sight slipped that much?"

"For your information, it was never that good. I ruined my eyes long ago, but now, since the stroke . . . Well, look at the size of this print! Even you'd need glasses to read it."

"Mother, I am wearing glasses." He leaned over. "Ah, more poetry." He closed the book. "I never had much time for poetry, only what we had to read in college. I never liked much of it."

Isobel shrugged. "I only read what I liked. It took me a while to warm to poetry. I never cared for that e. e. cummings, for instance. I always wanted to take a red pen and correct those silly stanzas falling off the page. What was the purpose of all that, anyway?"

Thomas shrugged and swabbed an antiseptic pad over the tiny sore on Isobel's hand.

"Shouldn't a nurse be doing this?" Isobel looked at the pinhole in her flesh left from the IV.

"This is a hospital, all the nurses are busy."

"I liked that Eliot, though. I even memorized parts of his poems. Would you like to hear one?"

"Certainly, love to."

Isobel closed her eyes and began in a wavering voice. *"Those who glitter with the glory of the hummingbird, meaning / Death / Those who . . ."* She frowned. *"Those who . . ."*

Thomas crumpled the gauze between his fingers and dropped it in the wastebasket. "You're not dying, Mother."

"And how would you know? Shush, I've got it. *Those who suffer the ecstasy of animals . . ."*

Thomas turned to wash at the sink.

"None of this is in order, mind you." Isobel rubbed at the spot on her hand. *". . . are become unsubstantial, reduced by a wind."*

Thomas waited but she'd gone quiet, was sniffing at the binding of the book in her hand.

"Mother?"

"Oh, I can't remember the rest of it now. Doesn't matter. Here, Thomas, put this in my closet, please. And see if there's a hairbrush in there, would you? I must look a fright."

He took the book from her. "You look just fine. If there was a beauty contest on this ward right now, you'd win."

He checked her closet. The skirt she'd been wearing when he found her hung crookedly on a hanger. He pushed it aside. Her suitcase was open and empty, the old, battered hatbox she'd asked him to bring sat high on the shelf. As he took it down he saw it was missing its handle. Inside were a few more books, a pair of tweezers, two bars of French soap in wax paper, a square of tailor's lead, and a leather photo album. He ran his hand over the worn gold lettering on the album. He slowly turned. "Mother?"

But her eyes were closed behind blue tissue lids. Thomas noticed how deeply they rested in their sockets. She had lost weight since being admitted, flesh stretched away from the rack of cheekbones. He watched her breathe for a minute and felt her wrist. When he let go her hand fell like a weight. She shifted under the blanket.

Thomas settled in the bedside chair and opened the album.

The first page was taken up by a formal wedding portrait. His father looked exactly as Thomas remembered — wiry, mischievous, his own younger face. His mother was tiny next to her groom, and his father had not been a big man. Thomas glanced over the blanket. She was even smaller now, a husk on the hospital bed. He realized he'd always imagined her to be larger than she really was. How long now since he'd seen her standing?

In the portrait she was a lovely girl, her angular jaw softened by the bridal veil and the sweep of blond hair draped over each temple. Her eyes were clear and large under arched brows, her nose narrow, and her lips smudged to look larger with a bit of lipstick. A face of delicacies and strengths, her mouth was a line of determination where any other bride might offer a smile. Thomas grinned.

He had the sense of being watched and looked up, startled to catch his mother.

"So, you're still with us."

"I was never gone."

"I thought you'd fallen asleep."

She looked at the photograph. "Oh, that one. My mouth always displeased me in that picture."

Her vanity surprised him. "It shows you're made of tough stuff."

"What bride wants to look tough?" She shook her head. "A thin mouth, that's a blight on any woman. I always thought, I always imagined that a generous mouth portended some . . . I don't know, largesse of spirit. Sensuality."

"Ah well, Dad must have found you sensual enough." Isobel smiled.

Thomas began to speak and swallowed, dropping his chin to avoid her eyes.

As they fell into an awkward silence, Thomas felt his mother's physical presence more keenly than he had in years. The sharpness of bones that had not always been sharp.

She would have once reveled in her physical self like anyone else. She would have run bare-legged as a child, danced as a girl; she would have nursed her babies, nursed him. She would have walked on ice without fear. She had carried him. He closed his eyes to the bright curtain of a memory patched together of primary colours.

A summer afternoon composed of deep blue sky, red geraniums, and a yellow dress. His mother grasping both his wrists and dragging him sideways, the movement difficult at first, his ankles raking the grass, but then she was laughing and he was spinning, suddenly airborne. As he left the earth, swooping in an arc just above the grass, blades skimmed and tickled his bare heels. He rose higher in flight, the joy of it spiced with danger. Above him flashed a zoetrope of endless sky and flapping laundry, a row of white dishcloths became rectangular clouds. Sky and dress and sky. Blue, yellow, blue. At that moment his world was fixed in colour and speed, and he believed his mother had conceived it all. Joy and danger both owned in her steadfast grip.

He looked at the now withered arms, the upturned claw of her weak hand. The hand was null, held nothing. His own hands still did his bidding, and he daily took for granted their ability to do what he set them to — maneuver a car along a winding road, soundly shake the hand of a client, or plant a hedge of oleander. Even arouse a woman. He wasn't dead yet.

She would have had desires once. Of course she'd had desires.

He shook his head.

"Where are you, Thomas?"

He stared. Her eyes burned with the same determination as the young woman's in the photograph. The same lovely woman.

"I'm right here, Mother."

When she woke again, he was gone. The photo album sat on the chair where he had left it, opened to another photograph, the one showing her surrounded by her children.

Her own face stared up at her. Not so different, really, than how she'd looked with Victor. She'd carried a young face her whole life. *Blessed,* some said. Until she was fifty, people often misjudged her age by at least ten years. But in this photograph her mouth was even more severe.

Of all, why that picture? It was the worst time, the worst possible reminder. She tapped a fingernail over the faces. Thomas, a gangly ten-year-old, stood stiffly at her shoulder, his eye grown steely, his childhood suddenly over. Louisa was fourteen but no taller than Thomas. She stood pressing toward her mother, and her hand trailed down Isobel's sleeve to rest protectively on her forearm. Henry stood serious in his navy uniform, aloof, already set apart. He was itching to be overseas, she remembered that.

The photographer had wanted her to prop a picture of Victor in her lap so the portrait would include him. "Have you ever heard of anything so ridiculous?" Isobel muttered to the empty room. "Victor would spin in his grave."

On the afternoon of her fortieth birthday, Isobel walked into the shop to find Victor slumped over his work-table. At first she thought he was pulling a prank. Typical Victor. She tiptoed forward, ready to pounce.

When she saw the thread of orange saliva connecting his lower lip to his sleeve, she recoiled, pitched forward, then back again, legs buckling precisely under her in sections, a pair of folding reeds. *You wouldn't. No, Victor, you wouldn't!*

For a full year she moved as if against a current. Walking to the grocery story she would marvel, I am walking to the grocery store, placing one foot in front of the other. I will buy eggs and meat and carry them home.

I am making a bed, as though it matters whether this bed gets made.

Louisa was fourteen and working in the shop after school. Isobel had decided to keep up with some of the easier tailoring, mostly uniforms and trousers. She continued to do alterations. Sympathy business was steady. There was just enough money. The millinery limped along, just surviving.

Thomas worried her. He began to hang around with older boys who cut classes and loitered openly at the curb of the drugstore as if to taunt the truancy officer. He and his pals attached themselves to buildings, smoking and leaning through the school hours until the bell finally rang and their task was over. Thomas's grades plunged, and he took to coming home late and sullen, rarely meeting her eye when she confronted him. When his dead father's name was mentioned he would rise silently and leave the room.

He began to reform only after Henry's body was returned from the South Pacific to be buried next to Victor's.

As Henry's coffin was lowered into the earth, Isobel watched paralyzed as Thomas and the other mourners turned. She knew what they were seeing, but her neck was stone. They were looking at the clay hump of the next grave. The other wound on the earth.

It was the last picture taken of Henry. Isobel peered at the outline of her elder son. If she'd had to describe him, she would need this picture to be able to pair words to his features. He'd been only nineteen when he was killed. She'd only been his mother that long.

~   ~   ~

The room was airless. A locker. Isobel rang twice, three times, for the nurse to come open the window. While waiting she closed the album over her lap, pressed a thumb over the embossed letters, pressing. Pressing as if to render them smooth.

~ ~ ~

CHAPTER NINE

Cathryn's new watercolours were no longer of remembered hats, but Isobel's own creations, painted in
crisp detail, but with one side fading into shadow or simply unfinished, so that the hats seemed to be emerging
from the thick watercolour paper by magic. The faces of
the models were regally simple, drawn with only a few
strokes of black ink to define a profile; a curving lip, one
closed lid, the sweep of a cheek.

As a surprise, Isobel had six of the paintings framed in
slim walnut. She smuggled them into the shop one morning and hung them over the register. Cathryn came in just
as she was climbing down from the ladder, hammer in
hand. Isobel gazed up at the display.

"Don't they look nice all fitted out and hung like that?"

"Oui! Très, très chic, madame."

She skipped over to Isobel and crushed her in a hug, kissing her on both cheeks.

On the pavement outside a man passed, movement inside the store momentarily catching his eye. He did not slow his gait but turned just long enough to glimpse two women through the wavering glass. Their backs to the window, the women stepped back in a seemingly choreographed motion, both raising their left arms at the same time as if to indicate something on the wall. One of the women held a hammer. Their arms dropped simultaneously and they both cocked their heads slightly. The man smiled and quickly moved on.

A large carton with Cathryn's name on it arrived at the shop, but Isobel could not get her to open it.

"It's a sur-prise," Cathryn sang, dancing around the carton. When Isobel reached out to run a finger along its edge. Cathryn slapped her hand away, clucking, "If you're naughty, Izzy, I'll send it ba-ack." The carton sat in the storage hall until Isobel forgot about it.

The shelves began to fill with hats. They transferred a dozen of them to the window, stepping in and out the front door several times to view the display from the sidewalk, making sure the hats were aligned at proper angles, and separating those that clashed. Cathryn hung pale blue tags on each and priced them with green ink.

"Green for summer."

Isobel read the tags and gasped. "For greed, you mean. Cathryn, these prices are far too high. I can't possibly ask so much. Who would buy them?"

"No one. They'd be crazy if they did. Listen, here's what you do. You price them high and make sure the tags are visible from outside. Women window-shop. It's simple psychology. We all covet what we cannot afford, right?"

Isobel crossed her arms. "I'm listening."

"You leave a set of these overpriced hats in the window for a while and then you have a big sale, mark everything forty or even fifty percent off. The good ladies of Cypress will stampede in, buy hats at a fair price, and walk out thinking they've gotten the bargain of their lives. It's a snap. Three or four seasonal sales each year, and in the times between, it will be very, very peaceful around here."

Isobel clapped her hands. "And the rest of the time I could just work?"

"Exactly."

The display in the window was slow to draw attention. Isobel noticed that only a few women passing stopped at the window. Some came to a full stop and openly examined the hats, but none came in to browse. Isobel felt defeated.

"I've spent so much money." She moaned.

"It's only been a few weeks, Isobel." Cathryn's cheerfulness didn't buoy her.

"I suppose I could take out an ad."

It wasn't long before the first hat sold. The portly wife of a mine supervisor came in and pointed to a netted cap she had admired in the window. She was given a mirror and fussed over by Cathryn, who affected a French accent as she placed the hat on the matron's head with a flourish. The woman turned left and right. "It is quite pretty, isn't it?"

"*Oui, madame.* Mizz Isobel, she's an *artiste,* no?"

The woman smiled broadly at her fat image. "I'll take it."

"Exzellent choice! *Un moment, madame.*" Cathryn skipped to the storage hall. While Isobel wrote up a purchase slip, she heard the squeal of nails being pried asunder and a sharp yelp of *Merde!* as something wooden hit the floor.

Isobel smiled weakly as the matron dug into her handbag. Cathryn, flushed and sucking on her fingertip, walked to the counter and set down a new hatbox.

"Zhese were just rushed to us by box maykars in Minneapolis."

The box was crimson with thin black stripes, the braided handle was dark gold, and on top an ivory oval was embossed with the graceful silhouette of a woman wearing a tiny feathered hat. Curling across the oval was a single name in simple cursive, *Isobel*. In smaller type under the silhouette was *Fine Millinery Since 1936*. Isobel touched the letters of her name and looked up at her friend, but Cathryn was all business, chattering in French-peppered English as she wrapped the hat in gold tissue paper. Isobel turned and stood dumbly with her hand outstretched as the matron counted eight stiff one-dollar bills into her hand. If the woman thought it odd that tears rolled down the milliner's cheeks, she did not show it.

Cathryn trundled the woman to the door, chirping, "*Au revoir,*" and gently nudged her on her way. She came back to Isobel and lifted three of the dollar bills from the immobile plane of her palm. "Izzy, can you stop leaking long enough to tell me where in this town I might buy a bottle of champagne?"

"Champagne!" Isobel wiped her eyes with the back of her hand, crumpling the remaining bills and laughing. "You'll be lucky if you can find wine, *ma chérie*. Try the supper club on Bay Point."

Cathryn slapped on her hat and made for the door, but Isobel stepped into her path.

"Cathryn, those boxes . . . I don't know what to say."

"Oh, shush, Izzy. Don't say anything, just find two glasses" — Cathryn held out her bleeding finger — "and a plaster."

The number of customers grew from one to a few, a few to a dozen. Women ordered custom hats and the millinery made its progress, steadily but achingly slow in Isobel's impatience. Summer would be over soon, and her best customers, the impulse buyers — tourists staying out at the resorts or summer cabins on the shores of Cypress and lakes farther north — would be gone.

When she realized that her fastest-selling hats were the more casual summer styles, she raced to make more, using lighter materials like canvas, linen, and straw. She adorned these "holiday hats" with twisted bands of red pine needles or silk flowers modified to resemble those from the forest — trillium, sweet woodruff, or bunchberry. Women tended to come in from the resorts on Saturday mornings, so Isobel, Louisa, and Cathryn worked late through Friday, trimming. Louisa padded green velvet so that it looked like moss, and Cathryn stripped thin twigs of willow, then stained and braided them into hatbands. Isobel bought a roll of canvas from the mercantile, a muted stripe of gold, red, and green intended for the slings of folding lawn chairs. That weekend, the linen bowlers she banded with this fabric sold as quickly as she put them in the front window.

As Cathryn watched the third of these hats leave the store, she chewed her pencil and then tapped it decisively on the glass display case.

"Izzy, I don't think you should sell any more than one or two of the same hat on any Saturday."

Isobel was tucking bills into the register. "Why not?"

"These customers are here on holiday, right? Usually for about two weeks at a stretch." Cathryn took her pencil to the wall calendar and ran it down the remaining weeks of summer. "You wouldn't want them running into each other wearing identical hats."

"She's right, Momma." Louisa, who had been sitting cross-legged on the floor, was busily constructing a miniature turban from a scrap of silk. Isobel picked up the turban and turned it over, amazed to see it was fully lined and decorated with a cluster of tiny feathers. "You made this?"

She looked from her friend to her daughter in disbelief. "By yourself?"

Louisa shrugged. "I've been watching."

"You must've been. This is really . . ." She laid a hand on the girl's shoulder. "Louisa, this is very, very well done."

The girl beamed. "I thought so too. It's for my doll. Can I have another scrap? I'd like to make a matching dress."

Cathryn led them to the storage hall. "Let's take a peek in the remnant drawers and find something."

Isobel's shoulders dropped. "But those drawers are such a mess!"

"No they're not. Not anymore. Look." Cathryn opened drawer after drawer to reveal neatly folded piles of remnants Isobel had dismissed as too jumbled to ever sort.

"See, I've organized it all. These far drawers have the smallest pieces." She pulled out a hank of nubby red silk the size of a pillowcase. "Here, Louisa. This is just enough to make a dress." The girl took her scrap and skipped out the door.

"Look, Isobel. All these short lengths are stacked by color, see? Patterns on the right, solids on the left." She pointed to a mound of stripes behind the glass. "Using these pieces, you could make hundreds of hats, and it won't cost you a penny."

Isobel hardly heard her. The panes of glass shone, and behind the glass fronts, all of Victor's supplies had been rearranged. The teetering stacks of boxes were gone, and all fabrics were folded, stocked, and tagged. The blackened floor had been stripped of ancient wax to reveal poppy-red linoleum. A dozen years of grime and disarray had been replaced by a gleaming order.

"Cathryn, when . . . ?"

Cathryn shrugged. "Oh, sometimes I don't sleep that well. When you gave me the key you said I should come whenever I wanted."

"Well, yes, but . . ." Isobel cocked her head with a frown. "Cathryn! What do you mean, you don't sleep?"

Cathryn's eyes were veiled. "Oh, a few restless nights now and then. I'm fine, Izzy. I'm fine now."

Isobel folded her arms.

"Izzy, don't look at me like that! Here." She handed Isobel a stack of light-coloured seersucker and muslin. "Oh, and look at this!" Cathryn rose on her toes, opened a high cupboard, and pulled out a half-bolt of black-and-beige mattress ticking. "Wouldn't this make a novel cap?"

"Don't change the subject, Cathryn."

Cathryn spun. "What are you, my mother? My husband? My nurse?"

Isobel shrank at the tone. "No, of course not. I'm just concerned —"

"Has Liam put you up to watching me? I'm sick to death of being watched. I'm a grown woman. I do not need to be baby-sat!"

"Baby-sat? What are you talking about? Cathryn, I . . ."

But she was turning as if she hadn't heard, her voice lowered to a mutter as she walked away. "Can't I be left in peace for one moment? One goddamned solitary minute?"

Isobel stepped back as if pushed.

She stared at Cathryn's retreating form and tried to blink some meaning into what had just happened. *Had* something happened? She stood alone in the hall for a long while, mindlessly wringing the remnant of muslin in her hand.

~   ~   ~

"You hardly mention the husband." Thomas sat back. "Liam, right?"

"Don't I? Well, I didn't see too much of him."

"Not too many husbands around that summer, were there?"

She didn't like his tone. "It didn't seem so. Liam was

very busy. I don't think Cathryn saw much of him at all."
Her voice was thin.

"What was his story?"

"Oh, goodness, Thomas, I barely remember him now."

"Really? You seem so clear about everything else, almost as though you can barely forget."

Isobel set her brow. "You want to know about Liam Malley? He was an Irishman, from Cork, I think. He was handsome and quiet, and awkward in company. He was a very proud man, and I think he was self-conscious about having married someone socially superior, someone rich. He didn't care about her money. He was devoted to his wife, there was no question. She was a complex person, difficult. Moody. But he was dutiful — to a fault, really — was willing to stick by her, take care of her no matter . . ." She was tiring, her guard falling away. Her next words were tinged with grief. "No matter what. Poor Liam. He couldn't have known what he was getting into when he took on Cathryn."

"Well, that's a lot of recollection for someone you barely remember."

She shot him a glance. "That's all speculation, Thomas."

"Speculation? Not what you actually know?"

"How would I know? Cathryn told me very little. You don't seem to understand something, Thomas. Personal things were not discussed in the way they are now, particularly marriage. Private lives were private. I would no sooner have asked Cathryn about her problems with Liam than I would answer if someone had asked me personal things about myself and Victor."

Thomas crossed his arms. "So, you admit you had problems with Dad."

She exhaled heavily, as if to breathe away all thought. "I'm done talking now, Thomas."

~   ~   ~

In July, Liam Malley was suddenly called away to a Michigan copper mine after two men were killed in a collapsed shaft. Isobel helped Cathryn pack his kit and shirts into a valise. Through the cottage window came the metallic slam of a tailgate. Liam was loading his fishing gear.

Cathryn sighed. "I don't know how long he'll be gone."

Isobel sat on the edge of the bed, picking at the loose threads of a pillow sham.

"You'll come stay with us. It's just Louisa and me, plenty of room." She looked back over the wide bed. "You can't stay in this gloomy old place all by yourself, Cathryn. Besides, it'll be fun."

Cathryn shook her head. "That's so sweet of you. Maybe I'll come and spend a night or two, but I really don't mind it out here. I rather like my time alone these days. And now that I can drive, well, there are so many interesting little back roads to explore." She snapped the suitcase shut. "I've been roaming a bit, in case you're wondering why I've not been in the shop as much lately." She seemed to be speaking to the suitcase. "You wouldn't believe some of the spots I've found."

"Mmm?" Isobel was barely listening. She'd risen from the edge of the bed and stood with her arms crossed at the doorway, gazing across the hall through the window overlooking the driveway.

"Isobel?"

Liam stood frozen at the driver's-side door, his hands high on the truck's cab, his forehead resting on the glass.

As she slipped from the room, Isobel tried to make her words sound cheerful. "I'll be right back."

"Hey!"

When Isobel turned, Cathryn handed her the suitcase. "Take this out for me, would you? Please?"

Outside, Liam was busy again, tightening a strap on a metal box and hoisting it into the back. Isobel shook his hand and wished him a safe journey. After a glance toward the cottage he pulled a slip of paper from his shirt pocket and quickly folded it into Isobel's hand.

"Here's the name of my hotel in Michigan. The telephone number for the mine office is on the back."

As Cathryn appeared at the kitchen door, he leaned down as if to fetch something, whispering, "Call if you need me. And try to get her to stay with you if you can."

She looked at the paper. "But she doesn't . . . I don't . . ."

She thought of Cathryn's outburst the previous week. The first day they'd met, Liam had said something then too, something about taking care with her, or *of* her, she couldn't say which. Liam *did* want her to watch over Cathryn.

He was in the truck and turning the key, while Cathryn was at the screen door, waving and smiling in her apron, a domestic scene like a glossy page from *Collier's*. Isobel looked from Cathryn to the back end of the truck bouncing down the lane.

She was not sure she even wanted to guess what might be between them.

In the end Isobel couldn't coax Cathryn to come to the house. She assumed she'd see more of her at the shop in the weeks Liam was gone, but the opposite proved true. From her daily junkets into the countryside, Cathryn would burst into the shop, flushed and cheerful, always bringing treasures for Louisa — an agate, a curled section of birch bark, bits of driftwood twisted into elegant serpents. She would stay only a short while, reading, helping Isobel with the finer tacking or beadwork, sometimes working on Louisa's frocks, ripping out entire sections for one mislaid stitch. She talked either a great deal or not at all. Sometimes she wrote in her small book, in the margins of her sketchbook, or even on scraps of torn paper or the backs of receipts. When Isobel asked what she was so busy with, Cathryn shrugged.

"Just words. You know, thoughts, things that come to me."

Sweeping up one afternoon after Cathryn had gone, Isobel found a dusty scrap under the desk, the hand unmistakable.

> *In saline seas we are formed, born standing distinct — we don't so much make our way as stay rooted to let life churn around us. Sky and clouds shifting above, tides stirring at our hems. Do we ever touch? Or is it merely the air and water we touch that shifts over to others, the ebbing ripples that reach them, diluted and wafting-weak. All our essence intended, but so little of our true selves divulged.*

On a cursory read it didn't sound particularly like something that might come from Cathryn, so Isobel assumed it was a quote, or copied from some book. She tucked it behind the register and promptly forgot about it.

Isobel was reading aloud from the serial novel in the paper. She got nearly to the end of the column when she realized no one was listening.

"Yoohoo, anybody?"

When there was no response, she glanced up to see Cathryn staring blindly at the wall, twisting her fingers around an imaginary object.

"Cathryn?"

She continued staring. Isobel watched for a moment and observed the almost imperceptible rocking motion of Cathryn's upper body. She laid down her paper and crossed the room. She crouched in front of the chair and stilled Cathryn's hands with her own.

"Cathryn. What's wrong?"

Cathryn blinked as though trying to clear a fog from her eyes.

"Cathryn!"

She blinked again, this time focusing on Isobel's face. She saw her hands covered by her friend's and looked up with a faltering, puzzled smile.

"Yes? What is it, Izzy?"

Isobel watched Cathryn, waiting for the days to pass, hoping Liam's return might calm her. On the afternoon before he was due back, Cathryn hopped nervously from table to table like a sparrow caught indoors.

Isobel sat her down, pressed a pencil into her hand, and asked her to draw and enlarge a picture of a turban she had torn from *Vogue*.

Cathryn laboured over the drawing, beginning, tearing up the paper, and beginning again. She was on her third sketch when her pencil snapped. As the splintered end hit the floor, both women raised their heads. Cathryn's hands tumbled to her lap and she burst into tears.

Isobel slowly took the thimble from her finger, folded her work away, and walked over to place her hands firmly on Cathryn's shoulders.

"Cathryn. I'm your friend. You do believe that, don't you?"

Cathryn nodded, tears flooding eyes.

She smoothed the hair at Cathryn's brow. "Then you must tell me what's wrong." The concern in Isobel's voice was ticked with exasperation.

Cathryn shuddered and wiped her face with the back of her hand. She nodded again.

"Izzy, there is something. I . . . there's some*one* . . ." She turned away, unable to face Isobel.

"Someone? Someone!" Isobel crouched down and took Cathryn's face in her hands, turning it so that Cathryn had no choice but to meet her eye. "Oh my God, Cathryn, some man? Cathryn, look at me!"

Cathryn scrabbled in her pockets for a handkerchief.

"Don't tell me you're in love?" Isobel fought not to show her shock. She pulled a stool close and fell heavily to it, sighing, "Tell me," and truly not wanting to know.

Through the afternoon, Isobel listened. As a dry wind listlessly pushed warm air through the screens, Cathryn alternately paced and sat, sometimes crying, sometimes laughing, as she described her first encounter with Jack Reese. She'd carried her secret nearly the entire time she'd known Isobel, and the relief in her voice upon telling was absolute.

CHAPTER TEN

~ ~ ~

W ith little to do in her first lonely days in Cypress, Cathryn had taken to wandering about on a bicycle left by some previous tenant. On one of her excursions she found a narrow road leading up to the fire tower. The tower stood on the highest point of land in the county, and the rutted road winding to it was so steep and rocky she had to get off the bicycle and push it along. It was the beginning of the warm weather, and by midmorning the temperature was near ninety. The hill ahead seemed endless, yet she felt compelled to climb to its peak. She hoped to see the town from above, but as her legs began to ache, and the perspiration trickling down her back reached the band of her skirt, she wondered if the whim was worth the effort. At the halfway point, she came to a smooth, flat rock. She stopped, thoughtlessly dropped the bicycle in the middle of the road, and made for the ledge, where she collapsed in the shade of a sprawling pine. As she regained her breath, she considered the sheer drop at her feet. She grasped a branch and leaned gingerly over the cliff, guessing at the distance between herself and the canopy below. A hundred feet? A hundred-fifty?

The town's tarred, shimmering roofs lay scattered among the treetops and steeples in the distance. The unpaved roads blurred into ribbons of sepia whenever a vehicle sliced through the grid. Cathryn laughed to herself. The whole of Cypress looked to be a child's board game laid out in a patch of wilderness.

Her foot slipped on the mossy ledge and her stomach leapt. She scooted backward to sit against a tree. Looking out over the lake she settled her backside into a safe crevasse and wished she'd brought something to drink; the glitter of the bays and backwaters made her suddenly thirsty.

To the west was the body of the vast lake, and though she had examined the maps, looked at picture postcards, and listened to Liam's descriptions, Cathryn was unprepared for the size and wildness of Lake Cypress. Not far from her home in Chicago, Lake Michigan had always seemed to her a mere accessory to the city, a mirror of approval as Chicago raised its skyscrapers, museums, and endless department stores.

But the wild lake below captured Cathryn's awe. Even at such a height she couldn't place the far shore. Directly west were many huge bays, some so peppered with islands as to seem solid land with only a line of water scrawling through. This part of the lake was called the Maze, and Liam had warned Cathryn never to row into it alone or she would most certainly become lost. Even if one was able to find the actual shoreline, it was apt to be either mosquito-infested bog or granite cliffs too sheer to scale. Beyond the Maze, open water stretched for undetermined miles before the patterns of islands and bays began again. The lake shone black, and only near its edges did the water lighten to a bluish grey.

Cathryn traced the road at the end of town which eventually turned onto the lane that led out to her own cottage. She located Granite Point by one of the chimneys. She was just thinking it would be nice to show Liam this spot, bring him up here for a picnic, when she heard a vehicle rumbling down the hill. As it neared the curve she suddenly remembered her bicycle. Scampering up, she ran blindly into the road to retrieve it. She grabbed the handlebars as the truck came around the bend and looked up to see it barreling toward her.

She froze. The driver leaned back hard, as if putting all his weight and strength to the brake.

The next moments warped and stretched themselves into and out of focus, as though viewed in a poorly silvered mirror. Time and sight became unreliable, so that what seemed a full minute was only a fraction of a second. What appeared a blinding flash of lightning from a cloudless sky was only a glint from the truck's windshield.

In the distended seconds it took for the truck to reach her, Cathryn saw herself as the driver would see her — a woman not young, not old, flushed with the heat, perspiration glistening on her upper lip, white hands pulling up a bicycle. A tall woman with dark hair standing dumbly in the wrong place. Alive, but only for the next abbreviated moment.

The heavy vehicle skidded on the loose gravel, spewing small stones and jets of dust from beneath each of its locked tires. There was no time to swerve, probably no time to consider swerving, she knew that much. Had she been just a few yards farther down the road, there might have been enough distance between herself and the truck for some action. The driver might have steered his truck in the only direction possible away from her, over the cliff, to become airborne for the last moment of *his* life. Or she could have dived to the side of the road to safety. But there wasn't enough distance between them, no split second for such options, no time for response of any kind.

The tires of the truck found temporary purchase, but it was too heavy. The sound of tumbling stones was layered with the sickening keening of brakes. Cathryn found herself looking steadily at the driver, into the last face she would certainly ever see.

Well, that's that.

Eyes locked, nothing between them but dust and her last breath. Cathryn took in the man's green eyes, his other features indistinct, blurred planes of flesh that fell away, unimportant. You poor man, I am so sorry.

Cathryn and the driver blinked at the same instant. This tandem gesture released them from their trance, and she closed her mouth and eyes. The truck lurched, skidded. Suddenly, the moan emitting from the vehicle changed pitch and the truck jumped and came to an abrupt, angry stop. A mad dog at the end of its chain.

Cathryn opened her eyes. As the engine died, stillness settled on the road, a silence broken only by the sound of distant crickets delivered on a hot, rolling wind. The chrome grill of the truck was an inch from her chin. Her nostrils flared at the heat of the engine; the distinct tang of oil and gasoline and the acrid smell of ground metal filled the breath she took. The air was thick with grit roiled loose from the road.

The driver and Cathryn stared at each other. The cab door squealed open and he climbed down to walk in measured steps to where she stood, each footfall distinct in its graveled wake.

The man took a huge breath before firmly peeling Cathryn's fingers from the handlebars. The bicycle bounced to the ground, one tire spinning lamely. He took her by the arm and steered her to the side of the road, where he was able to bend her into a sitting position on a boulder.

He crouched low in front of her and looked up to her face. "You," he said, gently resting one hand on each of her knees as though to settle their knocking, "are a stupid, stupid woman."

Cathryn nodded, unable to speak. The man waited.

"My name is Jack Reese."

Cathryn nodded again.

"I'm a ranger." He pointed up to the fire tower. "Forest service."

Shakily she touched the embroidered pine tree on the shoulder patch of his khaki shirt.

He looked at her closely. She was disheveled, dust on her forehead riven by two clear lines of perspiration. Her body slumped like a rag doll. When he examined her profile, Cathryn's eyes followed his, not breaking his gaze.

"Are you a mute?"

Cathryn opened her mouth, closed it, and shook her head.

Jack settled on the boulder next to her. "Well, how about if I talk for a while, you listen, and maybe you'll remember how?"

Cathryn nodded.

Jack cleared his throat. "I'm a ranger . . . right, I already said that . . ." He pointed out to the lake. "I live just over that ridge, past Granite Point. I have a small cabin there, on an island about a mile into the Maze. Not far by water, from Mr. and Mrs. Malley's place."

Hearing her name, Cathryn looked at the man with alarm and sat straighter.

He grinned. "Everyone knows who you are."

Cathryn sat dumb while the man talked. His voice was

a balm, settled her shaking, and as her heart calmed, she found herself listening intently, as if each small thing the man said was of vast importance.

He told her about the young ranger stationed in the tower up the road, a new fellow he'd suspected of drinking on the job. He'd brought the kid a deck of playing cards, a stack of newspapers from Duluth, and some jigsaw puzzles.

"I know what it can be like up there, days with no human contact . . ." Jack brushed the wavy hair away from his forehead. As his hand dropped to his thigh, Cathryn examined his broad fingers and the fine blond hairs on the back of his hand, the same golden shade cuffing the outsides of his square wrists.

She smiled. He was making conversation for her sake.

"With such a dry spring I can't afford having a man up there doing less than his job." He waved at the air shimmering over the hood of the truck and the valley beyond. "This could all go up in an hour with the right wind."

When Cathryn shuddered he quickly recovered the conversation and pointed to the tower. "If you're up there very long, you've got to find something to do. I studied botany myself, wanted to use some of that Latin from school. I read, of course."

"What did you read?"

At Cathryn's first words, Jack smiled. "There you are." He patted her hand and continued.

"What did I read? Philosophy, mostly. Works we'd only touched on in the seminary."

"Seminary? But you're not a priest."

"No." He shook his head, dropping it a little. "No, never made it that far."

Cathryn edged closer. "What else did you read?"

"Oh, the usual stuff. Novels. Poetry."

"Poetry!" Cathryn lightly touched his open palm.

They compared poets they read, but after a time words fell away, as something unnamed but fierce edged aside their conversation to possess the air between them.

They sat, unsure of what to say or do, certain only that neither wanted to be the first to rise, to make any movement that might stretch the distance between them, break the closeness.

Soon enough the sound of a car labouring up the road forced them apart. Cathryn stood and picked up her bicycle, feeling self-conscious and oddly guilty as the car appeared. She gave its occupants a halfhearted wave without seeing their faces. Jack jumped into the truck and rolled it to the edge of the road to make way. Only after the sound of the car died away did they dare to look at each other again.

Jacked leaned out the cab window. "Meet me tomorrow?" His eyes were pure intent, there was nothing to misconstrue.

"Yes." She straightened up and climbed onto the bicycle. "Where?"

"Here."

She did not remember her ride home. She bathed in the lake and made dinner for Liam as though it were a regular Tuesday evening.

Cathryn laughed. "God knows what Jack must've thought of me."

Isobel would later come to know exactly what Jack Reese thought. He'd written it all in the letter she found hidden in the satchel that Cathryn, in her flight, had left behind.

"We met the next day, of course, and the day after. When I haven't been here at the shop I've been with Jack. At first I cycled out to places to meet him, and later, after you taught me to drive, I'd take the car, but only on days

Liam was out of town with the company truck. I couldn't risk being seen in the car if he was around."

Isobel leaned forward. "So, these last two weeks? While Liam's been in Michigan . . . ?"

"I've been staying in Jack's cabin."

Isobel's hand drifted to her mouth.

Cathryn smiled. "We're lovers."

As Cathryn sat down next to her, Isobel quickly rose. She paced a distance away. When she did turn back she could only stare at Cathryn's hands, unwilling to meet her eye. In the silence she watched Cathryn's hands work the handkerchief in her slim fingers, the gold wedding band glinting through the lace edging. The hands finally settled for the briefest moment before Cathryn stood, her voice oddly high.

"Right. Well, I really ought to be going." She made no move to the door.

Isobel blinked. Cathryn had told the story so vividly, so eagerly, and with such relief. She should respond some-how . . . but none of her words would coalesce into clear sentences. None of her responses would be what Cathryn wanted to hear.

"I suppose you should."

They both turned at a sound, and Isobel saw a flash of blond under the pants press.

"Louisa?" She walked over to peer underneath. "Oh Lord. You've been here this whole time?"

Louisa squirmed in place, as if hoping for some distraction — a customer, anything — so she could slip away. "I wasn't spying, Momma, I was just here."

"Come out. Now, please." Isobel branded a look toward Cathryn. "What did you hear?"

The girl scooted out and stood, looking from one face to the other. "Um, everything, I guess."

"And how much . . ." Isobel fought the tremor on her lip. "Just how much do you understand?"

The girl held up two fingers. "Two commandments' worth. Auntie Cathryn has broken two, I think. But I can't remember the order."

Cathryn closed her eyes. "Jesus Christ."

The girl shrugged. "That makes three, for sure."

Isobel grabbed the girl's wrist with a harder grip than she'd intended. She opened her mouth, faltered, and turned to Cathryn.

"*You* explain this. I'm still trying to understand, but I can't. Not yet. You can't expect me to make sense of this for her? You explain." She let go of Louisa.

"Louisa, I'll see you at home."

The tear in her friend's eye did not stop Isobel. At the door she turned. "Lock up when you leave."

She walked. She found herself a mile from town before realizing she was headed nowhere. She was in the hills above the mine, moving quickly under great arms of pine boughs. Her legs moved her along with a will she did not feel. The air was sharp with pitch and needles snapping underfoot. The smell brought her back to the many times she'd raced along the same paths as a child. A thousand years before. She pressed over the length of a ridge until the trail began a slow decline through a birch forest north of town.

She was out of breath. *In love.* She recalled Cathryn's ecstatic voice relaying the impossible encounter with a stranger who now held her in thrall.

She could not shake the image of Liam's face, his earlier warnings to her. Did he know? Nor could she shake her overriding sense that even with the confession, Cathryn had not told her everything. As she trudged through thicket she broke her way through one image after another. The day she found Cathryn on the floor under a table, curled into a C and red-faced, claiming she'd only just fallen asleep there. The time Cathryn had Louisa in her lap, arms around the girl, when her focus had fallen suddenly away, her limbs taking on some sort of rigid somnambulance. She wouldn't let the girl go, seemingly couldn't, as if her suffocating embrace was involuntary, robotic. Louisa only laughed, thinking it was a game, had called herself Houdini and eventually wormed her way free.

What were the actions of a woman in love?

Only when she found herself on the trail leading back to the shore of Lake Cypress did Isobel tally how far she might have gone, how many hours she'd been wandering.

She couldn't think anymore. The sun began its drop and was just skimming the trees by the time she made it back to the band shell in the park.

It was completely dark by the time she opened her front door.

Louisa was asleep on the couch, her head in Cathryn's lap.

"Isobel," she whispered, "where've you been?"

Isobel's folded arms fell to her sides. "Walking." Her dress was damp with perspiration. "Thinking, trying to sort this out." She had planned to be patient, give Cathryn the opportunity to volunteer more, but her composure fissured, and the questions she'd planned to ask fell away behind terse accusations.

"You *lied* to me. I taught you how to drive. I was your alibi, wasn't I? I provided you an alibi, daily." She was shaking as she hissed, "Why didn't you tell me about Jack Reese before today?"

Cathryn eased herself out from under Louisa and stood. "That wouldn't have been fair."

"Fair?"

She smoothed the wrinkles of her skirt. "It wouldn't have been fair to put you in the middle of things."

"In the middle?"

"Yes, in the middle. Where you are right now, upset. I wanted to spare you this."

Isobel nodded stiffly at the couch. "And Louisa?"

"We talked. She's a bright child, Isobel. She understands more than you think."

"Don't tell me about my own . . . what do *you* know of children?" She went to the couch and gathered the sleeping girl up, sorry she had spoken. "Never mind."

At the foot of the stairs she shifted Louisa's weight in her arms and turned. "It's been a long day, Cathryn."

Only after putting Louisa to bed did Isobel remember Cathryn would be making her way home in the dark. She rushed back down the stairs and opened the front door, to find Cathryn was already out of sight. She hurried over the still-warm pavement to the corner, but the streetlight illuminated only the smallest circle of night. Turning in the dim disk she could make out nothing beyond, her movements as feeble as the light cast from above.

~   ~   ~

Isobel's hand tired of holding the magnifying glass Thomas had brought for her. Her weak arm could only hold down the pages like a weight, while the other alternately held the heavy glass and turned the pages.

As a figure moved into the room Isobel dropped the book in exasperation. Nurses. Doctors. Forever sneaking up behind you. She sighed and closed her eyes as a cheerful voice commenced.

"Hello there. What's that you're reading?"

Isobel placed the voice. She did not turn, but answered curtly. "A poem, Dr. Hertz. A poem, in fact, about a patient being etherized upon a table."

"Ah, even I know that one."

"Are you here for blood? If you are, please make it quick."

"They don't let me take blood. We have staff vampires for that. But I'll check your arm, if you don't mind."

"Fine. Just don't muss me — the nurses have me all bathed and powdered. I want to stay fresh." She straightened herself on her pillows. "Perhaps they could bring me a bed of ice."

She was beginning to find the man annoying. He laughed at his own jokes, but not hers.

"Where's my son?"

"Thomas? I just saw him in the hall, sent him down to have coffee."

"Why?"

He sat on the edge of the bed and lightly pinched the loose skin over the bones of her hand. "Nurse's report says you've sent back your trays untouched. Dietary confirms that."

She watched what he was doing to her hand. "I'm still drinking."

Their eyes met.

"Fluids aren't enough."

"I'm not going home again. I know that. It's a nursing home after this, right?"

"Probably. Yes."

"You have a grandmother, Joel?"

"I could order an IV."

"But you wouldn't have to."

He didn't answer.

"You know how old I am."

"Everyone in this hospital knows how old you are."

When she shifted under the covers the book fell to the floor. He leaned down to sweep it up and laid it back on her lap. A rigid corner of tan stuck out between pages.

"Let me show you something. My bookmark."

"It's a photo?"

"Yes, one I took myself." She handed him the overexposed, yellowed square.

The image showed a couple sitting in a small wooden sailboat in glaring sunlight. The woman's hair was swept up in a mass held by broad ivory combs. She wore tiny round sunglasses and the sleeves of her kimono drifted out from the stern, silk wings just brushing the water. She reclined, facing the camera, one slender foot resting on the man's knee. He was in profile, looking intently at the woman from beneath a curl fallen over his brow. The canvas sail swagged limp against the mast. The scene was reflected over a skin of water so still the photograph was halved into dual images, identical boats, twin couples.

"So that's him. The man who looks like me."

"You mean you look like him."

"So he does exist."

"I know you've doubted me. I'm frail, not addled."

"I know."

"I'm of my own mind."

"Yes. Yes, you are."

Joel held the photo gently. "It's very old." He handed it back. "Are they dead?"

"I don't know." Isobel looked at the faces, the real Jack and Cathryn and their warped equivalents, the palest of reflections. She shrugged. "I do not know."

She set the photo on the bedside table and closed her eyes.

Thomas got up and shut the door against the corridor sounds of nurses' rubber-soled shoes, the nasal drone of the PA system.

"You've talked in your sleep again, Mother." He was agitated.

"I wasn't sleeping."

He sat heavily and dug his elbows into his knees. He looked almost ill. "Mother . . ."

She tried to reach for him. "What is it?"

He wouldn't look at her, but took a deep breath and began again. "Mother."

"What? Has something happened?"

"No." He hung his head. "Yes."

She saw he was holding the curled photo of Cathryn and Jack.

"I thought it was you."

She waited.

"I thought it was *you* who had the affair."

She blinked, weighed the information. Waited.

He laid the photo away. "That winter, after Dad bought the island . . . you seemed so angry at him. Then, when we came back in August everything was such a mystery. Everybody whispering, weird gossip in town. Louisa acting strange. You and Dad both going away to Michigan. I was too young to grasp any of it. It was before Dad died that I found out some man had disappeared, maybe even died near Cypress four years before, during the time he was having an affair with a woman — a *married* woman."

"And?"

"And all this time I've thought . . ."

"It was *me?*" Isobel's mouth fell. She looked to Thomas's face to see if it was a joke. After a beat she saw it was not.

"Why didn't you come to me? Why didn't you ask me back then?"

"Why?" He spoke into the bowl woven by his fingers. "It didn't seem to matter after Dad died . . ."

"And?"

"And I was only ten. How would I have even brought such a subject up?" Thomas knit and unknit his fingers.

"Oh, Thomas."

He turned away, but not before she could see the shame on his face. It was a long time before he spoke again.

"We always knew that fire tower was haunted."

Isobel's voice wavered. "We? Who's we?"

"All of us kids. Town kids. The older ones used to dare each other to climb it. Louisa always knew something, but she never talked. Couldn't get her to. All we knew was that a man had died up there." Thomas leaned in. "Was it Jack?"

Isobel didn't answer. She was watching her son's hands, the folding and unfolding of them. After a moment they went limp and hung between his knees. When she looked up he was crying.

There was nothing to offer.

After a while he wiped his face and put on his jacket. He had to get out.

~   ~   ~

Isobel took Louisa to the Vermilion Hotel for Sunday dinner. Afterward she walked with the girl along the south shore, past the supper club, and onto a shaded lane where they might escape the heat.

"Louisa." She started twice, clearing her throat. "Louisa, I . . ."

The girl was dragging a pattern into the road behind her with a forked branch. "I know what we're gonna talk about."

"You do?"

"Yup. We're gonna talk about love and marriage and stuff."

"Yes, that's right. Love . . ."

"Cathryn says love can save souls."

Isobel frowned. "Save souls?"

"From sadness, you know, like when you're crying and sad and can't make it stop."

"What else did Cathryn say?"

"That she has to fix the mess she's in."

They walked in silence, Louisa pressing her stick into the dusty road.

"It's not bad to love someone, is it, Momma?"

"No, not bad exactly, but it's not so good to love a man who isn't your husband."

"Everybody knows that. But why is it wrong?"

"For a lot of reasons. It's more complicated than just being wrong."

"Is it bad for Auntie Cathryn to love you?"

Isobel stopped walking.

Louisa made zags in the dirt with the stick.

"Because she says she does. She says that because she loves you, maybe it's better if she's not your friend anymore."

Isobel wrote a note and Louisa bicycled out to Granite Point to deliver it. She wanted to see Cathryn, wanted to meet Jack. She wrote that Cathryn should bring him into the shop the next day.

Cathryn did bring Jack, and he spoke of saving souls, and Isobel looked into his oddly innocent eyes and saw him for what he was — a vulnerable boy walking through life in the shell of a man.

The very day after that meeting in the darkened shop, Cathryn asked for her help.

"Just a few afternoons, Izzy." Her eyes were wild. "Just a few hours here and there. To watch for Liam. To watch out for his car."

Isobel knew she wasn't thinking clearly, hadn't had time, really, but the next day she packed her basket with some handwork and a book of Chekhov stories. She walked home, and after feeding Louisa lunch, she started up the Ford and tacked through the back roads to the dock near Granite Point.

Jack met her on the road.

He directed her to a spot behind an abandoned fishing shack, a place to park where the car wouldn't be seen by anyone passing. "I'll meet you on the dock."

She parked and stepped down from the running board into powdery earth and fought her way through stiff blond reeds taller than herself, moving through beige curtains to the lakeshore.

On the dock Jack gave her a carved wooden bird whistle on a length of leather whip, looking uneasy as he looped it over her head.

"Just in case."

Isobel gave it a few practice toots. "So, I just watch for the car? Should there be a certain signal?"

Jack shifted. Deception seemed a new and uncomfortable posture for him. "No, I think not. If you see Mr. Malley's car, please just blow as loudly as you can."

He pointed to the flimsy-looking canoe nudging itself against the dock.

"Ladies first."

She almost laughed. "You're joking. In a boat?"

Jack looked puzzled. "Well, yes, in a boat."

"Can't I just sit on the shore? Or how about here, at the end of the dock?"

"There's no vantage point. The middle of the bay is really the only place you can see down the road."

She squinted out over the water. "You're sure?"

"You're afraid, aren't you?" The deepness of his voice reminded Isobel of shade.

"A little." It was as much as she would admit.

"Of water?" He bit his lip.

"Jack, I'm sorry."

"I didn't know. Listen, don't worry about it." His tone was an apology. "Cath and I will figure some other way."

"Wait. How deep is it?"

"Here? Only a few feet. See? There's the bottom."

"I'll do it. Really. I can do it."

He looked her in the eye. "You're sure?"

After Jack helped her onto the cane seat of the canoe, he climbed in behind and knelt between the ribs of the boat. His arms circled her as he showed her how to hold the paddle. He wrapped her fingers around the handle, shifted her other hand down the polished length of the paddle. He began a dipping motion, graceful arcs, one side, then the other.

"Okay, now you try. I'll keep holding on, but I want you to do the work."

She did not think of the water. She would think of other things. He was close enough that his chest was just brushing her back. For a moment she imagined leaning against him. Her back would touch his chest, the rumble of his voice would vibrate over each word. She suddenly shook herself and leaned forward.

"There, you're doing great. See how simple it is?"

They paddled a few circles, then made their way back to the dock, where Jack climbed out. He stood and smiled broadly. Isobel began to smile back but saw his eye trained over her shoulder. She turned to see Cathryn waving from the far shore.

After he pushed the canoe and Isobel away from the dock, he got into his own boat and began to row toward Cathryn.

When she turned to watch him the canoe suddenly tipped low. The floor of her stomach fell and she cast her weight too quickly to the opposite side. The gunwale dipped nearly to the water. She yelled, dropped the paddle, and froze.

Jack turned in alarm. "Isobel?"

"I can't. I'm sorry, Jack. I can't do it."

~   ~   ~

"Momma?"

No one had called her Momma since Louisa. She opened

her eyes to Thomas standing by her bed. His sweater was folded over a chair and his shoulder bag hung on the door. His posture was slack, and she had the impression he'd been standing there for some time.

She struggled up and drank some water. She slipped in her dentures, waving away his help, but she let him straighten her pillows. When she was settled she looked up. "Good morning." She knew her voice was clipped, but she couldn't control it.

He didn't speak but took her hand and folded something smooth into it.

"What's this?"

"Shale."

Shale. Had she seen it somewhere before? She waited.

"Do you mind if I sit?"

"Why would I mind?"

"All I can say is I'm sorry."

"Sorry for what, for thinking? For assuming?"

He touched her hand, the stone. "This was Dad's." He cleared his throat. "A stone from the island. I was with him when he found it. He spotted it on the beach. I remember when he reached for it; out of thousands, this one caught his eye. He picked it up and said, 'Tommy, this will be my lucky stone. Look here, when you turn it to the light it's the colour of your mother's eyes.'"

She touched the sheen of it, felt her scalp tighten.

Thomas sat. "After he . . . the day he died, I remember someone brought you home, and it was Louisa who took me outside and told me he was dead. You were asleep then — they'd given you something, I think. I went to the shop after they took his body away. It was there, in his coat pocket. His coat was hung in the back hall, just like it was any regular day. I knew it would be there. I was going to throw it into the Marko Dam. I figured it hadn't been too lucky for him after all."

"But you didn't."

"No. When I got to the bridge I couldn't do it. I kept it. I've carried it with me since."

"Oh." Isobel fought the tremble in her hand. "See how smooth it is. It's like glass."

Thomas smiled. "It used to be bigger, but see, it's all worn away."

She looked up at him, her mouth twisted somewhere between grin and grimace. "Like me, then."

"It's yours now."

Thomas stayed through the afternoon, ordering lunch in from a restaurant down the street. Isobel made eating motions, plucked at her tray. Afterward he went out and brought back iced coffees from the café next door.

He crossed his legs and propped a pillow behind his back.

"So, when *did* you become their lookout?"

Isobel bit the inside of her cheek and rolled to her side. "I always preferred the title of sentinel. It seemed less furtive somehow." She wiped a hand across her dry lips. Thomas uncapped a tube of Chap Stick and placed it in her palm. Catching his eye was like glancing into a tunnel opening onto other times, the clear gaze of his youth shining through. Her green-eyed boy.

She managed to apply the Chap Stick with minimal jerking.

"When? Only toward the end, really. It was only a few times, all told."

Isobel lay awake. She tried one of Cathryn's novels, but the words and snatches of description thinned before her eyes, comprehension falling away altogether as she reread the same passages. She walked the halls and sat for a long time on Louisa's bed, watching her slender chest rise and fall. When the children were tiny she watched over their sleep in amazement. Breath, so miraculous in its simplicity, need only pause in the chest of an infant for a few seconds to precisely fix a mother's hell. Losing a child had been one of her greatest terrors, but she was a mother and so not unique in that fear. Night unfolded its fears in many ways. Isobel scoffed at odd creaks or the idea of creeping strangers or anything else that might be scripted into a horror movie; nothing compared to the break in the rhythm of breath.

So much of night she loved. She embraced the darkness, yearned for the softness of midsummer nights in the way she'd begun to crave rain over the stale weeks of summer. Her real fears crept in with the dawn and seemed to draw strength in the light of day. The sun glared upon her failures — what she hadn't done right, what she hadn't said right, her own failure to define *right*.

There was a list of fears. Water was just the beginning.

Cathryn had said once, "I think I would like to be a fish, or a dove, to swim or fly. No! A flying fish would be best — then I could move through the water or air as I chose."

Isobel smiled against the words just behind her teeth but they edged their way out. "I'd fancy myself a wolf."

She knew even as Cathryn turned that her lovely brow would be sharp. "A wolf! Izzy, why ever would you choose to be a wolf?"

She shrugged, regretting the gesture as her shoulders rose. "Oh, so I could run, I suppose, through the woods. To run over moss under that spotty light coming down between the leaves." She did not say, *Because they fear nothing.*

She knew that even standing by Cathryn was immoral, she knew well enough that what Jack and Cathryn were doing was wrong.

But she could hardly condemn them. She envied and

pitied them, saw that the very depth and strength of their bond rendered them helpless. They seemed caught in a web she could not contemplate for very long or she would become trapped herself. But wasn't she already? Was their risk worth what she'd seen?

What had she seen?

Only Jack's and Cathryn's faces when they looked at each other, the ache of love, the collapse of wills.

Isobel envied Cathryn's bravery but in the end was perplexed by its irony. For all Cathryn's despair — those days when blackness visited her and she struggled to find some clear way through her shadowed mind — she stood unbowed by her misery like some heroine in a performed tragedy. Isobel had thought the doomed would be silent and expectant, but Cathryn trilled and smiled and shifted her shoulders in her beautiful clothes and kept her character in motion. Only in the odd glimpse — when Isobel caught her friend's rare, momentarily unfocused stare — did she slowly come to recognize an anguish that went beyond language.

Isobel went back to the raft of her empty bed, and when she finally fell asleep she dreamed of Victor. He was with her, had climbed in over the side of a boat, saying, *Look at us, Iz, look at us.* She didn't understand.

She woke crying, reaching.

She knew the chasm between herself and Victor needed mending; the fear between them was one only she could overcome. He had not changed, but she had. Had rolled from his side to embrace fear.

He'd bought the island for them, excited as a boy. Never something he meant to do behind her back. It was a gift. It was his adventure and she'd been invited along. But she'd refused, had ruined it, denied him that pleasure because she was too stubborn to admit a weakness and tell him just how afraid she was. For their marriage, of water. Of life.

In the weak light of morning the path opened before her.

She went back to Granite Point. She climbed into the canoe and sat, testing. She plunged her hands into water. She held onto the edge of the dock and rocked the canoe to get the feel of it under her. She strapped on the lumpy canvas life vest and imagined the worst. She tightened the straps until she was certain it could not come off. The life vest would keep her afloat.

The first few afternoons in the canoe were terrifying. Isobel held tightly to the sides and clutched the leather lace holding the whistle around her neck. The canoe was wide enough and watertight, but she still felt lurches of fear when it shifted under her or rolled in the black water. Paddling to and from the middle of the bay, she bit her lip and counted her strokes. On a calm day the trip took twenty-five dips of her paddle, on windy afternoons she counted forty or forty-five. Having achieved a fair view of the road, she dropped the makeshift anchor made of an old sash weight. She found that if she moved from the high cane seat to settle among the ribs of the floor, the canoe seemed more stable. After several days she was comfortable enough to hold a book on her knees, and, rocking along with the rhythm of the boat, she learned to shift her weight to compensate for swells.

Years later, Isobel realized the habit she had of propping herself between pillows when she prepared to read must have been acquired in that canoe.

As her unease faded she began to take note of her surroundings.

The bay between the road and Cathryn's cottage was called Ingress Cove for its access into the Maze. The surrounding cliffs rose straight up from the water. Much of the bay was like a room, its walls papered with textured lichens, chalky to the touch and coloured only on the side facing out, as if they had only enough reserves to cheer their facades, while their backsides imitated the exact shade of the stone they lived on, a dour grey.

She thought of Cathryn, her face brilliant and warm one moment, then turning silently, shifting without warning toward some inner gloaming.

After waving Jack and Cathryn off, she would open an umbrella and prop its handle through a tear in the cane seat. Every hour in the canoe was a battle against afternoon sun. With the lake reflection, brilliant heat came at her from every direction. She adjusted the umbrella and tucked her legs into the shade. She couldn't remember another such summer, the milky sky domelike above, its bright haze rarely broken. The sun had dried up the mosquito population so that dragonflies, deprived of their usual prey, hovered over the lake in opalescent battalions, desperate for the occasional gnat.

Louisa argued she was old enough to stay in the shop alone on the afternoons Isobel went to Granite Point. Isobel made the girl promise not to touch the sewing machine or the cutters and reluctantly left her daughter to work on her drawings or sew new pieces for her growing collection of doll clothes. She tacked a sign to the door reading *Call for Appointment,* and Louisa understood she was not to open the door.

On those afternoons, Isobel took up her post in the bay and watched for Jack to arrive at Cathryn's cottage. Sometimes he rowed over to say hello and they would talk awhile, but he could not hide his anxiousness to get to Cathryn, and Isobel would hesitantly shoo him off after a few minutes.

"Go on, Jack. The lady waits."

As the days wore on Isobel noticed that the hang of Jack's shirts became severe, the skin under his eyes took on a dusty blue, his thinness seemed tubercular. He had volunteered for the most brutal shift at the station, nine P.M. to six A.M. Bracing himself with coffee, he spent nights logging incoming telephone reports of campfires gone awry, false alarms, or heat lightning strikes. Crews were on alert around the clock with the dry conditions, and many worked double shifts. Jack dispatched crews and wrote long letters to Cathryn in the dawn, the time he felt most clearheaded. He cooked breakfast for the incoming shift and updated the pin maps. At six he drove twelve miles on an unmapped logging road to his mainland dock, then rowed the last mile home through the bog end of the Maze. On calm mornings he was home early and could sleep until noon. In order to be with Cathryn a few hours each day he cut his scant sleep in half, got back in his boat, and rowed east to Granite Point.

Usually when he arrived they lingered near the shore, talking. From her nest in the bottom of the canoe, Isobel didn't hear very much, but sometimes bits of conversation would drift over, amplified by the medium of water, and she would feel suddenly guilty, as if caught eavesdropping.

"We *will* be together, Cathryn. Always."

"Jack."

"Nothing can change what we have. I promise you that."

"You don't know."

"Nothing."

Other times, less often, they laughed. And sometimes, after a long silence, Isobel would glance over to see them only looking at each other, or sitting with their heads bent. She turned away when they touched each other, but sometimes she couldn't help but catch brief images — a hand reaching out to touch a face, a finger tracing a lip, a chin tilted upward for a kiss.

Eventually they would climb the ledge of granite and disappear into the cottage. Then Isobel tried desperately not to think what they were doing.

She busied her mind with other things — her children, her work, the book she was holding and pretending to read — but flashes of limbs and falling garments interrupted her. The book fell to her lap. She wondered if they made love in the bed Cathryn shared with Liam. She hoped they didn't.

Just before Isobel was to be married, her mother sat her down to explain what she could expect on her wedding night. She dipped a wedge of lemon cake into her tea and looked at her daughter with a rare expression of condolence.

"Just let him have vot he vants. It's easier than fighting it."

Isobel felt a stone in her stomach. "Fighting it?"

Her mother popped the cake into her mouth and crossed her arms, her smile sour.

But she found Victor's kisses pleasant! There was nothing brutal in his attentions. She was sure of it. Why, only the other day when he had greeted her in an embrace, he hadn't let go of her waist — and she hadn't wanted him to. They had smiled stupidly at each other the entire moment his hands cinched her ribs, moved down over her waist to rest on the swell of her hips.

They had danced together. The proximity of his lips to her ear, his breath in her hair, made her want to dance longer, forever. She had already made up her mind that the next time Victor's warm hands strayed upward to the bodice of her dress she would not stop him. Was there something she didn't know?

"Mother, it can't be all that bad."

"Bad? There's vorse tings in marriage, I suppose. But in

the bedroom? There's blood and there's pain." Her mother's tone turned suddenly accusing. "*Mein Gott.* You're not expecting pleasure?"

The stone in her stomach turned on end. Her mother made love sound like misery. Isobel glared at her. *Maybe for you it is,* she wanted to say. *Maybe for you.*

The pitying gleam in her mother's eyes and the weight of her own doubt shadowed Isobel the entire train ride back to Duluth. From the station she walked to the pier and sat on a bench. She had arranged to meet Victor by the bridge, but she was early. She passed the time watching freighters move under the lift-bridge and the families milling around the waterfront. On the other side of the channel children played on the sandy beach. They plunged into the waves, squealing and shouting as they were repeatedly knocked down. Parents lounged on blankets, and at the shore two girls swung their toddler brother between them so that his knees sliced the water. When he screamed with delight Isobel found she was vaguely irritated at his joy, envious at how free he was, the obvious ease with which he flung his body through the world.

Victor sidled up beside her, handing her a bag of popcorn in greeting. He kissed her temple. She felt her face where his lips had touched her.

"You're a million miles away."

"No I'm not." She frowned, remembering why she'd come.

As they meandered the boardwalk she tried to break their engagement. Victor, too stunned to be angry, hounded her for a reason, until she broke down and relayed the conversation she'd had with her mother.

Victor bent double laughing.

Isobel stared. "But what if it *is* awful, the way she makes it out to be? I just don't know, Victor."

He took her arm and led her away from a group of

tourists. Jokingly he offered, "Well, we could give it a go. If you don't like it, we won't get married."

Isobel stared at the seagulls feeding on popcorn strewn over the rocks at the shore.

"What do you mean? Try it out?"

He gave her a sidelong glance but did not answer.

She dug into the paper bag and threw more popcorn toward the swooping gulls. "Fine. Let's do it, then."

~ ~ ~

CHAPTER ELEVEN

Victor reserved a room at the Hotel Duluth. Saturday after her shift at the Pasal Millinery, Isobel rushed home to pack. She bathed, put on perfume, decided the perfume was too strong, bathed again. She raced out the back door of the boardinghouse so her landlady wouldn't see her leaving with an overnight bag. She'd left a note saying she was going to see a cousin. Like a criminal.

She had tried to make herself look as mature as possible, putting on a hat that was much too old for her face and a dress that fell nearly to her ankles.

Victor arrived in the hotel to find her just barely sitting on a velvet bench and kneading the beaded bag in her hands. He tapped her on the shoulder and she jumped.

When she turned he was staring at her.

"Victor!" She looked around the lobby and whispered, "Do I look like a hussy?"

He took in her long dress and borrowed eyeglasses. With his index finger he pushed the hat riding low on her brow up so he could look into her eyes.

"Ah, noooo. You look more like a young schoolmarm."

She kept her gloves on in the lobby to hide the fact she had no ring.

Victor steered her into the hotel restaurant. Once they were seated he pulled a bottle of cheap Bordeaux from the valise at his feet and began to open it. Isobel gasped, "Victor! That's illegal now."

Victor shrugged. "Look around."

Several tables had flasks openly set out, the waiters seemingly taking no notice. Victor poured the wine into coffee cups. They ordered. The wine was too astringent at first, but Isobel thought it grew more mellow after the first cup.

"Victor, what did you to today?"

"Don't gulp, now," Victor whispered, easing her hand down. He poured them each another cup when their food came. He ate heartily, salad, potatoes, and pork chops, while Isobel only picked at her salad between sips. "What'd I do?" He laughed. "Well, I had a little fella come in, nearly didn't see him over the counter. He wanted a pair of trousers let down two inches." Victor took a gulp himself. "I measured him and measured the pants and said, 'Look, they're right on the money for your inseam.' And he says, 'Let 'em down anyway.' And I say, 'But you got a twenty-two-inch inseam. I can measure again, but what you got is a twenty-two leg, and these pants got a twenty-two leg.' So, when the little guy puffs up like a blowfish, I throw my hands up and tell him, 'If I let 'em down you'd be draggin' your cuffs through the mud!' Then he turns all red and reaches down and slams a box on the counter. And what do you think's in it?"

Isobel had discovered that if she ran her finger around the rim of her water glass, it made a pleasing sound. She suddenly looked up at Victor. "I'm listening."

"So, what do you think's in the box?"

"I don't know, Vic."

"He pulls out these shoes with huge lifts built into them! Like something out of Frankenstein." Victor slapped the table. "Like Frankenstein!"

Isobel touched his arm. "Are you nervous?"

Victor looked around, suddenly aware of his loudness, though no one seemed to have noticed. He turned slightly red. "A little. You?"

Isobel nodded, and covered his hand. "Okay, so what happened to your little man, then?"

"Aw, not much. I told him, 'Well, hell, you shoulda showed me in the first place. I can even flare the cuffs out so nobody'll know you're wearing high heels.'"

"Victor, you didn't."

Victor waved his napkin. "Oh, he's all right, even had a good laugh by the time he left. Damnedest thing, isn't it, the things people try to hide. Like trying to hide a tumor from a doctor. People come in to see me and have some fault — a game leg or shoulders like a girl or a hump — but I can always figure out a way, I can make their problem less obvious. But they got to work with me, right? It's a matter of trust."

Isobel leaned back. "Trust?"

Victor held up the nearly empty bottle. "Yes, trust. You trust me, don't you?"

She bowed and blotted a tear, but not before he saw it.

"Ah, Izzy." Victor took her gloved hand. "We don't have to do this tonight."

She shook her head. "That's not it. I'm just . . . I had a bad day. And now all this." Isobel plucked the collar of her dowdy dress and pulled the borrowed glasses from her face. "I look like a fool."

"A pretty fool." Victor took her other hand and kissed it before picking up his cup. "Let's toast."

"To what?"

"To us. To now. Yes, *now*. Let's toast to that. To this moment. To tonight."

They clinked their cups and finished the bottle. When they rose to leave the dining room, Isobel felt a pleasant unfocusing, a cushioning with each step.

Upstairs, the length of corridor seemed endless. At their door, Victor fumbled with the key and it fell to the rug. They both bent down to get it, and their heads knocked together with a dull *crack*. Isobel slapped her hand over Victor's mouth to stifle his laughter, took the key from his hands, and unlocked the door herself.

But before she could step in, Victor pulled her back. He picked her up in his arms. With his knee, he propped open the door so he could carry her through.

"But, Victor," she whispered, "I'm not really a bride."

"Close enough."

He stepped over the threshold and deposited Isobel in the narrow vestibule. She took one step and stumbled over her suitcase. She found this somehow hilarious, and Victor had to reach out to steady her. He kicked the suitcase out of the way, making her laugh harder.

Isobel leaned back, misjudging the distance, so that when she met the wardrobe door it was a hard resting of flesh to wood.

"Whoops!" Her giggles died under the jangling of wire hangers.

When Victor placed his palms on the door at either side of her head, she looked at him and fell quiet. After a moment she whispered, "Well."

"Here we are." He kissed her lightly on the brow.

"Yes, right here."

Victor's lips moved to her temple, her ear, her throat. He lingered at her collarbone, breathing scent at the slight ridge. Isobel touched the back of his neck, her nails raising gooseflesh at the cowlick. She browsed the nape with her fingertips, his hair soft as a child's. He smelled of laundered cotton, starch, and pears.

She reached behind her, placed her hands on the wardrobe door to steady herself, and wondered aloud if she was very drunk or only a little drunk. The hangers rattled again, and Victor's response was muffled by the collar of her dress. She felt his lips and the smoothness of his teeth graze her. She felt the strain at the fly of his trousers.

"What should I do? I mean, what do you want me to do?"

"Do anything . . . anything you want to do."

Isobel reached up to unbutton the front of her dress. Victor's hands covered hers, and he smiled. "Except that. I get to do that."

He kissed her from the hollow at her throat to the slight cleave between her small breasts. His lips found the taut roundness at her belly through the silk of her chemise. The dress fell, pooling on the carpet, and he began to remove her underthings. Straps fell, a breast was cupped, kissed, cupped again.

When he stepped away she covered herself. He peeled her arms from her chest and looked at her. The softness in his eyes eased her embarrassment.

Victor's shirt peeled away, and she looked at his wrists for a long time, marveling at their squareness, the inner plane of pale skin, the bony ridge giving way to darker flesh and the abrupt line of hairs defining his forearms.

He guided her hands to the band of his shorts, hooked his thumbs over hers and helped her lower the garment over his hips. When she began to turn her face away, he demanded, "No. Look."

She did. His body was not ugly, not at all frightening. The opposite. He was beautiful; his arms and chest were hard, but his skin was soft under her touch. In the oval mirror of the wardrobe they were framed as if for a portrait. She smiled at the contrasts, she so pale against his side, his nipples tawny where hers were rose. His penis was not the shock she'd expected — she *wanted* to touch it. As she looked at their reflections together, then at herself, she thought for the first time in her life, *I'm pretty. My body is pretty.*

They moved away from their clothes toward the bed.

He lay down and opened his arms, but Isobel stood rocking in a moment of apprehension. He waited. After a moment she reached down to touch his lower lip, and when he tried to take her finger into his mouth she pulled it away to trail the shallow cleft at his chin. She stopped at a bristled spot where his razor had missed. Her fingers traveled the length of his throat, over his Adam's apple and to the shallow dip between his collarbones. She felt the slight depression halving his upper chest, the plate of bone beneath muscle. Laying her palm flat over the place where his ribs separated, she felt the flesh give and pulse slightly. His navel was a half-moon just below a soft fanning of fine hairs.

She knelt on the edge of the bed and bent low over his hip. When her hair swept over Victor's belly he sighed. She stretched on the bed next to him and arrayed herself as if she were an offering. When he began touching her she lost words. Under his hands she could feel parts of herself emerge, places that seemingly hadn't existed before. Isobel felt she was being mapped, compiled, and expanded, as though her flesh were an endless plane. Layers of her were uncovered, rolled, smoothed. Her hands occasionally found his, and when his hands pulled away her palms stung with the emptiness.

She felt his touch on her, over her, and down her limbs, the fine skin of him like wind. His breath on her ached. His palm was a blessing on her spine. As his hands traced her she was reminded of his working on the wedding dress she had yet to see completed. He took care with her as he would a fine hem, smoothing her as he would a dear length of silk.

Suddenly he was over her, separating her knees, and Isobel sighed. *This is it, then.* But it was his mouth that found her. A jagged breath of shock gave way to a shifting and blurring as Victor's mouth uncovered her layers. His mouth moved intently as different colours broke over the backs of her closed lids, lavender splashing into magenta and carmine. She lost her breath and found it, thought of asking him to stop, but knew there was no compelling reason to offer. She found herself pressing toward his mouth and felt his teeth over ridges of flesh her mother had told her never to touch except with soap and water.

A sin, surely.

She didn't care.

When he kissed his way back to her neck and over her chin to meet her open mouth, she could taste the slight sharpness of her own sex on his mustache, a mild pepper, shifting liquid from his tongue to hers.

He moved gently and there was a pressing in. Resistance where she expected pain. She imagined blood, but her concern dissolved under the instinct to meet Victor's rhythm of shallow movements. There was a sharp sting as Victor arched and forced his length into her. He stopped abruptly and looked into her face. "Are you all right?"

Isobel's empty hands drifted to the sheets. "Yes, I'm fine. It was fine."

"Was?" Victor smiled. "Oh, Iz, we've only just started . . ."

Afterward, Isobel lay with her head on Victor's thigh. A tiny ridge ran down the underside of his penis and flowed over the soft pouch, halving it with the tenderest of scars. Victor watched as she gently traced this line. He rose up on an elbow and whispered, "It's the final seam, Izzy. It's where the angels stuffed me before they sewed me up."

She sighed and rolled onto her back. "Ask me again."

Victor's fingers drifted to linger at her temple. "Ask you what?"

"Ask me to marry you again."

"Isobel, will you marry me?"

She pretended to mull it over.

Victor shot to his knees and pounced, straddling her and pinning her arms above her head.

Her face was serious, but a twitch pulled at the corner of her lip. "My mother, she was right, you know, about letting you have what you want. It *was* easier than fighting it."

A moan from the foghorn drifted in, its solemn tone drowned under their laughter.

Her time in the canoe often seemed to have no beginning and no end. The heat overtook Isobel by midafternoon so she would have to steer the canoe to the shade of the cliff wall. The life jacket absorbed and stored heat so that sweat ran continuously between her breasts. She felt safer in the shade, and in the cool pause she noted the stunted ferns curving outward from horizontal cracks of stone, vivid in contrast.

There was only sun and water, and of course the stone. Nearly every foot of the shoreline was defined by it — the sloped hump rising to separate Cathryn's cottage from the water, the cliffs casting Isobel's shade, and beyond the point, the jagged teeth flanking the entrance to the Maze. Jack's cabin was nearly a mile beyond, his small island set deep into the corridor, past the point where the cautious dared.

Isobel went as far as the cabin once, invited to paddle over for a picnic on a rare day Jack and Cathryn spent on his island.

Jack had given her a compass and warned that once into the Maze, she should aim straight west and avoid veering into the many channels to the north. On the map the Maze looked like an elongated torso with writhing limbs, its watery arms narrowed into thin hands with thinner fingers, and those channels tapered to curl back on themselves like a Chinaman's fingernails. Many passages were no wider than a canoe, and as many dead-ended at cliffs or widened to feather out once again into bogs or low tamarack forests.

"This map isn't accurate," Jack warned. "There are whole sections of the north half that were never surveyed."

Isobel set her shoulders and paddled into the Maze on a course taking her through the widest arm.

After a quarter mile the air shifted. Cedars grew outward from the banks like shepherds' crooks reaching to the open sky above. The banks were dark, ragged with moss draping just over the black water. As she paddled farther in she felt herself placed in a different time. It was cooler, and somehow the air seemed old, as if left behind from a previous age.

She negotiated the winding corridor, estuaries opening to the north like many open doorways. At their entrances, the water churned in gentle eddies as if beckoning her to enter. The rest of the world seemed to recede with every dip of her paddle. Isobel found this condensed atmosphere strangely soothing, was reminded of an empty cathedral. The corridor of water beneath her seemed less menacing, more benevolent, as if it might be the way to some haven. The silence of the Maze gave Isobel pause, and she let the canoe drift through this dense quiet, listening for some underlayment of sounds — of birds, or of foliage ruffled by breeze — but the pall was established, endorsed by muffling banks of ferns, guarded by sentries of ancient cedar.

Reluctantly, she resumed paddling, dipping gently so as not to disturb the cloak of silence. Rounding the last curve, where according to the map there should have been a bay, she felt a tug of panic. Instead of a bay, a low, ragged-edged island all but took up the space. As she looked down to check the map a third time, something shifted at the corner of her eye. The island in front of her had moved.

Moved? A trick of the light. Isobel sank her paddle into the mud bottom to still the canoe's movement. To make sure she was seeing right, she lined up the trees on the island with those on the shoreline with her index finger, watched them meet up, shift, line up again. The island drifted as if pulled by an invisible cable.

She had heard of floating islands, but had no idea they could be large enough to host trees. Carefully paddling around it, she hoped it wouldn't shift and trap her. She held back an image of the lapstrake hull of the canoe splintering around her knees. She paddled faster. Once around, she found herself freed into a large bay.

She could see Jack's cabin in the distance and noted with some relief that his tiny island was weighted by a shoal of sand and a solid bank of stone.

Her journey had taken a full hour but had seemed brief. Her shoulders knotted as the wide bay opened up, reflecting too much sky. There was the unlikely presence of a cabin, a dock, humans.

Cathryn saw her approaching and rose from her bench. Isobel had a sudden, inexplicable desire to turn back, or remain floating, but the boat slid under her toward shore, and Jack reached out to catch the tip of it, swinging it in one motion so it paralleled the pulpy dock.

She looked skeptically at Cathryn. "Is this safe?"

Cathryn blinked. "Liam's gone to Duluth for the day, Isobel."

"I know that." She pressed a finger into the spongy black wood of the dock. "I mean is it safe to step on this thing?"

While Cathryn prepared lunch, Jack showed Isobel his one-room cabin. Its logs were aged a deep treacle. A soapstone sink anchored the tiny kitchen. A run of small screened windows opened over a narrow counter bowing under the weight of stacked food tins and a pie safe. Open shelves held a disparate family of plates, assorted jelly jars, and mismatched porcelain cups. Iron skillets hung from rusted hooks over a blue enamel cookstove. A bookcase crammed with volumes separated the kitchen from the small living area, which held a table just large enough to eat at and two leather chairs flanking a narrow stone hearth. The ceiling light, a copper hooded lantern, sprouted ringlets of amber flypaper thick with corpses. The place wasn't dirty, exactly, but was imbued with an overall darkness that made it seem so.

Near the side door, an alcove held a bed behind a half-pulled curtain. Isobel stopped and stared at the space just above the iron bedstead where a dried palm frond was held in place by a hand-hewn crucifix. The bed beneath was covered by an intricate field of frayed flowers, an old pink lattice quilt, appliquéd with roses and vining stems thin as tissue, petals opening at burst seams to breathe out cotton batting.

The mattress sagged in the middle, deep as a hammock, and Isobel nearly laughed, shaking her head. Cathryn sleeping here?

When she met Jack's eye, he blushed and quickly pointed the way to the screened porch. He offered her a chair near a low table. The table was covered with botany books and glass jars of plants, their roots floating free beneath them. Handmade shelves lined the wall, with at least a hundred more plant specimens in jelly glasses.

"Some of them come from the bogs, like these pitcher plants." He pulled one from its jar. Isobel cradled it and peered at the red, veined interior. She looked up at Jack.

"Why, it's like a heart. Like a human heart opened up."

She put it back, carefully coiling its long root into the jar.

Jack showed her stacks of pressboard with dried, flattened specimens of anemones, spring cress, gentian, and dogbane, all glued into place and meticulously labeled.

"Most forest plants bloom white. A few have blue and rose tones, some yellow, like this lady's slipper, but at least eighty percent of woodland flowers are white or nearly white. They need light to produce color, just like anything else. You'll rarely see a bright flower in the shade of a forest."

Isobel did not look at the next board of flattened flowers. "Jack, what will you do?"

"Do?"

"You and Cathryn. What will you do?"

Jack carefully set down the boards. "I'm not sure. I've asked her to marry me."

"But she's already married, Jack. And Liam Malley is a Catholic. *Irish* Catholic. You don't honestly think he'd agree to a divorce?"

"Cathryn thinks he might."

"Cathryn isn't thinking, Jack. You know that as well as I." Isobel trembled with frustration. "Even if you could marry her. Then what? You couldn't stay here in this cabin, or even in Cypress. My God, Jack, how much longer do you believe this can go on?"

He looked through the screen to where Cathryn was setting food and glasses on the outdoor table. "I don't know."

"Someone's going to get hurt."

"If Malley lays a hand on her, I'll kill him."

"That's not what I meant. But Jack, something is bound to happen."

"Lunch!" They turned to see Cathryn standing just beyond the door, hands on her hips, a tea towel dangling from one slender fist. The fabric of her summer dress was tissue thin against the sun, revealing slight shoulders, the ridge of hip, reedy waist. She'd shed weight. Her face had tanned, and her eyes, all the lighter for it, had taken on an odd detachment that Isobel recognized but could not place.

Isobel angrily stabbed at the corner of her eye with a knuckle. "You'll both have to make some decisions. Soon."

Cathryn's hands fell. Isobel nodded, sure now where she'd seen the look, the posture. A newspaper photograph of a migrant, the hopeless gaze of a woman confronting despair.

Isobel was silent for much of the picnic. Cathryn served slivered melon, cold asparagus, salmon salad, and cress sandwiches with crusts meticulously cut away. Isobel sensed Jack's awkwardness with the dainty bits of food. It was an incongruous meal given the setting.

They ate under a white pine on a table Jack had salvaged from an abandoned fishing shack. A tobacco tin filled with bird-on-the-wing decorated the table, and their chairs were rounds of a fallen log Jack had sawn into rough stools. The faint smell of fish bled through the ironed linen cloth Cathryn had brought from her cottage.

Jack and Cathryn fussed over her, grinning at each other each time they offered Isobel another spear of asparagus, lemonade laced with ginger, a bowl of raspberries.

After they ate, Jack led them to his boat and ferried them through an estuary into the tamarack bog. They took off their shoes and, stepping from the bow, instantly sank calf-deep into the sponge of wet moss. Each step was an act of faith on the land shifting under them. Isobel stayed close to the lacy stands of tamarack, hoping she'd be less likely to break through with a web of roots beneath. Ahead, Jack and Cathryn picked green cranberries and pelted them at each other.

Isobel hung back and watched.

They were playing at being a couple, playing at being carefree. The meal had been more theater. She couldn't help wondering if it had been performed for her benefit or their own. She might be the doll at their tea party. There was no reality here. Isobel made her way back to the boat to wait.

Lunch churned in her stomach as she paddled back through the Maze, past Cathryn's cottage and beyond the point, over the stretch of open water to the dock. She pulled the canoe up in one motion and carelessly dropped it. Her arms were aching. When she stood and looked back to the ingress at the mouth of the Maze, she knew what a great distance she had come but barely remembered the journey. For the first time she'd forgotten to be afraid for herself.

~   ~   ~

The tones of the hospital altered after sunset, the corridors cleared of daytime bustle to give way to lesser noises — the thrumming of distant machinery, the constant rumble of the power plant in the basement. From midnight to the start of morning shift the muted sounds were amplified — the elevator's ping, the ticking tires of gurneys. The nurses' laughter, and even sometimes their whispers, came clearly to her, as if over water. These night sounds were comforting to Isobel. She tried to stay awake as long as she could, reluctant to abandon the hush and quiet predictability of night.

A white torso bent over her. The nurse handed her two tablets and a cup of warm water.

"Miz Howard?"

"What are these for?"

"Your temp's up. A hundred-one."

Isobel took the tablets and dutifully swallowed. She did feel hot, almost as if she'd been out in the sun for an afternoon.

The nurse's head was in shadow, faceless as she took the empty cup from Isobel's hand. Behind the white hip Isobel saw Thomas slumped in his chair, his jacket around him like a shawl.

"Oh dear. He'll be a plank in the morning. Will you wake him up and send him home?"

"Sure, hon. Want your reading light turned off?"

CHAPTER TWELVE

~ ~ ~

She asked Cathryn if she was ever afraid God would punish her for her sin.

"My sin?"

"Your infidelity."

"My infidelity. *Mine*. It has nothing to do with God. If anyone, it's Liam I'll have to answer to."

"But what about the church?"

"Izzy." Cathryn huffed as she stood up. "You're too intelligent a woman for that. Don't go righteous on me. Besides, Jack feels guilty enough for both of us."

Isobel turned away, feeling insulted.

After a moment Cathryn gently pulled her back by the shoulder. "Listen, I'm sorry. I keep forgetting where I am."

"Where you are? You blame geography? I suppose women in Chicago cheat on their husbands every day."

Cathryn crossed her arms. "Some. More than you'd think, probably." She looked Isobel in the eye. "In a different time I suppose I'd be exiled or beaten. Something. If I were in India my husband could burn me alive. Here I'll only be ostracized — doesn't sound so bad, really."

"And how do you think Liam will take it?"

"I've no idea. I suppose I'll have to tell him first."

"Yes. The first thing is to tell Liam. When, Cathryn?"

"When the right time comes."

"Do you really think there's a right time for this sort of thing? What's wrong with now?"

Cathryn looked down. "Everything."

If someone had asked her only a month before if she believed Cathryn would go to hell she would have said yes. Now she wasn't so sure she believed in the God who condemned souls after spreading temptation before them like a banquet. That God was man's creation, she decided. She couldn't have imagined any decent woman being unfaithful. Men, of course, strayed all the time. It was their nature.

Just after Thomas was born, when she was still nursing him, Victor traveled to Duluth on several overnight trips, always returning in a better mood than when he'd left. Her heaviness seemed more than physical as the months wore on, and she came to resent his trips. In his absences flashes of slim, sophisticated girls interrupted her daily chores. One evening after he'd returned, he found her in their bedroom, rummaging through his coat pockets. She blanched, slowly freeing her hand before facing him.

He stood unmoving in the doorway, blinking at her pale stare.

"Whatever it is you're looking for, you won't find it, Iz."

"And what does that mean?"

"It means what it means." He turned and went down the stairs.

Had he strayed? She didn't know. She wondered how well she knew her own husband. If he had been unfaithful she wouldn't want to hear of it now, would never want to have it spoken of. She herself couldn't take a lover and still sleep next to Victor in a charade of duplicity. It would be too confusing.

Cathryn was a good woman. Isobel knew she was. Sex, the sin end of it, was just an accessory of Cathryn and Jack's love. She could not believe the love itself was a sin. Nor could she believe Cathryn would have decided *I will sin now.* Her falling in love could not have been a thing she had sought or even chosen; rather it was a thing that had begun and she had not stopped its beginning. Her choice, then? Or had she allowed a fate to choose her?

What woman would choose a life so off-course, so imbalanced as Cathryn's was this day?

Her hand trailed languid figure eights in the water while Jack and Cathryn made love in the cottage. In her years married to Victor, she had never thought of another man with desire. She'd been momentarily unbalanced by Jack's frailties, even envious of Cathryn's possession of Jack. She'd fought having feelings toward him, but now she knew it was the ownership of Jack's somber heart she envied. A possession she'd never felt with Victor. That was as much as she was willing to admit. When she was near Jack now she wanted to turn away, not look at his serious eyes, not notice how thin he'd become. She looked away from the ruin he and Cathryn had made of love. Of sex.

In those first years with Victor, the two of them would race home from the shop at lunchtime to make love. Sometimes they stayed in the shop, flipping the *Closed* sign on the door and filling those hours with quiet sounds — the echo of shades hastily drawn, the soft falling of garments creased with haste. Chords of sighs and whispers.

When Isobel was feeling wanton, she would whisper into Victor's ear, "Thank you for your patronage."

Or he might slip behind her to wrap his hands over hers, gently prying until her fingers released the scissors, the pencil, or the cloth, whatever task was taking her hands.

Victor always looked into her eyes after undressing her. As he moved over her, in her, she often felt she was climbing toward something, reaching, and that he was reaching too for a similar thing. She felt a crush of love for him during these moments. When she felt her muscles move with their own purpose, the harmony of colours always returned to her. She and Victor were conspirators, united not only in flesh, but in something larger, some lovely collusion she could not name. At the first signs of Victor's immediacy — a harsh breath, his soft groan — something within her would swell and form itself into a wave of hues. Wild hands reached to crumple yards of fabric, to grab at a counter, to clutch the armrests of a chair; she would fall into the shades and tones, her fingertips and knuckles grown white in their grasping.

Once, during their lovemaking, she had rolled onto a yardstick and the impression of inches and the name of a hardware store were neatly embossed onto the plane of her shoulder blade, legible for hours.

Peering over Victor's back as he moved in her, she had watched an amber chunk fall from the ceiling to land on his spine and tumble its length before it sailed over his hip. She had whispered, *The sky is falling.*

She buried her face at orgasm, pressing her mouth to Victor's flesh, not wanting her sounds to be heard by anyone but him. With her eyes closed she pictured her breath as soft billows of purple, indigo, scarlet, colours matching the rhythms within them.

But that closeness had faded. Colours diluted. After Thomas was born, her fears of pregnancy twisted lovemaking into a mechanical duty, something the children might hear from their rooms, something she acquiesced in as seldom as possible without rousing some sulk from Victor.

A cruel reversal of nature had turned her third birth into the longest and bloodiest. She thought she and the baby would die in labour, and in those desperate last hours she blamed Victor should their children be left motherless. When Thomas was finally born, she looked into the baby's eyes and knew he would be her last. Had it been only self-preservation that made her avoid intimacy? In the last months she had actively denied Victor, avoided love. After he bought the island she didn't know how to show her displeasure except to withhold the one thing she owned that was of value to him. She knew now how wrong she'd been, that in denying him she had harmed them both.

Leaning against the gunwale, watching her still-youthful reflection in the mirror of Lake Cypress, Isobel smiled. Perhaps it wasn't too late. Once he came back, she would be herself again. Her old self. She would discuss contraceptives with Cathryn; she would defy the Catholic Church. She would buy a lock for their bedroom door and reclaim her desires. She would travel to his island.

When Isobel opened a volume of Teasdale Cathryn had lent her, a folded sheet of onionskin stationery fell out. Was she meant to find it?

Dearest Jack,

A poverty of words. How can I respond to your letters? You are indelible, branded on me for life. You know that.

If it were only you and I, alone! That's the thought I cling to, what keeps me aloft, that somehow, in a lottery of fate where we are winners, the world will dissolve and leave only us. A dream. But this is real and there are lives around us that will change — we are afflicting lives and fates of others. You must realize that wherever we go we will carry the weight of

It ended there. She dropped the letter to her lap. Since Cathryn exhibited no guilt or remorse over the consequences of her affair, Isobel had assumed that she hadn't suffered any. The letter indicated otherwise. Isobel knew she was one of the people Cathryn mentioned whose lives would be afflicted. *Afflicted*. A harsh word, dramatic. But then Cathryn was dramatic. Once she had used a Latin term when describing the force behind a person's actions, *modus operandi*. If Cathryn had one, Isobel knew, it would be distinctly labeled *drama*.

Isobel imagined Cathryn beginning the letter at her bedroom table, her pen trailing to leave the last line unfinished when she heard the purr of Liam's car through the woods. She would blush, quickly tuck the letter between poems, and hide the book. Feeling her cheeks, she would head down the staircase to greet and smile and make dinner for her husband as if he were the light of her life.

Isobel shook away the scene.

Who's being dramatic now?

The day after Isobel found the letter, Cathryn and Jack rowed into the Maze to visit his cabin. As afternoon shifted to evening Isobel drummed the seat of the canoe, peering often across the water. She should have been home to see to Louisa. She had no watch but could tell from the slant of the sun it was certainly past five o'clock. She laid her book aside and waited. What was she supposed to do? She realized they'd had no real plan in case Liam did come by. She felt like an idiot, and was suddenly angry with Jack. Even if she did blow her whistle now, they'd never hear her.

After another half hour, she pulled up the anchor and paddled closer to the entrance of the Maze, cupping an ear for sounds of their approach.

Had they fallen asleep? Isobel glanced repeatedly up to the road, sure Liam's car would roar into view any minute. She paddled in and looked down the channel. Nothing. She fished the whistle out of her blouse. Perhaps she should use it.

Just as she thought she might, she heard the creaking of oars and splashing, as if the boat was unbalanced. Jack's voice carried over the still water.

"Cathryn, please try to stop. Try."

Cathryn was sobbing. When they pulled into view Isobel could see her slumped and rocking in her seat.

"It'll be all right, Cathryn." Jack let go of his oar to reach out and brush a tear from her cheek. She jerked roughly away.

Isobel knew he was struggling to manage his tone. "Everything will be fine. We'll figure it out."

As their boat slid past the canoe, Cathryn dropped her face into her hands, would not acknowledge Isobel. But Jack looked at her, just long enough for Isobel to see the weariness, complete in the deep lines around his mouth.

The paddle in her hand felt like lead as she made her way slowly back to the dock. She tried to remember the last time she'd seen Cathryn smile.

Weeks before. The air in the shop had been still and warm through the morning. Louisa hung by the door, making as though to open it, but then retreating, listening to something at the window with anxious concentration.

"Why don't you go out, Louisa?"

"I'm waiting for it to stop."

Isobel looked up. "For what to stop?"

"The electricity."

Cathryn swiveled on her stool. "What electricity?"

"Can't you hear it? The buzzing in the wires. It's every-where."

"Buzzing? Wires? Oh sweetheart, that's not electricity! It's only the —" Both women chimed:

"Cic*ay*das."

"Cic*ah*das."

Isobel raised an eyebrow, her face deadpan as she began to sing in her terrible voice. "You say cic*ay*da, and I say ci-*cah*da."

Cathryn slid from her stool into an impromptu tap. "You say pot*ay*ta and I say pot*ah*ta." They sang. "Ci-*cay*da, cic*ah*da, pot*ay*ta, pot*ah*ta . . ." Cathryn's dance de-generated, her feet pounding vaudeville parody onto the floorboards, elbows flapping. They dissolved in laughter, singing. "Let's call the whole thing *off!*"

Isobel waited while Jack dropped Cathryn off at the ledge below her cottage. He pulled up to the dock, and climbing from his boat gave Isobel an unconvincing smile. She laid a hand on his arm.

"Jack, is she all right?"

He shrugged. "I'm not sure."

"Should I go to her?"

He looked up blankly. "I don't think you can help her. I'm not even sure I can."

She saw the tear form and she reached up. For the mo-ment his jaw rested in her hand she felt its faint tremor.

He looked to the cottage and spoke over the water. "We're all a little lost, I suppose."

Isobel woke too early, agitated and not knowing why. Her pillow was damp from sweat, the room close. The curtains hung slack against the sills. She sighed. If the heat kept up she'd move herself and Louisa down to sleep in the living room.

She plodded to the kitchen and turned on the tap. After several minutes the water was still running cool. Descending the cellar stairs, she felt the water tank to discover it was cold. She shouted for Victor to come down and relight the flame, too frightened to try doing it herself. When she was seven, a small gas explosion in her father's bakery had badly burned a young helper whose scarred face loomed whenever she whiffed a trace of gas. She went to the foot of the stairs and called again, tapping the banister for several moments before realizing that Victor wasn't home. She felt suddenly foolish and a little helpless. He was far away, across miles of water. Somehow, during the night, she had lost months.

She slapped the iron tank and sighed. "Fine. We'll do without." She turned off the iron crank that fed the gas line and climbed the stairs. In a large kettle she warmed water on the stove and called for Louisa to dress and come down. They hauled the kettle out to the garden along with a glass pitcher and a narrow brown bottle of shampoo that Cathryn had given her.

Louisa stripped off her summer blouse and stood over the old copper boiler while her mother poured water over her head.

It wasn't seven, yet the shifting bits of sunlight through the canopy of maple were mean rays. Light played over Louisa's thin shoulders and neck, and as Isobel massaged suds into the girl's scalp she looked at her daughter's half-clad body. Her chest was smooth as a boy's, and Isobel felt a pang of regret knowing it wouldn't be long before she would become a young woman. Grow away from her, independent.

Louisa turned her head to peer at her mother through a soapy curtain of blond. "It smells nice, don't it, Momma?"

"Doesn't."

"Well, I think it does!"

"I meant you should say *doesn't* it, not *don't* it."

"Well, *doesn't* it smell nice?"

"Yes, it smells very pretty." Isobel read the label aloud. "Jasmine Spice. For gloss and sheen."

"Sounds pretty too. Momma, can I wash your hair?"

Sunlight suspended itself in a drop of water as it trickled down Louisa's spine and was absorbed into the waistband of the girl's shorts.

"Sure."

After wrapping a towel around Louisa's head turban-style, Isobel heated more water, found a stool, and slipped out of her own blouse to lean over the basin in her brassiere.

Louisa poured a jug of warm water over her mother's head and massaged in the shampoo. Her touch, to Isobel's surprise, was not childlike. She'd expected soft meandering pats, but the girl applied firm strokes intent on their task.

Isobel began to drift under the rhythm Louisa rubbed into her scalp. She watched the girl's square feet shift, hop, and cross over each other as she worked. When she stood still, tiny violets poked up between the girl's splayed toes.

Isobel had lately found herself assigning bits of poetry to what she saw or felt, if only to see what she could recall or recite. *Whispers and small laughter between leaves and hurrying feet. / Under sleep, where all waters meet.* She couldn't remember the poet.

Tepid water washed over her, hove down her neck, poured into her eyes, threatened to flood her nose. *Under sleep, where all waters meet.* The dream that had left her tossing and restless during the night rushed back to Isobel and she sat up suddenly, knocking the pitcher against Louisa, drenching her, water washing over the girl's feet and into the grass.

"Momma!"

———

Water. So much water. The canoe nearly capsizing. She'd daydreamed, forgotten her post. Had forgotten to watch the lake, the road, the sky.

Where were Jack and Cathryn? She scanned the shore. No one. The cottage was boarded up as if for winter. There was a sailboat off toward the big bay, too far to tell if it was Jack's. She clumsily paddled out to look around the point. She took a breath and headed in, pushing along the Maze with increasingly difficult strokes. Clear water beneath the canoe churned to muck.

Jack's cabin was gone, had grown stone legs and retreated. To where? Wherever was too far. Too far to paddle, point after point to navigate. She scanned the north corridors yawning toward her, eddies singing, *Come in, Isobel.*

The tamarack bog? The wind caught hard at the bow and the canoe slipped backward. Every hard stroke only managed to keep the boat stationary. Rain began to fall, first in threads, then in great cutting sheets. She would never find the bog in such rain. Waves set the canoe to pitching, and Isobel moaned when water splashed in over her legs. Rain dammed in the brim of her hat suddenly ran in a gush down her back, a sinister caress. The paddle frosted with heavy mud. She threw it from her and let the canoe drift.

To shiver and drift, lost. For hours.

The canoe bumped against the side of the dock. How? Isobel looked up to see Liam's Buick skid around the corner, mud flying from its tires like brown birds, suspended a moment in air before crashing to the dock. Isobel grabbed for her whistle, but couldn't find it. Struggled out of the canoe. Groped at her soaking dress. Taillights of the car receded, red eyes of a night animal racing backward. Isobel clawed up the rough boards. Five pale buttons cascaded to the water as she tore the whistle from her dress. She held it to her lips and blew. No sound came out. Of course no sound came out.

~   ~   ~

Isobel tried to fill her lungs again, wheezing. Nothing came. No air at all. Her face felt hot, slick. She turned from the dock to face the road and suddenly there was Jack. He placed something over her mouth and she was free to breathe. Relief.

Where have you been I was so worried.

He had done something to her hand. Isobel saw the tip of her middle finger clamped and taped into a glowing thimble. An invention? Isobel smiled and tried to lift her hand. Wonderful, lit from the inside. Trim work will be so much easier with this. As she pulled her hand closer to her face she saw the thimble was connected to a wire. She frowned and looked to Jack to explain. She couldn't sew with a wire dangling like that.

He took her hand and held it up. "Just a thermometer, see?" He tapped the glowing red light and grinned.

Isobel tried to pull away.

Where is Cathryn? Her words made useless steam in the plastic gravy boat over her face. She pulled it away from her mouth.

"Where is she?"

The man frowned. "Who?"

"Where were you that day? Where was your boat?"

"Isobel, where are you?"

"I'm on my way home to get dry. What are you doing here?"

The doctor sighed, his eyes darting to the blinking monitor above Isobel's head. She followed his eye. "It's Dr. Hertz, Isobel. Joel. Do you remember me?"

She scanned the room. *This is not my house.* When she

tried to speak, words stumbled over bare gums and fell back into her throat.

The man took her shoulders and gently leaned her forward. He laid his hand over her bare back and put the stethoscope over a breast. "Breathe."

The man's touch was trained, careful. She obeyed, breathed as she was told, and afterward was gently laid back into her soft pillows. A bed.

She felt the rattle of pebbles burning in her chest. "Why am I so hot?"

"Because you have pneumonia."

"No wonder, out in the rain like that."

"You haven't been out, Isobel. You've been here. It's weeks now. You had a stroke, now you're ill. You've been here all this time."

Isobel touched the stethoscope. In its shining circle of metal she caught a small but clear reflection of herself. She took a sudden, difficult breath, which caught and seared. He adjusted something on the oxygen mask and placed it over her mouth again. Her words were muted, far away even to herself. "Yes, all this time, of course. Pneumonia . . . of course."

Isobel knuckled away a trickle of perspiration pooled at the elastic strap crossing her cheek. *Pneumonia.* The body drowning itself.

"We'll have you better soon. Up and walking."

"Walking? I don't want to walk, I want to go home."

Isobel knew as she spoke that the doctor would misunderstand. She didn't want to go to her apartment, she wanted to go *home.* To see Victor again, sauntering around a corner with a ridiculous paper flower. To sit in a rocking canoe, shielding her eyes from the sun to glimpse lovers strolling on a shore, bending to reach for the same stone. To settle on her work stool and choose something lovely for a brim. To be back in her old garden, washing Louisa's hair under the shade of trees long fallen. To rest.

They gave her a drug to make her sleep, and when she woke her throat burned, but she felt like talking. Thomas's eyes said, *No, Mother, don't, you need to rest.*

But when she began he scraped his chair along the floor to settle closer to the bed. When it was his turn finally to speak, it was almost as if he were thinking aloud. "What could you have been thinking, sitting in that canoe those afternoons?"

Isobel could feel the weight of each word pressing out. "I thought I was doing something noble, but not just for Jack and Cathryn. For the first time I thought about things that mattered in my own life, sorting out what your father meant to me, what kind of mother I was."

Thomas had to crouch forward to make out what she said through the plastic mask, her words echoing in vapor. "I couldn't believe I let Victor take you out there to that island, barely a roof over your heads. You were hardly out of diapers."

"I was almost six." Thomas was whispering now. "It was the best summer of my life."

"It was selfish of me, not to have gone."

"Selfish? That's silly. Besides, we were growing up."

"And away. That was the difficult part. You all seemed so independent of me. I wondered if I'd done all I could. So much of it was automatic, you know, most of motherhood is. All instinct and worry. Rocking and feeding and watching. Holding on until you were strong enough to climb out of my lap, and then . . ."

"Then?"

"Then you were gone. It seemed as soon as you were born you were moving away. It never occurred to me to follow any of you or hold you back. You were good children, bright. Well mannered enough to be let loose in civil company, as your father said."

Thomas laughed.

Isobel sighed. "It's terrible and wonderful to love children so much."

"Ah." Thomas nodded. "Louisa."

Isobel looked at him. "Yes, Louisa. Louisa and you. I knew from birth, something in your eyes."

There was a long pause before Thomas said anything. He looked down. "I suppose I did know that once."

"My two stars . . . poor Henry, I should've loved him more."

A yellow stain of evening pulsed into the room, glinting off the surfaces of the bed, the walker, and the porta-potty in the corner.

"Mother, I hardly remember him."

"But you didn't know him for very long, did you?"

Thomas picked up her hand. "It must be unbearable to lose a child."

"It's amazing. What you can bear."

Then someone else held her hand. She turned to see Louisa's profile, her Mona Lisa smile trained on the ceiling. Moonlight spilled into the narrow space between mother and daughter.

Isobel felt she should give something in return for the visit, but she had so little to offer. She wasn't surprised at seeing Louisa, but she felt unprepared. She couldn't think of a way to apologize for having lived when Louisa hadn't.

"I never made another hat after you'd gone. I closed the shop, couldn't leave Cypress fast enough. The building still stands in town. I'm told there is a bakery there now, *again*. Funny how things circle back.

"When you went out east to school, I thought I'd never see you again. Really, I didn't. And that year you studied in Paris? When all the other girls went to the countryside or Italy or wherever for the summer, *you* came home. . . . I didn't know how to thank you. You helped me keep that business afloat. You could have worked anywhere, but you came back, you *chose* Cypress. Those were good years, remember? You went on that buying trip and came home with sixteen bolts of raw silk and Robert. I remember Thomas walking you down the aisle, so very handsome . . . giving you away to the New Yorker. Everyone called him that, even after you died.

"Thomas should be here. He'd love to see you. He's still the same, too smart and tough as nails, doesn't need anybody. He's been a good uncle to your girls, sees them more than I ever did. I couldn't bear to somehow. They're middle-aged now! One of them made me a great-grandmother the day I turned eighty. I have great-grandchildren in college. I suppose that makes you a grandmother . . . imagine that!"

She could taste the tears. "Oh, my my . . . it's good to see you." She turned in the dim light to see her daughter's serene face give way to a stranger's. Plump, with an indifferent chin, the lapel of Louisa's fine suit folding itself over into a nurse's collar pinned with a red enamel cross.

Isobel eased her hand from the nurse's and reached up to drag the oxygen mask away, her voice hollow even to herself. "Tell Dr. Hertz he can have this thing, and tell him I won't have any tubes up my nose either."

She drifted along familiar passages; her grade school with its mold-green halls, the narrow, many-doored second story of her house in Cypress, hospital corridors throbbing with light, the stacks at the library smelling of wax and the dry pages of thousands of books, the twisting channels of the Maze. As she moved, small images caught her eye; a seed-eyed grackle atop her lunch pail, a door opening onto a child's empty room, her own face peering up from a gurney, books falling to crack their spines on marble floors, an eye-shaped leaf that seemed to stare at her from shore. Though she drifted easily, she couldn't seem to reach her own bed. She couldn't get to it.

Light shifted. The voice was happy. "Look at you! What on earth do you have on your finger there? You look properly silly, trussed up to all these machines." She looked up to see Cathryn halfway through the door, a fistful of flowers under her nose. As she slipped in, her voice was a conspiracy. "Don't look so worried, no one saw me. Look, Izzy, *tulips*. What a morning I've had. Do you know how difficult it is to find tulips in summer? I practically had to go to Holland! Now don't go saying 'you shouldn't have.' You'd do the very same for me and you know it."

She looked very beautiful. Wearing the same summery outfit as the day she first came into the shop, her face flushed as if she'd run.

The flowers were bound. Isobel touched the familiar ribbon.

"You've got to recognize that! It's from those matching tams you made for me and Louisa. I was going through some old box or other and found mine. Moths had at the tam" — she let the ribbon flow over her hand — "but this survived."

Isobel moved her dry lips.

"Now don't say anything, Izzy. I know exactly what you're going to ask."

She was no older or younger. She settled on the bed with a fine weight, and her smooth hand lit on the covers. "Before we get to all that, I want to show you something." She offered her wrists for Isobel to examine, and then raked her skirt high to show her thighs. She pointed to her neck. "Notice anything?"

After a beat her face grew impatient. "The scars, Izzy! My scars are *gone*."

There was movement outside the window. "Don't look. Don't look away. It's just the old street, dusty as ever. Lord, did you ever know such a summer? Remember when we went down to that abandoned quarry to get out of the heat? You saw that itty bitty snake. I never in my life saw anyone move so quickly to get away from something so small." Her laughter ushered a silvery echo. "Whoosh, you scooped up Louisa so fast she didn't know what hit her. A *garter* snake! It might even have been a baby garter snake, hardly bigger than a worm! Didn't you know, Izzy? Didn't you know nothing would harm you?"

Her eyes flickered toward the door, then back to Isobel, her voice urgent. "I'd better go, sweetie. I just wanted to see how you were getting on."

She took a step away but suddenly turned, her smile broad. "I was so dramatic, wasn't I? Nobody ever took themselves as seriously as I did back then. I could be such a complete ass . . . remember that harangue about being an island?" She cleared her throat to recite.

"Sky and clouds shifting above, tides stirring at our hems. Do we ever touch? Or is it merely the air and water we touch that shifts over to others; the ebbing ripples that reach them, diluted and wafting-weak. All our essence intended, but so little of our true selves divulged . . . blah blah."

She laughed. "Horse hockey. Truth is, it all balances out in the end. I found that out. You do get to touch those you're meant to, after all."

The kiss to her brow was warm. "Enough divulged, Izzy. Enough."

Her sleep was dreamless, black. When she woke she was encased in an oxygen tent and propped with pillows into a sitting position. She stared through the plastic for a long time; its crinkled surface warped light and shifted contours. She had imagined it a thousand times. Dying underwater. She raised her stronger hand to touch the plastic.

The IV tube caught stippled light so that it might have been the silk ribbon from the tams she'd made for Cathryn and Louisa. They'd posed for her. While she fiddled with the camera, their heads bent together, and with pointed forefingers sunk in their cheeks, they winked *Poo-poo-pee-doo.*

"Louisa." Isobel's voice echoed around her in the confines of the tent. She closed her eyes.

It had been so cold, the kind of winter night Isobel found eerie for the dry, cloudless skies, silent save the distant reverberations of a world freezing: boughs snapping, stones fissuring, the unearthly gong of lake-ice cracking.

The trilling of car tires skidding on ice.

The lake had opened up, had taken her in. Ice formed quickly again over the car, so that by the time the rescuers reached the lake the next day, they'd had to take axes to the sheet, a jagged oval framing the top of Louisa's green Chrysler. A jade trinket in glass.

She'd died with her eyes open. Looking straight ahead, calmly touching the windshield, as if pointing to something interesting. A chunk of slowly sinking ice. A wavering beige stalk left from summer, its colour sapped away. The ice above was already thickening into a shroud, a wretched weaving of water and cold.

The definition of cold, Isobel read once, was so simple as to seem utterly benign: *the absence of heat.*

Isobel clearly remembered the pattern of the tie the sheriff wore when he came to tell her. Blue with yellow diamonds. She despised him for being out of uniform. His ski jacket was casually unzipped to reveal the polyester tie, a poor choice over his grey work shirt. He looked like his father, who had been the sheriff more than thirty-five years before, the man who hounded her about Jack and Cathryn, and had later come to tell her about Liam Malley.

She'd stood numbly in the doorway, a pair of scissors

dangling from one hand, the other fluttering through the cloud of her breath. The sheriff shuffled in place, stamping his feet on the icy stoop.

Louisa? Not possible. It was a mistake. She had been born with a caul. Everyone knew that was lucky, everyone knew that kept a person safe from drowning. Isobel dropped the scissors.

The young sheriff's hat hung at his side, pinched between two fingers of his glove. He swung it back and forth by its brim. A casual, stupid gesture. "Mrs. Howard, I'm real sorry. I went to school with Louisa, you know."

Isobel stared at him.

"So, then, I guess I'll go tell the New Yorker."

"His name is Robert."

The sheriff looked down at the scissors, wondering if he should pick them up. "Right. Sorry. I s'pose with their girls away at school he'll be wanting them to come home. Well, I'll just go on up to the house and tell him now."

Her sudden fierce clamp on his arm made him wince. She was over seventy if she was a day.

"No you will not." Isobel reached to the peg near the door and grabbed her coat. She stepped outside. "You take me to that lake. Do you hear? You take me out there, then you bring me home. I'll tell Robert."

Why hadn't she insisted Louisa learn to swim when she was young? Why hadn't she begged Victor to teach her?

Isobel's own father had tried to teach her to swim, but she'd been too young. She ignored his coaxing, and when he lost patience, he hoisted her up against his wet stomach and carried her to the public dock. His flesh was soft, and Isobel found herself pulling away from the clammy suction of his vast chest.

A line of boys were launching themselves cannonball fashion from the end of the dock. Her father bounced her up higher on the shelf of his paunch. "See how much fun those boys are having? That's the way. Just jump. Shall we try that?"

She unglued herself from his shoulder to look. The boys' feet pounded the dock, stork knees pumping to meet bony elbows. When they reached the end of the dock, their bodies hurled outward to sail through the air for an untethered moment.

Isobel bit her hand. "Okay."

Before she had a chance to change her mind he started forward. "Just plug your nose when we jump. I promise I won't let go."

But he had. As he trotted down the dock, her father's weight set the boards rumbling, his torso not quite in sync with his stride. As he came down on the last two boards, there was a sharp wooden *crack*, and his foot wedged into jagged raw space.

Isobel flew from his arms, a projectile. Arching backward over the water she saw the reflection of her father's wobbling form, a blunt body with arms windmilling comically. She laughed to see his great mustache twitching, his mouth stretched and contorted.

And then she met the water.

Hadn't she just been laughing and flying? As suddenly she was sinking into blackness. Her arms, so limber in the air, made lazy wingbeats as she descended. Water flooded her nostrils. Instinctively, she kept her eyes open.

She sank to the bottom. The way out. Way out. Where?

The wooden pilings of the dock were cloaked in viscous algae, lime-green tatters waving in the current; the pilings were slick phantoms as she grabbed at them. Toward shore, the legs of wading bathers made a shimmering pale fence.

The instinct to inhale broke her, and as she took in water white pain hammered her chest, her breath a betrayal.

As her toes found the bottom she knew she would have to find purchase in the muck and walk against her pain in the direction of the bathers. She knew at the same time she would never make it. Feeling an abrupt and piercing sadness, she thought of her room back home, her bed with its oft-washed sheets, the soft cotton of her eyelet duvet. Her doll, Amanda, propped ladylike and waiting against the matching pillow. The angle of sun coming through the shutters to wake her on Sunday mornings, her favorite time to be in bed. Cinnamon toast. Now sand in her throat like sugar that wouldn't dissolve. Burning sand.

Leaving.

She closed her eyes against the wavering world.

Sadness backing away now, just as a fierce comet exploded into the water and her eyes opened against her will. A ball of boy unfurled himself before her, scrawny limbs the colour of shells, hair wagging like the algae, streams of bubbles trailing upward from each corner of his mouth like a sea horse's bridle of pearls. He reached for her, fingers digging deep into her armpits. He tried to pull her to the surface. She fought him, making herself solid and willing herself to sink. *Leave me be. I'm on my way.*

Other arms joined his and she closed her eyes to deny them, feeling her feet leaving their slippers of mud.

Coughing and vomiting on the shore, she would never forget her father's breach of faith, or her own brief flight over water.

She knew exactly what it had been like for Louisa, could reconstruct a drowning to the finest detail, if she chose.

If she could take back just one moment it would have been to spare her daughter. Maybe teaching her to swim would have been fruitless. Even if she'd made it out of the car alive, she probably would have frozen to death.

Twenty-five years. Isobel still wanted that night back. Just long enough to walk the long road out of Cypress and lay her body down between the skidding car and lake ice.

~ ~ ~

CHAPTER THIRTEEN

When Thomas walked in, her face was turned to the window and she was reciting something. Her voice was muffled by the plastic tent. He stepped closer.

As she turned, her voice became more clear. *"And woodthrush calling through the fog / My daughter."*

Her eyes were hooded; even through the barrier he could see the sharp bones of her skull.

"That's Eliot, Thomas. You must've read some Eliot in school?"

As she dozed and woke she felt she was opening her eyes as she would open doors. Each door opened to someone waiting. Sometimes it was the nurse she mistook for

Louisa. Other times it was Thomas, the real Thomas, expectant and rigid in the chair.

In these waking moments she could see that her son wanted to communicate somehow, and she was glad for the oxygen tent between them. She had a vague sense of a child troubled, and while she wanted to comfort him, she had nothing to offer; the best she could do was lift her hand and let it drop.

The crinkled plastic fractured every movement beyond, turned every visit into a brief cubist film. Shards of colours stacked, broke apart, stacked again. Figures federated, coalesced into humans only in moments of stillness. The television in the high corner of her room displayed moving jigsaws of Toyota commercials and sitcoms jerking to canned laughter. The evening news tumbled over itself in a somber kaleidoscope. Tom Brokaw's features shifted, blurring to match his drunkard's voice.

Nurses hovered, dipping like great shattered cranes.

~   ~   ~

The sky remained steadfastly empty. No wind, no bugs, no birds, no sounds.

Isobel tugged at the straps of her swimsuit and sat up to watch Louisa and Cathryn from her lawn chair. They had made their way over the hot slope of granite shelf to the shallows, and were stepping along the slippery bottom, arms outstretched like rope walkers'. Louisa only ventured in up to her knees, but Cathryn pleaded, promised safety, and pointed to her shoulders, bending so her hair nearly touched the water while the girl climbed up on her back.

Cathryn spun, suddenly furrowing through the water in a gallop. She sang an old tune, jouncing it breathlessly out along with her pegging motion.

"Pony boy, pony boy. Won't you be my pony boy?"

Louisa giggled. "Auntie Cathryn, I'm a girl!"

Cathryn stopped abruptly. "Oops. So you are. Okay, then." She pivoted in the other direction and galloped faster.

"*Pony girl, pony girl. Won't you be my pony girl? Carry me, carry me, right across the sea . . . Ooooh!*"

A plowing of water, and they disappeared under their own wave.

Isobel's heart skipped. She stood.

Louisa rose first, coughing water and blinking. Cathryn's head popped up, her hair pasted to her forehead. She screamed with laughter. "It's so coooold!"

Cathryn called to the shore. "Izzy, how can the water be so cold with this heat?"

Louisa dunked down again to her shoulders. "Cold!" She shot up into the air. "Hot!" Cathryn struggled up and joined the girl. They rose and fell out of sync, holding hands, red and yellow swimsuits like pistons in the water, "Hot! Cold! Hot! Cold! Hot cold hotcoldhotcoldhotcold!"

~ ~ ~

Underneath his coat he wore the plaid shirt again.

"Jack, what did you do with her?"

He bent low. "Isobel, did you say something?"

She peered through the tent, tried to piece together the shifting view. Hot. I'm hot.

The doctor cocked his head.

She looked at him. Hadn't she spoken?

Thomas suddenly stepped out from behind the doctor. Or was he next to him?

His face was creased in concern, and as he leaned down she could see his features waver beyond the membrane of the tent. She licked her lips and this time could hear her own voice whispering, "Cathryn came to see me."

Thomas shook his head.

She nodded; at least she meant to nod. Her muscles did her bidding less and less often. "Louisa too. She was here."

"Mother."

The doctor was patting Thomas on the shoulder. Then he moved away, a white-coated mannequin rattling his limbs out the door.

Thomas lifted the corner of the tent so he could slip his hand under. He cleared his throat. "I came yesterday, but you were asleep all day."

Her mouth tasted milk-stale. "What's the temperature?"

He lifted his glasses and glanced at the monitor connecting the thimble to her finger. "A hundred flat. Much better."

"Not mine. Outside. What's it like outside?"

Thomas shrugged. "Ninety. Too hot for September. Maybe ninety-two. Dripping."

Isobel squinted at the fractured sunlight. "That's right. It was so warm we went wading, at least Louisa and Cathryn did. I only watched from the shore."

"Rest, Momma."

With an effort she turned her head. "All I do is rest. May I have some water?"

The air in the tent smelled of foul breath and eucalyptus. Thomas grimaced as he handed her the glass.

Getting the water down required a swallow that burned the back of her neck. She imagined gulping ground glass, she imagined her spine drying, the disks turning to chalk. She managed to twist her face into a smile for Thomas.

He thumbed something in his vest pocket. After a moment he cleared his throat.

"Mother, was she older than you or younger?"

"Who?" Isobel turned to peer through the tent, her son's expression warped by the plastic.

"Cathryn."

"She was younger by a year. Why?"

Thomas shrugged. "Just wondering."

She was tiring; he had to lean close to hear. "We were a year apart. Her birthday was the day after mine."

"Do you recall, by any chance, her maiden name?"

"Is this some test?"

Thomas grinned. He could have been Victor sitting there, up to something.

She blinked slowly, so slowly he feared she was falling asleep but then she said in a high voice, "Yes. I remember."

A charred image flickered over Isobel's closed eyelids: one of Cathryn's burned traveling trunks, its monogram blistered but still legible. *CLM.*

"Leigh. That was her maiden name. Cathryn Leigh Malley."

When she opened her eyes, Thomas was slipping a pen and a small notebook into his vest.

~ ~ ~

Although she had promised she would, Isobel didn't go to Granite Point that day. She dried her hair, wishing she'd never remembered the dream. She marched Louisa to the shop, pulling the girl along for several blocks until Louisa twisted from her grasp and dropped to a shady patch in a stubborn heap. She rubbed her shoulder.

"Momma, you're pulling me too hard!"

There was a sheen of sweat on Isobel's brow, and she wiped it away with the back of her hand. She fought her exasperation and crouched at Louisa's side.

"Was I pulling? I'm sorry, sweetie." Isobel fanned herself. "Good Lord, it's warm."

"Momma, why are you so angry?"

"Angry? Oh, Louisa, I'm not. It's just that I'm so hot and, oh, I don't know . . ."

"Upset?"

Isobel looked through the shade toward the lake, a span of sheer glare in the distance. She wondered what Cathryn and Jack would do when noon came and she wasn't there to sit sentinel. Would they see each other anyway? Would they risk it? She hoped they had enough sense to stay away from each other.

She was tired of worrying for them. Like children, they seemed to have little sense of their own danger.

Louisa tugged her sleeve. "Momma, are you? Upset?"

"I suppose I am. But not with you." Isobel helped Louisa to her feet, using a name she hadn't since the girl was a toddler. "C'mon, Lulu. I'll make us some iced tea when we get to the shop."

Isobel lagged behind while Louisa hopped from crack to crack in the sidewalk, leaving impressions from her rubber-soled sandals in the narrow ridges of softened tar.

"Hey, there, what about your mother's back?"

"Oops. Sorry, Momma."

Merchants loitered outside their empty stores under the cover of deep awnings. Some fanned themselves with newspapers. A few customers drifted slowly along, sagging with their net bags and parcels. Isobel nodded to them. The sidewalk heat made its way through the soles of her shoes. Turning the key in the lock, she stopped to look the length of the street. She had the vague feeling of being examined.

The shop was stifling, even with the shades drawn. She worked through lunch, her mouth set. She had to wipe her hands continually to avoid getting sweat on the cap she was trimming. The room was still, save the occasional scratch from Louisa's pencil, the flutter of paper, the constant *chik chik* of the overhead fan, her own exhalations.

"Momma, can I go home? It's cooler there."

"No. Go out to the alley and run cold water on your

feet. Or go over to the butcher's and ask Mrs. Sima for some ice chips."

"But Momma, why can't I go home?"

"Because I want you here."

"Why? It's boiling! Why do I have to stay here?"

Isobel tugged too hard on her needle and the thread snapped. She slammed her fist on the table. "Because!"

Louisa fell asleep on the floor. The chain of the ceiling fan made a slow pirouette, and Isobel wondered if the room would be more comfortable with it turned off. Heat rises, she reasoned. The warm air seemed only to be pushed back down on them, heavy as a damp hand.

The sky had begun to thicken with dark clouds. She raised the shades and opened the front windows in hope of a breeze. But the air was still and mournful, the street deserted. The drone of cicadas joined the dull stutter of the crushers at the mine.

She'd hoped Cathryn would come in. They needed to talk. She sat in such a fixed torpor that it didn't occur to her that the ache in her back was from the edge of shelf she'd been leaning against for the past hour. The hue of grey outside deepened under the hood of clouds. Perhaps the weather was keeping Cathryn in; perhaps she didn't dare ride her bicycle under skies that promised lightning.

She knew what she needed to say now. Too much had gone unsaid.

She could drive out to Granite Point, she supposed, but she'd hate to take Louisa, could hardly leave the girl to wake up alone in a storm. Just the thought of starting the car and sitting on hot leather seats made her tired.

When the chimes above the door sounded, Isobel was so startled she nearly cried out. Doug Green, the mail-boat operator, stuck his head in, but she didn't rise to greet him, waving him in instead. He was drenched in sweat and moved slowly as he handed her the note, dimpled between his thick fingers. "Got a message here from Victor, Miz Howard."

She eased open the damp envelope. The note said only
The boys all home Thursday!

Isobel took in a breath and looked at the wall calendar.

"It can't be." Isobel shook her head and Doug tipped his cap.

"Yes, ma'am. I bet you're anxious, huh?"

A flash of heat lightning suddenly froze the room in a blaze of silver. A quarter minute passed before thunder rumbled in the distance. She looked outside, waiting for the next strike. When she turned again, Doug was backing out the door with a half wave.

CHAPTER FOURTEEN

~ ~ ~

Through the afternoon, lightning illuminated the room's farthest corners in jagged flashes.

"One-thousand-one, one-thousand-two, one-thousand-three . . ." A staccato clap of thunder shook the building. The storm was three miles away. Or was it? Isobel tried to remember: did you simply count, or did you count and then divide the total in some mathematical formula? Turning on a small lamp, she sat down on the floor and watched Louisa sleep. So much lightning. She leaned against the felt bolts on the floor and played with her daughter's hair, curling it into damp loops over her cheek, dabbing perspiration from the girl's skin with the hem of her skirt. A brilliant flash rendered Louisa's flesh white, the blond cowlick tracing an ephemeral confluence down her neck.

Lightning and racking thunder lit and shuddered the windows, but oddly, no rain came. The waiting between the flashes and roars reminded her of childbirth — the bracing, droning tightness before the spasm, the release and ominous stillness bringing the brief arc of relief before it began again. She lost track of the time as she waited for the first drops. Then the clock tower chimed.

Four . . . five . . . six.

As the last chime died away a new sound emerged, a distant whine like a swarm of mosquitoes. The sound grew, revealing itself as a far-off siren, and Isobel sat up. Acrid air from the open window seized halfway down her throat.

The wailing wove around and over itself until it broke into two distinct sirens, two fire engines. As they rumbled into town Isobel watched their revolving lights hurl crimson over the storefronts and awnings. Louisa slept on, but when the trucks bore closer she tossed restlessly as if trapped in a dream. The building trembled, loosening shards of ambered varnish to rain from the ceiling and settle among shelves and floorboards.

Isobel looked over the sill to see three green forest service trucks fall in behind the fire engines; a dozen men weighted with water packs clung to the sides. She strained to recognize Jack among them. As the cortege veered and skidded, men swayed out and away from the vehicles, the water on their backs threatening to yank them from their moorings. When she stood she saw the trucks turn at the narrow road at the edge of town.

The road to Granite Point.

Isobel blinked and slid back to the floor, sitting very still until the sirens died away. Urgent footfalls met the pavement, and distant shouts were drowned in the bursts of car engines firing. Louisa moaned in her sleep, and Isobel crawled to gather the girl in her arms and rock her.

She looked at the pattern of the pressed ceiling. To still

her mind she began to count the sections. Rocking, she counted twenty across the breadth of the shop and then started on the length, counting as far back into the room as she could see, until sections fused in shadow.

An erratic wind rose, and when the door flew inward the rope of chimes hit the wall in sudden violence and windows rattled. Through the open door she saw the street, scraps of paper sailing along in a dusty regatta. She was about to get up and close the door when she heard a footfall.

She stiffened and turned away as someone stepped in. A heavy footstep. Isobel peered up, and ducked back when she saw it was Liam Malley. He was scanning the room, taking in its empty corners. He began backing out the door, but slowly, as if doubtful, as if sensing a presence. Crouching, Isobel scooted into the bolts of fabric, dragging Louisa with her. Her elbow caught on the electrical cord and the small lamp on the counter hit the floor.

Liam spun.

The lamp rolled, sending a weird sway of yellow over both their faces.

Louisa woke at the noise and began to cry when she saw the man's ash-streaked face. Liam strode to where they huddled. Isobel gripped the girl.

He towered over them, his voice barely controlled. "Where is she?"

Isobel lifted Louisa from her lap and set her into the bolts under the table. She looked at Liam and tried to control the tremble in her voice. "I don't know. She's not at the cottage?"

"The cottage is gone. So are half the woods on the south shore." When he crouched down next to Isobel she could smell the fire on him. His voice was hoarse with smoke. "So is Jack Reese's cabin."

Isobel bit the inside of her cheek. A copper pool collected on her tongue. They looked at each other until Isobel blinked. "Gone. You mean burned?"

"To the ground. Where is she?"

"I don't know. I . . . where can she be?"

"That's what I'm asking you, Mrs. Howard."

"I said I don't know."

He pulled her up by her elbow, dropping her arm the instant she was on her feet, as if touching her was unpleasant. The tone of his voice made Isobel cringe.

"Where is my wife?"

"I do not know."

"You" — he was shaking — "are the only person she would have told. I will ask you one more time. *Please . . .*" His soot-blackened hands curled and uncurled into fists. "Will you tell me where my wife is?"

"And I will tell you again, Mr. Malley." She knew he was misreading the waver in her voice as a lie, her growing panic pleating every utterance. "I have no idea."

He raised his fists and a cry tore from him as his arm swept the counter clear. A mug of pencils hit the wall and shattered, account books tumbled open and grazed the chair like drunken gulls. The heavy adding machine pounded to the floor last, its thud followed by a metallic *ching* as keys struck, the machine ejecting a curled tongue of paper. They watched dumbly until the paper worked its way out and the machine ticked to a stop.

Liam spoke with barely strained patience. "Can you guess?"

She tried. She could only picture them at Cathryn's cottage or at Jack's. All places beyond those charred points were voids, her imagination remained unyielding. Her sigh was an apology.

"No, I can't."

Liam's posture suddenly went slack, the anger draining from his face, a grey mask of exhaustion filling in.

The rain began to fall, thrumming the tin roof over the entrance like hoofbeats. Louisa had stopped crying and was hugging her knees, staring from her mother to the man.

There was a pause in which all three seemed to be casually listening to the rain. The stale air in the shop shifted as smells of wetness and burnt timber blew in the open door, heat ebbing under the strong wind.

Liam rubbed his face thoughtfully, as though to check the growth of his stubble. He whispered, "Mrs. Howard. *Isobel.* There are things you don't know about Cathryn. She suffers periods of blackness. There are weeks when she cannot rise from her bed. The doctors have tried to explain these episodes to me, but the plain fact is that you and I — healthy people — can never understand what it is like to live with her particular anguish." He looked into Isobel's eyes, his fingertips darting over his temple. "She told me once that on her bad days she feels she's being held under the surface of a cold ocean, a bottomless, soulless place." His hand paused to cup his chin, as if to support the weight of his head, and he looked away, out the window, through the rain.

"Jaysus. I always knew it would end. But this. *This.*"

Isobel inched closer to Liam, touched his arm. She opened her mouth to speak, but her tongue was thick. Liam saw her struggle and felt for her hand to cover it with his own.

"Isobel. Jack Reese can't help her like I can. He can't know how. You see, Cathryn denies her illness even to herself. She needs . . . she needs to be taken care of."

Isobel's voice was a dry whisper. "But if . . . if you find Jack Reese, you'll find her."

Liam grunted. "And where might I find him? In the ashes of his bloody cabin? I don't think so, though it'd serve the bastard right. His boat's gone too, y'see." Liam shook his head. "In the morning, when the fires are out, they will search the cottages. They'll probably try dragging the lake, but I'll wager Jack Reese will never be found. I've even gone into the Maze, past his place and into the bogs, but there's no sign of them there." Liam moved away from her, reached down, and meticulously brushed the knees of his pants with his large hands. "No sign."

Soot and pine needles drifted to the floor. Isobel stared at his pant legs and crouched down to pluck a burr from the floor.

He straightened. "I love her, you know." He stepped away. "Loved her."

"I'm sure she loves you too."

He scowled. "You know nothing of us," he said, speaking to the window. His tone was acid. "I dread leaving her in the morning and I dread coming home at night. I can't read her moods anymore; you'd think it would be the opposite, by now. This many years. I don't know when I can make love to her, or when she might scream for me to leave our bed. I don't know when it's safe to leave her alone. You've seen the scars?" He reached up to his collar. "The one she calls her 'surgery'? She tried cutting her own throat. I was only out for fifteen minutes, gone out for milk. She said she wanted a milkshake." He inhaled. "You cannot conceive how much floor a few pints of blood can cover. The bottle fell from my hands, and then there was the milk mixed in. Glass everywhere . . . her head on the edge of the tub, just resting, like. She could have been sleeping there, her neck dripping, dripping . . . the whole floor grown pink with milk and the blood. Rivers of it between the tiles."

Isobel leaned onto the counter.

Liam straightened. "There've been other times, you can guess."

Isobel closed her eyes to the ridge on Cathryn's wrist.

She'd claimed she'd been caught on a barbed wire fence as a child. When she and Louisa had played at the shore, Isobel had noticed the strangely uniform white hatches on her thighs just below the hem of her swimsuit. Cathryn cheerfully dismissed them as ancient. "Oh, some old bicycle crash or fall."

She shook herself as if waking when Liam spoke.

"I wish you hadn't taught her how to drive." There was no recrimination in his voice, only exhaustion.

"We've got to find her."

"No." He touched the doorknob, studying it as though he'd never seen one. "*I've* got to find her." The door opened. "The sheriff will be by. He'll have questions."

Isobel nodded.

At the door she watched him walk toward the road to Granite Point. Halfway down the block he paused, pulled up the collar of his jacket against the rain, and turned slowly on his heel to set off in another direction.

She sat down hard on the floor, still nodding, the motion uncontrollable.

Louisa crawled out from her nest of bolts to touch her mother's shoulders. She rested her cheek next to Isobel's and whispered, "Momma, you're bleeding."

Isobel looked down. A thin trickle staining her dress at the knee. She opened her clenched fist to see the burr from Liam's trousers crushed into her palm.

"So I am."

"Momma, let's go home."

They walked in darkness, Isobel unaware of the rain until it suddenly stopped. She looked up in surprise. Inside, she dried Louisa's hair and helped her into her pajamas. She tucked the girl into Victor's and her bed. She negotiated the hallways by weak light. Out the bathroom window she saw the storm moving off, lids of clouds sliding away to expose stars. She ran water into the tub, tempering its chill with a kettleful from the stove, then stripped off her wet dress, and stepped into the bath. In the darkness she examined the bar of soap in her hand; it was colourless, as was the towel she had laid on the floor. The robe she'd draped over the chair, brilliant in daylight with red-and-gold dragons, was indistinct and dull. The room and all its furnishings became a monochrome of dead greys. She imagined blood on tiles; a horrible pool.

Cathryn owned a book of paintings that held both colour and black-and-white plates. The black-and-white reproductions had the same oatmeal texture as the bathroom at midnight, condensing all shades into points of dark and light. Isobel remembered the name of the painter, *Cezanne*.

She closed her eyes and tried to imagine the voice of Cathryn's illness, her haunting blackness. Did the greyness and darkness of Cezanne's shifting dots represent the bleak periods Cathryn endured, her episodes? The book had a few colour plates scattered throughout, as joyous as the others were bleak. Did those rich colour renderings paint her high and energetic periods?

Isobel wondered where the book was now. At the shop? In the ash of Granite Point?

She wrung the sponge over her face. *Why didn't she tell me?*

She didn't have to. From the very first day there was something just off in the light of Cathryn's eye, beautiful but damaged, a chipped prism.

Padding along the hall and down the stairs, Isobel tried to concentrate on her footing, feeling the polished wood with the balls of her clean feet. As if putting her flesh to something solid might keep her from drifting, each step an anchor to keep herself from floating away. She could nearly make out the grain of the risers with her toes.

She turned off the lights. She locked the back door and

made her way to the front hall, stopping suddenly in the foyer to look through the small window in the door. Storm clouds moved briskly over the face of the moon. The air was tinged with a dirty orange light. The moon glowed and then disappeared altogether as more clouds swept over.

Was Cathryn at the mercy of her mind in the same way as the moon had no control over what obscured its face?

Isobel steadied herself by putting her back to the door. What was she doing? Walking through her house, locking doors. She slid to the floor and tipped the weight of her head into her hands.

The next morning Isobel walked to the shop. Louisa trailed a few steps behind. The scene they encountered after turning onto Main Street jarred them. A search party of bedraggled men had gathered outside Jem's Diner, their trousers and boots blackened and wet from walking the charred woods. They drank from dented thermoses and bent their heads in consultation with the fresh crews going out. The new recruits appeared anxious to move on, shuffling in place like restrained horses. Spent men drooped against parked trucks; Isobel recognized a few as miners, but most wore forest service uniforms.

Two men who had been braced against a wall straightened when they saw Isobel approach. Their eyes were expectant, as if she might address them, give them something, a word, some clue. She reached for Louisa's hand and kept walking. One man stepped forward to stand in her path. She did not slow her pace, and as she walked toward him she stared defiantly at his questioning face. She had no answers for him. She had none for herself. When she was upon him he turned from her gaze and stepped away, suddenly examining the smoke curling from his cigarette.

New crews put sandwiches and bottles of lemonade into their packs. At a signal, they hoisted their gear in unison and adjusted the weight of their loads. One man balanced a long bundle of dowels and canvas over his shoulder. Isobel swallowed. A stretcher.

They walked to the edge of the town, where they spread to form a line. Isobel stood motionless as, one after another, the men dropped from the road to the ditch and then scrambled up the opposite side into a thicket of birch.

Louisa tugged at her arm and pointed to the window of Jem's Diner. Isobel turned to see two dozen faces crowding the window, looking out at her. As she met their stares, some turned away, went back to their tables or to the counter, but others continued to gaze.

The smell of fire clung to the evaporating dew, and the air was vague with drifting ash. The flag at the post office was grey with it, hanging limply from its pole. Several merchants had swept up whatever had settled on their stoops overnight. A few had even washed their windows, and they gleamed to reflect the scene in the street. The mercantile had enameled wheelbarrows parked out on the sidewalk, and a neat line of pitchforks leaned against the brick.

As if nothing had happened. As if it were just another day. Isobel unlocked her door and walked in, her exhalation jagged in the silence. As if it matters they sell a rake or a can of paint. Her footsteps echoed on the bare floors. Louisa squeezed past to put the kettle on for tea. Isobel locked the door and walked to the large front windows, yanking down each canvas shade. She surveyed the mess at the base of the counter. When she picked up the adding machine, its crank snapped away in her hand. She put it in the trash and gathered up the strewn account books. She swept the pieces of broken coffee mug and plucked up scattered pencils.

Louisa left a cup of tea for her on the counter. The girl found her sketch pad and settled back among the bolts of fabric where she had taken refuge the night before.

"Louisa, what are you doing? Come out from there."

"But won't that scary man come back?"

"Mr. Malley?" Isobel crouched down to look into her daughter's face. "I don't think so, sweetheart. Besides, he's not scary, he's just sad."

"He won't hurt us?"

"Of course not, he won't hurt anybody."

"How can we be sure?"

Isobel gently pulled her daughter into her arms. "Listen, Lulu. You're safe with me. Always. Now stand up. I've got a chore for you." She put the girl to work tagging and rolling bolts. "Start with the smallest number, pull the bolts, reroll them, and arrange them all in a row. Can you do that?"

"I think so."

She looked to the corner where Cathryn kept her things: a paintbox and a slender folding easel, a stack of books on a chair, the gramophone records in their wine-coloured cases. Leaning against the chair was the scuffed satchel Cathryn always seemed to be lugging around.

"Louisa?"

"It's going to take me a long time, Momma."

"It will, but you'll do a fine job, sweetheart." Isobel picked up the satchel. "Listen, Momma has to do some work in the back for a while, all right?"

She walked the length of the storage hall, beads of light glinting off brass Cathryn had polished. Sitting cross-legged on the floor, she lifted the satchel to her lap. She examined its tiny keyhole and lock. There were small sewing machine tools and curved darning needles she might try to pick the lock with. She could do it. But when she tested the clasp with her thumbnail, the latch sprang with a sharp click, startling her.

Cathryn hadn't locked it.

Her hopes fell. If it wasn't locked, it couldn't hold much in the way of clues. She took a breath and opened the satchel. Reaching in, she took out the items one by one and placed them around her. A bottle of Evening in Paris, two polished round stones, a handkerchief with Cathryn's initials embroidered in spidery floss, two brown envelopes with Cathryn's name written in a hand Isobel did not recognize, a small, leather-covered notebook, and a loose receipt.

One of the envelopes held two small cardinal feathers, one brilliant, the other the duller hue of the female. The other envelope held the thinnest layer of birch bark, nearly translucent. It had been intricately folded and patterned, then unfolded and smoothed flat. She recognized it as an Ojibwa pattern for beadwork. The designs were made not with tools, but with the gentle indentations of human teeth. Isobel had once seen these being made when she was a girl, the folded arrows of chalky bark slipping in and out of the squaws' lips, the women measuring and spacing their bites with little more than the rhythms of some ancient chant, as if singing the designs. Isobel held the bark to the light to expose its floral pattern. She had never known the proper name for the craft, but had assigned it one with her childhood vocabulary: *mouth lace.*

She laid aside the birch bark and feathers and picked up the receipt. American Custom Box. The receipt was stapled to a card with the outlined silhouette Isobel recognized as the one from her own hatboxes. It read:

```
SPECIAL ORDER
12 dozen rib-band 18-inch round,
   stripe/gold braid
Customer to provide artwork — to be
   returned
Custom embossing of silhouette 175.00
Raw boxes 75.00
   Total 250.00
```

She gasped at the amount and lifted the card to examine the black-ink silhouette Cathryn had drawn.

How could she not have noticed before? It was her own profile, unmistakable. Cathryn had taken the liberty of sweeping her hair to a style more elegant than Isobel would normally have worn, but the face and neck were definitely her own, the sloping brow, the evenness of the nose, the narrow upper lip.

She could not cry now, there was no time.

Isobel tucked the artwork and receipt back into the satchel and picked up the last item, a slim leather journal with lined pages, about half of them filled in with Cathryn's small handwriting. Alternate pages were adorned with small designs and sketches.

The first pages described Cathryn's arrival in Cypress. As Isobel read, she detected a petulant quality in the writing, as if Cathryn had come to Cypress grudgingly.

> *The best thing about this strange house, Granite Point, is that it is away from prying eyes. I'm glad Liam didn't rent a place in town, but why couldn't he have let me stay home in Oak Park?*

Some passages were barely structured, muddled with Cathryn's random musings and snatches of unfinished thoughts. Nonsense. On these pages the pen had been pressed harshly, letters nearly cut through. Here and there lines were crudely inked out.

The writing in the middle section of the journal was more lucid. A very sweet description of Louisa and some cursory notes on the visual highlights of the town, along with a list of sites to consider painting: the old teepee out at Chalmer's Point, an abandoned fishing shack near the boat landing, a Finnish farmstead south of town. The next two pages were missing, followed by a section briefly describing Isobel.

The charming milliner with magic hands, who cannot sing to save her life, but can do nearly anything else. I envy her capable ways, her naive heart.

There was nothing about Jack except one cryptic passage.

Today I nearly died. Should have been killed. I woke up in one place, and now I go to sleep in a different world, another place altogether.

All pages beyond this passage had been torn out.

Isobel let the book fall to her lap. It offered no clue as to where they might be now. There was nothing to tell the sheriff when he came. Nothing to offer Liam.

Sighing, she rested her head against the cupboards. She should find something for Louisa to eat. She'd not made any breakfast, couldn't think of food. She idly turned the book in her hands.

She noticed the back cover was slightly thicker than the front. She pressed it and felt a bubble of something under the leather. When she ran a thumbnail along the edge, it came easily unglued, to reveal thin stationery. She peeled back the flap to expose a letter. She carefully eased it out and unfolded the page. It was penned by the same hand that had written *Cathryn* on the envelopes containing the feathers and birch bark.

Jack's hand.

Isobel took a deep breath as she smoothed the letter flat on the floor.

A typical love letter, flowery, almost embarrassing. *My dearest, Until a month ago my life was ordained to be common, though I sought splendor it eluded me . . .* She scanned down the page.

. . . A fate can change in an instant, as mine did when our two fates became one.

It all happened so fast, yet in my mind that moment was slow and fluid as a dream. I'd rounded the curve, driving too fast, I knew that much. And there you were. The sight of you burned itself into me. I see it still, the scene outlined in surreal colour. The red of your bicycle, your pale hands, the impossible green of trees behind you. I noticed your posture, the fact that your face was flushed, a strand of hair along the edge of your cheek, caught there by perspiration. I remember being surprised at that detail, so fine. Your blue skirt had dust caked on the hem, a pattern of low hills. Your lips were slightly parted, and I marveled that your expression was not one of terror, quite simply, you looked as if you had misplaced something and were about to become annoyed. Your eyes though said something different. They were the eyes of a woman about to die. But when they looked into mine I saw — of all things — pity.

You would be killed, of that I had no doubt, but more, I understood I was looking into the eyes of my fate. The truck would strike you, there was nothing I could do about that. My plan formed in a fraction of a fraction of a second. After you were struck I would press my foot to the gas, deliberately turn the wheel of the truck, and drive over the cliff to my own death. My only regret was that we would die separately, you broken and alone on the road, and me down among rocks and scrub pine. I wanted our death bloods to mingle, hated that our ends would not be simultaneous, that you would precede me, if only by an instant.

But the truck stopped. I've gone over it in my mind a hundred times and I can find no logical reason why a two-ton vehicle on a slope of gravel would come to stop so suddenly. It's inexplicable. Intervention? Re-

prieve? I wonder what else we will escape? I no longer question fate.

In Delirium Amorus.

Jack

Isobel shivered at his Latin closing. At the bottom of the letter there was a line added in Cathryn's handwriting. *What else can I be, in the face of such revelations, but powerless? Willing. To go anywhere with you. Anywhere.*

Isobel reread the letter. "No." She spoke aloud, her voice echoing in the emptiness of the hall. "It's not enough. It proves nothing." She placed the letter back in its hiding place, pressed the glued edge back.

"Nothing."

She hid the satchel in the farthest cupboard.

~ ~ ~

CHAPTER FIFTEEN

"Did you believe she was powerless, as she claimed?"

Isobel grew thoughtful. After a moment she turned to her son. "I saw a television program once, I think it was during the Vietnam War, some panel discussion. Four famous and respected men were asked for their personal definitions of power. The writer said, 'Beauty,' the general said, 'Fearlessness,' the rabbi said, 'Madness,' and the businessman said, 'Money.' Does that answer your question?"

"I suppose it does."

"Jack and Cathryn left me something that summer, something that to this day I cannot define. It was a different view, an awareness that life was bigger. It seemed they left open some portal — perhaps the very one they escaped through — and I was left with this open gap where a wind carrying all the racket and texture of life came rushing back at me."

Thomas rolled his pen back and forth over the surface of Isobel's bedside table.

"I couldn't ignore much of anything after that. Life grew bigger after them, at least it seemed so."

He opened his mouth to ask a question, but she drifted on. "In a lot of ways things were easier before them. I didn't have so much to think about."

Isobel tapped her temple. "Memory. Stubborn contraption, isn't it? Most of what I try to remember now is a blur. I have to scrape for the simplest things — a telephone number, whether or not I've taken my pills, the name of a street I've walked a thousand times. But some memories come racing from nowhere of their own accord — those are like visitations. Clear as glass, more detailed as I grow older. Isn't that strange?" Her voice was out of sync, as if the oxygen tent delayed her words.

Thomas whispered, "Not so strange, I expect."

"I can remember every nuance, every angle of light at certain moments. The sudden rising of mist on the lake after a storm, the feel of your father's palm against my ankle while I stood on that old Ford. That time you fell from the big maple out back! I thought you'd broken your neck." She wheezed, and reached under the plastic to touch his elbow where the pin had been set. "I was in the kitchen when I heard you scream. I can remember the sound of my feet pounding the porch floor, the blades of grass you lay on, the fact that the clover near your head was blooming and the flower matched the white of your face. I was afraid to touch you. I dropped down to lay my ear over your heart, but just then you opened your eyes and looked at me — and I remember this so clearly — you said, 'It's beating fine, Momma, don't worry. It's not my heart that's busted, but you should take a look at my arm.'"

Thomas grinned. "Snapped like a twig. Do you remember the blue sling you sewed to match my scout uniform?"

Isobel frowned. "You were never a scout. That was Henry."

"Yes, I . . ." Thomas cocked his head, paused. "Never mind."

"Thomas, have you been here all day?"

"No. Not all day. I was working this morning."

"But I thought you retired."

"I did. Last Friday."

"Oh, your party. How was it?"

"Embarrassing."

"Oh, yes, the whatzit? Karaoke? Did they make you sing karaoke?"

Thomas picked up his pen and let it dangle between his fingers like Sinatra's cigarette. "Wanna hear a few bars?" He plucked an imaginary microphone from the air and began to sing into it. *"I'm gonna waaaake up . . . in a city that ne-ver sleeps . . ."*

"Enough." Isobel's weak laugh turned into a racking cough. "You're every bit as gifted as me." She gave in to the weight of her head and sank into her pillow.

"The proud mother." Thomas poked the plastic. "You should sleep."

"Where are you going?"

"I have a few errands." Thomas bent over the railing. "That reminds me. I won't be here tomorrow. I have to go out of town for the day."

"Where?"

He reached into the tent to tuck her blanket back up over her sharp collarbone. "Only Chicago, in and out. I'll be back tomorrow night."

She grasped his fingers, suddenly anxious. "Tomorrow night?"

"It's okay." He pulled his hand away gently. "Just a day trip."

She sighed heavily. "All right. I'll wait."

"Wait?" He looked at her, but she turned and didn't answer. He stepped to the door.

"Goodnight, Momma."

~   ~   ~

At four o'clock the sheriff came. He sank into a chair, took off his hat, and wiped his brow with a grimy forearm. Isobel offered him a glass of cold water, which he drained in loud gulps.

"Mrs. Howard, I got two crews out there searching now, and forest service got another two truckfuls coming up from Duluth." He looked her in the eye and hitched his shoulders. "I know you've nothin' to do with this mess yourself, Mrs. H, but folks think you might know something, since you're so friendly with Cathryn Malley."

Isobel swallowed. "My being friends with her doesn't mean I know where she is."

"Malley was here yesterday, wasn't he?"

"Well, yes, but only for a few minutes."

"What did he want?"

"He was looking for Cathryn, of course."

"No one's seen him since yesterday, no sign of his car. Nobody up at the mine's seen him neither." The sheriff looked intently at his empty water glass. "There's some think Liam Malley knows something, or maybe even did something."

"Did something? Did what?"

"Maybe something bad, like killed his wife and killed Jack Reese too. What do you think of that?"

"That's ridiculous." Isobel folded her arms tight against her chest. "He's killed no one."

"You seem awfully sure. Just how come you're so certain?" The sheriff stood, came too near to her, and rested his hand on the wall above her head. The smell of spent cigarettes and sweat made her stomach pitch.

"I'm certain . . ." She faltered. "I'm certain because I know Mr. Malley had only concern for his wife."

"Had?"

"Has."

"Well, I don't know much about Mr. Malley's personal relations with his wife, 'cept of course that she was whoring round behind his back."

She glared. *"Whoring?"*

He nodded. "Y'see? I do know somethin' 'bout what's between Reese and Mrs. Malley, or what *was*. That's the one thing I know." He mopped at his neck with a stained kerchief. "The other thing I'm certain of is that you're about the only person who was onto what they were up to. Their plan, so to speak. Now I'm gonna ask you one simple question, and all I want is one word. You got any idea where Jack Reese and Cathryn Malley might be right now?"

Isobel saw Louisa staring at them from the corner, hands behind her back. The child was pressed against the window as if trying to become part of it.

Isobel shook her head; she was able to look him in the eye. Her answer was a low whisper. "No."

"No idea? Not even a theory?"

"Sheriff Graham, you've been watching too many detective films."

He sneered. "No cause to be snotty. Well then, let me offer a few of my own theories, see if any of these sound plausible to you." He tapped his nostril. "How 'bout they might have run off together?"

"You want me to answer that? Because I can't."

"His boat's missing."

"Yes?"

"You don't think that's significant?"

She stared at him.

"Okay, try this one on. Drowned?"

She shrugged. "They were both fine swimmers."

"Lost in the woods?"

"Jack? Lost?" She shook her head as if he were pitifully stupid.

"So, you have thought about this. Maybe they're both dead. Maybe they could be . . . ah . . . suicides?"

She dipped away from him, slipping out under his arm to get the counter between them. For a second she thought he might reach across and grab her, pull her back, and force her to look at him. The tears she'd been fighting all morning ran freely down her face.

"They could be any of those things, I suppose."

He grunted. "Or none."

"That's right. Or none." She would not reach up to wipe her face. She would not let him see her struggle.

"You understand what 'aid and abet' means? You understand that's a crime?"

She glared at him.

"I could've hauled you down to the station, you know. I could've questioned you there. As a favor to Victor, I didn't." He turned. "Mrs. Howard, if you hear from any of them, you call me, understand? If your memory happens to shake anything loose, you call me."

After locking the door she went into the bathroom and vomited. When Louisa stuck her head in the door, Isobel was washing her face.

"Momma. It's time to go home. Please, can we?"

Stepping out of the shop, Isobel felt eyes on her, stabbing, and shifting away just as suddenly. She kept her head down the length of Main Street, walking at a clip, Louisa skipping alongside to keep up.

There were more people, crowds now. Volunteers had filtered into town, strange faces. A busload of teenage boys from Arrowhead Camp came to help search. Newspaper reporters had driven from the Twin Cities. Side streets were clogged with cars. Both hotels were full, and tents had been set up near the band shell to house spillover crews.

She ducked into an alley and walked to the edge of town, her hand tight on Louisa's. They climbed the grassy hill on the worn path the children had pounded out.

Ahead they saw a group of Welsh miners milling on the slope beneath the Finnish shacks. The smoke from their pipes and cigarettes gathered into one column.

One of them shouted, "There they come!"

Isobel ducked off the path behind a sumac, shielding Louisa with her body. But the men were turning in another direction. She peeked out to see them gesture, not toward her, but to a line of a dozen Finnish miners zagging down the steep alley from their rows of blue and grey houses. They met at the plateau, and the groups merged and began talking. They were too far away for Isobel to make out specific words.

A fat stranger in a fedora huffed up the hill, oblivious to Isobel and Louisa. He lumbered toward the men, close enough that Isobel could hear his laboured breathing. He swore as his bulky camera banged against his side, its dish of silver reflector fanned out and ready.

Twenty yards past their hiding place he stopped, mopped his forehead, and called up to the group of men.

"Where you fellas off to? Looking for the lovebirds?"

The men turned as one unit. They forged into a line to begin descending the hill, snaking along the path. No one answered the photographer until they were nearly upon him. One of the Finns brushed past, jostling the camera.

"We're not looking for dem. We're looking for da husband."

"Malley?" The man skipped sideways along next to the men. "Liam Malley? What the hell, he take a powder too?"

Their strides were long, and the man couldn't keep up. He stopped, flipped open his notebook, and pulled a pencil stub from the brim of his hat. "Say, anybody know how Malley's spelled? That with an *e* or just a *y*?"

One of the men passing by inclined his head toward the sumac and Isobel. "Ask her."

Isobel sat at the table watching Louisa make iced tea.

"You sure you don't want something to eat, Momma?"

Isobel shook her head.

Louisa sat and ate a crude sandwich made from uneven slices of bread. A glob of butter and something pale dripped out one side.

Isobel shuddered. "What's in that?"

Louisa wiped her lip and held the sandwich aloft. "Boiled egg and coleslaw. Want some?"

Isobel took her tea out to the screen porch off the kitchen. The wicker rocker cracked as she dropped into it. She rocked, staring out at the garden.

Victor would know what to do.

How would she ever explain . . .

She thought about finding someone to fetch Victor, bring him home now, tonight. But all available men and boys would be out looking for Jack and Cathryn. Liam too.

Her hands curled to fists over her knees.

Isobel froze in this posture, the rocker still beneath her. *Where can they be?* She tried to recall every word that had passed in her earshot that might offer some clue — places Jack or Cathryn had spoken of, offhand remarks about cities or sights they'd seen or wanted to see.

She pressed her knuckles to her temples, as if the pressure would bring some revelation.

When it grew completely dark she shifted into the living room and turned on a lamp. She sat on the couch and resumed where she'd left off. Her head was thudding. Louisa had dropped onto the living room rug, curled around a pillow and a book.

Isobel slept, at least for a while, for the night she'd been staring out at had somehow slipped from the window and the mantel clock was chiming five. She felt drugged as she rose to lay an afghan over Louisa, asleep on the carpet. She limped into the kitchen to make coffee. Her foot had fallen asleep, and she kicked it against the stove leg to bring back feeling. Her dress was wrinkled. She poured water, ground beans, ran her fingers through her dirty hair, pulling it back in a hank. She was staring at the glass button on the coffeepot, willing it to perk. With hairpins in her mouth, she used one hand to hold the twist of hair and the other to pin it up. The doorbell rang.

Cathryn? She ran, skidding on the tiles of the vestibule in her stockings. Fumbling with the lock she cried, "C'mon, c'mon!" Pulling open the door she sobbed, "Cathryn."

Sheriff Graham, his cap held to his middle, gave her a wearied look as she stepped outside. A young deputy stood just off to the left, yawning and plowing his fingers through his whiskers. Isobel sagged against the doorframe. Both men looked as if they'd been up all night. She looked from one to the other, gathering spit to ask, "Has she come back? Have you found her?"

The sheriff pulled at his earlobe with sooty fingers. "Nope. But we found Liam Malley, Mrs. Howard."

"Where?"

"In the woods at the bottom of the fire tower. Dead."

"Dead?" Isobel staggered.

"Momma?" Louisa had crept up behind, rubbing her eyes.

"Inside, sweetheart. Go back inside." Her voice broke as she pushed the girl back and pulled the door shut behind her.

"How? How did he die?"

"Dunno, Mrs. Howard." The sheriff's face was devoid of emotion. "Maybe he fell. Might have been pushed. Could've jumped."

~   ~   ~

"Please. Please, can you take this tent away?" She had buzzed the nurse and was feebly scratching at the plastic.

The nurse leaned over to tuck the loose side of the tent back under the mattress. "Doctor Hertz said since you wouldn't keep the mask on you have to have it."

"I don't care what he said." She slapped the plastic. "I'm trapped! If you don't take it down, I will."

The woman sighed. "Fine, but it means either the mask again or tubes. Your choice."

"I don't care. I don't care. Just please, get it away."

The old woman's tone made the nurse pause. She examined the crumpled face and, lifting a corner of the plastic, slipped a tissue into Isobel's hand.

"There now. Wipe your eyes, dear."

~   ~   ~

Victor told her later how he and the boys caught a ride in from Chalmer's Point in a forest service truck. As they climbed up into the truck bed, their lopsided bundles in tow, he saw his sons as she would. Thomas, his front milk teeth gone, had also lost much of his baby fat. Henry had grown two inches in as many months. Both were in need of haircuts, and the fine shag over their eyes had gone platinum from the sun. Their faces had browned to burnt butter, Thomas's eyes more green than ever. Legs and arms were bruised and perforated with insect bites and scrapes. Victor had mended and washed their clothes the best he could, but the frays and stains of bacon grease and berry were immutable. As he hoisted Thomas onto the truck bed, he gave him a noisy smack on the cheek. The boy giggled, rubbing furiously where Victor's whiskers had swiped him. "Papa! You're all tickley!"

The pale softness of spring had left their bodies, but as ragtag and scraped as they were, the boys were smiling, had flesh on their cheeks.

Victor climbed into the cab next to the young ranger and laid his brown arm out the window to catch the breeze.

"We could smell smoke all the way out to the island night before last. You boys been busy?"

"Shit, that was just a campfire, Vic. We got lucky with the wind, only lost about eighty acres over at Granite Point."

Victor nodded toward the row of trucks lined up at the landing, the men, the long boats with the odd tackle. "Then why all these fellas hanging around?"

The ranger glanced over his shoulder. "Can you roll up your window, Vic? You won't want your kids to hear this."

Isobel was in the storage hall pushing the rolling ladder on its track. She had limbered the wheels with sewing machine oil and was pushing it along to distribute the oil. Louisa was on the floor at the far end of the room, watching.

Isobel was thinking of the day Jack and Cathryn had taken her to climb the lookout tower. Cathryn had climbed far above her, nearly to the top. She had risen fearlessly, surefooted as a chimney sweep, until that last step, its half-inch difference compensating for the trapdoor above. She'd tumbled on that odd step, almost pitching over the low railing. Jack caught her.

Once they were in the tower, Jack explained to them that the mind's subconscious physical memory was so powerful, so adroit in its calculations, that climbing only two or three stairs set the formula. When a step of a slightly different measure was encountered, a person was sure to stumble over that fraction of space not recognized by the body's swift memory.

Isobel listened to Jack while she clung to the stovepipe in the middle of the tower room, the sway of the structure working on her stomach. Cathryn was leaning far out the window, as if on a dare, her arms eagle-winged, looking out at all that was laid before her, crowing, "Isn't this glorious!"

Liam must have fallen. That was it, then. It was an accident. Liam went looking for Jack and Cathryn at the tower, had climbed up in a rush — in the dark — and the last odd step had tripped him up.

But pushed? Isobel shook her head. The sheriff had lost his mind. Out of the question. Liam Malley was a large man, agile. Tough. The idea of someone pushing him from the tower was idiotic. Besides. Who? Not Jack Reese. Certainly not Cathryn.

Jumped? More nonsense. Liam was too level-headed. It would take more than Cathryn leaving for him to do such a thing. He was a devout Catholic, he knew suicide was a mortal sin.

Besides, the search had just begun. Liam would never have lost hope so soon. There was still a good chance Jack and Cathryn would be found. Unless Liam had known differently. A sliver of doubt wedged into her mind, the sight of his pleading eyes. *I love her you know.* She remembered how he had corrected himself, said *loved her.*

The gruff voice of the sheriff grated in her ear. *Killed his wife and killed Jack Reese too.* Isobel's knuckles were pale on the ladder. No. Absolutely not. Never.

"Momma, please stop now."
Isobel looked up. "But I'm almost finished."

"But you've been pushing that ladder forever. You've walked a mile with it, at least."

"Have I?" Isobel tested the ladder again, pushing it with her fingertip so that it glided easily to the far end of the hall.

"What time is it, Lu?"

"Five. Can we go now?"

"You go ahead." Isobel wiped her hands on the oily rag. "I'll come home soon and make you something to eat."

"You said that twice before. I'm hungry."

"Okay, you go home and make yourself a sandwich."

Louisa got up and dusted off her bottom. "Momma, can suicides go to heaven?"

Isobel took a long breath. "I don't know, Louisa."

"So, Mr. Malley? We don't know if he's in heaven" — the girl's eyes grew round as she whispered — "or hell?"

Isobel steadied herself by gliding her palm over the counter as she walked to her daughter. She pulled the small body to hers, fighting a sob.

"Mr. Malley was good. He was a good man. I'm sure he's in heaven."

Louisa's small arms circled her mother's waist. "Is Cathryn in heaven too?"

Isobel let go and knelt down.

"Cathryn isn't in heaven and she isn't in hell either."

"But the sheriff said — "

"Never mind him. He doesn't know anything."

"But how do you know?" Louisa's eyes filled.

"I know because I know. If they were dead I would know." Isobel gently wiped the tears away.

"How?"

Isobel pressed Louisa's hand over her heart. "I would know it here."

Louisa had rolled up all the shades, and evening light filtered into the room. Isobel abandoned the hall, washed her hands, and sat. Fine work was out of the question; she shook too badly. But she felt the instinct to stay busy, hoping work would steady her, quiet the odd rattle of what had come loose. She tried to concentrate on the beret she was lining, knowing full well the whole thing might have to be torn out and redone later. The satin under her hand creased, her needle regularly missed its mark. She thought of the flurry of activity going on out at Granite Point. Scrabbling through rubble for bones. She envisioned the great rafters of the cottage fallen like a spine, a shipwreck in a burnt forest. Wisps of smoke posing thin questions in the air. Exhausted men searching the woods, futilely dragging the lake. She could stop it all with one word to the sheriff.

I could stop it.

She had gone through Cathryn's satchel again. Couldn't believe she had missed it before. Opening the satchel wide, she flipped it over and shook it. The gold wedding band bounced into her lap. The ring was in her dress pocket now, the sparse weight of it resting on her thigh.

"I could stop it all now."

She touched the ring through the fabric. Or could she?

Maybe they hadn't run off. Maybe they were dead. Maybe their bodies would be found.

She felt as if the skin had been raked from her palms.

Victor stood outside the shop for a long moment before he rapped on the window. The light tattoo of his knuckles on the glass startled Isobel so she nearly dropped the beret.

If he was surprised at what he saw — the rows of hats, the new sign, the sudden order — his face didn't show it. Isobel watched him, her needle still poised, bracing herself as he walked in the door. His blue eyes shone pale under the brim of his hat. When he turned she saw his neck was brown save the white crescent of skin under his jagged cowlick, as if he'd just cut his own hair.

He stepped lightly into the shop. He did not speak but

scanned the room, taking in the additions of the tacking table, the framed watercolours, the bolts of labeled felt, the stack of hatboxes. He picked up one of the box lids and examined the silhouette, then compared it to Isobel's profile. His eyebrow raised in approval. After carefully replacing the lid, he gently took the beret and needle from his wife and settled his hands upon hers.

"Hello, Izzy."

When she began sobbing he wrapped his arms around her and rocked her, his next words a whisper nearly lost among her cries. "There's my girl. There's the girl I married."

Isobel clung, fighting for space between sobs. "Victor, I . . . you don't know. Cathryn, this woman who . . . my friend, and this man, Jack . . ."

"Shh, Isobel, I know. I know all about it. I've just come from the sheriff."

"My God." She shook her head. "What have I done?"

CHAPTER SIXTEEN

*I*sobel testified at the inquest into Liam Malley's death. Victor stood close as she gave her curt answers. *Yes, Your Honor,* or *No, Your Honor.*

She embellished nothing. She did not take off her hat or her white gloves.

Afterward Victor held her hand and walked her to Our Lady of the Lake, where she lit a dozen candles for Liam's soul. At the church door she hesitated, then went back and lit another dozen for Cathryn and Jack. Wherever they might be.

Once home Victor poured her a neat gin, which she gulped before taking the purse from her arm. She spoke of the memorial service to be held for Liam in the chapel at Our Lady, but Victor was hesitant.

"Maybe you better sit tight, Iz."

"I can't do that."

"Malley didn't have too many friends, Iz, but I reckon those few might not be very friendly to you. Those miners are a pretty tight crew."

"They blame me?"

He wouldn't meet her eye. "Well, I wouldn't say *blame*."

"Call it what you like, Victor, blame, responsibility. I do own a share in it. If I didn't go to the service it would look like I was denying that. Besides, I need to go. I owe it to Liam."

Could Cathryn really know all this was happening and stay away? Isobel was almost reassured by not hearing any word. It meant Cathryn and Jack were spared, oblivious, off somewhere to begin their new lives.

There was no casket. Liam's body had been shipped back to Chicago. Isobel couldn't help but wonder to whom. The service was brief, and afterward coffee was served in an awkward gathering in the private dining room of the Vermilion Hotel. Victor stayed close, and it wasn't as bad as she'd expected. It was a simple matter of meeting looks and not crumbling.

She gave Cathryn's gramophone and seventy-eights to Louisa for safekeeping. She wrapped the wedding ring in tissue and put it in Cathryn's satchel in a corner of the attic. She could keep them for her. For her return.

"It's not over, is it?" She pressed closer to Victor in their bed.

He tucked her in against him, trying to warm the chill length of her back. "No. No, it's not."

They watched the shadows of trees on the ceiling and listened as sounds of summer softened behind breezes.

The children were back in school. After they left each morning Isobel waited at home for the mail to arrive. There was no word. She knew Cathryn had a sister in Toledo. After a week of rehearsed starts she gathered the nerve to find the number. The operator came back on the line to say the phone had been disconnected and there was no forwarding number. She tried Cathryn's house in Oak Park. The phone there was answered by a man from the real estate firm hired to sell the house and its contents. He would not say who had hired him, that information was "privileged," but when she pleaded, he caved in and told her he had been contracted by a Mr. Colin Malley of Cork, Ireland. The real estate man's voice was effeminate and haughty. "I believe he's the father of the deceased. My client is a rather elderly gentleman, and frail. It wouldn't do to upset him."

She resumed going to the shop each morning. It was better to work. Better to be sitting next to Victor with something to keep her hands busy.

The banks of sumac along the road out of Cypress heralded autumn by shifting nearly overnight to scarlet. Cool winds brought days of steady rain until muddy water flooded the gullies and ditches and soaked the hay-coloured lawns back to a last striving of green. The *Fire Danger* sign at the edge of town had its arrow repositioned for the first time since May. Aspen and maple began their change as the last search party drifted away.

A bulldozer leveled the remains of the cottage at Granite Point.

Victor drove Isobel out to the spot.

A crop of green spears poked up at the base of scattered logs, a mantle of moss already spreading over the shallow depression where the cottage had been.

The two chimneys had tumbled into conical piles of granite, twin cairns at either edge of a void.

The only other evidence that a building had once stood there was the uneven stone path and the columns of the stone arbor, still framing a vista to the lake. The leaves of climbing rose had curled away to expose charred thorns. Bits of glass blown out from the cottage windows were imbedded in scorched mortar like shrapnel. Isobel pried a piece loose. It was jagged on the piercing end, while the outer edge had been melted smooth by the heat of the blaze.

Isobel stood in the arch and looked out toward the lake. She had clung to the notion that Cathryn or Jack would make some contact, a sign, send her some cryptic hope. But it had been nearly a month since the fire and Liam's death. The accumulation of anxious days — and now the destruction at her back — gnawed dull this hope. She wondered how many more days would feel like the glass in her hand, two-sided and jagged with disquiet. Only the nights were tolerable, burnished indistinct by a sleep that came only when she drank the merciful concoction the druggist had given her.

Victor stood next to her in the ruins of the arbor. She pointed down to the granite slope at the water's edge and managed a smile. "Louisa waded there with Cathryn once. You should've seen her, Vic. She went in all the way up to her neck, wasn't the least bit scared!"

Victor laid his arm over her shoulder, scanning the slope and the lake for a moment before whispering to his wife, "That's what you should be pulling from this wreck, Iz, the better bits. You've got to let go of the rest."

Jack's cabin had been similarly burnt. Arson was suspected, but there was no real proof. The newspaper accounts had speculated that whoever had started the fires had known exactly what they were doing. Someone accomplished in the ways of fire. Others said lightning was the culprit.

She did not go to Jack's island, but Isobel could easily imagine that scene: An empty square of singed foundation ringing a mound of debris. Perhaps a remnant from Jack's quilt tagging the branch of a nearby tree, a cotton rose trailing a faded cotton vine. Sky reflected in the shards of glass jars that once held wild mint and trillium.

Victor came home smiling and fluttered a pair of train tickets in front of Isobel. "We're going."

"Going where?"

"Vacation. To Michigan."

Isobel sighed. "We can't, Victor."

Business had been slow, and Victor was just catching up from being away. He had lost the contract he'd had supplying uniforms for the mine's band, as well as several customers connected to the mine. It was hard to say if Liam's death had anything to do with it, but Isobel knew she would be punished one way or another, through Victor if not directly.

She knew she wouldn't be doing much trade in Cypress, at least not until the next June, when the summer people came, strangers who didn't know. She'd managed a few large orders of spring hats and Easter bonnets for two department stores in Duluth. Kathleen from the millinery had recommended her. She was busy working on those orders, glad for them, though she would only break even after costs.

She looked at the tickets in Victor's hand. "Have you lost all reason? We can't afford to go anywhere."

"Yes we can, Iz. I've already borrowed the money."

"Victor. Borrowed?"

"Izzy, you need to get away."

"And the children?"

"All arranged. Sima's oldest girl will stay at the house with them."

Isobel moaned. Victor pressed the tickets into her hand and insisted, "Just a couple weeks, Izzy. You need the rest."

They changed trains in Duluth and got a sleeper compartment heading east through Wisconsin. A blurred palette of gold-and-white birch throbbed past the rain-streaked compartment windows. Isobel spent most of the last leg of the trip in her window seat, her forehead on the pane, letting her head loll gently with the sway of the train. As they neared the Upper Peninsula of Michigan, rain and birch trees gave way to shaded pine forests with ticking shafts of smoky sunlight.

Victor came back from the smoking car smelling of cigars and spearmint chewing gum.

"I talked to some folks from Sault Sainte Marie. They recommended this little resort." He handed her a slip of paper with a name scrawled on it. "It's on the mainland."

"But what about Mackinac Island?"

Victor smiled at her. "It's an island, Izzy. We'd have to take a ferry to get out there."

"I can do that." She sat up and tested the buttons at her throat. "I can take a ferry."

The Island Inn was close enough to the shore that Isobel could hear the surf *shush* through the night. They spent the days walking the beaches, gathering shells, and building afternoon fires nearly invisible in the daylight. She napped before dinner and wrote daily letters to the children.

On the portico Isobel let her tea go cold while the last of the leaves fell to upholster the wicker in ragged cushions of ochre. Victor often reached for her hand, but they spoke very little in their first days alone. He never asked directly about Jack and Cathryn. In fact, he was strangely silent. Days went by until his patience seemed almost another presence in the room, waiting next to him while she gathered the events like strewn playing cards and put them in some order.

In increments, she found her voice and spun out scenes until they were knotted into the flawed length of summer. She began with the cloud of mayflies that ushered Cathryn into the shop that first sunshot day in June. She finished her story with the odor of seared pine cloaking the very wind that swept Cathryn away.

Isobel leaned toward Victor. In the cold mornings they clung to each other, made love upon waking, and afterward lay spooned against the sharp air whispering through the half-opened windows. They burrowed under blankets and looked out at clouds thickening above the bones of oaks. And then she would tell him more, filling in hours to build days.

She told him about teaching Cathryn to drive; about the many kindnesses Cathryn had showered upon her and Louisa; about the snake in the quarry; about making the daisy-chain crown that made Louisa sneeze in fits. About the day Cathryn lured them underground . . .

The mine held its annual company picnic. Cathryn, Louisa, and Isobel went together. It was the anniversary of the mine's founding, and the company opened the shafts, inviting anyone from the picnic down to tour.

Louisa held back, but Cathryn urged the girl on.

"Louisa, you know what the world looks like up here. Why, you can even imagine what mountains and tropical lands are like. For heaven's sake, we've seen all that at the cinema. But underground? Now that's another world, that's something I'd like to see. Won't you come?"

Just then a miner next to them barked in a sour voice, "You'll catch me down there on my one day of rest when Satan hisself sends me." He leaned over and spat, just missing Cathryn's foot.

It only fed Cathryn's resolve. Her response was determined. "See? It's the least we can do, experience one hour of what these men live day in and day out."

At the entrance, a volunteer outfitted them with helmets and old-fashioned headlamps of the type original miners used. The helmets were heavy and the stench of kerosene burned Louisa's nostrils. She was frightened, but if Cathryn was going down, so was she. They were herded into a metal box, pressing in with giggles at the intimacy. The volunteer told them the elevator usually held fourteen men. There were fewer than ten in the group, but still they were close and uncomfortable, limbs finding space among limbs like jigsaw pieces.

When the door closed they were jerked downward. Pulleys and rattling chains and enormous hooks followed them. The rough wall of the shaft was just visible in the tiny square of wired glass. The racket and bumping made Isobel fight off an image: a metal coffin slipping down a stony well.

Deeper into the shaft, the bit of light from above suddenly went black and Louisa pressed into Cathryn's side, moaning.

Isobel was on the opposite wall, separated by bodies. The girl burped, her face grown blotchy in the light cast from the flame in Cathryn's headlamp. "I'm gonna v-v-vomit."

In the crush there was no getting to Louisa. Cathryn licked a thumb and reached up to pinch the flame on her lamp and tipped the helmet off her head, saying, "In here, that's a girl."

Most passengers groaned against the sound of retching, the splash onto metal. Cathryn paid no one any mind. "We'll get another helmet just as soon as we're down." Somehow people made room so Cathryn could crouch down and wipe Louisa's chin with a handkerchief.

The descent took a full five minutes, but it seemed longer, with the heat of iron walls and the smell of vomited knockwurst and potato salad. At the bottom, the door clanged open onto a damp corridor lit by a string of hanging bulbs. Pools of red water reflected lamplight. Wind moving through the tunnel was icy, and the volunteer proudly offered, "Fifty degrees year round. That breeze you feel is shifts in air pressure." He led them around the puddles, Louisa still fitted to Cathryn's side.

The volunteer spoke as if the mine were one big house, going on about hallways and rooms. The group was quiet, flames of headlamps winking with each step. There was just enough room to squeeze single file next to the line of small rail cars.

"The ore's brought out in these here cars."

The rusted open boxes bulged with huge dents. Everything Isobel could make out was reddish brown, a phalanx of pickaxes and curved truncheons the size of men's legs were lined up against a tunnel wall of the same bloodlike hue. The whole corridor was in monochrome; even the bulbs cast dull iron light.

At the end of the tunnel, they pulled themselves up a narrow winding staircase to emerge into a vast, unbraced cavern. The man lit a sulfur torch and held it up to the wall so they could see the linear striae of the stone. "Layers of history right here to examine, folks." He held out his free fist as if to represent the earth. "The landscape, the earth's crust, looks secure up above, but below, down here, there's ceaseless change. You can see it in the stone."

The women shifted in place, occasionally ducking and covering their hair against swooping bats.

"The greenstone in this region is some of the oldest known in the world. You can see it here among the veins of ore. That's a metamorphic rock, altered from lava flows of basalt tens of millions of years ago, before man." He traced an oval in the stone. "This stone here . . . come closer, see these shapes next to the veins? That's your greenstone. Like eggs trapped in ice."

He gathered the group into a half-moon, and they took turns touching the stone.

"What I'm gonna show you next is something most people never experience, 'cept maybe the blind." He extinguished his torch and licked his thumb and forefinger, chuckling. Without warning he reached out and swiftly pinched out the wicks of their headlamps. One by one they sizzled under his damp squeeze. "Welcome to true darkness." His smile was mischievous as he reached up to put out his own flame.

The last Isobel saw was his hands covering his forehead in shadow.

There was a moment of shocked silence as the black engulfed them. One of the women gasped. Isobel reached for Louisa but found only air.

"Hold your hands out in front of yer faces." The volunteer's voice echoed in the cavern. "See? Total blackness. Even babies in the womb have more light. Jonah in the whale had more light."

The air around Isobel became tangible, wrapping her in seamless velvet. The sounds of breathing and a bat squealing overhead became amplified. The falling of a pebble skipping down a rock slope might have been a boulder.

And then all sound stopped.

Isobel felt she was being absorbed into herself. It was extraordinary, the loss of light. She let herself dissolve. Were the others experiencing the same sense of tranquillity?

"No, no," someone moaned. "Light the lamps. Please!"

There was a rustle of clothing, the striking of a match, movement as the volunteer lit his torch. The face of the terrified woman was illuminated.

It was Cathryn.

She lunged for the torch. "Give it to me!" The box of matches was knocked from the man's hand and the torch fell to a puddle. Blackness again and the smell of phosphorus and cold sweat.

Louisa cried out then. Isobel heard a thud of frantic footsteps and another cry. By the time the man got the torch lighted again, everyone was glassy-eyed with panic. Bitter breath came hard into her face. Louisa had somehow reached her side. A moan rose up from the ground to their right. The man quickly lit their lamps and they turned as one to see Cathryn splay-legged near the rusty puddle, her skirt up to reveal the cut on her shin where she had met the ground. She looked down at the blood, and her next sound was an animal whimper.

Isobel and Louisa each took an arm and got her up, but when they tried to help her walk to the stairs, she shook them off. When they reached the elevator Cathryn rang the bell furiously to trigger the ascension.

The elevator clanked up the shaft and away from the rest of the group, who hung back, whispering and nodding.

No one spoke until they were above, out and safe. They squinted in the brightness and gulped warm air.

"Cathryn, are you all right?"

"Sorry I panicked so." She laughed, spit on her hankie and dabbed the cut. "Silly isn't it? Guess I should add claustrophobia to my list."

As they walked back toward the picnic, Isobel asked casually, "Where's Liam today?" She was hoping she might have Louisa fetch him to come take Cathryn home.

Cathryn shrugged. "Oh, home. Maybe fishing. He can't stand a crowd."

Isobel studied her friend, but all the anxiety in the mine dissipated in the sunlight. She tried to think of something to say.

When Cathryn bent to brush away the red dust defining the folds of Louisa's dress, Isobel and her daughter locked eyes, their shrugs minute.

———

Isobel smoothed the fine hairs on Victor's wrist as she spoke. "By the end of the picnic Cathryn had taught the fiddle player an Irish reel and showed Louisa all the steps, as though she had forgotten her panic in the mine, as though nothing had happened."

Victor nodded but remained quiet.

Isobel rolled onto her stomach. "Now that I'm telling, I see it so much more clearly. Nearly each day was like that, Cathryn leading us up and down, from light to dark and back, showing us very tops of hills and the undersides of valleys, but never anywhere in between."

Their hotel room was small, enough space for a wardrobe, the walnut sleigh bed and, just under the window, a small writing desk. The contents of Victor's pockets were spread on the polished surface: his wallet, fawn-coloured and molded to the shape of his hip, the ring of brass keys, coins gritty with sand, and the odd flat stone he'd carried since coming back from the island, its grey the same shade as the October sky. Under the desk his shoes lay pitched on the hooked rug as he'd dropped them, nudging each other, vaguely pigeon-toed, like him.

Isobel would often go back to that time on the Michigan island, reconstructing a vignette of Victor's strewn belongings framed by the simple architecture of their room. With that memory came the feel and fit of his chest against the wings of her shoulder blades, the weight of his arms resting over hers, the proximity of his unshaven chin to her ear, a thumb idly brushing her nipple as he relayed a dream or mumbled, "Good morning, Mrs. Howard."

In the raw years after his death she would lie in their old bed on fall mornings, the room robbed of his scuffed shoes, the bureau clear of the loose change he always seemed to have too much of. The space where his comb and wallet used to lie gleamed, empty. When she rolled over, her temple on the sheet where his shoulder would have been, the salt of slow tears pulsed into starched cotton.

She would not wear black. Victor had told her once it made her look peaked, but she knew he meant sallow. Her mourning clothes were watery greens and the blue shades he liked best. She ignored the raised eyebrows of the gossips in town. She wore hats the colours of another hemisphere, trailing feathers of tropical birds.

Later, after the customary period of grief had passed, doubled itself, and passed again, she reluctantly changed the sign on the shopwindow. She insisted on scraping away the old letters herself, and as the gold and black shavings of *Victor Howard — Tailor* curled and fell from the putty knife, she braced herself against rungs of the ladder.

The new name had been Louisa's idea: the same elegant type of her hatboxes, *Isobel,* and just under, *Fine Millinery Since 1936.*

Men, a few even Victor's old customers, would shyly come into the shop to nervously finger hats, test brims, touch cloth flowers and bands. They would cough, clear a throat, or scuff a toe before rousing the spit to ask Isobel to go see a movie, attend a concert, or have dinner at the supper club out by the lake. She was always able to make her refusal seem as if she were doing the man a kindness by declining.

She simply couldn't imagine it, what they might talk about, what she would ever have in common with a history teacher, a union organizer, a widowed resort owner.

Midforties seemed an absurd age to start again. She had her work and she still had children to raise. By the time Thomas and Louisa went away — to Michigan Tech and design school in New York — Isobel had settled into resolute widowhood, even affecting a less contentious attachment to her garden. Instead of trying to control it, she let it grow around her. She read books on horticulture and learned to prune delicately, began to give plants space instead of trying to corral them. She learned to mulch and fertilize, and standing one day with her shovel poised in a heap of manure, she came to consider her garden as she might a painting or a hat, flower beds as schemes to which she might add colour here and height there, texture and tone. She laid out curving beds that set her eye on roving journeys, constructed unexpected corners of compositions: blue delphiniums and salmon poppies wading in white baby's breath; trumpet vine covering a fence flanked with ivory canna. She planted trout lilies along the path of flagstone she'd laid along the creek's edge, and put back the same types of old-fashioned perennials she had once torn up: hollyhocks, peonies, old roses, and climbing hydrangea. She devoted a balsam-shaded grove to ferns and wildflowers: bog rosemary, gentian, tender bloodroot, and pasqueflowers so pale and small one had to kneel low to appreciate them.

Her patch of lawn shrank year by year until there was only enough space for her chair and table. Here she read, looking up occasionally, each time surprised by something in her garden. It was like a room, as beautiful as any described in the novels or poems resting in her hands. She cried less often.

Sometimes she spoke to Victor, and sometimes she imagined him responding, his laughter muted behind vines of bittersweet.

She had known moments of trepidation and regret would come, knew even as she and Victor were mending themselves back together on the island in Michigan. She tried to articulate her fears to him during the evenings after dinner in the hotel's empty dining room. He told her a truth: that she would find herself to be stronger than she ever thought she could be.

She believed him. But only after he was gone.

———

Much of the hotel had already been shut up for the season, and the hallways had ghostly airs, as if the footfalls and laughter of departed summer guests were held in thick carpets. She found a side door and stepped out onto the sloping lawn, walking slowly toward the marina, dew cold on her ankles.

She detoured the groomed path leading to the docks of neat sloops and mahogany power cruisers. Finding a narrow footpath she ventured to where a line of old fishing shacks slouched, softened and greyed by the wind like old men, shingles fallen away like teeth. The uneven docks were blanketed with nets laid ready for mending. Gulls arched down but did not land, swooping only low enough to pluck at the nets, pulling up bits of rotting bait here and there.

Beached fishing boats knelt in postures of supplication, bows fast in the sand.

A battered sailboat thumped against the pilings, and in its rhythm a line of Eliot came to her. *Bowsprit cracked with ice and paint cracked with heat.*

She stepped lightly among the nets. *The garboard strake leaks, the seams need caulking.* There was something in between, but she could only recall the last bit. *The awakened, lips parted, the hope, the new ships . . .*

She smiled.

She told Victor how she and Cathryn would find a bench close to the water and the words would flow from Cathryn to pool around her. She told him how she'd learned early on that when Cathryn began it was not worth interrupting her — anything Isobel might say butted up against Cathryn's phrases like strings of hackneyed words competing with birdsong.

Isobel lay in bed in a hotel by water and told it all in the best words she had. At the end of her story she turned to her husband and said, "You see? I could never tell anything the way Cathryn could."

Their last evening on the island was truly cold, dusk somber with the waning of autumn. Victor and Isobel put on thick sweaters and gloves and walked to the harbor. Bending forward into the wind, they climbed the jetty and made their way along the crooked finger of black stones. Their clothing slapped against them from all sides, the black air ruthless around them.

Bracing each other with arms around waists, they fought to stay upright until the gusts lessened to a steady blow. Isobel cried some then. Victor dug for his handkerchief, but the wind dried her tears almost as they fell.

Isobel held a peach-coloured scarf around her throat, and when she let go to regain her balance over rough stones, it was suddenly lifted from her, spiraling in an upward vortex. She and Victor watched the scarf, a pale wing rising.

The moon crested, tipping each wave with a pale lip until the bay swelled in an undulating field of black violets. Isobel stepped away to the very point of the jetty. The icy breath of Lake Huron felt like baptism, permeating clothing to burrow into her pores. She felt an almost corporeal sense of herself lightening, a few scales of sorrow blown away, lifted and carried off like the scarf. She resolutely wiped her nose and turned to Victor.

"I'm ready now. I'm ready to go back."

~ ~ ~

CHAPTER SEVENTEEN

When Louisa came to visit from New York she saw her mother's hair wild with grey, her demeanor oddly complacent, and her tongue a little dull. The shop was dusty, and when she examined the account ledgers she found payments past due and orders well behind schedule.

"Mother, what's this?"

Isobel looked up from her book on the Canadian fur trade. "Oh, I'll get to it. I've been so busy with the garden. I've laid a new stone path — it's taken me ages." She glanced back at her book, her voice brightening as she held up a finger. "A leading cause of death among voyageurs?"

"Ah . . . freezing?"

"No."

"Scalped?"

"Nope."

"I dunno, Mom, exasperation?"

"Close. Constipation!"

In the short time she'd been home, Louisa had noticed that her mother's routines had grown into stubborn habits; if the newspaper didn't come, she would be out of sorts all day for not having done her crossword. On Wednesdays she ate chicken salad for lunch; if there was no chicken salad, she did not eat lunch. She'd let the house go, had closed up most of the rooms and lived in the kitchen, her bedroom, and her tangled acre of garden. When Louisa laid her suitcase on the bed in her old room, dust rose like smoke from the coverlet.

"C'mon, up you go." Louisa pulled her from the chair by the shopwindow. "You're only fifty, for God's sake."

"Pardon?"

"It's been ten years since Dad died and you've done nothing but read weird books and fertilize your annuals."

"Not true. I work. And I read other things."

Louisa glanced at the stack of library books obliterating the cash register. She bit the inside of her cheek. "No kidding. By the way, half of those are overdue."

She took Isobel to Seleskar's beauty parlor to have her hair dyed back to its ashen gold. Louisa unpacked the dove grey organdy suit she had designed and sewed for her mother and made a reservation at the supper club.

Over dessert she asked innocently, knowing the answer, "Have you rented the apartment above the shop, yet?"

The Welsh widow living upstairs had died in April, but Isobel hadn't roused herself to place an ad.

"You know I haven't. I wrote you."

"Great. So I can move in?"

Isobel paused, the spoon of sugar suspended over her

coffee. "You can't honestly want to stay here, Louisa. What would you do in Cypress?"

"Dresses." Louisa pulled her portfolio from under the table and cleared a space on the cloth. She showed Isobel her designs, and a rough sketch for a new floor plan for the shop. "I know you have room for me."

The next month Louisa returned from New York and brought Robert. Isobel liked him immediately. He said little, but when he did speak his words were measured and well placed, economical as poetry. He smiled easily and adored Louisa. He settled quickly, and bought a canoe-outfitting service and a bankrupt float-plane business.

Isobel offered them the house after Louisa's first daughter was born.

"But Mom, where will you live?"

"Upstairs of the shop." She laughed. "You're being evicted. I want my old room back."

"But what about your garden?"

"Have Robert clear enough space for a swing set, but don't let him touch my perennial beds. I'm still the gardener."

The comfort of routine melded time and work into a solid if sometimes reversed line. Their orders for dresses and hats always placed them seasons ahead; autumns were spent on spring styles, in winter they planned summer. After a time it did not seem odd to be working with heathered woolens in the heat of July. Years were compartmentalized and remembered by trend, cut, line, decades defined by styles. The fifties were a blur of comical patterns and flared skirts; fads of darted tunics and unadorned caps were quickly forgotten during the sixties, when neat suits with covered buttons in nubby wool came into fashion. Isobel made endless variations of pillbox hats inspired by President Kennedy's wife. They watched every movie starring Audrey Hepburn and raced to fill orders for look-alike garments. Louisa and her helpers sewed hundreds of sheath dresses, and Isobel topped them with broad-brimmed black hats with white bands.

In the early seventies, Isobel threw up her hands at the wide collars and polyester fabrics, the loud patterns.

"Ugliness defined. I'm retiring before this drives me insane. No one's worn a hat since Eisenhower. I'm too old for this. I'm almost seventy-five."

"Seventy-four, Momma."

"If you say. Besides, I have other things to do."

Louisa nodded patiently. She'd heard the threat before.

"Can't you hang on just one more year?" She was nearly fifty herself and was ready to spend more time with Robert. Her daughters were almost grown, and the town was falling in on itself. The mines had laid off men, then laid off more. Finally the crushers had gone quiet. Houses went on the market at half their value and still did not sell. One store closed, then another. Louisa gave up on local sales when ready-to-wear clothing from Hong Kong began turning up on the shelves of what few shops still operated.

Isobel read from an article in the paper. "Well, here's some good news, finally. They say tourism will boom. That's good for Robert, then." He'd bought up two more resorts and had been expanding his canoe-outfitting business.

She and Louisa stopped going to the annual fashion shows in New York and on buying trips to Chicago. On her last trip, Isobel caught a cab near the Loop and told the driver to take her to Oak Park.

Just to see. *Just to peek,* she told herself — at what kind of house, block, neighborhood, Cathryn had lived in. The ink on the paper in her hand was barely legible. As she counted off numbers on the quiet street, she felt a creeping dismay as the house grew near. She tapped the driver's shoulder.

"Back downtown, please." She suddenly knew she couldn't bring herself to look at the house. She didn't need to see it. It was just a house, after all, peopled with strangers now. Nothing left of Cathryn. The confines of the car tightened around her. She crumpled the decades-old scrap and let it fall to the floor.

After Louisa's accident, Isobel closed the shop and wrote the same abbreviated notice to patrons and suppliers alike. She sat at her desk and held the pen as if it might crumble in her fingers. *Due to a death in the family . . .* She settled accounts and let go the women who had worked for Louisa since the late fifties, having made sure their pensions were in order. Robert helped tape newspapers across the windows, and contacted an equipment broker to sell the machines and shop fittings. Robert would be lost, she knew, but she had no choice. She would not stay to embroider his grief; she needed to be alone with her own.

As she moved through the business of closing out a life, Isobel felt a strange lightness to her body, as if her heels made no mark. She unplugged the telephone and worked in silence, folding away a hundred garments Louisa had put her hand to. She found herself running her fingers slowly over seams, suddenly pulling the raw edges of an unfinished blouse to her mouth.

Louisa's body had gone directly from the lake to the undertaker and into the casket. Isobel had not seen, had not touched her daughter in death.

On her last day in Cypress she visited the shop a final time. She emptied the register and walked the worn path to the door, lingering only for a moment. Her bag was light; she had chosen only two items — a folded collage of horses made from fading wool, and a carved doll with a nail splitting its neck. She flipped the *Closed* sign behind her.

This time she did wear black.

She moved quickly. It took her less than a month to find a place in St. Paul. Thomas was twenty minutes away in one of the north suburbs. He sent a moving van up for her things and took a week off from his business to get her settled. In the days he spent helping his mother unpack and arrange furniture, she didn't mention the accident, never spoke his dead sister's name. He imagined she was in shock. Once everything was in place he bought her a grocery caddy and a bus pass and took her shopping for plants for her window ledges and terrace. In the hot aisle of the greenhouse she stopped, turning among the waxy ficus and the towering tropical palms.

"Skip the plants, Thomas. I only want pots and dirt. Vermiculite. A few grow lights."

She wrote a letter to Robert that evening. *Put my grandchildren to work. I want bulbs and seed pods from my garden, anything that blooms white.*

In the fall she found a volunteer position at the new performing arts theater, and on Saturdays she altered and patched costumes and kept the production wardrobes tagged and in order. It was an endeavor she imagined Louisa would have chosen herself.

There were free tickets for her work, and she saw productions of Shakespeare and Beckett. Dickens was so overdone during holidays that by January the Cockney accents went up her spine. She never wanted to see another Tiny Tim costume.

She liked Tennessee Williams, Horton Foote, Edward Albee, and Mr. Wilder. She went back to watch Williams's plays twice, sometimes three times — of all he seemed to have the best insight into the human condition, could understand the depth of grief.

She was polite with the actors but rarely spoke to them, didn't care to know them outside their roles. She admired their work onstage, then she brushed out and pressed their costumes and stitched seams they burst in their gesticulations of bogus ardor, or fury, or joy.

She kept moving, kept her apartment spotless, fed coffee grounds to the potted ivory azalea, ground up nutshells for drainage under her pale impatiens. Scraping pigeon droppings from the tile on her terrace, she mashed them into the soil of troughs containing velvety flowers that bloomed in hues of eggshells and bones.

After a year she was able to organize her photo albums, but she did not let herself linger over any image of Louisa.

The cold midnights of February were worst. The whine of tires skidding, the sounds of sheet-ice cracking, invaded her dreams.

In her free balcony seats she watched ballet and modern dance, and she felt the constriction sealing her own bones as the elastic bodies of young dancers soared like shot liquid. They spiraled over the stage, over each other, and she envied their ease, the beautiful leaping of them.

It was a progressive theater, and so tradition paused to allow performance art and experimental theater, and she didn't dislike all of it, was even amused by the vast narcissism, the incredible focus and self-absorption it took to expose aberrant lives to audiences in the name of art.

It was nice, the theater, the excitement. The prop builders and stagehands called her Gran, and she didn't mind. She looked forward to the ballet season, though the dancers propelled their near-naked bodies through the wardrobe room on the balls of their feet and said outrageous things. They liked Isobel, she knew, but she imagined they enjoyed the thought of shocking her, by using words like *fuck* or *fag,* or by leaving the bathroom doors open when they loudly vomited up their lunches in fits of bulimia.

The dancers were ambitious and focused boys and girls, but Isobel was dismayed that people so young could be so neurotic. When the boys augmented the front pouches of their tights with layers of tissue and gauze, she offered up handfuls of cotton batting as being a more natural-looking substitute. She tried not to smile. The young men went by the full names their mothers had given them, never nicknames; always William, Andrew, or Christopher, though occasionally they called each other pet names like Stella or Kitten. By the end of a run they would all sign her programs and always promised to remember her once they were famous.

Sunday mornings she took a bus to Como Park, where she wandered through the zoo and watched the apes and giraffes. She bought paper cups of chum to feed the seals. She rested among the warm boulders of the Japanese garden, and on cold days she stayed inside the great glass conservatory, breathing in the odors of dirt and foliage and sneaking pinches of crushed Rice Krispies from her pocket to feed the white carp swimming under the bridge.

There was a woman in the conservatory gift shop who looked a little like Louisa. Isobel's refrigerator door grew crowded with the magnets and postcards emblazoned *Como!*

Weekday mornings she walked, and in the afternoons she went to the library, where she read the paper in dusty squares of light fallen through the great grid of skylights.

Thomas complained she was never home.

The edges and borders of Cypress began to soften in shadow, as if set farther back on her shelves of memory. Glassine envelopes of images pulled forward less frequently. As the sting of Louisa's death diminished and grief became less stabbing, Isobel began to enjoy the routines and habits she'd adopted.

She avoided staying in her building during the day. *Senior housing.* The very name wearied her, and she could think of nothing less natural than being housed with a hundred people her own age. Nearly all were women.

She heard their conversations in the lobby, in the laundry, passing the game room. Volleys of one-upmanship as to who might have suffered most, proudly crowing their widowhood and relaying bouts of ill health as if they were their most defining moments. All seemed to have children who did not visit often enough and ailments that never healed. Isobel knew some of them must have had children who had died, but she would not let herself get close enough to compare losses. She remained stubbornly aloof and avoided these women who scheduled their days around soap operas and spoke of the characters as if they were family members or personal friends.

When they died their replacements were nearly identical.

She considered moving to a neighborhood, to get an apartment in a smaller building with families or students or couples. But Thomas wanted her to have the convenience of elevators and the shuttle bus to the grocery store, the safety of bathroom handrails, the emergency buzzer in her bedroom. *Just in case.*

She relented. The building was adequate, the utter quiet of deep carpets in her hallways pleased her. Her twentieth-floor windows looked out over the state capitol and the somber dome of St. Paul's Cathedral, with the city fanning beneath. She could walk to the river, the corner store, the theater, and, of course, the library.

An asylum. The entrance to the library was like the vestibule of a church, darkly paneled and soaring; the reference room was as serene as a parlor, despite its size. Puddles of hushed light from table lamps colonized small areas, and people bent into these tiny sanctuaries, the concentration on their faces reflecting the pages in front of them; pondering, amused, confused, enlightened.

The librarians were always kind, always a "Good afternoon, Mrs. Howard," sometimes a "Beautiful day, Mrs. Howard." She learned their names, and from hushed, overheard conversations she knew a little something about each of their lives — when one was having trouble at home, when another was gone sick because she'd had her uterus removed. She knew which ones hated their mothers-in-law, and which were only mildly annoyed by them; she knew which were worried about their children, or were having affairs, or were otherwise overwhelmed. It amused Isobel that they knew nothing of her. They never asked questions, as if only accustomed to answering.

She sat near the main desk and listened to the strange and varied requests from patrons. Information that the librarians retrieved as if it were absolutely vital to know how to eviscerate a shrew mole, what the capital of Bolivia was, where to find the statistics on incest in rural Canada, or how to spell Ceausescu. Three librarians retired during her tenure. At holidays she left them small parcels — handkerchiefs or soaps, sometimes candy — but she knew by their puzzled smiles that they would probably never use the soap or eat the candy. She didn't care. Their curious thanks were enough.

Her presence impressed them mostly for its longevity. Three or four days a week, years compiling first into one decade and then another, she could be found in the same corner, a well-dressed elderly woman, reading or just sitting. She was a stooped figure in the afternoons, as much a fixture as one of the worn leather chairs. Isobel's presence affected the librarians and regular patrons even if they did not know it — when she was settled near her table, everything was as it should be in the great room.

Ever older, always with a fresh flower on the lapel of her overcoat, even in winter. Always a white flower. Her face shadowed by the brims of her odd, outdated hats as she bowed into her newspapers, licking her pencil to begin the daily crossword, looking up only when the sun shifted or slanted away from the glass skylights above.

She stayed away from the library on rainy days. Those days she mended or did laundry, wrote letters, or cooked things to freeze for the next week's meals: a stack of Welsh pasties, a pot of soup. Once a week she made bread.

The making of bread was a reflex. The recipes for German rye or Vienna loaves were imprinted somewhere in her so that she was hardly aware of tapping out the proper amount of yeast into water. She didn't count handfuls of flour, simply stopped when there was enough in the bowl. Testing the dough for air bubbles and kneading them down were memories in her hands. Baking was a task of the body, its remembered motions a kitchen waltz, steam rising from the brown loaves like so many notes.

Her health held, but with an odd exception. At the close of three singular winter nights in three consecutive years, Isobel was hospitalized with breathing difficulty. Thomas took her to the emergency room after she'd called in the middle of the night, gasping and nearly incoherent. By the third trip he had grasped the connection the doctors never could. All of those nights were threaded together by the possibility of ice, the air cold enough to freeze lakes, even rivers. All shared the same sapphire cold stillness as the night Louisa died.

On fine mornings she walked the city, leaving her building promptly at eight o'clock as if due at an appointment. She was downtown by eight-thirty, when people were still streaming in from the suburbs.

Men poured from car pools and vans in front of office buildings, their posts of low or middle management obvious by the cut of their off-the-rack suits. The CEOs and bankers arrived later, faces less harried over their crisp collars, camel lapels, cashmere scarves.

Unless it was very cold no one wore a hat.

St. Paul was usually a quiet city, so she relished this frenetic early hour. Delivery trucks double-parked to incite choruses of honking and the hiss of hydraulic brakes. The mornings smelled of diesel fumes, fresh tar, and a prickling coolness. She walked past the office buildings, greeting the security guards and the other familiar faces she encountered — doormen, policemen, the old German at the newsstand who always called *Guten Tag* as she passed.

She took care of errands in these hours, making her bank deposits, dropping off dry cleaning, paying utility bills. The last time she renewed her driver's license the clerk's eyes had widened in shock when reading the numbers on the date of birth line. Isobel rose up on her toes to lean over the counter.

"Don't look so frightened," she reassured him. "I don't actually drive anymore."

She knew the blocks of the city, the facade of each building. After reading books on architecture she could pass buildings and assign them styles: *Italianate, Federal, Gothic, Baroque.* Certain gargoyles caught her eye, and she nodded to them in stony greeting, wondering over the generations that had walked under their gaze. Thousands of people walking thousands of steps. As many histories.

Jack's long-ago words had stayed with her, and she often said them aloud like a credo. *Take note of small, seemingly inconsequential things.* She watched and opened herself to what the streets offered and discovered the endless small tableaux that made up the city.

Crossing the green square of Rice Park she would sit to watch the people. Sometimes when a certain old man passed she was reminded of Victor. He would've enjoyed the squirrels. She followed their progress for him under the ginkgo trees; autumn after autumn the idiotic creatures buried their stores in the same spot — just where the skating rink would ice over to seal their food away from them. Whenever she saw a tall elderly couple she could not help but scan for relics of Jack or Cathryn in their profiles. Who was to say that some ancient woman might not turn from the arm she was linked to and exclaim, wonder in her lined face, *"Isobel Howard, as I live and breathe!"*

She smiled at herself. Lottery odds.

Thomas didn't like her being out in winter and encouraged her to use the enclosed skyway system, but she wouldn't. The skywalks were loathsome carpeted tunnels with uneven heat blasting at her. He saw he was defeated and so took her to a medical supply store to at least buy her a cane to help her along outside. He'd watched her gait degenerate to a shuffle, but he knew she still wandered heedlessly along the icy streets and cobblestone alleys. She was indiscriminate in her routes. He saw bags in her kitchen from a fruit vendor and thrift shop on the other side of the river, the wrong side. He knew she looped through the warehouse area on her way home in the dusk, as if she hadn't enough sense to know she might stumble in some remote alley.

She stood blinking at a display of rubber-tipped canes and walkers. After five minutes she turned and walked stiffly out of the store. Hurrying after her, Thomas couldn't hide his impatience.

"*Ma.*"

"Don't call me Ma. That's what a cane looks like now? So ugly, those aluminum things. And did you hear that god-awful clanking? They sounded like the monkey bars at the playground." She smiled sweetly at Thomas. "I'd rather fall."

He opened his mouth, ready to raise his voice, when she

turned away from him, the conversation over. She could be that obstinate.

He sent away for a catalog from a London manufacturer of wooden canes and umbrellas. He chose a polished lilac-wood walking stick with a sterling orb he thought would fit well in her small hand. When it arrived it looked so much like a weapon he was almost afraid to give it to her. He turned the polished handle to show her the engraving of her initials on one side.

"Oh, now isn't that something?" She kissed his cheek. It looked like something Cathryn might have carried. "It's lovely Thomas. It's almost too nice!" She winked up at him. "It'll be a shame if I have to bludgeon a hobo or a river rat with it."

The rat comment wasn't so far-fetched. In the year before her stroke, the river became her most frequent destination. Now, almost daily Isobel drew a straight bead through downtown, tapping her route with her new walking stick to one of the three great bridges. On fine days she could watch the boat traffic for hours, cars whizzing just behind her, the city throbbing to the west.

She imagined living on one of the barges or houseboats beneath, tidy existences of labor and rest, constant maintenance against wind and wave and rot, the enforced economy of space, the leisure of floating. She thought of a life unfettered, days ruled less by reason or ambition than by eddies and currents. She could easily picture Victor on such a vessel, his curious gaze always ahead, anticipating what might present itself around the next bend, the next mystery. She could see him, grey and gliding into the future.

Perhaps the two of them living on a boat. Wouldn't that be a picture. Carried along, watching the sky and ever-changing riverbanks.

She came to sense when the river was about to freeze,

noting the changes in glassy motion below the bridge trusses. Water slowed to undulate in sluggish swells before forming the thinnest vellum of ice. She wanted to see it freeze solid before her eyes, but it never did. Cold would drive her back to the shelter of the city, and the hard freeze would happen in the night. If she were younger, hardier, she would have posted herself on a bridge for a night to witness it, to be there the very instant water would cease being water.

A sunny May day — her last in the library — Isobel faltered even as she stepped through the revolving door. Something was off. Shadows tipped oddly over the polished floor, and when she looked up she saw the workmen walking in the air. Figures tiny for their distance, their forms greyed by dirty glass, they balanced just over the grid of skylights on external catwalks, laying a false roof over the panes.

She read the public notice salted with words like *liability* and *danger*. As if laying tiles on a game board, the men floating above darkened one square of daylight after another. For a long time Isobel stood in the large room gazing up at the sections of sun being extinguished. The great room had no other source of light save the table lamps. Suddenly her underarms were damp, her throat closed against the smell of old books, and she was swept backward to see herself awaiting a storm, gazing up to count the panels of tin ceiling in the tailor shop. Liam Malley stepping through the door to tell her Cathryn was gone.

As the workmen laid the last tile she heard a low moan and looked around before realizing it had come from her own throat.

One of the librarians touched her elbow. "Are you all right, Mrs. Howard? Can I get you something? A glass of water? Tea?"

She did not break her gaze from the ceiling. She felt her ankle churn sideways, the heel of her shoe pressing oddly into the terrazzo, as if her body were bearing the weight of the past.

She blinked and looked at the librarian as if to say, *I know where I am.* She spoke slowly, "They've closed its eyes. This room will grow blind."

"But the glass wasn't safe, you see? I'm afraid it's very old." The librarian looked at her with the soft pity reserved for the ill.

Isobel peered squarely at the young woman. "*I* am old. Older than this room, in fact. I am ninety-nine years old today."

~   ~   ~

Thomas had a thin manila envelope tucked under his arm. He set it on the bed.

"Mother, where's the oxygen tent?"

Her lids fluttered. "I made them take it away."

Someone had put an electric blanket over her, yet her wrist felt icy under his touch. He frowned and sat down.

"I have something for you."

"Hmm?" It was becoming difficult to swallow.

"You remember I told you I had to go to Chicago on business?"

"Yes."

"Well, when I was there, I did some digging."

"Digging?"

"Research, I mean."

Isobel took in a breath. "That's nice."

Thomas dropped his chin, laid the envelope on the bed, and weighted it there with her hand.

Isobel blinked at him, suddenly missing the barrier of the tent; she even thought of asking Thomas to have them bring it back. She looked suspiciously down at his offering and remembered him quizzing her about Cathryn's full name, her age. Research?

"Thomas." Isobel looked down, her hand pressed woodenly onto the envelope. "What have you done?"

"I found out. I know what happened to Jack and Cathryn."

"You what?"

Thomas grinned. "It's all in there, your mystery, all these years of wondering."

He eased the envelope away and turned it over. In bold font were two names: *Jack Alan Reese — Cathryn Leigh (Malley)*.

With an effort Isobel reached out to touch the names, to run a yellowed nail along the block letters. As her hand turned, her wedding ring slid over her knuckle and rolled onto the blanket.

They stared at the ring for a moment before Thomas picked it up. "Here, let me help you put it back on."

Isobel shook her head. "No, that's all right. I don't think so." She examined the knot of her knuckle, the crepe and gristle. "It will only fall off again."

"But . . ."

"It's not as though I was born wearing it. Just put it in the hatbox in my closet, would you?"

Thomas held the gold band. It was molded to the shape of Isobel's finger, not round, not perfect, a more human shape, thin as foil in places where decades of repeated movements had worn the gold away. The ring was still warm.

He held it gently so as not to bend it further. He tied the ring to the frayed cord of her photo album and as it fell to the cracked leather the last of its heat rose from the metal. He laid her sweater over the album and closed the lid on the hatbox. Its covering had faded, and the edge had worn so the cardboard showing through was coffee-coloured fuzz. The embossed silhouette was worn as well, but the outer edges were distinct. Thomas examined the profile and looked over at his mother.

It was her, still, unmistakable. The face had changed, as faces do, jowls develop, noses lengthen, hair thins. But the strength of the silhouette on the box still belonged to his mother, still unrelenting.

He pointed at the envelope, his voice less sure. "Aren't you surprised?"

She smiled. "You must've gone to a lot of trouble."

He knew when he was being humored. He sat on the bed. Her narrow form made only a slight ridge under the blanket. He felt suddenly angry at himself for wasting a day tracking down the fates of strangers when he could've been spending the time with her.

She nodded at the envelope. "I suppose you spent a lot of money."

"Nah, it wasn't too bad. Want me to open it for you?"

"No, not yet. Can you just sit here awhile? I'm so tired."

She tilted her head slightly to receive the kiss he stamped on her forehead. She held his fingers. The other limp hand tapped out a dull rhythm on the manila.

It's all in there.

As if any such thing could be contained by an envelope! There could be no scenario, no fate within of simple ink pressed to paper, which Isobel had not already assigned a vision to, had not already imagined.

Sixty years had produced a loaded archive of possibilities. Isobel could walk down a phantom aisle and glimpse the scenes, each plumped and shaded with the minute detail of years of conjecture. Some possibilities were waking and deliberate, while others had come in dreams. For months after Jack and Cathryn disappeared she'd dreamed of them almost nightly, but only one dream stayed with her, followed her into her later years.

Pulling her canoe up onto a shaded rock ledge, Isobel takes a compass from her pocket, though she knows this is the place without looking at the needle. She sheds her skirt, blouse, and layers of underthings until she is naked. Sits on the stone ledge until it burns her thighs. She stands in the terrible heat; it is as if all the days of one summer have been simmered down to a single afternoon. She has paddled many arms of the Maze, portaged over bogland to this place, and her thirst is vicious. She climbs the cliff face, her white torso glowing in the shaft of July sun. It is an effortless climb. Knowing nothing of the depth of the water beneath her, she dives with blind faith into the channel. The dive is precise and quiet, the water achingly cold. Concentric rings form after her small feet disappear into the black sheet.

She forces herself deep, kicking. Six feet, then ten, surely she must be near the bottom. Deeper, and her ears sing with the pressure. Just as she knows she has failed — that she must arc to ascend, to save herself — she sees them.

Perfectly preserved in the icy waters, the bones of Jack and Cathryn lie entwined on a ledge, as casually as if they'd tumbled back into bed some lazy Sunday. The colours of Cathryn's Chinese silk wrapper are still vibrant, the seams intact. The tail of a lake trout turning near Jack's temple creates just enough stir to cloud the pale bone with silt. They embrace undisturbed. Safe in the tomb of Lake Cypress. *Safe.*

Her timing is exquisite. There is only a fraction of an hour each day — minutes, to be precise — when the sun is straight overhead and can penetrate the channel depths. The portion of the ledge where Jack and Cathryn lie is lit for only several seconds of those minutes. No one else could ever find them. Ever would.

The sight is hers for only those fleeting seconds. Hers alone, a tangle of ivory bones anchored to a block of granite. Even as she kicks upward — aware of her own danger now, and panicking toward the sunlight — she knows this is already a memory, and perhaps an unreliable one. As she rises she is disquieted by the irony of silk outlasting flesh. Her lungs will explode.

But they don't. She breaks the surface, choking on her own breath and heaving in great drafts of air sour with mildew. She remembers then that she cannot swim, thrashes, slips under, thrashes again, reaching the rock to embrace its slick haven just in time.

Isobel knows this to be one of her more romantic visions of Jack and Cathryn, a drama born of love, one which spares them any of the mundane existences they might have lived had they fled and tried to hew out a life together. She knows they could have as easily faded into a more realistic scenario, but these waking dreams are bitten with practicality.

She has pictured them seaside, somewhere on the West Coast. Places she only knows of through television documentaries or picture books — gull-populated islands in the Strait of Juan de Fuca, the bitter coast of British Columbia. On some wind-bruised beach far from the Midwest, Jack has fashioned a cottage, weather-battered and sagging by now. He and Cathryn are companions to dunes, reedy grasses, relentless surf. Perhaps she paints seascapes at her easel near the windows, while Jack is off performing some menial task, mending nets, repairing engines of trawlers, or working in a cannery. Jack is a dogged and reliable employee, if sometimes slow to reply when he is addressed, never having become accustomed to the lie of his assumed name. John or Jake or Mike.

Mornings are spent combing their stretch of beach to see what the tides have offered up: a crate of ruined electric toasters; a case of fan belts; cleats and bits of sails torn from passing sloops; a squat yellow vase; a heavily worn leather dog collar thick with slime. More often they find garbage, and Cathryn walks along with an open canvas sack while Jack stabs refuse with a stick he has attached a nail to. He impales chip bags, six-pack rings, bottle caps. The detritus of human functions accumulates in the sack; condoms, diapers, tampon applicators. Some days there is so much plastic their haul of garbage will barely burn.

Cathryn has days of grey silence even Jack cannot penetrate, her illness compounded by age, the distant weight of Liam's death. Does she even know of it? The local villagers consider Jack and Cathryn as they would any other aging couple, noting their infrequent forays into town — to buy groceries or lightbulbs or watercolour paper — with genuine indifference.

Perhaps they obtained false papers and emigrated. To France, or Italy, where Cathryn might flourish but Jack would not. He cannot grasp the language; their Parisian neighborhood is filthy. The presence of prostitutes in Rome depresses him. They try a village in Portugal, but Cathryn contracts a parasite or some strain of hepatitis. Her health at stake, they move on. They might have returned to live in some odd state, perhaps Alabama. Isobel does not know why that particular state came into her head, perhaps because it was one of the least likely places she could imagine for Cathryn, who would have abhorred the weather, the lazy drawl of the natives, the abysmal food. She has imagined them in a row house or an apartment, where they would have begun again with high hopes. After a few years, the drama at Granite Point would have faded like a coloured photograph, freeing them to move through the world like any ordinary couple, time chiseling a space for problems suffered in any normal union. It could be that the very things that drew them one to the other — Jack's sensitivity, Cathryn's dark frailties — eventually weakened them and frayed the bond. Jack easily overwhelmed by Cathryn's neediness. With no one strong enough to take care of the both of them, they might have drifted into separate despairs, one of them going out one day to buy sherbet or cigarettes, instead wandering to the depot to book a one-way coach ticket to wherever the next train was bound.

One of them would have died before the other, but Isobel has tried not to think of which. She realizes how few of her scenarios picture the couple anything but united, even in death.

But she has tried to imagine them apart. Jack alone, or Cathryn. Teaching art or French at a private school, perhaps in New England. Moody and known to the girls for being erratic in her grading and prone to favoritism. An elegant character who walks the campus on moonlit spring nights reciting dead poets. More tired than usual at the close of each dusty August and never sure why.
The body's memory.

There were other images Isobel pushed away altogether. The flashes that would sometimes come at night, as she lay alone.

She made herself consider possibilities that she was previously unwilling to accept, possibilities that might await her in the envelope Thomas was so eager to offer.

Perhaps Cathryn had succeeded at the grisly chore she'd attempted times before. Found another razor to drain her-

self with. A horrified landlady or one of her students finding her, slipping backward on the tile floor, weak moon
lighting Cathryn's pale face, the dark pool at her lovely
throat growing.

Together? Two rigid corpses in a wood.

Blood seeps through the makeshift shrouds Liam has
fashioned from a one-man tent, or perhaps the lattice quilt
from Jack's cabin. With his camp shovel he battles roots
and stones at the base of a white pine, his task hampered
by darkness, his vision clouded by tears. His brogue gone
suddenly heavy, as it does when he's exhausted, he speaks
to Jack's body. "Bastard. Bloody bastard," he demands,
"why'd you make me do it, man? *Why?*" He hacks at the
stony soil until finally two graves gape up at him. Deep
enough that they will not be disturbed by animals. Found.
Jack's body rolled in, propelled by Liam's boot and landing
with a thud. Cathryn laid tenderly, as if only put down to
sleep. More shoveling. Covering the ground with pine needles and gathered brush.

His task finished, he moves onward, overland, not sure
where he's going, until he finds himself at the base of a fire
tower just before dawn.

No. Not that one. Hardly likely.

Their fates, which are by now their histories — Isobel
knows she has outlived them — might have been better,
and these scenes creep through her armor of cynicism.
They could have settled in New York on a tree-lined street
in a sunny walk-up, or in the green haven of Brooklyn, perhaps on a quiet lake upstate. They could have as easily had
a beloved retriever, a knowledgeable doctor to help
Cathryn through her dark days, a small sailboat for Sun-
days on the bay. Perhaps Cathryn sold her watercolours in
a gallery and had a few artist friends. Jack with a job he
didn't mind, whistling homeward to calm suppers on their

porch or the occasional dinner party peopled with sculp-
tors and weavers. A garden with yellow tea roses. They
would have grown a little plump with the French recipes
Cathryn was always trying out. Spending their evenings
quietly with the *Times* book review, Cathryn with a lap of
embroidery, Jack carving willow whistles. Sometimes reading aloud to each other, their words occasionally punctuated by the shift and pop of logs on the hearth.

Perhaps in those quiet evenings they remembered Isobel.

Unkempt graves side by side on a hill of cedar, false
names etched on twin headstones.

But over the years she kept coming back to the same
image — lovers under a lake — perhaps because of the
vividness of her recurring dream.

The prelude to the dream: They sit in Jack's boat at
dusk, Cathryn wearing her beautiful silk robe. An open
vial of some botanical potion passes from his mouth to
hers. A bitter cocktail he has extracted from purple night-
shade or hemlock. Lengths of rope around their waists,
tied to the same heavy stone so they will not be separated.
A hand ax ready to punch a hole in the bottom of the boat.

A final kiss, long and dreamlike, as the poison begins its
end. A respite under the water, together. Peace. The kind
you get once or twice in a good life. The peace of a small
girl lying in twilight under the curve of a winter sky.

~ ~ ~

Thomas cannot move his hand from the envelope, has not
been able to for some time. His mother has told him of her
dream of lovers at rest in a bed deep under a wavering surface. He is astonished at the detail, the haunting accuracy.

How?

Would she be surprised at what eerie knowledge she holds?

He has advanced degrees, has read and learned and traveled, has paid attention, has run a company. He can perform intricate card tricks, knows statistics, can forecast economic trends, track a deer, identify any constellation in both hemispheres, is proficient in Latin, can order in French. Can do countless other things; has a thousand other small knowledges.

He looks over at the woman he has known and loved and sometimes not loved for almost seventy years, and realizes he knows nothing.

~ ~ ~

CHAPTER EIGHTEEN

*I*sobel's eyes closed to a veil of sleep. She had fought to stay awake, to run through more possibilities. By all, she could no more be certain of the fates of Jack and Cathryn than she could know what to expect when the splashing within her own chest would cease.

~ ~ ~

Her own chest. When Victor tapped her collarbone she woke up in a bed of life vests lining the ribs of the rowboat. Victor had gathered stones into a ring on the sand and had built a fire of driftwood and birch bark. She had dreamed, but the memory of it was already ribboning away; dreams eluded her as they finished, just as the woodsmoke curled skyward. Clouds had lowered the sky while she slept and the air had cooled.

Victor had rowed her to this island from his own. Somewhere along the way she had dreamed in the cradle of the boat.

She could hear happiness, laughter pealing over the water. She sat up to hear her children hooting and shouting across the broad channel as they chased one another through the underbrush. A game of hide-and-seek? Looking back toward the source of the voices, she thought she recognized the view of the island. The same angle as in the snapshot.

"It must have been taken from this shore. That picture. The one you brought home with the deed."

He glanced over the water. "Yes, I think so."

"It's a fine little island. We'll have to name it someday."

Victor helped her out of the boat. "Let's name it now, while we can see it whole."

They sat on a log with their knees touching, and as they thought of different names Isobel wrote them in the sand with a stick.

"Tailor's Island?"

Victor shook his head and took the stick from her hand. "How about Milliner's Island?"

She swatted sand flies and rubbed the name away.

They passed the stick between them in turns.

Summer Island. Giant's Foot (for the shale formation at the shore). *Sanctuary. Berry.* None seemed fitting.

Victor slapped at his neck. "Mosquito Island?"

"No."

"Would you like to name it after someone, a person? Your friend maybe?"

She began to write Cathryn's name in the sand, but the stick in her hand went still at the lip of the C. Isobel smiled. "Thank you, Victor, but no."

It was her third and last visit to the island. Each summer since Cathryn and Jack, she and Louisa were ferried out on the mail boat and stayed for a week over the Fourth of July holiday.

Isobel felt sudden taps of rain on her neck. The beach dimpled before her, drops pocking the C. Victor rushed to turn the rowboat over.

They moved into the cover of trees, Isobel looking back once over the water, straining to hear the voices of her children.

"Do you think they'll have enough sense to go into the cabin?"

Victor took her hand, laughing. "Does it matter?"

They hurried through the woods looking for shelter and stopped in a copse of birch as the sky opened. Victor shielded her with his jacket. Leaves shuddered around them, and he shouted to be heard over the thrumming. "C'mon! There's a fishing shack on the other side."

They skidded on the slick path. Isobel was out of breath by the time they reached the far end of the island. The shack turned out to be only a lean-to with a mud floor, but it sheltered them. They waited, watching curtains of rain cover one island, then another. For an hour sheets swept across the lake, grey gauze waving over the shores. Chill ripples scarred the lake surface.

The storm moved slowly, shifting west and away from them. When it was over, the sun broke through to gild the thick mist rising from the lake.

As they walked back over the island an erratic breeze shadowed them, danced just off the path in whorls, stirred the branches overhead, tipping the wet leaves so that they spilled their loads in false showers, the drops bright with sunlight. Wet pine needles and moss soaked their shoes. Isobel stopped, shivering in her wet blouse, and pulled Victor to her. Rainwater from his mustache met her parted lips.

———

When she sold the island after he died, she found it penciled in over the old name on the legal deed. Victor's handwriting.

Isobel Island.

~   ~   ~

The sun had shifted. Thomas had changed clothes.

Her mouth tasted sour. Another night passed?

"You didn't open it?" Thomas's whisper was in her ear. His voice held no surprise as he pushed the envelope across the bedside table, the thinness of the manila under his fingers, its nearly weightless contents. Two recent single-column clippings, one from the Cypress newspaper, reprinted in the *Chicago Tribune,* describing the grim catch of a vacationing fisherman — the bones of a man and a woman, a gold four-leaf clover pin, shards of silk. Speculation. Jack's and Cathryn's names posed as questions.

"No. Perhaps today."

Her voice had taken on a strange echo, as if she were speaking through the bellows of a split throat, as if her lungs were working independently of each other. She tried to motion for him to sit. He scanned the floor. "I've called Robert. He's arranging for the girls and their kids to come in tomorrow."

"Call them back. Tell them to stay home."

Thomas looked into her eyes. Her gaze was resolute. They sat this way, nothing between them but the rhythms of breath, until a car horn outside lifted the silence.

"You've been a wonderful son to me."

"Mother, I . . ."

"It's glorious outside, isn't it? I can't see much today, some sort of eye-fog. But I can feel the sun. It must be strong."

Thomas looked out. It was overcast and smoggy. "It is.

It's a beautiful day, Mother. High clouds moving on a breeze, coming from the north, I think."

"Feels lovely."

"Maybe you'd like to go outside? I bet we could get an orderly or a nurse to help wheel your bed out onto the terrace. I saw other beds out there yesterday. They must roll them out through the conservatory doors."

"Outside?" She closed her eyes to storm-washed skies, a lake rippled gold in a breeze.

On the shores of lakes she fell in love with Victor. Twice. He broke her heart only once: the time he'd not been joking. The slump of his shoulders, the string of orange saliva connecting his lip to his sleeve. The sudden lead of her intestines as she forced herself toward his worktable. There had been a bubble in his spit, a tiny bubble of all that remained of his last breath. She watched as it made its way to his sleeve with a slow deliberateness Victor seldom had in life.

Had he time to think of what his life had meant, its impact, its triumphs, the gifts he'd imparted? Or was his going as fast as the shutting of a door? When the bubble met the starched cotton, it laid itself open, was lost, absorbed.

Later, there were terrible moments when she was glad he'd died. Driving to the depot in Duluth to meet the railcar carrying Henry's coffin.

Sitting in the cold cab of the sheriff's pickup and listening to the chime of pickaxes breaking the ice to get at Louisa's car.

When she was sixty and looked at her body in a mirror and realized it was no longer desirable. She was glad then too, even in her vanity and selfishness.

Other times she couldn't help wondering what life might have held for them together, what it might have been like to grow old with him, to have had his side to lean into.

She wondered if she would see him.

Any belief in God, any notion of heaven or religion had unraveled over the years. Threads that must be gathered up now into some semblance of faith. She had no idea where to begin this chore. More than anything else, this urgency made her so tired she had to press the idea of it away.

"Once, as a joke, your father told me he was made by angels."

Her voice jarred Thomas upright. "Did he?"

"You are just like him. You know that, don't you?"

"Dad?" He reached up to his thinning hair and grinned. "Yeah, same shiny dome."

"No, not that. You're kind, like he was. Made of fine stuff."

Thomas opened his mouth to speak, but some slight and sudden shift in her face dissolved his words. Something. He leaned closer, perhaps a trick of the light. The furrows between her brow had softened, the hollows under her eyes and cheeks were not so chiseled as they'd been only that morning.

The angle of light, surely. Thomas felt the coolness of her hand and peered again at her languid face. Flesh giving up its century-old grip on bones.

Isobel remembered the evening he returned from his first summer on the island. An angular brown boy, his voice whistling through the void where his front teeth had been. Isobel had walked into her house and Thomas had been the first to reach her, jumping up and wrapping thin legs around her waist, planting damp kisses on her chin. Victor behind him, circling them both in a squeeze.

She laboured to take in breaths, made herself slow until her lungs relaxed, each shallow inhalation slowing the spin a little. A little boy's face. The hand around hers a warm tether.

Faith. Walking along the St. Paul waterfront where the railroad tracks snaked along the river, she turned inland to find herself in an unfamiliar block of warehouses. A rare fog had risen from the Mississippi to obscure landmarks, and she made several wrong turns before considering she might be lost. She contemplated her plight while picking her way along the broken sidewalks, nudging along scraps and bits of glass with the toe of her old woman's shoe. She didn't feel fingers of panic tighten around her, did not tense against her own insides as she might have expected, but she did feel a vague inner displacement as her mental compass shut down. She didn't care, really. The surroundings had taken over her will; nothing to do but give way to the strange geography deeming every step aimless. After a few blocks of walking with no destination, no real purpose, she began to enjoy the idea of being nowhere she could name.

The fog was lovely, a mantle settling over her to round her sharp shoulders. As she grew less rigid, her mind pleasantly dulled. She could feel Victor at her side. Could hear his voice through the lush air. *Izzy, there is nothing you know here. Nothing to fear.*

He'd been lost. Often. What had it been like for him. She thought of the vulnerability, of being at the mercy of the next stranger met, not knowing if the next corner might offer a familiar landmark or a darker, more sinister alley. She wondered at the vast trust he must have had in life.

Just as she wished she could reach forward through the damp veil to touch him, by some theater trick, he was standing behind her. When she began to fall she fell backward into his arms. Let herself fall. Perhaps that was faith?

Fall backward into arms, into scenes and lives so far in the past as to be trimmed in fine mists.

One cold February morning when the children were very young, the boiler had broken down. They had all three crawled into her bed, wearing the woolen jackets Victor had tailored. While he went out to find a wrench they played rhyming games with Isobel, reciting every riddle and tongue twister they knew. They sang nonsense songs and watched the thick snow plaster the windows in great swatches. Passing that morning in the simple necessity of keeping her children warm and entertained gave Isobel an awareness of that endowment she alone possessed, the ability to care for these children and keep them safe. Love them as no one else could.

Eventually Victor had banged into the house with a tool he'd found in the garage. The children spilled away from the bed, a plaid caterpillar snaking out the door. A soft avalanche of stocking feet thudding down the stairs to spiral to the basement.

She stayed in bed, running her hands over the nubby bedspread, listening to the clanging pipes and young voices cheering as Victor worked a father's magic.

She heard distant whoops and a throaty rumble as the furnace came to. Fifteen minutes later Victor stomped up the stairs to their bedroom with a steaming cup of tea in his hands. He wiped his oil-smeared fingers on his shirt and grinned, kicking the door shut behind him.

She sat up and took the tea. The house had gone quiet. "Where are they?"

Victor suddenly stooped in a hunchback's posture and dangled one arm to his knee, undoing the buttons of his shirt with his free hand. His voice took on an expansive lisp. "The children? Why, locked in the coal-thellar, my thweet." He jumped up on the bed in one agile motion, shifty-eyed and rocking in a menacing crouch. "Not to worry, though, I've left them thome water and thtale bithcuits . . . the thtub of a *candle*."

She giggled and screamed as he crabbed over her, wobbling the mattress. Tea sloshed over the bedspread.

A stained bedspread. Tea spoking across chenille. Other fabrics passed through, over, under her fingers; the textures and hefts of years. The dress of a doll whose name she'd long forgotten, its blue gingham as distinct to Isobel as if she were holding it now. Amelia? Anna?

The hem of a nightgown she had used to wipe an infant's mouth ringed with bluish milk from her breast. She could recall the detail of the scalloped edge of the nightgown, could see the baby's mouth. Which of her babies had that been?

The linen tea towel she had used to soak up spills of coffee during the endless afternoon of Victor's funeral. Innumerable handkerchiefs damp with blotted tears, handkerchiefs bloody from scrapes, purple with jelly lifted from a soft cheek. Harsh corduroy of boys' trousers worn at the knees, the satin lining of her favorite winter coat, thin cotton dresses covering the aching vulnerability of a child's shoulder blades.

The rigid trifold of the American flag on Henry's coffin.

The perfect, perfect laying of lapels on Victor's suits.

The impossible smoothness of ivory velvet trailing Louisa's wedding gown.

As she remembered, her hand twitched a little and clutched softly at the hospital blanket.

"Mother?"

He was closer now, and she could make out the deep lines in his face. She reached out to touch his jaw, his ear. Behind him the envelope slid to the floor. Neither took notice. Isobel brushed back her son's hair.

———

Filament woven into a summer that began as a boat moved away, watching her husband's face dissolve behind sun-riddled smoke.

"Mother? Would you like to go outside?"
By this grace dissolved in place.
Cupping her son's chin in her palm.
The boat stopped in the water. The engine reversed itself and the stern backed itself out of a yellow fog.
Isobel raised her other hand from the blanket in a gentle gesture. She waved the air in front of her face, the motion in her arm suddenly fluid, its dead weight rising. What she had been trying to remember for weeks came to her without hesitation; the lines had been with her all along. How could she have forgotten? Words rising to greet her, uttered softly as if from the mouth of a lover, a sweet child, a benevolent father. Lines she had balanced in her memory and conserved for others like consecrations turned slowly to make themselves heard and precious to her, whispering for *her.*

What seas what shores what grey rocks and what islands
What water lapping the bow
And scent of pine and woodthrush singing through the
*   fog*
What images return
. . . this face, less clear and clearer
The pulse in the arm less strong and stronger —
Given or lent? More distant than stars and nearer than
*   the eye*

"Outside? No thank you, Thomas. Too much fuss."

. . . what granite islands towards my timbers
And woodthrush calling through the fog . . .

Her fingers trailed away from her son's face. "I believe I'll stay inside. Stay put."

My daughter.

She turned to a brilliance throbbing through the glass. "But do something for me before you leave, please. Open that window. As high as it will go."